Dimmed

Dimmed

To my foggy friends. Enjoy
SB

SK Brown

Copyright © 2009 by SK Brown.

ISBN: Hardcover   978-1-4363-8955-6
          Softcover   978-1-4363-8954-9

All rights reserved. No part of this book may be reproduced or transmitted in any form or by any means, electronic or mechanical, including photocopying, recording, or by any information storage and retrieval system, without permission in writing from the copyright owner.

This is a work of fiction. Names, characters, places and incidents either are the product of the author's imagination or are used fictitiously, and any resemblance to any actual persons, living or dead, events, or locales is entirely coincidental.

This book was printed in the United States of America.

To order additional copies of this book, contact:
Xlibris Corporation
1-888-795-4274
www.Xlibris.com
Orders@Xlibris.com
55567

DEDICATION

I dedicate this book to Joann Strickland
whose tireless encouragement and badgering helped get it out
of my head and onto the printed page,

To my little sister, Sue Clemens, who has patiently listened to my tales,
and giving me the confidence and support to finish a thought.

And my parents, my Dad, a special man who taught me
how to laugh at life, and gave me the strength to live it.
And my Mother who still assures me that I'm not loco.

Chapter 1

Dimmed, I know I have dimmed, I'm looking at the mirror in my hallway I see the reflection of the room in back of me *through* me. I have a tingling feeling in my limbs, my vision is sharpened, textures are richer but in black and white and shades of grey.

Heredity has little to do with it. Checking with my parents and family members and investigating ancestors have not explained what happens to me. I still look for a explanations but I don't have the passion I once did to find it.

After 22 years I have accepted it. I try to work with it. But most times I try not to think of it.

Most of my family regards me as a bit strange due to the fact that they have almost seen me as I have helped them at times. This is not a topic that comes up. It was not really acknowledged.

My parents seemed relieved when I found my first apartment. I know they love me but my *achievements* were not something that they could really brag about.

This is not a recent occurrence, or even a sometimes occurrence. This is my life. When it happens I know that am not readily visible. Some might catch a glimpse, or maybe feel a shadow pass; if you were paying close attention you would think I was just a *trick of the eye*.

Animals and small children seem to have a clearer vision, most are not alarmed. I don't have an explanation; I've never met anyone like me to ask.

I do know is that once the dimming starts I should be wary of my surroundings. Some form of danger is near. To my family or friends or even a stranger, it didn't take any time at all to realize the *urge* I felt with my dimming would lead me to whatever needed to be done.

As a child I never questioned it. Helping a stray animal, or a neighbor kid, I was there, I helped. It was a rude awakening when I realized that no one else shared my ability.

Grade school was a strange for me. Getting odd sensations while sitting at a school desk, watching my hands fade and my vision change into textures of grey was a little unsettling.

The *urge* would compel me to follow a path that could lead anywhere. Once I was led behind the school building. Where Jimmy Winters, voted *Most likely to do time,* was slapping Allan Woods calling him *Wimpy* and demanding his lunch money.

I jumped on Jimmy and hit him with his World Geography book. Both boys stopped to look around. They both saw the Geography book fly through the air. They screamed in unison and I laughed as they ran away. Alan never had a problem with his lunch money again.

I attended a small school with the problems that all schools have. Petty, stupid, jealous, puberty stunts, some pretty vicious. Bullies came in all sizes and ages, either gender, tall or short, and some as they grew older became more malicious.

This ability caused many problems growing up. *Disappearing* with no explanations, I would feel the *vibes* as the tingling started. I would excuse myself and if I did not return to class I would be counted as absent or accused of skipping class. My parents would sign my bogus absent slips and mumble about priorities with the admonishment of *did I ever expect to graduate?* My explanations did not make for believable excuses.

I realized that my problem was unique. When I started Junior High it really hit me that *my problem* was mine alone. It took a while to sink in but I began to realize how strange I really was. My folks couldn't help. When I brought up the subject there were no answers, just uncomfortable pauses and a change of subject. I never knew if they were embarrassed or just worried that some neighbor might mention it.

I don't think anyone actually *believed* what they *may have seen;* it was a taboo topic in the house. Apparently if it was not talked about it didn't exist. Sometimes I felt I didn't exist.

Puberty was the beginning of a whole new set of problems, the skinny little girl I knew, was not a skinny little girl anymore. As I started to *fill out* I constantly worried about how I could stop my odd behavior.

The *episodes* were coming more frequently with more intensity. The *tingling* was deeper, and the urge to move overwhelming.

I tried to ignore it; I held my breath, thought happy thoughts. I tried to tell myself to not let it happen.

I read about all kinds of illnesses. Maybe I had a brain tumor. Did my dad drop me on my head as a baby? Did I get hit by lightening? There didn't seem to be a cause. I got the reputation of being a serious girl that acted strangely.

Half-way through the 7th grade I found a miracle. I call it a miracle, it was something that I could do to stop the tingling, or delay it for a minute while I made excuses to leave a room. Later I learned that it worked to help me return to normal more quickly.

Deep breathing worked. I had started to take swimming classes and I loved to be under water. I didn't have *episodes* while I was underwater. I made a conscious effort to deep breath whenever I felt the tingling start. I joined the YWCA for swimming classes and then signed up for a Yoga class they offered. I was filling my spare time trying to find a way to control the change.

I had finally found a way to work around it. It helped me to distinguish the degree of the urges. What was minor and non-threatening or major and immediate.

I didn't date much, I wasn't a popular girl. I wasn't totally a recluse, just quiet and standoffish. You might say studious. The one time I did have a date I freaked him out by *disappearing* at a movie, long enough to be missed and found *fading* in. My date didn't completely believe me when I told him it was the lighting in the theater. I was home in record time and he never asked me out again.

When I graduated from collage I was at a crossroad, I had studied parapsychology hoping that I would get a better handle on my gift.

I now called it a gift because I was really tired of it being a problem. The fact that I did help others even in little ways made it more like a good thing. I covered every avenue I could think of studying and contacting various groups. Occult, witchcraft, alien life forms but didn't find any information that would help me understand my *special gift*. I also took classes in self defense and marshal arts. Some of the more hands on problems had taught me that I needed to protect myself. Dimming did not stop bruising.

Working was a big problem. I had to be really creative when I was asked to explain my absences. I couldn't explain my condition. I couldn't even explain it to myself. I would go from job to job waiting for the pink slip.

The idea came to me during a fairly painful marshal arts class. I was lying on my back looking at the ceiling. My instructor was leaning over me with a puzzled look. I felt the familiar tingling. I jumped up and as I ran past the admitting desk it came to me that I needed to get paid for catching the bad guys. I could pay my bills without having to worry about explanations.

The urge led me to older lady. She was screaming that her bag had been stolen. Following the direction she pointed I ran after a boy as he made a quick turn into an alley. He stopped behind a large garbage bin.

I caught the purse as he tossed it into the receptacle. His mouth was wide open as the purse flew back from the bin and wavered in thin air. A small yelp came from him as the wallet flew from his hand and returned to the bag, seemingly hovering in space. He screamed and ran like his clothes were on fire. I'm sure my laughter compelled his legs to run faster.

When I returned to the lady she was shaking so badly she didn't notice my dimmed condition. I could feel my self fill in as I touched her shoulder and asked her if it was her purse. She looked inside as she thanked me over and over while she checked the contents. She had a large smile as she pulled out a $10.00 dollar bill and pressed it into my hand.

This was the first gratuity I ever received for using my gift. It was also the beginning of a plan that would be the first step in my new career.

My name is CJ Mason; I am a Private Investigator. Hopefully, a name for my new line of work will come to me.

Chapter 2

I have lived in the city for almost six months and have had many opportunities to use my *gift*. I made my decision to move after trying to find a way to make money in my home town. I was not surprised that I was starving. It's a fact that people don't talk to shadows. I knew almost everyone in my home town and no one took me serious as a person much less a professional investigator. My odd behavior was well known. The fact that I look more like Orphan Annie then Nancy Drew didn't help. I decided to move to the big city, hang a shingle and wait for people to come to my door.

I had emptied my savings account and found a 2nd floor flat in a nondescript red brick building that had three rooms with a small kitchen and smaller bath. I converted the entry into a reception area, the bedroom on the immediate left into a fairly respectable office. To the right of the entry/reception area was the kitchen and adjoining bath that led into a small closet size bedroom. My front door stated that you had reached the office of:

CJ Investigation
Privacy Guaranteed
512-For Help Fax 512-449-2112
www.cjpi.com

I had a small wooden sign made for the entry of the building, 1000 flyers, business cards and an ad in the local neighborhood paper. I sat by my phone and waited.

I found that my dimming came on more often due to the exploding population around me. Many times I would have that inner beast call me at the most unlikely times.

I would follow a trace and come to the aid of whoever needed me. Small fixes mostly, returning purses, finding misplaced children and pets, or taking the keys out of the hand of some thug trying to steal a car. Most of the time the look on the perpetrators face was reward enough. But rent had to be made and my cupboards were bare.

I now used my skill more then I ever had in the past. I had taken the tests and received license that declared me a licensed Private Investigator. I framed the certificate and hung it proudly on my wall.

I decided to go to where all the bad guys usually end up, the local police station. I was thumbing through the Wanted Posters that decorated a wall. Several were listed for petty crimes and for some reason or another missed their court date. Their bond had been revoked and I would find them and collect a percentage of that bond. There were several that sounded like they were up my alley. I would track them down, pick them up and receive the reward.

It sounded simple but I needed more information. I waited for the desk sergeant to finish speaking to an officer who had a very intoxicated person with him.

I stepped up to asked for information regarding Wanted Posters. A huge man sat man behind a counter. His badge read that he was Sergeant Dombrowski. He had a half smile with a leer as he looked me up and down. "A little woman like you is biting off more then she could chew."

The hair on the back of my neck stood up at his insult. I glared at his face and then checked the badge on his wrinkled uniform. I counted to ten. His smile got wider. "You should wander back home before it gets dark."

I counted to ten again as I put my hands on my hips. "Is there a real police officer in this building? One that's a little more politically correct? From where I'm standing you are a poor excuse for a public servant."

His eyes bulged as his face turned a strange color of red. He seemed to grow out of his seat as he bellowed for me to take a one.

I stepped back but I did not sit. We glared at each other for a heartbeat or two, he then picked up the desk phone and barked. "Keyes, get up here."

We were at a standoff, neither of us budging an inch. I was not going to be the first to look away. As I stood locked in my standoff I thought, *great, my first contact with the local boys and I piss off the first one off that crosses my path.*

Our stare-off was interrupted by a voice at the side of the desk.

"What do you need Dombrowski?"

We both looked up at the man who stood at the side of the counter. He was tall and strikingly handsome. He wore a dark brown corduroy jacket, and a cream colored shirt, the top button open showing a strong neck. Thick sun streaked brown hair worn fashionably long framed his face and set off a magnificent smile. But eyes held me. They seemed to be hazel but shifted to grey, or maybe green, the lighting was not the best in this room.

I stood frozen as he again asked what the desk sergeant wanted Dombrowski seemed to puff up larger then life behind the huge counter. He hitched his head my way and spat out "This lady needs some help. Get her out of my lobby."

When *Keyes* looked at to me I realized that my mouth was open. I shut it and looked into his face.

"I'm Detective Keyes, what can I do for you?"

I was trying to remember why I was there.

"You seemed to have put a knot in Dombrowski's necktie come on back and we can talk about what I can do for you."

He appeared beside me and held my elbow as he led me through a door. We entered a large cluttered room. He walked me through a maze of desks that held a strange assortment of human beings.

We arrived at a desk where he pointed to a chair. I sat down and tried to gather my thoughts as he took a seat behind the desk that was cluttered with file folders, scribbled notes, a computer and a phone. He moved the folders to the side and leaned back in his chair. I felt like I was sitting in the principal's office.

He was patient as he watched me take in the people around us, the noise, the ringing phones, and the occasional loud angry voice.

I turned back to the desk and he appeared to be waiting for me to speak.

Taking a deep breath and found my voice I introduced myself and told him why I had come to the stationhouse. His face showed little of what he might be thinking. As I talked I saw that he was taken in my dress, my build, assessing my words with my appearance. I didn't feel as uncomfortable as I had with Dombrowski. I knew that I could do what I had planned. But to be so openly assessed added to my anxiety.

I took out a business card as I explained my training and license. He calmly took everything in. After I had explained what I wanted I waited for his response.

I was beginning to get uncomfortable and wondering if I was ready to hear the lecture on *Women in a man's world* speech again when he surprised me by saying that he recognized me.

He explained that he had seen me downtown putting up fliers. He opened his desk drawer and pulled out one of the bright yellow flyers that I had plastered, stapled and taped all over town. "So you're CJ? I thought you were putting fliers up for someone else. It never crossed my mind that CJ was a female."

I wasn't sure if I was offended. His intense stare would not leave my face. I was locked in his gaze. My mouth was dry and I had no response.

He reached over and took the handful of fliers from my hand and ruffled through them.

"This guy is Max Wiggins he was last seen on 4th street at a bar that he sometimes frequents, the bartender will give you a good lead if you handle him right, start with a ten dollar bill." He laid the poster on his desk and held up another. "This is Rosie Cross; she has a house on West Vine, she didn't show up for a court date. She'll go easy, I'm surprised she forgot. This last one turned himself in yesterday. I'll check on these others, I let you know if they are still at large."

By the time he screened the flyers I had to again close my mouth. I didn't expect this much information. I expected more sarcasm.

Detective Keyes explained bondsmen the procedures for bringing in a *client* and the paperwork it required. He also said that if I needed any help in the future they would be available to help. I assumed he meant the police department

I started gathering up the posters and thanking him for his help when he put his hand on my mine and asked if I had spoken to any of the bail-bondsmen. I told him that I hadn't but it would be my next step. He looked at me with a smile and said that he would like to help and we could discuss it over dinner.

For the third time in an hour I had to tell myself to close my mouth. I had never had an invitation like this one. Before I could say a word, he stood up and walked me out of the room past Dombrowski's station, calling over his shoulder that he was off duty.

We walked to the street, his hand still on my elbow. The sun was setting and a breeze was flitting around us. Gentle wind was sending little whorls of dust in the street; the sky was red, yellow and pink. The street lights were lit up, white globes marking our way down the street.

He looked down at me and said that he knew of a nice place to eat. *Good food at a good price with great atmosphere.* He led me down the sidewalk, turned the corner and walked another two blocks to a little café with a yellow awning. *Magpies* was stenciled on the window with friendly little birds wafting around it, he ushered me through the door.

It was a very comfortable restaurant. Candles and flowers decorated blue and white checkered table cloths. Pictures of the restaurant with family and patrons filled the walls.

Detective Keyes ushered me to a booth in the back. As we sat down a waitress made her way to our table. She placed water and menus in front of us with a big smile. "Its about time Jess, it's been a while, mama asked about you just yesterday."

He had a big smile as he gave her a hug and said, "Tell mama that I always come back."

The waitress gave him another hug, turned around and said "I'll let her know you're here."

I buried my head behind the menu through this exchange. *Mama? Was this his sister? His lover?* I checked out his ring finger, *not the wife*. Hoping this was his sister and then chastising my self because his marital status was no concern of mine.

As she left the table he looked my way and told me that the food was good and filling.

"They have a great Ruben, but the roast beef is out of this world."

I glanced over the menu that I had been hiding behind and saw his clear grey-green eyes gazing back, a hint of a smile in them.

"I think the roast beef will be fine." The back of my mind was already anticipating the doggy bag for my imaginary canine, known as lunch.

I realized that I was hungry. I hadn't eaten since morning and the wafting aromas from the kitchen were heavenly.

It was then I realized that this was the only clear thought I had since we left the precinct. The walk here was filled with thoughts that flew through my head with no real clarity, rhyme or reason. I didn't remember anything we may have talked about. It was a relief to just know that I was famished. All thoughts stopped when I looked up and saw those green grey eyes looking back at me.

The waitress had chosen that moment to come for our order. We both ordered the roast beef. Detective Keyes ordered a bottle of wine.

The waitress was collecting our menus when a portly woman came bustling up to our table with a wall to wall smile. She was short and wore a bright white apron. She was a bustle of energy. Her grey streaked hair was held back in a bun and her eyes were twinkling as she came to the table.

Jesse rose to greet her. Stepping on her tiptoes she held her hands on each side of his face.

"Jesse where have you been, no calls, no stopping by, did you forget about us?"

Jesse bent down to give Mama a kiss on a very rosy cheek, "Mama, I could never forget you. Here I am. Your food was calling to me."

As hokey as that sentence was, he had made it sound sincere.

"Mama, I would like you to meet CJ, She is a friend and I've told her what wonderful food you have."

Mama turned to me and looked me up and down. *This seemed to be my day for inspections.* I stood up to shake her hand but she took each of my hands in hers. She looked into my face. "Jesse, she is special. You must take care to keep her close. You, Miss CJ, must come often and let us feed you with good healthy food."

She turned back to go back into her kitchen as she told us to enjoy our meal.

I was left standing there, again with my mouth hanging open, trying to get a grasp on all my whirling thoughts.

"Is that your mother?" was all I could stutter out as I returned to my seat.

"No that is *Mama*. She is the only mother I know. Most of the people who work here are here because of Mama, we all love her, she takes in strays and watches us grow. She expects only the best from us. Annie, the waitress, was a run away; she ended up at mama's door. Mama fed her, made her go to school, she will graduate this year. She wants to be a nurse. We'll all help her get through school."

My mind was swimming. This man had a real talent, giving me answers to unasked questions. Each time he opened his mouth I found another unexpected side to him.

I changed the subject. "Detective Keyes, I can look up the local bonds men, I do appreciate all the help you've given but I really can't take up all your time."

"Call me Jesse, and you're not taking up my time, I'm here because I want to be here. And I'm hungry. You surprised when I saw you squaring off with Dombrowski, not many can do that. I like your spunk. I'm just doing my job as a public servant making sure all our citizens are safe."

"You might want to remind Dombrowski about that. You don't have worry about me; I can take care of myself. If you have a list of bondsmen it would be great, but I do have a phonebook."

His eye brow lifted and his smile grew wider.

"CJ, I saw you posting your notices a while ago. Since that time I seemed to see you everywhere. Coming from the cleaners, at the diner on 5th, you popped up here and there and I knew that some day I would find out who you were. Today you turned up at the station and do something I have tried to do for years, tick off Dombrowski. I'm in awe. It was an amazing sight. I want to know more about you. I was going to follow up on your posters you saved me the trouble."

Now I was totally flabbergasted. I took the glass of wine he offered and gulped it down. My eyes had to be a big as saucers.

"What? Detective Keyes, uh, Jesse, I don't have relationships. I have a business to run, I don't date." Words were spouting out of my mouth but none of them seemed to be filtering through my brain.

Detective Keyes put one of his hands over mine. "This is just supper, and I just want to know you better. You're a beautiful, intelligent woman. You have a business. You have spunk. What's not to like? If you are not interested then just say so and I'll wave when I see you in the street. But I would like to be a friend. Besides I'm really hungry and would like to have dinner with a really attractive woman."

Our salads had come and still I had no words. I was grateful for the distraction. I was fiddling with my fork silently making a list why this was impossible.

I was not a normal person. I could not have a normal relationship. I was socially inept. I never really had a date.

On the other hand, here I was with a handsome kind man who offered friendship and a meal. I looked up and studied Detective Keyes, *Jesse*, as he enjoyed his salad. I decided to enjoy my meal too.

The roast beef was the excellent, tender with carrots on the side, home baked rolls and mashed potatoes with gravy. The meal was topped off with a wonderful apple pie.

Jesse made the conversation easier. We talked about what I had done to start my business. How I liked it. He offered to get me a list of bondsmen and volunteered to go to the few that might be a bit rough around the edges. I found out that he did not have a significant other. His life was centered in the area and he knew almost everyone.

People came and went around us some nodded at Jesse, but no one stopped at our table. I found myself genuinely enjoying his company.

Jess walked me back to the station and then led me to his car. My address was only a few blocks away but he insisted on driving. As he walked me to the door he said he would call when he had the list together, "Unless you want to try charming Dombrowski again." I laughed as he took my hands in his and his steady gaze darkened. and I thought he might kiss me. Before he could, I panicked and pulled away.

"Thank you for the help and the wonderful meal!" I called behind me as I ran up the stairs.

I stood with my back to the door wondering what I was doing. I needed some quiet time. What had just happened? What was this attraction? I had a business dinner with a fine looking man. Don't go thinking that it was more. Experience had taught me that I had too much to hide. Eventually it would all come out and I would have to deal with it. Not a pleasant thought. Disappointment and heartache wasn't part of my business plan. Just enjoy the moment and concentrate on my livelihood.

It was fun though, I could still dream, and this was a really nice one.

Chapter 3

I woke up dreaming wrapped up in warm fuzzy feelings. The events of the previous evening were still floating in my head as I drifted on air. I shook my head and told myself to get down to business. The events of last night would have to stay a dream. I still had to eat.

I pulled out the wanted posters and studied the faces while I read the minimal data. There was not much to go on just the bare bone facts.

I touched the flyer on Rosie Cross and started to get my old familiar feeling. Rosie's file read that she had stolen items and had resisted arrest. I folded the poster and stuffed it in my back pocket.

I left the office and walked the seven blocks to Rosie's listed address. A sad unkempt looking house, one shutter was hanging off the side of the window and the whole house needed paint. I went down the side alley and saw that the back yard was fenced; a section sagging and partially bent back. There were houses on both sides and one behind it.

After scoping out the area I went to front the door. It was slightly open. My tingling increased as I walked in.

Rumpled newspapers were strewn on the couch and floor, dirty dishes and cups were on the coffee table. Ashtrays were full and overflowing. The tattered furniture looked too nasty to sit on.

I followed a hallway that led to the kitchen. The sink was piled with dishes; the garbage reeked and was overflowing. There were more large plastic bags on the back porch. Not a hospitable place. I couldn't imagine the kind of person who would want live this way.

There was an open door at the end of the kitchen. Walking through it I saw a shadow of a woman sitting in a chair. She seemed to be sleeping.

This room looked tired but was much tidier then the rest of the house. Old dolls and photographs were on the dresser a scarf was folded neatly next to them. The bed was made.

The woman's face was turned to the only window; the sun seemed to make her glow. She looked younger then she did on the poster. Her dress was worn but neat. She had on a pair of well used house slippers. I sat on the edge of her bed and spoke softly to her.

"Rosie, you missed your court date. You need to go to the police station with me."

She slowly opened her eyes trying to rouse herself awake. I knew she could not see me, the tingling was getting stronger and I felt an overwhelming urge to leave the room.

I looked out of the half closed door and heard him before I saw him. The man was tall; his clothes were dirty and rumpled. He was loud and clumsy as he roared through the house. Greasy long hair and a scraggly beard added to his menacing aura. Cold dark eyes darted in every direction as he moved through the rooms. The smell of sweat, beer, and cigarettes was overpowering as he reached Rosie's door. Throwing his coat on a chair he bellowed "Rosie! Where are you? You can't hide! Get your ass out here you lazy ole bitch!"

The intensity of my feelings rose with the tone of his voice, he totally pissed me off. I stepped aside as he stomped past me and entered her room.

"What you doing sitting here? Where's your check, it's the 15th. Give it up!" He stomped angrily to the side of the bed raising his hands ready to strike her. "I got things I got to do. Hand it over!"

Rosie was now wide awake; fear had her cowering in her chair. Years seemed to rush into her face. She looked up afraid not wanting to confront him.

She said quietly "Ralph, I need that money. I have to pay Mary for this room and I have to go to the police station."

His face screwed up and his eyes grew round as he raised his hand to strike her. "Your gonna give me that check, and I'm gonna make damn sure you don't go see any police."

Rosie shrank deeper into her chair. "I can't Ralph, I need that money."

Ralph took a step forward. I didn't wait. I darted behind him and grabbed his arm twisting it high up his back. He screamed out and tried to turn around. I kicked him in the back of his knees and he went down. "wha . . . the?"

Ralph could feel my hold but not see me. He went from angry to alarmed He had no point of reference for what was happening to him.

When he tried to rise I kicked him back to the floor. My heel was pressed hard on the back of his neck. His hands were reaching back trying to feel what was holding him down. I had grabbed the scarf from the dresser and started winding it around his wrists.

Trying to see behind him, staring at the scarf as it tied itself around his wrists, he called to Rosie. "Rosie? Rosie! What's going on . . . what's happening?"

His wrist secure, I took the other end of the scarf and forced one of his legs up and tied it tight. I reached around me and touched a dresser. I grabbed the first thing out of a drawer, a ball of material and shoved in his bellowing mouth. I stepped back and watched as he fought to get out of the bindings while muffling curses through a pair of bright red socks.

Rosie had risen and was hugging herself behind the chair. Shaking and terrified. I could only guess what could have freaked her most, a big mean-mouthed bully or the disembodied scarf.

I couldn't go over to comfort her but she needed help; she was working up to hysterical.

I went back to the end of the bed. "Rosie, listen to me Rosie, leave this room. Leave this house now!"

Rosie hesitated and looked around and then took off at a fast shuffle. She didn't want to pass Ralph so she skirted around the bed. I placed my foot back on his neck. He froze.

As Rosie shuffled out of the room I went out the back door, breathing deep and trying to regain some form while I rushed to the front of the house. I reached Rosie as she reached the edge of the sidewalk. She was shaking her head back and forth trying to figure out which way she should run. Her arms were wrapped around herself. Big tears ran down her face.

I walked up to her. "Rosie? Are you all right?"

She opened her mouth once and then again but nothing came out.

"Rosie, My name is CJ; I came here to see you."

"See me?" You want to see me"?

I took her hand as I said, "Rosie, I came to see you, I want to help you. Do you have a minute to talk? Let's go over to the Diner and have some tea."

She looked at me as if I offered her sanctuary. We walked slowly, her slippers making shuffling noises on the sidewalk. She laughed and made a comment about forgetting her shoes.

We sat a table halfway to the back of the diner; I ordered us both an iced tea. After a bit she was calm enough to talk, she looked surprised to be sitting across from me. "Who are you?"

"My name is CJ, and I have come to help you. But you have to help me. Will you help me?"

She looked at me and sighed. She sipped her tea and cleared her throat. "How can I help you? I can't even help myself."

"Who is that man Rosie, the one you ran from?"

"Ralph, Ralph is a bad man. He likes to hurt people. He steals, He's a bad man." Large tears were forming in her eyes. She lowered her head.

"What did he do to you Rosie?"

"He steals my money. He hurts my daughter and won't let me see her. I don't know what to do." Tears were streaming down her cheeks. "If I tell you, or anyone, he said he would kill us and nobody will find us." She shrunk back into herself, her head was down.

"That's not going to happen Rosie; I'm going to help you."

Her head came up fast "How? Nobody can know," she pleaded, "He will kill us!"

"Rosie, you can't live like this. I am going to find your daughter. I am going to get you out of this mess. We are going to the police station and report this. You will be safe. I am a private detective and I went to your house because I wanted to talk to you about the court date you missed. I will ask that you be allowed to stay there until I get some more information on your daughter."

We sat for a long time. I listened as she told me about her daughter and what she knew about Ralph. I found out Mary was Rosie's landlady and was in the same boat. I wondered how many others he preyed on to get what he wanted.

After a while we walked to the station and she turned herself in. I waited for my receipt relieved that Dombrowski wasn't at the desk. I gave Rosie a hug before she was led to the back and told her I would come back for her as soon as I could. I thought about asking for Jesse, but decided to wait until later. I wanted to get back to Ralph and get some more information.

I was half way to the street when I heard my named called. I looked up and saw Jesse lopping across the parking lot heading my way.

"Hey CJ, what are you doing back so soon, come to get my list?" He was pulling a sheaf of papers out of his jacket and handed them to me.

He looked so handsome. I was happy to see him and startled that he was in front of me. My heart did a little flip.

"I just dropped Rosie Cross off. She's a nice lady, she has several problems that I hope to help her with, is there anyway she can stay for a while?" This came out all in a rush; he had a look of disbelief on his face.

"My, you have been busy." I couldn't help noticing that his smile matched mine. "We will have to talk about this, Can you meet me later? I have court most of the afternoon but I should be done about four."

I told him that would fine but I had an errand and I was already late. He took my hand and held it. "I'll call when I get out."

I left him and walked in the direction of Rosie's house.

As I turned the corner to Rosie's I began to feel that old familiar feeling. I knew that Ralph was still trussed up like a pig and he had to be angry. I walked into the house quickly. I was fading fast.

Entering the bedroom I stepped over Ralph and sat on the bed. He must have felt the air disturbed around him and the creak from the bed was a dead giveaway. His head came up his eyes were wild as he looked around. He was scared. I could hear him muffling through the socks that were still lodged in his mouth. I didn't even try to understand him.

I sat for a minute before I came up with an idea that might give me the advantage I needed. I stepped over Ralph again, his eyes latched on the dresser as a drawer opened. His eyes bulged as a scarf flew out. His eyes grew even larger and he started to bulk, his mumbling got even louder as I wrapped the scarf around his eyes. I kicked him in the side and told him shut up.

I sat on the bed again. His head came up. He waved it around trying to sense what was next. I gave him a moment and then I spoke.

"I will take the gag out of your mouth. When I do you will answer my questions. You will not fight, you will not lie. If you do I can promise you a trip to hell with no return ticket."

I was pretty proud of the last sentence. I had heard it in a movie and I thought it was pretty hokey, it sounded pretty good here.

Ole Ralphie was settling down. I reached over and pulled the socks out his mouth.

He was shaking his head while stretching his jaw. Moving his head around he wanted to play tough. "You got any water?" His raspy voice had an edge to it.

"Maybe later, when and if you earn it. Where is Rosie's daughter?"

"Who the hell are you? What do you want? I don't know nothing!"

"That's your first lie. Where is Rosie's daughter?"

"Margaret's my girl. I take care of my girl."

"I'll bet you do. Where is she?"

"At the house, what's it to you?"

"What house? What's the address?" I gave a less then gentle kick to his head.

"Hey, stop it. She's at my house, Cherry St. 438 Cherry Street. You dumb bitch."

"Here's the story, Ralphie boy, you're a pig. You will never come back here again. You will leave Rosie and Margaret alone. I will find you're other victims and I will make sure that they will never be bothered by you again."

He opened his mouth and started to bellow at me. I stuck the sock back in his mouth.

I grabbed his wallet as I walked over him and rummaged through it for his drivers license. He had a little over $300.00 and I wondered who it belonged to.

I walked back into the kitchen went to the phone on the wall and dialed the number from Jesse's card and was told to leave a message.

I told him that there was a thief trussed up at Rosie's and I needed to get some information on him, as in reward? I glanced up at a clock and realized that most of the day had passed but I still had an hour or so before Jesse would be available. I called the precinct and asked to talk to the desk sergeant. I was put through and again counted my blessings that Dombrowski voice wasn't on the other end. I spoke to a Sergeant O'Riley and asked if there were any sheets on Ralph W. Mooring. I rattled of his drivers' license number and wondered if I would get any information.

Sergeant O'Riley asked who I was and why I wanted to know. I told him my name and that I was a private detective. I had Mr. Ralph Mooring and would appreciate some help bringing him in. There were two victims willing to press charges for extortion. O'Riley asked for the address and told me that a squad car was on the way.

It didn't take long. I was myself again and sitting on the top step of the porch when the squad car pulled up. I explained that Mooring had threatened to hurt Rosie because she would not give her money to him. I needed to pick up a lady who would sign another complaint. *I hoped she would after I explained that her mother was in jail.* I also told them that there were other victims and I would get their names and give them a list as soon as I contacted them. "Moorings in the back bedroom I'll meet you back to the station."

As I left I heard one of the officers the officers laughing. "Hey Mooring, we've been looking for you. I like your scarf."

I could hear him raging behind his sock. I wanted to stick around and hear Ralph's version but I really needed to get to Cherry Street and talk to Margaret. Maybe I could get Rosie out since Ralphie boy was going in.

I ran the eight blocks to Cherry Street. I stopped in front of the house and saw that it was in sad condition too. I knocked on the door hoping that Margaret was there. It was a good ten minutes of constant knocking before the door opened. A woman opened the door a couple of inches.

"What do you want? I'm not buying anything!" I pushed the door open. She glared at me.

"I said I don't want to buy anything!" The woman at the door resembled Rosie. She had long stringy matted hair and a tattered robe that had seen better days. At first glance I saw that she been crying. Looking closer I saw that her cheek was red and swollen and she had the beginning of a black eye. Her movements were slow and painful. Her feet were bare and the look on her face was one of lost hope. Before me stood a woman that had been beaten down and held very little expectations.

"I came here to talk about Rosie, I met her today and she needs your help."

She looked at me and said "The only way I can help is to stay away, I can't help you."

I was on a timetable I didn't have time to argue. "Look, let me come in; I have a lot to say and not much time."

I pushed her aside and walked into a room that must have used Rosie's decorator.

She followed me holding her arms around herself. "What do you want? You have to leave, someone's coming over and you can't be here."

I looked her in the eye, "Ralph is not coming back. He is on the way to the police station and we're going to keep him there. I need you to help your mother and yourself."

I could see some hope flicker, but she wasn't ready to believe me.

"My name is CJ, I am a Private Investigator." I gave her one of my cards. "I was picking your mother up for skipping bond when I met her. She explained that Ralph was in the house and demanding money. That he would hurt her. She is in jail and safe. As soon as Ralph is charged I will try to get her out. I need you to come with me and back up your mother's statements, if you have any charges, you can make them at that time. I am here to help Rosie, but this is a good time to stop Ralph, I can't do this without your help."

She gave me a steady gaze. I could see the change in her posture and the look of determination that replaced the hopelessness that was in her face.

"Let me get dressed. Mom's okay, right? She's not hurt is she?" She went into a room and within minutes she returned wearing sweater and a pair of jeans.

"Your moms okay, she's scared, I told her I would do all I could to help both of you."

She slipped on her shoes and grabbed her purse while quickly brushing her hair into a ponytail. She looked ten years younger. She was a very pretty woman even with the bruises.

As we headed for the police station, she gave me some background on how Ralph operated. She knew others that Ralph had been fleecing. She would get me get me the names and addresses of those she knew. She told me of another man named Art who worked with Ralph and he did more then help Ralph scam money.

"Your going to have to tell the police all this."

"If you can help my mom I'll tell you everything I know." She seemed to grow stronger with each step.

When we arrived at the station I asked the status of Rosie and what had happened to Ralph. I explained that I was the one that made the call on Ralph. I was told us that Ralph was in holding and the officers were taking statements. He laughed as he confided that Ralph was telling ghost stories. That statement made me a little uncomfortable but I didn't comment on it.

I introduced Margaret as Rosie's daughter and asked if we could see her. He called someone from the back and asked us to take a seat. Margaret was pacing beside the bench while I checked to see if anyone had been added to the poster collection. Margaret was determined to make sure Ralph paid for his crimes.

I looked up just as Jesse walked into the room. He was returning from court and I could tell that he was distracted. He was surprised when I called out to him. He walked over to me with a questioning look and a big smile.

I took a step back and introduced Margaret while I explained that she was Rosie's daughter.

"We came in to sign a complaint on Ralph W. Mooring. I need to find out if there is a reward on him."

His smile lit up lit up the room, "Mooring has been off the radar. We've been looking for him for a while. He's wanted for questioning for a couple of things. How did you meet him?"

"It's a long story. We're waiting for Rosie. Is there anyway you could help speed up the works?"

We followed him back to his desk. The room had more people and noise than it did the last time I was here. I found out that Ralph was worth a whooping $1,500.00.

It was quite a while before we left. Rosie was allowed to leave after an appearance before the judge. She explained that she could not make her court date because she had been beaten by Mooring so badly that she could barely move. The Judge set her court date and released her in Margaret's custody. They left the building holding each other.

Ralph was wanted on several counts, he was not going anywhere. The word was out that he was talking to ghosts; rumor had it that he would try to plead insanity. Jesse called the bail bondsman who held Rosie's bond and my share was $50.00. I would take the receipt to the bondman in the morning. Jesse would be tied up with the complaints and interrogation.

It was going on seven. The sun was setting. It had been a long day and I was thinking of the roast beef in my mini fridge. I stopped on the way home and picked up some orange juice for the morning and six-pack of Beck's. As an after thought I added milk and muffins to the mix. I counted out the change and I had left in my pocket $11.44. But on the happy side I would have $50.00 in the morning. I had given the $300.00 from Ralph's wallet to Rosie to pay the rent.

I walked up the last few stairs thinking about how nice a bubble bath would feel. I put the groceries away, and started to run water in the bathtub. I undressed and leaned back into the water letting the warmth take all the strain and dirt away from me. I went underwater closing out the world.

When I opened my eyes; the water was cold and the bubbles were gone. I lifted myself out of the tub and grabbed a towel. I was ready for supper.

Chapter 4

I woke the next morning feeling wonderful. I did a mental run of *things I gotta do*. There were several items on my agenda, but none as important as my $50.00 bounty on Rosie and the possible $ 1, 500.00 on Ralph. I looked at my alarm clock that was just about to ring and turned it off. I had two hours before *Fred's Bail Bonds & Pawn Shop* opened. I went into the kitchen, started the coffee and ran back to wash up and get dressed. There was a nip in the room and I reminded myself that the days were shorter and I needed to work harder.

I listened to the answering machine while I sat making notes on yesterday's happenings. The landlord called. He would be by to fix the window. Someone wanted to sell me insurance. The next call sat me straight up in my seat.

"CJ, Jesse here. Sorry I missed you. I have a couple of questions but I wanted to tell you that you're incredible. I will stop by in the morning and introduce you to Fred. There is another bondsman in the same area. If it's a problem call me, I'll be there by seven."

I stared at the phone and checked the time. I had my calendar out and entered Rosie's new court date. My file cards were updated with all the new names and numbers I had. I still had time before Jesse was due.

I never considered myself a glamour girl. I went to the hallway and looked in the mirror. I really tried to be objective. But the skinny little girl I grew up with was still in there. My hair was short and the curls were running wild. Not to tall, fairly decent legs and eyes to big for my face. I thought of putting on makeup but I didn't know where it was. Every flaw I ever had seemed to be staring back at me. My inspection was interrupted by a knock on the door. I took a deep breath and went to answer it.

Jesse stood in the doorway. He was so handsome his smile lit up the room. He looked great in jeans and a dark blue shirt. He walked past me waving a paper bag under my nose.

"Are you hungry? I brought some bagels, do I smell coffee? I take mine with cream."

He was taking in my surroundings as he found the way to the kitchen. It was small and cozy before he entered; it was now wall to wall male. I had a nook table and two chairs. He sat the bag on the table and turned around and bumped into me. I felt myself stumble backward and caught my balance when he pulled me to him. He held me for a heartbeat, then he placed his hand on my cheek and looked into my eyes, I felt a rush.

I felt my knees weaken. I took a deep breath as I stepped back "Err . . . a, thanks Jesse." I stuttered

"Have a seat, I'll get that coffee." I wasn't sure if my legs would work.

Jesse reached behind me and picked up the bag of bagels. He had also brought some cream cheese and made one for both of us. I placed a cup of coffee in front of him.

"Do you have any cream or milk?" he asked. I went to the mini fridge and opened the door and winced as it hit his knee. I handed the milk to him. We both were quiet now. I couldn't find a reason to speak. If I tried I was sure it would come out garbled.

He poured the milk into his cup and took a sip. "Not bad, you make a wicked cup of coffee."

We both reached for the bagels. He backed off as I took one he then took one for himself. We sat eating the bagels listening to the silence. It seemed to grow around us.

Jesse cleared his throat and said "You are so beautiful."

I nearly choked on my bagel. I was speechless how does one respond to a statement like that? I came up with a weak "Thanks"

I spied the clock on the wall mumbled something about my jacket and ran from the room.

I sat on my bed wishing I had a book on how to talk to good looking guys. I had no experience. How were we going to work together if I lost the power of speech every time we shared a space? Being beautiful was not something I as ready work with. That was personal. I don't do personal.

I glanced up and saw Jesse leaning on the door frame. He had a smirk of a smile. Damn he was handsome.

"I'm sorry if I embarrassed you. I pretty much watch what I say, but with you words jump out of my mouth. I was out of line."

I looked up, "Jesse. I don't go out looking for men. I am concentrating on my business. I really don't have time to play around."

Jesse's eyes turned to a cold steel grey, his face, and his stance seemed to turn hard. His body language was on alert.

"You think that I want to play around? Hell girl, I want to get to know you. I want to go to dinner, maybe dancing once in a while, I don't play around. If you just want to be friends, I can do that."

He turned around and walked back into the kitchen. I could hear him rinse the cups and ball up the bagel bag.

Damn. The guy cleaned up too. I walked out of the bedroom and went into the kitchen.

He turned as I got to the door. He looked defeated and leaned with his back to the sink.

"Jesse, I'm sorry. I don't have much experience. I don't know what to say except that you've helped me so much already. For some reason I can't think around you."

"CJ, we'll go slow and learn about each other. No pressure. I want to be a friend. Lets get over to Freddie's, I'd like to catch him when opens his up."

As we walked out and I locked my door, Jesse stopped to read my window.

"Nice sign, next time maybe you can show me around. I have a leather sofa that will look good in your reception room. Its in storage, It might as well be used."

"I would pay you for it. You'll have to wait until I get some more work. But I could find a place for it."

He stopped in the street. "You sure have a hard head. I'm paying to store it. I'm giving it to you so I can save money."

"You are not a very logical man. I'll think about it."

"How about this, you borrow the sofa until I find a place for it."

"So your can save on storage fees?"

He stopped dead in the street and threw up his arms. I kept walking, thinking it was so nice to see that smile again.

He had parked his car in front of my building. It was an old Chevy Nova in mint condition. It smelled like him and he smelled so very good. I wasn't surprised to see him pat the steering wheel before he turned the key. When he turned on the engine I was sure that it would go very, very fast. I buckled myself in, leaned back and watched as he maneuvered into traffic. The time and effort he had put into his car reflected in his face.

As we drove he told me about Freddy. He lived and worked on the other side of town. Freddy's was a landmark. In business when he was the only business. He had put his two children through college, His wife of 52 years died several years back. He could retire but the pawn shop was his baby. Rain or shine he was open. He rarely denied anyone bond. He had many friends and loved to play cards.

Freddy's business was in a square dark brick building with a well worn green stripped awning. The window was full of all kinds of items, guitars, horns, drums, necklaces, and large ugly dog that had a chip on his ear and a missing tail. There were hundreds of other items that I'm sure he didn't remember he had.

We waited in the doorway commenting on all the different items when I spotted a man come down the street. He wore a battered suit with wide lapels and a bright red bowtie, His hair was combed over a shiny bald head. He was short and stooped. He looked up and saw us standing by his door. He squinted at us through thick glasses and then smiled showing a mouth full of teeth.

"Jesse boy! How have you been? Are waiting for me? Am I late?" He was looking at his pocket watch. He looked relieved that he was on time. He put the watch back and pulled out a key. Fitting it into the lock he jiggled it a few times and opened the door. A bell jingled at our entry.

The shop was dark with wall to wall clutter. I walked slowly behind them until he turned on the lights. It didn't help the room's ambiance but at least I could see what I was walking into. The whole time he chattered on, not waiting for an answer before he launched into the next question.

"Jesse you catch any bad guys? How is Mama? What wonderful thing did we want from his store? Who is this pretty lady?"

We made it to the front of the store and waited as he went around the counter and turned on a multi colored desk light. He adjusted his glasses and made him self comfortable on a high stool and listened while Jesse answered his questions.

"Fred, this is CJ. She just started a business on the other side of town. She's a Private Detective."

I pulled out one of my cards and handed it to Freddy. He looked at it closely and then looked at me.

"This is a strange line of work for a lady, but ladies do all kinds of work nowadays. Police work, fire fighting work, carpentry, stocks and bonds, you be very careful Miss CJ, you are so pretty, you must not let anything harm you."

I was blushing. Now I was pretty. Before I could answer Jesse spoke up "Oh, don't worry Freddy, I don't plan on letting anything happen to CJ."

Freddy raised his eyebrows and looked at Jesse, he nodded his head as if he approved. "CJ, I am proud to meet such a beautiful lady. Jesse,

I'm pleased to meet your friend, but I can see by your face you need something."

Jesse looked at me to explain.

I looked at Freddy and said "I picked up one of your bond skips yesterday." I pulled out the poster and a receipt that I received from Sergeant O'Riley.

"I am here to collect the reward for retrieving her." He looked at the receipt and then again at me. "You brought Rosie in? Such a nice woman."

"Yes she is" I replied. "She is imperative to an ongoing investigation. She did not mean to skip on the money you paid for her bond."

I wanted to explain more but I felt that what I knew was still being investigated.

Freddy looked at me again and replied. "It is a reward well deserved, come to my office and we will make it right."

We followed him behind the counter into a room that was just as cluttered as the room we left but with papers and books and a big roll top desk that had pidgin holes over flowing with papers. Post-its were stuck on files and in various places.

He pulled out a large black well used ledger book and opened it; he flipped a couple of pages and found the entry he wanted.

"I have that I would owe you 10% of the poster value. That would be $50.00 dollars. Is that correct with you?"

I told him that it was. He reached for a pen and made out a receipt. It had the date, Rosie's name, and the amount and asked me to sign that I had received the money.

I borrowed his pen as he reached into a pocket and pulled out a handful of bills folded in half. He counted out $50.00 in $20's and a $10 and placed it in my hand.

"I thank you for your service." he said as continued to hold my hand that held the money. "If I can help you in the future please come to me. I would ask some help if you are not too busy."

He turned around and picked up a dog eared paper that was another face on a poster. "I would like to find Matt Dawson. If you could look into it I will pay twice the reward."

I looked at the picture and saw that the reward was for $500, 00. I looked at Freddy "I will do my best."

Freddy walked us to the door. He shook Jesses hand and told him to come back soon and be sure to bring me with him. He looked at me and told me that he would make sure to let people know if they needed my help.

"Both of you be careful. Come and see me again soon." A big knowing smile was on his face as he gave a wave and a wink.

"Let's go get some coffee." Jess said as he opened the car door. "I have some time before I have to set in on a conference and we have a few minuets before you meet the infamous Vince."

Chapter 5

We ended up sitting in a shabby little diner that had sandwiches, bad coffee and not much else. We sat at a table by the window. There was a lot of foot traffic. It was a good people watching place. If I were alone I would be amusing myself by thinking up lives for the pedestrians that walked by. Not today. We sat down and gave our order to the waitress. When she brought the coffee we both sat doctoring it in silence.

After I had my first sip Jesse opened the conversation by telling me that I accomplished much more then picking up Rosie. I had helped to bust a ring of abuse that was bigger then the police were aware of.

"Some reports had come in but no one would admit it or come forward. Most of the people that were contacted last evening were still afraid to speak up. We have a task force looking into the names that you gave us. I don't know how you accomplished so much in one day. I read your report and it's pretty straight forward. But a few questions came up and I hoped that you could help fill in the blanks."

I looked over the top of my cup and I took a sip. I told him that I didn't know what I could add, but if I could help ask away.

"CJ, Mooring said a ghost tied him up, the same ghost demanded to know where Margaret was. We didn't pay much attention at the time; we figured he was working to plead insanity. It wasn't until I read Rosie's report and she stated that a Guardian Angel helped her and that this angel told her to run out of the house. That doesn't explain how Mooring got tied up. Rosie didn't do it, and she swears she saw an invisible guardian angel do it."

"This Guardian-Ghost was not visible to either of them. You said you came up to Rosie as she came out of the house. Did you see anyone around? I need to know exactly what you saw, and if you can tell me something about these invisible phantoms."

It seemed he had the story. My only hope was that he would accept what I was frantically trying to come up with. I put my cup on the table. He was intent on what I was about to say. I did not want to lie.

"I came up on Rosie in front of the house, she looked lost and confused. She was upset and crying. I went to her and told her who I was and I would I help her if she came with me to the police station. She was pretty hysterical. I took her to the café for some ice tea. She was really scared."

Jesse wasn't going to stop there.

"How did Mooring get tied up?"

I evaded the question. "Rosie told me he was there. I dropped Rosie at the station and went back to the house and there he was. Rosie told me it was Mooring, and what he had been doing to her, I called the police." That sounded simple.

Jesse countered with, "Mooring said that the ghost asked him about Margaret. How did you know about Margaret?"

"Rosie told me about Margaret at the café. Like I said she was upset. Mooring had been hurting her and threatened both of them. He said that he would kill them. He was using them against each other. The next logical step for me was to contact Margaret."

I waited for the next question. I could almost hear the wheels in his head spinning as he went through every sentence I uttered. I realized I was holding my breath as his eyes looked into mine. I took another sip of coffee.

I hadn't lied; I did omit a few things in the time frame. But I would never be believed if I told the absolute truth. I was hoping that I sounded sincere. The bare bone of my story was true. It was just that some of those bones needed to stay buried

Jesse looked at me. "Mooring had an outstanding warrant. We cannot give the reward to a ghost or guardian angel. The fact that you called it in and had him in custody to be transported to the station means that you can request the bounty. It's in Bales County so we will have to go there to collect. Maybe while we're there we can get a lead on his ghost."

Apparently my answers satisfied him for the moment. I could think of few things that could complicate my story. Like the fact that I got Margaret's address from Mooring. Or that Rosie and Mooring had heard my voice. I was not going to bring that up.

Jesse looked at me and put his hand on mine and told me that he could think of a hundred things that could have gone wrong. "The way it went down was a lucky break. The way that all of the pieces fit together are pretty hazy. There are a couple of things that don't quite jive, but we are interviewing the other victims. I want a solid case when it comes time for trial."

I back tracked the conversation to the bounty of Mooring. "I can collect on Mooring?"

"Yeah, you'll qualify. I'm not exactly sure of the amount but I can drive you over. I have the bondsman's name and address in my desk."

His attention was drawn to the street. I looked up just as he grabbed his jacket and said "Come on, one of your possible employers just opened up."

I followed Jesse down the block to the street crossing. I could almost see the wheels turning in his head and knew that our conversation was not closed. He was in his *cop* mode. This was a side of him I hadn't seen, it was disconcerting that it was on my behalf. I walked beside him concentrating on our conversation. We reached the other side of the street when he said that he was *relieved to know that that I could handle myself.* I was wondering just what he meant when we reached a small shabby building.

At the counter sat a little man on a stool. He had a heavy accent when he greeted Jesse.

"What can I do for you Keyes? Haven't seen you in this part of town for a while."

We stood in front of the counter. "I just thought I would come and visit the neighborhood. I wanted make sure that you were safe Vince."

The air was palatable; these two men did not like each other. I was wondering why Jesse would introduce me to this guy. There had to be other bondsmen.

Vince was a sleazy little man. Extremely skinny, his clothes were hanging on him and they were not too clean. Stains marked his shirt and a thick smell of cheap cigars was hovering in the air. He had thin greasy brown hair and really bad teeth. His eyes were red and he had deep circles under them. A birthmark on the left side of his face added to his sinister look. I was having second and third thoughts about working with this man.

"I had a particular reason to see you Vince. This is my friend CJ; she just started a new business that might interface with yours."

Vince leered at me over his counter. "Cute little piece Keyes but how can this little bit fluff help me?"

I felt like I wanted to go home and take a shower. His beady little eyes were undressing me while he smiled like a Cheshire cat.

Jesse cut him off. Before I realized what was happening Jesse had yanked Vince's shirt collar pulling him up to the counter bringing them face to face.

"Vince, CJ is under my protection. I will stick your balls in your mouth if you touch her."

Vince didn't look intimidated but he was defiantly paying attention.

"CJ has a business on the other side of town, she is a Private Detective. She happens to be looking into one of your skips; we came to get some information."

Vince looked at me and then at Jesse and said "She's a private dick? She doesn't even have one."

Jesse, who had yet to let go of Vince's collar, yanked it so hard that Vince was pulled halfway over the counter. Vince finally showed some fear.

"Watch your mouth. She can walk out of here and you'll never know what she can do for you."

"Okay, Okay, Sorry Keyes, you too CJ, but we don't get anyone in here like you. Who are you looking for?"

I wanted him to take me seriously. I took a deep breath and tried to sound confident. "I need any information you have on Max Wiggins. I need contacts, phones and addresses."

"You're going after Max? Max can't be found his whole family hides him. You get close and you have a swarm of Wiggins's hiding him behind their skirts, giving you bad information. I should have never bailed him out. That family is bad news."

"*Poor Max couldn't stay in Jail. Poor Max would be tortured.*" Vince said in a high whiny voice. I should have let him rot. Max's mom had the water works going, the brother kept saying he was set up. They said they would make sure that he showed up for court. I think I did it to get them out of my office. I did it! I hate being anyone's fool. The whole family should be behind bars."

I looked at him and was amazed at the change in him, such passion when it came to money.

"Just give me the information. I'll get back to you if I need more. I gave him my card and took one his from the counter. I felt like I should disinfect it before I put it in my wallet.

We waited as Vince went to get the information. He came out of the back office with a dog eared file folder. He eased himself over to a loaded piece of furniture that turned out to be a copy machine. He copied every page. He came back to me and handed me the copies.

"Good luck honey, I hope you find him. You better stay close to her Keyes; the whole family is crazy-mean. They don't' mind breaking things like arms and legs and heads."

It was a relief to get back on the street. The sun was so bright after Vince's dark and smelly office that my eyes hurt. I looked at Jesse and thanked him for his help. He looked down and his eyes grew soft as he looked at my face.

"Anytime CJ, I know Vince is a strange fellow. I didn't want you to go here on your own. He will let it be known that I stand behind you so the seedier elements won't bother you. But promise me you won't come around here alone, especially when it's dark."

I was quiet for a moment but I had to tell him. "Jesse, we just met, but I can take care of myself, not everyone works the day shift, and not everyone's going to meet me under a street light. If I think I need help I will call you. I don't have a death wish."

Jesse kept with the *look* and finally said. "You *will* call me if you need help."

It sounded more like an order then a request. I chose to ignore the attitude.

I gave him the *look* back and said "Who else would I call. You're the only person I know."

Jesse began to laugh; this was the first time I heard him really laugh. Before I knew it I was lifted off of the sidewalk and swung in a circle. Before I could tell him to put me down he lowered his face to mine and kissed me. Just a peck but I got a jolt. I think we were both thrown by it. He held me as he looked in my eyes, "Baby there's something here."

He put me down and opened my door. He went to the drivers' side and got in, buckled up, and turned the key. He looked at his watch, "I have to get you back. I've got twenty minutes to get to my meeting."

Jesse stopped in front of my building. It was a quiet ride; both of us were lost in thought and I wondered if he was thinking what I was thinking.

"Don't bother to get out; I know your running late." I said as I opened the door. I walked behind the car and as I stepped up the curb, he called me to his window.

"CJ, I'll be by later. Please wait for me before you do anything."

I was in a hurry to get to my office and think about what just happened. I looked at him and said, "I'm going to stop in and see Rosie. I should be home after five."

I flew up the steps and fumbled with my keys, I entered my office I took a long deep breath and decided that I needed to calm down before I did anything.

The light on the answering machine was blinking. I ignored it and went into the bedroom and started to take off my shirt, I changed into comfortable skirt. I washed my face and hands and other ordinary non-thinking actions that helped to calm me down. *One thing at a time,* I went into the kitchen and put some water on to boil; while it was heating up I picked up the mail that was lying on floor from the slot in the door. I started leafing through the envelopes and saw the usual bills. It was getting to be that time of month. Then I remembered the $50.00 dollars and my spirits lifted.

I had made money, I could make more. The time and money spent setting up my business had started to pay off. A small beginning, but it was a start.

The tea kettle started to whistle. I went to the kitchen, poured water over a teabag, picked up my cup and mail, grabbed my purse from the door knob and headed for my office. I spent the next two hours making notes and updating my files. Names addresses and phone numbers of my new *associates,* Vince also loaned money, that wasn't a big surprise.

Jesse had given me a list of all the bail bondsmen in the area; I logged them into my files.

Rosie was on my to-do list. I called her number, Margaret answered and she sounded chipper, she and Rosie were in the process of cleaning. Rosie had just left to pick up some more cleaning supplies. I flashed a mental picture of the house and told her she had her work cut out for her. Margaret had moved into the house. Mary had gone down to the police station that morning to file her complaint against Mooring. They had been talking others into doing the same.

"If you hadn't come to get Rosie we wouldn't have gotten out of that mess."

"Well. I need you guys to stick to your guns and he will be put away for a long, long time."

I reminded her that I'd be at court for Rosie. When I hung up the phone I was feeling good for these women who were so happy to be free and reunited.

There was a nagging in the back of my mind about the holes in my story. I ignored them and decided it was a good time to look at Max's file.

Chapter 6

I started to read the charges and realized that looks could be deceiving. Max was charged with extortion. I looked at the picture again and wondered how he did it. The picture on the poster, even with the number he was holding in front of him, was that of a baby-faced, over weight choirboy. The poster read that he was worth a thousand dollars.

Max was 6'1", 320 pounds, a big boy, 36 years old. Black hair and brown eyes that looked beady on the flyer. Last know address was about nine blocks away in an area that I might want to scope out before I did any heavy prying into his life. Vince had left notes that he had a mother and a brother.

I looked at the clock and a couple of hours had turned into four. I looked out the window and saw the sky was dark and wondered if it was going to rain. My tea was cold. If Jesse was going to call it would be soon.

After the frenzy one little kiss had caused I wondered if I could handle another. I stopped myself from thinking about it. I was not going to start a relationship with someone that I would have to lie to. How do you tell someone that you were someone's Guardian Angel?

I filed my papers. I looked at the clock again trying to decide if I should start my check on Max. I rinsed out my cup and decided that I couldn't face Jesse. Not this evening.

How could it be that when I am so sure of my direction, with goals solid in my mind, that one good looking, sweet smelling man with *melt me* eyes comes around and turns me into jelly? No, I did not have time for a man in my life, not any man.

I decided it would be a good time to take a nice long walk, clear the cobwebs. I realized that I was running away from his phone call. I picked up my jacket and with a last look in the mirror I opened the door.

I stood face to neck, a very nice neck, a familiar sweet smelling neck. I looked up into his face, red with exertion and the smile that came into my mind whenever I thought of him.

"Good, you're here. I would have called but I was really rushed to pick up a friend and bring this over."

I looked behind him and saw a leather couch sitting at an angle in the stairwell. The other end of the couch was held by a man whose face was beet red and had rivulets of sweat running down it. It looked like a very heavy piece of furniture.

"Jess can we get this in, I'm going to drop it." A deep strained voice boomed from behind the massive black leather couch. I looked at Jesse and the strain that showed on his face.

"You didn't have to do this."

He looked past me and said "How about that wall?"

The two men lifted it up and angled it into the room and set it down. They both plopped down, one at each end. The torso man was good sized and handsome in his own way.

"That sure is one heavy sofa; I'm surprised you didn't find another flight of stairs to go up Jess."

I was stunned. Before I could speak he suggested "Why don't we put this couch against that wall, what do you think, it's really heavy and hard to move, you have two hearty men right here, right now."

I stammered that the wall was fine. I turned to Jesse and again told him that he didn't have to do this. The other man looked up at Jesse and then me and said, "Well I'm not going to *un*-do this. Jess, I'm going down and get the tables."

I stuttered "tables?" Jesse looked at me and said "Sure one for each end of the couch. I also brought a chair for your office, I hope it fits, can I see where you want to put it?" He got up from the couch and walked to the office. The door was open. He looked back and said "Nice room, I think it will look good on the other end of your desk. You could use another one; I'll keep my eyes open for something that matches."

Jesse's friend had returned with two tables stacked precariously in front of him as he maneuvered them into the room. He set them down as Jess came out of the office.

Jesse grabbed one of the tables and placed it on the far end of the couch; his friend set the other one in place. The change from a just a large barren room to a comfortable reception area was unbelievable. I had no words. This act of kindness overwhelmed me. I stood in the middle of the room speechless. Jesse came up and put his arm around me and introduced his friend.

"CJ, I want you to meet Walter Bass, We call him Bass and he has his sights set on Annie."

Bass rose from the sofa and held his hand out to shake mine and said

"I'm glad to finally meet you CJ, you are better looking then Jesse said. You have anything to drink? All this moving has made me thirsty."

I was still shaking his hand when I told him that I had some Beck's.

"If it's cold it will be exactly right." He replied. "Jesse, why don't you get that last chair while I help CJ get the beer?"

Jesse looked from Bass to me, "You better behave yourself or I'll tell Annie."

I looked around the room and saw *MY* new improved reception room. I shook my head and as gracefully as I could said "Thank you both. You have just made this room look like a real business." I knew I was blushing, "I'll get those beers."

I went into the kitchen and took some glasses from the cupboard. Bass was right behind me. He reached around me to get to the refrigerator. He grabbed three beers. We walked back into the reception area as Jesse came through the door with an overstuffed straight back chair.

"Jesse, that chair looks valuable."

Jesse saw my look of surprise, "It looks exactly right."

Bass took a long drink and asked how long before we had to be at Mama's. I looked at Jesse as he explained.

"We have been invited to Mama's to celebrate an anniversary. Bess and Carlos, they met at Mama's and have been regulars ever since. You'll like them."

"I can't go to Mama's I don't know anyone. I don't want to barge in. I don't have anything to wear!" I exclaimed.

Bass looked at Jesse and then me and said. "You look exactly right. It's casual; we prefer comfort at our gatherings. You have to come." Bass said sheepishly.

"When Mama heard we were coming here she told me to invite you she can't wait to see you again."

"She was really angry when she heard Jesse forgot to invite you yesterday." Bass piped up.

"You can't disappoint her. She's been working on this all week and she insisted that I bring you."

Bass took another sip shrugged his shoulders and said "You can't disappoint Mama."

I looked from one face to the other. They looked like petulant little boys that had their toys taken away.

"After what you two have done I guess I can't refuse."

Bass stood up to leave saying that he needed to take a shower and had to get going. Jesse said I looked great and he would give me a ride but we would have to stop at his house on the way to change his shirt.

Bass was right there with "That's a great idea saves time, let's head out."

It all sounded so logical, especially coming from two bossy men. I grabbed my purse and followed. On the way down the steps I wondered how long my brain would be frozen. I am not a social person. I avoided social events. I'm the one who stands on the sideline and watches.

Chapter 7

Bass dropped us off at Jesse's. "See ya at mamas, bout hour, okay?"

Jesse gave a wave and walked me to the side of a tidy well kept white house. He opened the door and waited for me to enter. I stepped up to a small back porch that led into a kitchen that was well cared for and homey.

"Just go through that door and you'll find the living room. Can I get you something to drink?" He was holding my elbow as he guided me into his living room. "I have lemonade and iced tea or if you prefer a beer."

"Lemonade will be fine." I looked around the room taking it in, this was a man's room and comfortable. The sofa and chairs were overstuffed and looked well used.

He returned with a tall glass and handed it to me. "Make yourself comfortable I won't be long." He turned and jogged up a short set of stairs and a minute later I could here his shower running.

I stood in the center of the room. I took in his surroundings. Another facet of Jesse emerged. This was a cozy home. No hard angles, No chrome and black, just basic comfort in shades of brown. He looked so good in brown. I look at the fireplace it was well used. A wall of bookshelves, I was surprised to see many law books. He had westerns and science fiction. Some were real classics. It seemed that Jesse was an eclectic reader. There were a few sculptures. A cowboy on a rearing horse, a carved totem, and a glass or crystal sculpture that should have looked out of place but didn't.

I wandered into the dining room admiring his oak dining set with a matching sideboard. I peaked in the drawers and found that he had real silver and linens. I wondered if he entertained much.

The kitchen had a small dinette table and chairs. Napkins, salt and pepper shakers sat next to a covered sugar bowl. I rinsed my glass in the sink and looked out the window. A narrow side walk led from the house to a side yard. I followed it into the back yard. A garden was beginning to go to seed but still bearing a few vegetables. I kept walking through the yard and noticed that it was well trimmed. I continued through the yard. I looked in glassed enclosure and realized that this was a sun porch that had to be connected to the end of the living room.

I was turning around to go back into the house when I heard the side door close. Jesse was standing on the walk. His hair was wet and he had changed into a casual shirt. I could only stand and look at this man. He held out his hand and asked if I was ready. I walked to meet him and thought *I'm as ready as I'll ever be.*

Jesse opened the door to his car and with a bow said, "Your chariot awaits."

The drive started out quiet. I was set on mute. I couldn't think of anything to say. I didn't know where to start. Jesse patted my knee. "I hope you don't feel railroaded into coming with me tonight; I meant to ask you yesterday, but it slipped my mind."

"Jesse, this has been a day of surprises and I would like to see Mama again but I wasn't expecting a party."

"You're a shy girl aren't you? You don't say much about yourself."

I couldn't disagree. I didn't talk about myself. What could I say, *Oh yeah, Jesse, if I happen to . . . a . . . disappear don't worry, its only me fading away . . . . I'll get right back to you.*

Just the thought of that conversation brought a rude snicker from me. Jess looked over at me. "And what are you laughing about?"

I looked out of the corner of my eye. He was smiling; "I'm just anxious; I would like to see Mama again."

"She liked you. *A good wholesome girl, but skinny.*" he said in a voice that I assumed was to mimic mama's.

"Skinny? Mama thinks I'm skinny?"

"Well I think you're just right."

We had arrived at *Magpie's*. The street was lit up and music was flowing from the open door. As we entered Jesse was greeted by almost everyone we passed. He said hello to every one and introduced me. I smiled and nodded and tried to pay attention but I knew I wouldn't remember all the names.

We were weaving through the room and spotted Mama sitting with a couple in their vintage years. Mama rose and came up to us. "CJ! I am so happy you could come. I want you to meet Carlos and Bess, old and dear friends, it is their night tonight!"

I told them I was happy to meet them and congratulated them on their years together and I hoped they had many more. I turned back to Mama and told her it was good to see her again.

"Jesse was to tell you yesterday. I found out today that he had forgotten. I am so happy you could come. I want to see you eat and dance and have fun. We must find a minute to talk."

Annie and Bass came up and greeted us. "We have a table but hurry or we'll loose it." We followed Bass and Annie to the table. We sat and Jesse ordered a bottle of wine. Bass looked good in the candlelight. He had shaved and showered and wore a shirt on that brought out his blue eyes. Annie was glowing and glued to his side. They made an adorable couple.

Bass started to introduce me when Annie interrupted him to say that she had already met me. "I met CJ when I waited on them the other night. Jess came to show her off."

This surprised me. I repeated "Jesse brought me in to show me off?"

Annie blushed, "Well, not to show you off, but he never brings his girlfriends here." Now she blushed even deeper.

Bass looked at her and said "Uh, maybe we should dance honey." He pulled her up and out of her chair and made their way to an adjacent room where the band was playing.

I turned in my seat and looked at Jesse. "So, Jesse, just what are you telling your friends? I thought we had a business dinner."

"Honest CJ, I'm didn't say anything. The only one I really said anything to was Mama. I told her is that we were working together. Bass asked about you because Annie told him about our dinner. I just told him you were beautiful and that I hoped to get to know you better."

He was at least gracious enough to look embarrassed.

"So buying me dinner? That makes us a couple?" I looked at him and said "Jesse, we are not a couple. We came here for a business meeting. This is not a date. Does everyone think it is?"

We were sitting next to each other in the booth the dimmed lights and candles on the table were only adding to the closeness that brought out the enticing scent of this man.

I began to feel heady, almost panicky as I realized that I had no control over what people thought, and even less over the way I was responding.

Jesse must have seen my confusion; he pulled his arm away from the back of the booth and looked at me. He had lost his smile. "I'm sorry CJ; I really don't know what everyone thinks. I know that I am attracted to you. I find you refreshing. I didn't realize that you were not attracted to me."

I couldn't think. I didn't know what I wanted. I was attracted and I wanted more. I had a secret that no one would understand. The thought of living alone for the rest of my life suddenly felt bleak. Where was the determination I had to fight the world alone?

I was playing with the wine glass watching the wine flow around the glass allowing my mind to free fall.

My thoughts were interrupted when Jesse took my hand, I looked at his face and he said "I'm sorry. I wouldn't hurt your for the world. I'm sorry that my friends presume so much. I'll set it straight."

I stared into his eyes. I knew that I needed to try to explain.

"Jesse, you need to know something. I am socially inept. I don't date; I don't go out cruising bars. I tried to explain this to you before. You need to know that I don't have time for a relationship."

Damn, I sounded like an idiot. Hearing my words come out of my mouth made me feel like a total fool. I couldn't believe what had spewed out of my mouth.

I grabbed my purse. "Oh god, I'm so sorry Jesse, I have to go. I can see myself home, stay and enjoy your friends."

I bolted from the table, spotting the back door I ran through it and didn't look back.

I found myself in the back alley. I stopped long enough to get my bearings and followed it until I came up to the main street. I had walked about a half block when I heard Jesse calling me.

"CJ, stop! Hey, CJ! If you want to go home I will take you. When I take someone somewhere, I take them home."

I stopped dead in the street. I waited for him to catch up. I stood there not really sure of what I wanted to do. He took my shoulders and turned me around to face him.

"Come on baby, it's been a long day."

We walked toward the car. His arm was around me and he was holding me close but not tight.

I didn't realize my eyes were wet until he took his thumb and wiped a tear away. Now I was really embarrassed. He held his hands lightly to each side of my face, the next moment he was lowering his head and kissing me. I felt his tongue lick my lips and leaned into him. His hands dropped to my waist and he held me close.

"Let's go home CJ, it's been a long day."

We drove to my office in silence; he walked me up the steps, unlocked the door and walked me in. I was numb and had no clue what to do next. He leaned over and kissed my forehead.

"Get some sleep." I heard the click of the lock as he closed the door behind him.

I went through the paces of washing my face, brushing my teeth. I pulled out a large t-shirt and put it on. I couldn't understand what was wrong with me. I just bit off the head of a very nice man. He had done nothing but help me and treat me with respect. I cried for goodness sake! I must have looked like the biggest fool. I never cry. That had to impress him about my career choice. I crawled into bed and cried myself to sleep.

Chapter 8

I felt lousy; my eyes were red and puffy and stuck together. My head ached. I didn't want to climb out of bed. Images of last evening kept flittering through my brain. I remembered the look on Jesse face. I slowly roused myself out of the bed figuring that I pretty much solved the Jesse problem. I went into the shower the warm water didn't take away the forsaken feeling I woke up with.

I made coffee and carried it to my office. I continued my lousy day by calling Vince. I was getting cross-eyed over his handwriting. I needed to find out what the two men, one woman, and now two teenagers looked like. When we were at Vince's he said there was a mom, but it was actually Max's sister, she must look as old as Max looked young.

He had one brother, but now I had another man and the two kids. After he untied the family tree I had a better idea of who these people were. I wanted to boil the phone when I hung up.

I warmed up my coffee. I was adding milk when someone started to bang on my door. "CJ, it's Bass, Let me in!"

I opened the door. "Is Jess here?"

"Hello Bass, nice to see you too." *Did he think he spent the night?*

"Look. It's really important. Have ya seen him?"

"Not since last night, what's up Bass? Is he okay?" I began to get that ole tingling feeling. "Bass, when was the last time you saw him?"

"Right before Annie and I went to dance. He was supposed to meet me at six this morning. He didn't make it, thought he might be might here."

"No, he dropped me off and left. We both had early mornings." The tingling was getting stronger.

"Bass, where are you going now?"

"Thought I go over to his house, I called but got no answer, I figured you were my best shot."

"What about Mama's?"

"I didn't want to worry her." Would you call? You can say you're looking for Jesse?"

I picked up the phone and dialed Mama as Bass rattled off her number. Mama came right on the line. "Mama, this is CJ, how are you?"

"I'm fine CJ; I missed our chance to talk last night. Did you enjoy yourself?"

"It was fine Mama, A good crowd. I just needed to get some sleep. It was a long day and I had a very early morning. Next time I will stay longer. I promise. Mama, I called to see if Jesse was around?"

"No CJ, I haven't seen him. But I will tell him to call if he comes in. Is everything alright CJ?"

"Oh, yes everything is fine; I think I left my purse in his car." I lied. "Thanks Mama, I'll call soon."

Bass was listening the whole time. "Thanks CJ, I'm going over to his house, you want to come?"

"I can't Bass." *The tingling was getting deeper.* "Let me know what you find out. I have to keep an appointment."

"I'll tell him about your purse. Call me if you hear from him." He was already halfway down the stairs.

"Bass!" I called after him. "Find him!"

The tingling was getting serious. I was in a definite fadeout mode. I rushed out behind him. I jumped into the bed of his truck as my feet disappeared.

Bass was really worried. He was speeding and almost stopped for a stop sign. I kept getting rattled with every turn. I grabbed some blankets that they must have used when they moved the furniture for me.

Bass stopped in Jesse's driveway and ran to the garage looking to see if his car was there. He went to the side of the garage and picked up a pot of dead leaves and grabbed the spare key.

I followed him into the house. I walked through the rooms as Bass called.

"Jess, Hey Jess! Are you here? Where the hell are you Dude!?"

I made the rounds downstairs and then went up. I felt like a sneak. I was invading his space. I looked to the right, the bathroom. A dry towel was thrown over the shower curtain.

I went through the connecting door and figured this to be the Master Bedroom. It smelled like Jess and the urge was pulling me. I crossed the room I looked down into the backyard. All seemed quiet.

Bass was leaving a room opposite the bathroom. I slipped into the room directly across from Jesse's room. This was his office.

I snooped on his desk and saw that he had brought work home. I saw a lone phone number by the phone and got a rush when I touched it.

Bass was coming my way; I slipped out of the room and went into the room that Bass had come from.

A spare bedroom it looked ready for company. I heard Bass as he headed downstairs. I ran to catch my ride.

Bass stopped at Jesse's phone in the living room. I listened as he called the station. He held a brief conversation and then I saw him repeat the number that he had in his hand.

It was the same paper that was on Jesse's desk. Bass held the phone to his ear with his shoulder as he wrote on the back of it.

"Do you have a name for the number yet? I'll call back." He said and hung up the phone. One thing was certain, Jesse was off the radar.

I followed him to the truck and as he fished in his pocket for his keys I slipped in the cab of his truck. I knew I was taken a chance but I didn't want to miss anything.

Bass looked at the paper and tossed it on the dash board. He turned the key and laid rubber as he took off. The urge was pounding. We were on a trail. I wanted to grab the wheel and drive.

We drove a ways out of town. This was an area I was not familiar with. Bass pulled over at a curb and pulled out his cell-phone. He dialed a number and asked for Dave.

"I need that name Dave, you got it yet? Shit. I'll call you back."

That did not sound promising. He sat there for a minute and I blew at the paper making it waver on the dashboard. He picked it up and studied it. Turned it over and read the address again. I wanted to pull the cell-phone from his hand and call it myself.

He stuffed the paper in his shirt pocket, put the truck in gear and took off. We passed a suburb when he started to slow down. He seemed to be looking for a street. He turned left and went down a winding street. Two blocks later we took a left onto a dirt road. We were going slowly. My instincts were running wild. He truck crept down the trail. I was ready to get out and run.

We stopped behind a grove of trees. Bass reached over into the glove box and took out his gun. He checked to make sure it was loaded and stuck it in the back of his jeans. He opened the door and left the cab. I rushed out behind him. He was looking over the field at an abandoned house partially hidden in tall weeds.

I flew out the door. I heard the door quietly close as I started to make my way to the house. I knew that Jesse was here. I could feel him. I could hear Bass as he made his way to the back of the house. I decided to take the far side. I looked into every window as I trailed around the house. There had been cars parked earlier, two vehicles, a car and one with big wide tires, a truck.

I needed to know if there was anyone in the house. I climbed through a window frame, the glass was long gone and just a part of screen was blowing in the wind. I made my way into the living room.

Discolored paint was chipping off the walls. Water marks on old moldy wallpaper hanging in strips off of one wall. The house was musty and thick with dust. Several sets of footprints could be seen. I walked around the periphery of the rooms. Following the hall to the kitchen I saw the counters littered with styrofoam cups, fast food bags, and beer cans.

I looked up as Bass come through the back door. I heard footsteps. I backed into a tall cupboard that turned out to be a broom closet. A shadow passed my hiding place heading toward Bass.

I reached for a weapon and my hand touched a piece of wood, a mop handle. I waited for an opportunity while judging the weight of the handle.

The shadow seemed to sense my presence. I turned and swung the wood with all the muscle I had. I hit him in the temple and clipped a good part of his ear. He screamed and fell to the side and grabbing at the counter.

Bass came in just as the man stood up holding the side of his bleeding head.

I took the mop handle and headed in the direction that Bass had come from.

I heard Bass say behind me "Go ahead scumbag. Give me a reason to shoot you. Where's Keyes!?"

I knew he was close. I made my way through the kitchen and saw an open door. I looked down a dark stairwell and heard a kicking sound. I flew down the steps into a dark room. Jesse was kicking his feet at a wall trying to break the chair he was tied to.

I ran over to Jesse and moved my hands over his face. I untied the dirty cloth that covered his eyes and mouth. I took out my pocket knife and cut the rope on his wrists and then his feet. Jesse was as blind in that dark room as I was. I was shocked when I heard him say "CJ?" I froze.

I couldn't say a word.

"CJ . . . tha . . . you?" I saw that he had bruises and a swollen lip, I watched him struggle to stand with the help of some shelving, He was holding his ribs but I saw no flowing blood but his shirt was torn and covered in it.

I backed off as Bass came down the steps. I wanted to hold him so badly.

Bass helped Jesse up the steps; Jesse was leaning heavily on his friend and holding his ribs. Every step added to his pain.

"Jess, son of a bitch, how did you do this to yourself? Why didn't you call me? How did you get in this mess? I've been looking everywhere for you!"

Jesse said "Basss, wh.ere's . . . CJ?"

"CJ? Jesse you ok? CJ's fine. She wants her purse."

"What? How . . . you know . . . I waz here?"

"There was a rumor that Bad Ass Jack was out and he was after us. We had out his old hideout staked out. I remembered this place was one of the places he used. I thought it was demolished. I took a long shot."

"Bass, who's wi' you?"

"Nobody, hey you okay buddy? We need to get you to a hospital!"

"Bass . . . my gun . . . asshole . . . . upstairs . . . took it . . . Four al . . . to . . . ether. backup? not leaving . . . get them."

"Help is on the way. I told them to park in the burbs' and walk in the back way through the fields. When they due back?"

"Not . . . long." Jesse was bent over, he was in such pain. "BA . . . a plane . . . . wants me de . . . d first."

I shuddered at the thought. I was trying to be very quiet. Jesse was looking around trying to figure out what was out of place. He lifted his head and looked around the room.

One eye was swollen shut and there was blood on the side of his head. He lifted his face and smelled at the air. "Bass, whos . . . wi'ou?"

"Jesse, there isn't anyone here but me. Let's get you cleaned up and figure how to get the out hell of here."

"Cut m . . . ropes? Som . . . body . . . did."

Bass was checking out Jesses' face and ignored the question. "Let me take a look at your pretty face. Mama will kill me if your not 100 %"

Bass sat Jesse in a chair and looked at his face. He spotted a liter of bottled water and brought it over. I winced as Jesse took a swallow swished it around his mouth and spit out blood. Bass pulled out a handkerchief and started to dab at a cut on his eye. Asking questions about how he got in this stupid mess.

"Got a call . . . Althea . . . inform . . . ant, BA . . . . after me . . . went to meet her . . . . set up . . . ."

I listened as they started formulating a plan. It was clear that they worked well together. Ideas were brought up, bantered about, set or rejected.

I followed the inside wall keeping an eye out the front door. I saw the man that Bass had tied up sitting against the wall. The effects of my mop handle were evident and I wished I still had it on me. I could hear every word in the kitchen and Bass was really pissed when he saw Jesse's side. Apparently he had been held by two of the thugs while they took turns beating him. Bass said it looked like he might have some broken ribs. As I listened to the growing lists of wounds I kicked the sitting man. He yelped. When Bass made a comment on welts on his back and sides, I kicked him again, really hard. He started freaking.

"Hey stop kicking me! Who's kicking me? Hey! Asshole! Untie me!"

This brought Bass to the doorway. "Shut up or I'll gag you. I don't have any reason to let your live."

"Don't kill me, I don't know nothing. I just needed the money. Let me go, Oh lordy, the devils here and he's taken me to hell."

"Sound's good to me. I don't want to hear another word. You sit. One word and you'll wish you were dead."

"I tell you this place is haunted, it's kick . . . ."

"Ok asshole I've had it." Bass grabbed a rag and gagged him.

I sat on the floor beside him and started to laugh quietly as Bass went back to Jesse.

I watched him as I continued to watch the front yard. "You sure look like a stuffed pig." I whispered as I watched his eyes go wide and he tried to scream through his gag.

I watched and listened as Bass continued to clean up Jesse. Jesse was getting some of his color back; his face was red and swollen. He was going to be bruised for quite a while. As they continued their planning I thought of places where I could be of use.

Jess was flexing his shoulders but I could see him wince and hold his ribs. He would need stitches on his forehead. His left eye was swollen shut and his jaw looked red and ready to bruise.

He walked around the kitchen trying to get his circulation back and limping badly. Bass helped him as they limped out the back door and I watched as they scoped the area around the house.

I followed them out walking a little behind them. Jesse turned once and looked right at me. For a moment I thought he could see me. His right was eye clear and searching. He shook his head as if trying to clear it. He looked up and continued to survey the horizon.

Bass and Jesse were watching the road as a car turned onto the dirt trail. Bass pulled out his cell-phone hit a button. "Company's here, come up the front."

We went back to the house. Bass went down to the basement where he would wait. Jesse took his post between the kitchen and living room. I walked past Jesse.

The man that was tied up was out cold. Well, one down.

I heard the car before I saw it. A cloud of dust enveloped it as it came down the dry road. I saw the big black flashy car stop in front of the house. Through the grimy cracked window I watched a cloud of dirt hovered around it as the doors opened. Voices were laughing and I heard a gruff voice say "Get it over with, I want him dead." I counted to three.

My urge had just topped out. I was ready. I bolted behind Jesse to pick up my mop handle. Jesse looked my way when he felt the air shift and turned. I returned to my post behind the door. Jesse stepped deeper into the shadows. The three men entered one after another and tromped toward the kitchen.

I let the first two make it through the door. I jumped in front of the last one and swung the mop handle with all my might. I caught him above the ear. He held his head and howled as I gave him a kick to the back of his knee. He dropped to the floor screaming. I kicked him in the ribs and then went for his neck. I put him in an elbow lock and whispered in his ear.

"Don't make a sound. Don't even try to move or I'll stick this knife in your heart."

I moved my leg and leaned on his neck. I picked up a thread bare faded drape and tore it in two. I quickly wrapped it around his hands and tied it off. I went down his torso and tied his ankles. He was loosing it. He watched a flying piece of material wrap itself around him. He started screaming. I cut off a strip of excess drape and stuck it in his mouth. I went to help the boys.

Jesse was hand to hand in the kitchen and I could hear fighting from the basement. I came up to the man who was cornering Jesse. I swung around and brought my leg up and thawopped him in the rib cage. His head came up as he doubled over bellowing. He tried to turn to see what hit him when Jesse gave him a good hit to the jaw and he went down. Jesse pulled cuffs out of his back pocket turned him over and cuffed him. He was barely holding himself up leaning on the counter.

He turned to go into the basement just as the last of the trio came barging up the stairs. Bass was in close pursuit. They both looked like they had been through a war. Jesse struck out as he got to the top on the stairs catching him in the jaw. I tripped him from my side of the door and he went down on his face. Bass pulled him up by the collar he was sporting a bloody face and bleeding nose. Jesse grabbed a fistful of hair pulled his head back so that he could look in his eyes. "BA . . . ni'ce to see . . . you again."

I heard the sound of sirens in the distance. I let myself lean against the counter. I looked from Bass to Jesse they both looked like they could use an ambulance. They both had big goofy smiles. First Bass and then Jesse stepped over BA and walked to the front door.

Bass looked at the guy lying on the floor. "*Good work*" and took a step over him. We were in the living room as the Calvary barged in the front door. Jesse looked at the floor and then at Bass. He shook his head back and forth with a quizzical look on his face.

Bass stopped the last uniform "Can you fella's clean up this mess? I need to get Detective Keyes to the hospital; I'll be at the station later."

The uniform looked at the floor stepped over the tied up body, and went to join the rest of the officers. I followed them back to the grove climbed into the bed of the truck curled up on the blankets and closed my eyes.

I thought we were headed for the hospital and was surprised that we stopped at Jesse house.

I pulled the blankets over my head. I was again visible. I heard Bass argue about stopping and Jess saying he wanted to check something. Bass argued that he would do it . . . . Their voices faded as they went into the house. I climbed out of the truck thinking I should head home. I was beginning to feel a couple of twinges. I wondered where the closest bus stop was. I knew there was one close to the hospital. I'd wait and grab a ride.

I looked at myself. I really needed a shower. I ducked around hedge in the front yard as Jesse and Bass came out of the house. "Jess, we'll call again, I'm sure she's fine."

Jesse was wearing some sweats and a baggy t-shirt. Bass had cleaned him up a bit and added some bandages.

"Neees a cell-phone . . . not a teleph . . . ne . . . on ev . . . ry corner. How . . . is she" asked Jesse as Bass opened the door.

"She was okay, she was concerned . . . ."

I lost the conversation. I followed the hedge up the driveway and cut through. I was even with the bed of the truck and climbed in. I had not been seen. The trucked backed out and headed toward town.

When we arrived at the hospital Jesse leaning heavily on Bass as they went through the emergency ward door, he was bleeding through his shirt.

I waited until they entered the hospital and went to the corner and met a bus that would eventually get me home. I was tired. Dimming was draining.

I took a shower, checked for abrasions and contusions, and changed into a broom skirt and green sweater. No blinking light on the phone. I was in my office when the phone rang.

It was Jesse. "CJ, tho . . . ht . . . I call . . . ee how yur day went. I'm wi' Bass . . . he tol' you I waz MIA."

He sounded tired and his voice was slow and slurred. I could picture his poor face in my minds eye and my heart went out to him. He was the one beaten and he wanted to make me feel better?

"Jesse. Is everything alright? Bass was really concerned." It was hard to play dumb. "You sound a little weird." *Slurred, drugged, hurt, half dead?*

"Yeah, tha's why I call . . . ing, tell youz all's well. I want t . . . stop . . . . by but I'll . . . tied up . . . while."

"That's okay Jesse; I have plans for this evening." I lied.

"What's up? Where . . . you . . . goin?" He sounded anxious.

"I'm going over to Rosie's; I want to check up on her."

"Tha's nice." He sounded relieved. "I call . . . you later?"

"Well, I don't think I will be back too early" Maybe tomorrow would be better."

"CJ" There was a long pause. "I wan . . . . see you."

"I'd like to see you again too. I have to go. Call me Jesse."

I felt like a coward. I knew that it took a big effort for him to make that call. He needed to be in the hospital and didn't have to call me. Why did that make me feel better? *God, how sick was that.*

I looked at the clock and decided that I needed to mellow out. The call from Jesse put me back to square one. I thought of all the strange things he must have seen. He would be reviewing the whole day. He was bright enough to figure out at least one or two of the strange happenings. I shook my head I couldn't think of anything that could really explain them away.

Chapter 9

I needed to work out the aches in my bones, I had a bruise on my hip where the jerk had kicked me otherwise I was fine. I decided to walk over to Rosie's. *Covering my lie?* I went up to the door and before I walked in I could feel the changes. The house was no longer oppressive. The porch was swept; there was a flower pot with bright yellow Zinnias on the step.

I knocked on the door and was greeted by Margaret. She gave me a big hug and thanked me for everything I did.

"I didn't do it Margret, it was Rosie and you. You two stood up and said *no more!* I'm proud of you."

Margaret looked great. She looked younger, more vibrant. Her eyes were bright, her hair clean and done in a stylish fashion. I could hardly believe that she was the same battered woman I met just a few days ago. She was lively and bright and open.

We went straight to the kitchen. It was a totally different room. Everything had a place, and the dishes were done. The walls and floor were squeaky clean. I turned around and admired their warm homey kitchen. They must have been working round the clock. They threw anything out that reminded them of the past. I could see bags of garbage ready to hit the curb.

There was a vase of mixed flowers on the table. The smell coming from the oven was a heavenly apple pie. Rosie was frying chicken on the stove. My stomach growled.

"You have really been at it. This is beautiful!"

Mary came into the room her smile transformed. She pulled me into a big bear hug and thanked me. I was invited to stay for dinner and I couldn't refuse. I was starving, after all the activity of the day I was a little light headed. We sat down to eat while they told me what they had been up to.

They were searching for others that had been part of Moorings extortion and convinced many of them to file a complaint, sometimes they went with them to the station.

We talked of how Rosie and Margaret had tried to protect each other. Not knowing how badly they were being used against each other. Rosie said that she lived in fear every day. "I dreaded coming home. I never knew what was going to happen."

I looked at these courageous women and my heart went out to them. I told them that if anyone ever tried to hurt them again to call me.

Rosie piped up "CJ, I'm not afraid. When the Guardian Angel came in to my room I was really scared. He tied up Ralph. I'm not afraid anymore; I know we'll be safe."

I patted her hand. This was the opening I was looking for. "Tell me about the Angel."

Rosie took a deep breath. "I was so scared. Ralph had that look he gets it when he's been drinking and he gets mean. I was sure he was going to kill me this time. He was cussing and telling me to give him the money. He started to come at me and all of a sudden he was on the floor. I thought he tripped. I screamed and hid behind my chair. The Guardian Angel stuck a sock in his mouth! I couldn't yell or scream. The Angel told me to run and get out of the house. It was a mystical experience. I talked to Father Bart and he said that the mind does strange things. I told him that he was real and it wasn't in my mind. I would think a priest would believe in Guardian Angels!"

"What did the police say?"

"I don't think they believed me. They think I'm crazy too. They want to come over and talk to me. Do I need a lawyer ya think?"

I looked at Rosie. "I don't know Rosie, A lot of people will only believe what they can see and touch. But sometimes, someone up there listens and they send help. It would make it easier for them to accept that it was the stress of the moment. I believe you but most of the world would call us both loco."

Margaret got up and freshened our coffee "Who's' ready for some pie?"

We talked about how lucky they were. The fear they had all lived under so long was gone. I left feeling a unity with these women. On my walk home I realized that I had friends.

I was exhausted as I trudged up the last steps. I thought about Jesse. I hoped he was doing okay. The last time I saw him he was on his feet. I wanted to call but my feeling for him was still to raw. After spending the night as a guardian angel I didn't want to pop my own bubble by admitting to whatever I was.

I opened my door and saw my message button blinking. I sat down totally exhausted and listened to the message. There was only one.

It was Bass. "CJ, Jess is doing fine. He was held up with a police matter and he'll give you a call tomorrow. Thought I'd call and let you know."

I hung up the phone and dragged myself to bed. The last thought I had was the vision of Jesse tied to a chair and fighting for his life. Knowing how hurt he was hurt me. He had sensed me, how would I ever explain myself?

Chapter 10

I woke up with the sun full on my face and groaned as I turned over. I was stiff. When I finally made it to the shower I let the hot steamy water stream down all my sore muscles. Gradually my body began to move a little easier. I had a couple of new bruises and they seemed to be taking on a life of their own. It looked like a long sleeved shirt kind of day. The bruise on my hip was purpling up, it could have been worse.

I took a cup of coffee into my office and started to make notes of yesterday's events. It occurred to me that I might have to have a separate file with out the deletions of some of my actions. I would give that more thought.

I was getting up to refill my coffee cup when my phone began to ring. At the same time someone started to knock at my door. I looked from one to the other and went for the door.

I was surprised to see Bass standing in front of me. He had a black eye and a line of stitches on his forehead. His nose was swollen but it didn't look broken. His jaw was red and tender.

"Bass, are you alright? What happened?" Sit down and tell me what happened!"

Bass looked at me and said "I'm fine, but you need to come with me. Jess is at his house and he's asking for you. He was kind of hurt yesterday; and he thinks your sore at him."

"Bass, why would he think I would be sore at him?" Is he ok? I had a message from him yesterday and he told me he would call this morning."

"CJ, Please, Just get in the truck he really needs to see you. I have never seen him this way."

"What way Bass? What happened? Is Jesse all right?" I had already grabbed my purse and was following him to his truck wondering what Jesse was so anxious about that he couldn't call me.

As Bass drove he explained that Jesse had been working on a police matter. He gave just the facts. His story was clear and precise facts. "Jesse was pretty beat up. We got home a couple of hours ago. He's sedated and needs to stay down. I need to be at work. He'd been talking about you. He really wants to see you, something about how nice you smell. He started talking crazy. Stuff about angels and ghosts and how nice you smelled. He must have a concussion so someone needs to be around. I have to get back at the station. Can you stay until I get someone over?"

I realized as he talked he wanted me to watch over Jesse. Not talk, just spend some time until got someone to come over or until he returned. I didn't really know how to be a nurse. I would be in his house. He would probably be asleep. I had a myriad of mixed reactions.

"Bass what's he doing home if he's hurt so bad? I'm not a nurse."

"He wouldn't stay, I had to keep him up because he had a concussion but he should sleep most the day. I'll get back as soon as I can. Look, CJ, every time he wakes up he asks for you. I'll try to get someone over as soon as I can. He's in bad shape."

We parked in the driveway and he pulled a key from his shirt pocket. "This is the key to his door. If you need anything call me. Tell Jess I'll be back about six. Thanks CJ." He started to back out of the driveway before I could answer.

So I was going in cold. I hoped Jesse was sleeping and his gun was somewhere safe. I let myself in. The sun was streaming through the window lighting the kitchen up and making it gleam in the light. The only thing out of place was a shirt thrown on the back of a chair. I walked in through the living room and up the stairs straight to last door on the right.

I went in, room was dark and the drapes were pulled closed. I saw the outline of his body under the covers.

I walked over to the bed and looked down at him; my heart broke as I gazed at his poor face. Vivid colors of red, black and blue. White bandages hiding some of his wounds, making others vibrant with the contrast. His eye was swollen shut and it looked as if he had stitches above his left ear and on his head. I wanted to reach out and touch him; there wasn't a place unhurt.

My eyes were adjusting to the dark room. His blankets moved slightly as I watched him breathe. Looking down at Jesse I could barely recognize him as the same man. My heart was breaking. This broken and bruised man was the same vibrant beautiful man who just yesterday with a flash of his smile took my breath away?

I brushed my hand on his forehead, fighting tears that he had suffered such hurt. I felt him try to move and then settle into deep sleep again.

I turned to leave. I thought I would see what I could do to make some nourishing food for him. Chicken soup was nourishing and if my mother was right it cured everything. Fighting tears I went back downstairs and headed for the kitchen. Checking his cabinets and then his refrigerator, I found some chicken in the freezer. I located the pans and started what I hoped would be chicken soup. I'm no cook; I really hoped it would taste good. I found some frozen vegetables, and the spice rack.

The more I snooped the more I revised my thoughts. The most used utensil in my kitchen was the can opener. I was thrilled when I found the mother load, a well used dog eared copy of the *Joy of Cooking*. I thumbed through the pages until I found a recipe for Chicken Soup. I collected all the ingredients that I needed and placed them on the counter.

As the chicken thawed I started wandering. I picked up the shirt from the back of the chair and saw that it was the one Jesse had worn yesterday. It was torn and dirty and covered with dried blood. I dropped it in the garbage can and went back upstairs.

The bathroom was a mess. I picked up his jeans and they were cut up and crusted with dirt and blood. My tears were getting harder to fight. I put all the dirty cloths along with his boots in a pile. Bandage packages were in the sink and on the floor along with bloody towels and washcloths.

Each discovery was a stab to my heart. I felt tears fall as I took the basket of bloody cloths down stairs. The washer and dryer were on the back porch. I threw out all the bloody and cut clothing. I started a load in the washing machine and went back upstairs to clean the bathroom.

I spent time cleaning the sink and floor wiping up every trace of blood and dirt. I thought of Bass and how he must have helped Jesse get this far. *True partners*, then I remembered the thoughtful acts that they both had done for me.

Back in the kitchen I put the chicken in a pot and added all the ingredients I could find. I spent time cleaning Jesse's boots. Poking at the chicken until it was time to dry the second load of cloths. I had to keep busy.

I had checked on him several times and he had not changed his position. This time his leg was outside the blanket and his hand wrapped in a thick bandage was on the pillow beside his head. The bruise on his shoulder practically screamed it was so raw. His leg was a patchwork of black and blue. I moved the blanket as gently as I could over his leg and shoulder. He was sleeping in his briefs and from what could be seen he was well muscled. I had never been this close to a nearly naked man. I feet myself blush. I spotted a medicine bottle and the instructions said to take one tablet every four hours. I had been here at least that long.

I thought this would be a good time to call Bass. I went to the phone in the living room and dialed the Station House.

"4th Precinct, Dombrowski."

I almost groaned at this voice from the past. I asked for Bass and was told he was in a meeting; there was a pause, "Is this the Private Eye? How's Jess? I can get Bass out of that meeting."

This was a big turnaround; I could hear the concern in his voice.

"He's still sleeping. I was calling Bass to ask about his medication. If you could have him call I'd really appreciate it."

"Sure thing . . . Uhm . . . ? Take good care of him."

"You bet I will Sergeant."

I hung up the phone thinking that somewhere under Dombrowskis' skin there might be a real person. I also wondered how many of Jesse's co-workers and friends thought us a *couple* now.

I went to poke at the chicken again when the phone rang. It was Bass.

"How's it going CJ? How's the kid?"

I paused and said "He moved a little the last time I checked but he's still out."

I asked him about the meds and he said that he took the last dose early in that morning before he came to pick me up.

"He's due for another dose. I had a devil of a time getting it in him,"

"Bass, some of his wounds look brutal. Is there anything I should know?"

"He's got two cracked ribs. He's lucky, they could have been broken. The bandages on his shoulder should be changed. He's got a cracked ankle and has to stay off of it. Multiple, abrasions, contusions, and a concussion; I tried to keep him up as long as I could."

"He hasn't moved much and I'm watching him closely, I don't want to wake him up. I'm not a nurse Bass."

"Has he said anything?" Bass asked. "He wasn't making too much sense this morning. He should be in the hospital but he wouldn't stay. CJ you okay with staying there? I can call Mama and have one of the girls come over."

"He hasn't said a word. I'm fine. I don't mind being here. Tell Mama I'll take care of him."

"I'll be back after this shift. Are you sure your okay with this? Call me if you need anything, anytime."

"I'm alright Bass, I'll see you later."

I hung up the phone and decided to check on Jesse again. If he was awake I would need to get another pill down him.

I went upstairs and Jesse was struggling to sit up. I ran to the bed. "What do you think you're doing? You have to stay in bed!"

Jess looked at me with unfocused eyes and said "Ceeej" that you? wha . . . Yoo ca . . . me?"

I was at his bed straightening out his blankets

"Jesse you will not get up. I came because you asked for me. Bass came to get me, and as long as I'm here you're going to do as I say or I will leave."

He looked at me as if I was speaking Chinese.

"Yoo cam . . . e."

He stopped struggling. I took the glass from the table went into the bathroom and filled it with water. I took a pill out of the bottle and I handed it to him.

He shook his head no.

"Do you want me to leave?"

He looked at me while he swallowed the tablet. "I nee . . . ba . . . th . . . room."

He winced with pain as he tried to pull off the blanket.

"Oh, no you don't buddy, you need my help."

I grabbed his robe off the bathroom door and put it around his shoulders. Even this small action made him grimace with pain. I helped him hobble to the bathroom. He leaned heavily on me and was shaking as he walked. The pain was etched on his face.

I discretely stood outside the door. When I walked back in he was leaning on the sink.

"Come on Cowboy lets get you to back to bed."

Leaning heavily on my shoulder he was resigned to having my help. I sat him on the bed and fluffed his pillows. I gently guided his head down to them. His eyes were closed, the medicine was taking effect. I pulled his blanket up to his chin. He whispered my name as he drifted off.

I sat at the side of the bed and went over his bruises and wounds. I saw how massive they were as we hobbled to the bathroom. This man should be in the hospital. I would do my best to make sure he got my best care.

The trip to the bathroom had opened some of his wounds. I drew back the blanket and saw that some of the bandages had blood on them. I went to the bathroom and brought out a washcloth and gauze, ointment and tape. He didn't wake up but he moaned and flinched several times as I worked to repair the injuries that I could get to without turning him. He had several on his shoulder. The wound on his side was bleeding through the bandage but the stitches were holding. I re-patched the best I could. I took a long look at his poor face and gave him a kiss on a part of brow that was clear of bandages or bruising. I sat in a chair by the window watching his face.

He was resting comfortably. I watched as he breathed in and out and went over the horrible events of the day before. He was so lucky to alive. Those men meant to kill him.

I couldn't sit any longer, I had to move. I got out of the chair and went down to beat up the chicken.

Bass came in around six. He looked beat and bruised and I wondered how much pain he was hiding. He had brought Annie. They asked about Jesse and Bass left to see for himself.

Annie started taking things out a bag that Bass had put on the table. Milk, juice, bread, she pulled out the makings for salad.

"Mama added some soft creations, pudding and broths. Home made rolls, a whole chocolate cake." Annie said as I helped her put everything away. We talked about what was needed to get Jesse up and around.

"Bass was worried that Jesse was seeing things and that he had a concussion. When he left this morning he'd been up with him all night, he wouldn't let him sleep until he came for you. He's riding on fumes."

"I can stick around for a while Annie. If you want you guys could stay in the spare bedroom. I can sleep on the couch."

"That's so nice of you CJ, but I have to get to work. I'm so glad your here. But if you could convince Bass to get some sleep it would be great."

We talked until Bass came down. He said that he didn't want to wake Jesse. We told him of my intentions to stay and he seemed relieved. I offered some of my chicken soup, salad and rolls and we ate while we figured out some possible solutions on what to do about my work.

I called Margaret and asked if she could help me out. I needed a part-time secretary/receptionist. Annie could drop off my key on her way home. She could call me and I would tell her how to get to my messages in the morning.

Margaret jumped on it. She would do it for nothing. We decided that 10 to 2 would be great. I told her pay was in the future and right now I was bare bones. Margaret said we'd talk about money when Jesse got better.

I offered Bass the spare bed. He said he would rather sleep in his own bed if I could do with out him.

He'd check on Jess before work. When they left I cleaned up the kitchen and filled the dishwasher. I folded the last load in the dryer. I went upstairs thinking how I just moved in with Jesse and he didn't even know it.

I checked on Jesse, he seemed to be sleeping comfortably. I opened his door, went to the spare room, stripped to my t-shirt and panties and climbed into bed.

Chapter 11

I sat up fast wondering where the hell I was. My hands and feet were tingling and I felt an overwhelming urge to bolt. I ran to the door. When I hit the hallway I realized that I was at Jesse's.

I fled to Jesse's room and found him sprawled on the floor holding his bandaged ribs. I rushed to him not sure where I could touch him. I ended up sitting on the floor holding him as we leaned against the side of the bed.

"Jesse, it's ok, I'm here. Don't move baby. Let me see if you're alright."

His eye was not focusing, and he was moaning with every movement.

"CJ, tha . . . you? I dre . . . am . . . . yoo . . . here." His words were really slurred.

"I'm right here. We have to get you back in bed. Do you think you can help me?"

"Shhur baby". He put his head on my shoulder. I didn't know if I could get him back in bed with out opening his wounds. He was so drugged and weak.

"I'm going to get up; then I'm going to pull you up. You just move with me, lean on me, we'll sit you on the bed."

I could feel Jesse try to gather his strength. I counted to three and wrapped my arms around him just under his arms. I pulled him up. His good leg added to our momentum. We were sitting on the bed panting from the effort. I laid him back and then placed his legs on the bed. He was lying on his back and in intense pain.

"You need to rest." I saw that his eyes were closed and sweat beaded his face. I went to get water and a pain pill.

"Come on Jesse you need to take this. Come on Cowboy, do this for me." He was hurting to much to argue. I put the pill in his mouth and he swallowed as I held the water glass.

I went to the bathroom and brought back a cold wash cloth and bathed his face as gently as I could. I continued down his neck, all the time telling him that he was going to be okay, I was here and I would help.

He was out. I examined his wounds. He had a fever; I rewetted the cold cloth and continued to bathe his face neck and shoulders. I decided that I would go over each and every sore spot he had in the morning. Meanwhile I didn't want to pull him off the floor again so I covered him with his blankets, brushed my hand over his hair and walked to the other side of the bed. I laid down beside him and fell asleep listening to him breath.

Bass's voice was intruding on my dream. "Hey, is anybody here? Get decent I'm coming up!"

Jumping out of the bed I grabbed Jesse's robe and started for the door just as Bass's large frame filled it. He looked at me and asked "How's he doing?"

"Mostly sleeping, He tried to get out of bed about two this morning. It took awhile to get him back in. Bass he should be in a hospital."

"Tell me about it." He was looking down at Jesse who was still out. I looked at the clock by the bed it was 5 a.m.

"Mama's sending Dr. Wenz over this morning, bout eight . . . He's a good friend and has patched us up since we were kids."

"I'm glad; I don't know how to help him. I was afraid that I might break a rib."

Bass came over and gave me a bear hug. "Honey you amaze me. Jesse is lucky to have you. I gotta get to work, I'll to stop by later."

He was gone as fast as he came. I was awake and in bad need of coffee. I saw Jesse move as Bass came in but he settled back down. I went too start the coffee and looked down at myself. I needed clean clothes.

I ran back upstairs and ran into the bathroom and took a quick shower wishing I had clean clothes. I wrapped myself in a towel and ran to the spare bedroom; I took a good look at my clothing and decided to wash them. I tiptoed back into Jesse's room and opened a top drawer and saw his t-shirts. When I opened the last drawer I found his jogging cloths. Bingo! I looked for the smallest pair and pulled them out. I dropped the towel. I heard a gasp behind me and Jesse's one good eye was staring at me.

"Oh. Sorry, I needed uh . . . to wash my clothes. I didn't think you'd mind. Do you?"

I knew my face was red and probably the rest of me. I grabbed the towel and put it around me. I couldn't dress in front of him. The shirt I had confiscated was bunched up and covering, I hoped all my pertinent parts.

"No pro . . . lem" he said in a slurred voice as he fell back on the pillow. His eyes were closed.

I put on the sweats and ran to the bed.

"Jesse? You okay? What can I do for you?" I went to him and brushed my hand over his hair. I was looking at his face trying to read it through all of the bruises. "Jesse. Tell me what you're feeling?"

"wunerfull . . . ."

"Jesse, you have to tell me what hurts. I need to make sure your bandages are alright."

"You are sooo . . . buteaful . . . ." His words came out a slurred.

Deciding to change the subject I said, "Oh Jesse, I'm so sorry, don't try to talk, save your strength."

He chuckled, I kept babbling on. "Dr. Wenz will be visiting you this morning. Bass was here earlier and will be back later. I made some chicken soup. Are you hungry?" I was talking a mile a minute.

He raised his good arm very gingerly and put it to my face, He looked in my eyes.

"Oou ca . . . . me."

The door bell rang and I jumped up." That's probably Dr. Wenz. You stay right there. Don't you even try to move!"

I opened the front door to a little wizened looking man. He could have been an encyclopedia salesman. Wire rim glasses, brown hat and suit. He was looking at his watch as he said he had come to look at Jesse. I was so relieved.

"He's upstairs last door on the right." I was so thankful to finally have someone who knew what they were doing.

I followed and watched as he entered the room.

"Jess, what you have done to yourself?" He immediately opened his bag that he had placed on the bed. "You could have lost this eye Jesse; you will need to see an eye doctor." He kept on talking, how this looked good and how that cut was deep and this might hurt because it needed re-stitching. He took each bandage off and went over every injury.

I left the room and brought back some warm water, washcloths and a basket that I put all the bandages, tape and ointments in from the bathroom. I made another trip for some ice.

While the doctor checked over Jesse I went downstairs' and had a cup of coffee. The phone rang and Margaret was on the other end. I let out a sigh as I told how to retrieve my calls and gave her Carte Blanc with the office. There was little to do but I felt better that someone was there. I thanked her again and told her to call if she had any problems.

I put my cloths in the dryer and thought of how nice the fleece from Jesse's sweats smelled. I laughed as I folded the towels from the dryer.

Dr. Wenz had finished with Jesse when I went back up. The sweat on Jesse's face told me of the ordeal he had gone through. Dr. Wenz was putting his instruments back in his bag.

"I'm glad your back, CJ, right? Jesse is in pretty bad shape. Keep a close eye on him. He needs to stay off that ankle. Make sure he takes his medication, pain meds for at least the next two days, antibiotics until they are gone. If you need me I left a card on the end table."

As he started to walk out he turned and looked at me with a strange look on his face.

"Someone needs to be here for the rest of the week. If you need a nurse call me. Mama may know someone too. I can let myself out."

Apparently I had moved in for the week.

I warmed up the soup, added some crackers and a glass of milk. I went outside and plucked one of the last flowers of the season and placed it on the tray. I picked up the tray and went to Jesse's room.

Jesse eyes were closed until I set the tray next to his bed.

"Are you hungry? I made some soup and I thought if you could live through my cooking you just might make it."

I heard him snicker. I helped him sit up. The pain had to be excruciating. His face was washed in sweat and he was pale under the bruises. I took the washcloth by the bed put it in the cold water and patted his face. Even my light touch seemed to cause him pain.

"Oh Jess, I really don't know what I'm doing here. I'm not a nurse."

He looked at my face and whispered out of the side of his mouth "yur best med . . . cine."

I fluffed his pillows helping to sit up straighter. "Let's see if you can handle my soup."

I spooned the soup to his mouth. After a while I think he enjoyed the attention. He had a soggy cracker and drank a little milk. I removed the tray to the dresser and helped him to the bathroom much as we did the last time. We both seemed a little more comfortable.

I gave him his medicine and distracted him by telling him about how Margaret was helping me out at the office. I kept the cool cloth on his eye until he went to sleep. I went to the other side of the bed and laid down beside him, I put my hand over his chest so that I would know if he moved and then I fell asleep.

We slept until I heard Bass's voice in the doorway, I popped right up. He had a walker and set it at the end of the bed. He looked down at

Jesse and said that he looked like shit. He blushed and he looked my way "Er . . . he's looked better."

I told him what the doctor said and I would be willing to stay at least until the weekend.

Bass looked relieved, "We all appreciate you doing this CJ, I know you have things to do. We'll help you out all we can. Just call."

"Well, I do have some errands, if you have some time could you stay with Jesse?"

As we walked downstairs I realized there were several plans swimming in my head.

We were sitting at the kitchen table discussing what Dr. Wenz had said, and how Jesse seemed a little bit better each time he woke.

"He's glad you're here. He was so insistent. Jess could only say he needed to talk to you. He was so drugged and hurt and all he wanted was you."

"We don't know each other well, only a couple of days. He might change his mind after I bully him into talking pills and nagging him about moving about."

Bass looked at me. "CJ, I have never seen him this way. He's always been a take it or leave it kinda guy. With you it's different. Don't you like him?"

We were getting a little personal. I decided honesty was the only way,

"Jesse is special. The first time I saw him I was attracted. I don't have much experience with the boyfriend thing and I have to admit I don't know what I feel."

"Give it time girl. Jess is the most patient man I know. That's what makes him good at what he does."

"Bass I see him lying in pain. I see his bruises. I feel his pain. My heart goes out to him. I don't know much about him. All I know that he's got good friends and a good heart."

Bass leaned back. "You're scared, Jess won't hurt you, but I think you could hurt him. Just give him a chance."

A loud knock came to the side door. Bass jumped up and put his hand to his back at the same time motioning me to be quiet and stay where I was.

Another loud knock and a big booming voice rang out. "OK BASS, I see your truck out here man! Let me in!"

We both shouted "Dombrowski?" and started to laugh. Bass went to open the door. Dombrowski filled the door. I had only seen him sitting high behind a huge counter at the station. Seeing him face to face in real life he was gigantic. He had a huge bouquet of flowers that were dwarfed in his fist.

"I came by to see about Jesse. How's he doing?"

Dombrowski shrunk the kitchen with his size. I took the flowers from him and he looked relieved. I told them to go on into the living room and I would bring them something to drink. I pulled out the last two beers in Jesse fridge, grabbed some glasses and went in to the living room. They both had made themselves comfortable. I could picture Jesse and his friends sitting around watching a ballgame, talking and cheering the home team.

I excused myself and went to look for a vase. I found a large picture and took my time arraigning them. I knew I was stalling. I could hear them talking about what was happening to BA and his gang. I eased-dropped; I knew if I entered the room they would change the subject. Dombrowski was telling Bass about how one of them was crazy, said he got beaten up by a nobody and swore that the house was haunted.

Opps . . . seemed being dimmed did not mean missed. Now I wanted to interrupt. I came in the room with the flowers and said I was taken them upstairs.

"Their beautiful Mr. Dombrowski, it was very thoughtful of you." Dombrowski turned a bright red.

"Call me Grady Miss. He pointed at the flowers, "These are from the Station, we all chipped in. I guess I owe you an apology, especially since you're taken such good care of the kid."

"Grady, I'm glad to meet Jesse's friends; I would like us to be friends too."

He reached over to take the flowers and said "let me carry these for you."

"Thank you Grady, why don't you call me CJ?"

We came to Jesse's room and Grady stopped in his tracks. His face went hard as he took in the damage that was done to his friend. Bass went around to the side of the bed and looked down at Jesse. I put the flowers on the bureau so that they could be seen from any angle in the room. Bass was at the bed calling Jesse's name telling him to wake up and say hello to Grady.

Jesse woke up fighting to rouse himself from the hold the drugs had on him. He tried to focus and get his body moving as Grady walked up to the bed, and looked down at Jesse.

"Jesus kid, you look terrible."

Jesse put out his arm for help to sit up. His smile was weak but genuine. I had time to adjust but looking at him through Grady's eyes made my heart hurt all over again.

The two men helped him sit up, fluffing pillows, making him comfortable, I went to the office and brought another chair so that they could talk.

I went downstairs and let the boys have some alone time. I went to the kitchen to make sandwiches and dish up the last of my soup. I heard laughter. Sometimes Grady's large voice, sometimes Bass, I heard them fill him in on precinct happening's.

After a while it quieted down they seemed to be getting ready to leave. I set the table for the two men and took a tray up for Jess.

"I made something for you two, downstairs in the kitchen. You have to be hungry."

They both told Jess they'd be back and went down the stairs. Jess looked tired but content. The few minutes that he shared with his friends had done wonders. I looked around the room and saw that they had rearranged things. The walker had been moved and they had helped him to the bathroom.

I sat on the side of the bed and asked how he was doing. I had begun to spoon him some soup. I told him about Grady's flowers. He looked at them and I could see him try not to laugh. He was speaking better. This time he ate all of his soup. I told him to get some rest. He was tired, sore, and happy. He took his pill with no protest. I pulled his blanket up and kissed his forehead. He smiled as he drifted off.

The boys had finished when I came back down. The dishes were piled in the sink. They were sitting in the living room.

"Hey fellows, I need to go to my office tomorrow could you ask Annie if she could come over for a couple of hours." I explained that I needed to get some work done and pick up a prescription for Jesse. I needed to start out early and catch the bus. I would be back about three or so.

Grady looked at me. "You don't have a car?"

"I do have it on my to-do list right after rent and electricity."

He laughed and said he had a car. He had just fixed up a car for his brother. It wasn't classy enough for him. "You can have it."

I sat with my mouth open. "Are you serious Grady? That would help a lot. How much is it and when can I get it?"

"Don't you listen girl? You can have it. I picked it up at a police auction and tinkered with it and it runs fine. You'll have to get insurance."

I tried to hide my disappointment.

"Grady, that's my catch 22; I need work to pay for things. At the moment my resources are low. If you can hold off, I'll get back to you."

Bass popped up. "Insurance ain't no big thing. I'll cover that. Grady give me the info, and CJ give me yours. I'll put you on my policy."

"Fellas, you can't do this. You're both being very generous but it's way too much."

"CJ, you need to be here. Mama can't do it and Jess will be really pissed since you're the only one he wants here. I will cover the insurance because you won't take money to take care of Jesse."

I looked from one face to the other. I was overwhelmed, "I don't know what to say!"

Grady said "It's settled. Bass you stay here and we'll go get the car."

I was rushed out the door and was almost shoved into Grady's Oldsmobile. He needed a big car. We took off and traveled across town. He talked all the way.

"I thought you were one pushy broad when I met you. But Jess, he's been walking on air. I shouldn't have told him you were trouble. But you got me on a bad day; I'm usually a pussy-cat."

He went on about the most nonsensical things. We finally got to Grady's house, a big ole monster house. It was huge and well cared for, I could picture a whole family of giants. He told me his brother and his wife, their two kids, and his mother lived in the house.

His brother really did need a bigger car but this one was such a deal. He had tricked it out, inside and out. It was a hobby of his.

He opened the garage and turned on the light. There sat a dark blue Volkswagen Beetle. It was beautiful. The tan interior was just like new. He took the key off his key ring and told me to start it.

"It's a little supped up but I think you can handle it."

I took the key from his big hand and then on my tiptoes I threw my arms around his neck and gave him a big long bear hug.

"Thanks Grady, I owe you big time. And you are a big ole pussy cat."

"Just don't let that get out. I have a image ya know."

Grady waved me off saying he'd see me the next day. I slowly backed out of the garage and managed not to stall it. I pulled out in the street and it road like a dream. I had a car. A major item on my metal list could be crossed off.

I got back to Jess's about 9:00, I drove into the driveway and walked around my new car admiring the color and the style and the fact that it was all mine. I walked around it several times. When I looked up I saw Bass wearing a smile to match mine.

"Bass isn't it beautiful! I don't know what I expected but I didn't expect such a beautiful car."

Bass laughed and said "You gotta have wheels. We take care of our own."

I stopped short. "I have some pretty extravagant friends"

Bass just smiled and said "Yes you do. I gotta go CJ, Jesse is comfortable and I gave him a pill about an hour ago. I'll stop by tomorrow after work. Annie said she'd be here at nine." He was heading for his truck and fishing in his pocket for his keys, he waved as he walked away. "Thanks CJ. Take good care of him."

I walked through the door and locked it behind me. I went through the house picking things up, a glass here, a plate there. I turned off the lights off as I left each room. I walked upstairs and used the shower. I checked on Jesse. He was asleep. I walked to the other side of the bed and climbed under the blankets. I rolled on my side to face him and put my hand on his chest so I would know if he moved. I dreamt of flying down the road in a little blue car.

Chapter 12

I was cruising down the highway, the wind in my hair. I had freedom. To go where I wanted, do what I wanted, when I wanted too.

The light breeze on my face, a gentle rushing, so light that it felt like butterfly wings. My face was nuzzled warm and cozy on a warm soft . . . shoulder?

I lifted my head; I was looking into his eyes. I could feel myself blush. He looked at me with such longing, still stroking me with his butterfly touch.

"I've dreamt of this." His voice came out husky.

I was snuggled up close to his body. My arm was across his chest. How wonderfully natural it felt to be lying next to him, feeling the warmth of his body, breathing in his scent, watching the sun streaming in the window surrounding us in its warm glow.

"I dreamt of you next to me. I was afraid to open my eyes; I thought I might be imagining you."

I *WOKE* up. I was frozen in place like a deer in headlights I was trying to think of something clever to say that would explain why I was where I was, practically naked and snuggled up with my arm around him. "How are you feeling?"

He glanced at my hand on his chest and then at my bare shoulder.

"Better and better, you have the best bed-side manner."

I could feel the heat of my whole body blushing when I pulled away, trying to cover myself and at the same time missing the warmth.

I looked around, hoping to find a robe or towel, something that could cover me while I climbed out of bed. Jesse's hand fell to the pillow when I sat up.

"Could you uh . . . I need to uh . . . ."

Jesse's smile changed to a grin. "There are some shirts in the closet, help yourself."

He turned his head away while I got up and grabbed the first shirt that my hand came to. I slipped it on and ran to *my* bedroom where the clothes I washed lay neatly folded on the bed. I jumped into my jeans and only hesitated long enough to catch the scent of Jesse as I buttoned up the borrowed shirt.

Jesse was trying to sit up when I came into the room. He seemed to be a little better. The color around his bruises still looked angry. The light yellow was a contrast to the deep black and blue. Trying to sound cheerful I said "Your eye looks better. The swelling seems to have gone down quite a bit. Your speech is clearer too. I can understand you now. What can I get you for breakfast?"

"I would really like some coffee. Maybe some eggs?" He said this as he felt his face feeling the growth of his beard. "And I would really like to clean up."

I brought the walker up to the bed. Getting around was going to be a little bit easier. I picked up his robe and helped him put it on. We leaned on each other for balance. I helped as he maneuvered the walker nursing his ankle. He was in quite a bit of pain and straining not to show it. I walked with him until we reached the bathroom. Not wanting to leave the room. I stripped his bed and found linens in his closet and remade it. I fluffed his pillows and I picked up the room. I went in his drawers and retrieved a t-shirt, some briefs, and what looked like a well worn and comfortable pair of sweat pants. I put them all on the bed.

I heard Jesse thrashing around in the bathroom and I knocked on the door. "Hey Jesse, you need me?"

I heard him grunt and then swear "Damn contraption, I want a shower."

I laughed as I opened the door, "Can't help you with that right now."

Jesse stood with his robe open I could see his bandaged ribs and angry bruises. He had a pitifully sad face.

"Let me get you back to bed. I'll get your some breakfast. We'll figure something out."

Jesse looked at the room, his remade bed, the pile of dirty cloths and the fresh ones on the bed.

"CJ, how can I ever I thank you?"

"I'll think of something."

Moving slowly Jesse was back in bed. He smelled so good. He had shaved and I couldn't imagine how much of an effort that must have taken. He was more alert. His eye was clearer.

I helped him change into a clean t-shirt, and sweats. I went into the bathroom for water for his antibiotics. We decided to hold off until after breakfast for his pain pill.

"You've been pretty busy. Thanks for cleaning up; I'll make it up to you."

"No need, I have been well compensated for my act of mercy. Grady and Bass worked it out that I have transportation. The prettiest little Blue VW, they didn't have to do it. I didn't agree to help for pay."

"Grady always surprises me. The car's a great idea; it's a nice little car. It fits you. I bought my Nova the same way. He's a mechanical wizard."

"Considering I was ready to punch out his lights the moment I met him."

"You surprised him. He thought you were a tough broad. Said you ate nails for breakfast. I told him he'd eat his words."

"Grady is such a pussy-cat. I would never have thought it. Annie's coming in this morning. I have to check on my office."

"I don't want a baby sitter. CJ, tell Annie she doesn't have to come over."

"Fine Cowboy, I'll just stay here then."

"CJ, really, there's no where I can go, I'll be fine."

"Well then you won't need me anymore. Just give me a call if you need something."

"That's not what I meant. I'll probably sleep until you get back."

"I can't do my job if I have to worry about you."

"You are a pushy broad; I'm going to have to talk to Grady."

I laughed. "Go right ahead. He was the next choice of babysitters."

He groaned and leaned back on the pillow.

He ate some scrambled eggs, a half piece of toast, and drank orange juice. I could see that he was hurting. I convinced him to take a half of a pain pill. "Just to dull the pain."

He was asleep before I gathered all the dishes to the tray.

I started some laundry, loaded the dishwasher, and was finishing the kitchen when Annie arrived. We talked over coffee about Jesse's meds, the surprise that Grady turned out to be, and how close the three were. They were family in everything but name.

As I walked out the door she told me to take my time. Bass was coming over after his shift. Mama wanted to me to stop by if I had the time. She had some things for Jess.

Chapter 13

I cruised to my office in my *new* car. I parked in back, and went in. It felt good to be there. The phone was blinking but I passed everything to get to my room. I pulled out my overnight bag and packed some undies, shirts, jeans and socks. I picked out some clothes to wear and ran into the shower. I let the shower wash away all the confusion in my life. There had been so many changes. I needed to make a list. I ended my contemplation as the water went cold. I dressed; I put on Jess's shirt again. I left it unbuttoned over a deep blue tank top.

I went into my office and picked up the mail. Mostly ad's, I read through the notes Margaret left. Her handwriting was clear and precise. *Call Jacobs—regarding reward"* That would be for Mooring. I immediately called and Jacobs's secretary put me through. I agreed to meet him that afternoon.

The other message wasn't so clear. I was from someone called Pete. The number was disconnected. I checked the date, yesterday; I made that notation and put it aside.

I picked up the Wiggins files and began to read the notes I had.

I wondered if Margaret typed. The door opened as on cue, Margaret entered disguised as a very large, leafy green plant. I wouldn't have known it was her if I hadn't heard her prattle as she entered.

"Good you're here, how's Jesse? Poor man, they sure do get beat up a lot. Is that a man thing you think? Got this plant on sale in front of *Eve's Garden* down town thought it would look good in here. Did you see the picture?"

I came out of the office and watched as she dropped her purse on the desk, set the plant next to end table. She was taking off her coat and turned to me "You need a coat rack."

I laughed "That's a great idea. We need to start a wish list." We gave each other a hug. She was such a whirlwind. Her personality lit up the room.

"CJ I hope you don't mind, the furniture is really nice but I added some character to the place. Margaret pointed to the wall across from the couch. I looked at the picture. It fit the wall across from the couch perfectly. I instantly liked the feeling. It was an abstract that was bold and bright and fitting. I would enjoy the feeling it emoted.

"Margaret it's great, I like what it does for the room. Thank you so much for working the office."

"Oh honey, don't thank me. I'm working this into a full time job. Right now we are helping each other get off the ground."

I asked about her typing. She had been the office manager for a small furniture company and had good skills. I explained what I needed. How I had my files, but she could organize something that would work for the both of us.

In between she talked about Rosie and Mary and how happy they were. She had moved in with them.

I told her about the Grady-mobile, how I first met him and my first impression. How he turned into a big pussycat. I brought her up to date on Jesse's condition.

We started talking about my plans for the Wiggins that afternoon. We went through the files; her suggestions were clear-cut and precise. I should have taken some computer classes but with Margaret's skills I wouldn't have to.

She would be glad to follow up on bondsmen, check to see if we could get some work hot off the press. She told me I needed to get a cell-phone and make sure I kept it handy.

I wanted to check out the Wiggins. I grabbed my duffle bag. Added a few canisters of pepper spray and had to remind my self I had a vehicle. I put my bag in the front seat and went to see Mr. Jacobs. I left the office in Margaret's very capable hands.

I arrived at Jacob's office 20 minutes early. His office looked like an office. After the last bond shop I had visited I was surprised to find Jacob's was neat and tidy with plants and chairs. He even had magazines. His secretary looked very efficient sitting behind a big desk. She looked up as I entered. "Good afternoon, can I help you?"

I handed her my card and said "Good afternoon, I am from CJ Investigations. We spoke this morning. I have an appointment with Mr. Jacobs."

"Ms. CJ, It's good to meet you. Mr. Jacobs will be right out." She picked up the phone and within minutes Mr. Jacobs came out to greet me. As we shook hands he led me into his office.

He was of average height and wore a well pressed expensive looking suit. His white hair was neatly combed and he wore horned rimmed glasses. He looked more like a professor then a bondman. His office was tastefully decorated with rows of books on his impressive book shelf. He motioned for me to take a seat.

"I am happy to finally meet you, bringing in someone like Mooring is no small feat. When I spoke to Detective Keyes he told me that you not only picked up Mooring, you were also responsible for several other arrests. My hat's off to you."

I thanked him for the compliment and told him that if he had need of our services we would be happy to work with him in the future.

"I'm sure we will be working together in the future. Meanwhile we have some business to conduct. The amount on Mooring was $1,500, 00. Detective Keyes informed me that you were directly responsible for his arrest. I made out a check and Rita has it at her desk. I hope that we can continue to do business."

"I'm happy that this worked out for both of us."

We talked a while longer; he seemed impressed by my choice of vocation. Commenting on the fact that I didn't look the part and commenting on the danger involved.

I left my card with him and rose from the chair as I held my hand out. He stood up from behind his desk shook my hand and said that we would be in touch.

Rita stood up to hand an envelope to me as re-entered her domain. I signed a receipt and took it from her and thanked her. "You're CJ the PI?"

"Yes, I'm afraid so."

"Good work CJ, It's good to meet you." She gave me Mr. Jacob's card. "Don't be a stranger."

I had a big smile as I left I read his card as I waited for the elevator. *Jacob's Loan and Trust.*

The radio was blaring as I drove back to the office. I was on cloud nine. I pulled into the back of the office. Ran up the flight stairs and shouted to Margaret to grab her purse, lock up, we were taken a ride.

First stop was the bank where I had a business account. This was the most activity to date. I wanted Margaret as co-signer. She started her own account when I advanced her $300.00.

I instructed Margaret to pay the rent and electric on the office, as an after thought I told her to get us both a cell-phone and coat-rack.

I had the $50.00 from Rosie's bail and about $6.00 and some change of my own. I felt so rich.

I dropped Margaret back off at the office and drove over to Magpie's. Mama welcomed me with open arms.

"It's so good to see you. We have been talking about how nice you are to take care of Jesse. Bass stopped in and said you had him eating out of your hand."

"I don't know about that. He's been so drugged I doubt he knows who's there."

"Oh, I don't think so CJ, but I want to come and visit. When is a good time? I can get Annie to take over. After the breakfast crowd would be a good time, I want to make it easy on you and Jesse."

"Mama, anytime you can come you are welcome, no phone call needed. You will make Jesse so happy."

Mama looked at me. She gave me another big hug and said "You are good for that boy, come to the kitchen I have some things for you to take home. Some things for when the boys come over too."

"Danny, Can you get those two boxes on the counter and take them and Ms. CJ to Jesse's?"

I remembered I had wheels. "Oh! I have a car. There's a blue VW we can put them in the boot!"

Mama looked at me. "I'll explain later. I will see you very soon." We each took a box and put it in the car.

I beat it over to Jesse's. I carried in one box and passed Annie as she went to get the other. There were two kinds of homemade soup, a large pan of Lasagna, two pies (apple), banana's apples and grapes, milk, tea and orange juice. Not to mention the homemade bread and biscuits.

"Am I having a party?" I asked as we put the food away.

"No. that's just Mama, she takes care of all of us."

I left Annie to go check up on Jesse. He opened his eyes as I walked through the door.

"You finally came back. I missed you."

"Don't see how, you slept most of the time. Are you hungry? I stopped by Mama's and she made a feast for you. She must really like you."

He motioned me over to the bed and I sat down beside him, I studied his eye and saw more of the grey-green then I had in the past but the red that surrounded it looked nasty. "How's your vision?"

"I can see you clearer, and what a sight you are."

"You are such a sweet talker. What can I do for you" He gave me a smile that told me more then I needed to know.

"Let's get you up in the walker. I'm going downstairs and bringing you some of Mama's soup. You are going to the bathroom and do whatever it takes to make you feel better. You will not leave that room until I get back."

"You are so bossy. Grady pegged you right."

"Okay big boy, on three."

I noticed that when I leaned in to help him up he seemed stronger. He moved into the walker pampering his ankle. He took a deep breath; his ribs were still tender. His walker was taking his weight as he hobbled across the room, he paused twice, but I knew better then to try to help. I followed him to the door. I called out that he had 20 minutes.

I ran down the stairs and Annie already had a cup ready for the soup, some biscuits and a piece of pie on the tray. I thanked her and we sat over cups of coffee while I filled her in on my day. She was thrilled that Margaret was working out.

She said that Jesse woke twice and both times asked where I was. She was laughing when he refused his meds, he didn't want to miss me when I came in. He was grumpier each time he heard that I hadn't returned yet.

I filled a cup with soup. Another with tea and carried the tray up the stairs. I entered the room and set the tray on the dresser. I knocked on the bathroom door and asked if he was hungry.

He opened the door and he looked so much better. He had combed his hair and I could smell his soap on his skin. He stood in front of me bare from the waist up. Even bruised and bandaged he took my breath away. I felt a familiar tingling in my stomach and watched as he slowly made his way back to the bed. When he met me at the bed he leaned in and kissed my nose. "Thank you CJ."

I pulled my head back "Okay, Cowboy, back to bed."

He snorted and said "I would like to sit up and eat."

I laughed and said "Dr. Wenz will be here in the morning. You are going to do what I tell you to do or I will take your walker away. But I'll let you sit up."

He looked at me, shrugged his shoulder and asked "What's for dinner?"

He started feeding himself. I just sat beside him telling him of my day. Thanking him for paving the way with Jacobs. I described Mr. Jacobs and the possibility of work in the future. He listened as he worked on the soup. I continued with the news about Margaret and how she was a godsend. It was a comfortable feeling, just talking, enjoying each others company.

He finished about the same time I ran out of prattle. I gathered up the tray noticing that his appetite was improving. His jaw was still tender.

But he looked stronger. He was still in pain but he was healing. I handed him his antibiotics as he finished off his tea. I was getting up when he asked me to stay longer. I looked at the clock and had about 20 minutes until Bass made it back over for Annie.

"No, you need rest until I get back." He wouldn't take a pain pill but did take two aspirin. I would force one down his throat later.

Bass came for Annie and they both went up to tell Jesse that they were leaving and he would stay longer when and if the doctor cleared him.

"We got strict instructions not to wear you out."

Annie gave him a kiss on the cheek and told him to be nice for me. Jess said goodbye and when they left he patted the bed next to him.

"Sit down CJ, we need to talk."

I sat on the edge of the bed. He seemed to be hedging around what he intended to say. He put his hand in mine and asked if I would help him sit straighter. I leaned over him and fluffed his pillows then helped him pull himself up. The bandage on his wrist was smudged. When he was comfortable he pulled my hand and I sat down beside him. His arm was behind my back. I lifted up so that he could move it and he lowered it around my waist.

"CJ, I know that you got roped into this. I have been trying to thank you. Now that your here I don't know where to start."

I started to protest and I told him we could talk later. Right now it was working out. "Just call it payback for all you've done for me."

"No, CJ that's not what I wanted to say. I need to let you know that I came on too strong. You told me that you didn't have relationships. I thought you meant you didn't want one. I seem to have time on my hands, a lot of time to think. And I like us. Thank you for being here."

I began to relax, it felt good to just sit and listen. We talked about the strangest things. His pill was working and he began telling me how he met Bass in 4th grade, how he was such a tough kid.

"Bass started coming over to Mama's. I swept floors after school and took out the garbage. I made sure tables were clean and put candles and flowers on them for the dinner hour. Bass started to help. At first to get me out earlier so we could go out and play basketball in the alley. Mama eventually put him on a bus boy. Mostly weekends but for special parties too. We were allowed to do our homework in a back booth. I always had a curfew and Bass started keeping it with me. After a while Bass was just there. We both did more the older we got. Mama never forgot his birthday. Holiday's he spent with us. Bass didn't go home very much. There was no one there. If his dad was home he was out of money and booze and looking for a punching bag. Bass spent the nights more and more. I had a bunk bed and we shared the room over the kitchen all through school. When we graduated we both went into the service. Mama wrote us every week and sent packages to the both of us."

"Mama helped him too. What about Grady?"

Grady; He was always bigger then life and loud, he was a grade ahead and into sports big time. His parents were good friends with Mama and Henry. We were the Three Musketeers.

We all went into law enforcement. And that's a story for another day."

I turned my face to him and asked. "How did you get to Mama's door?"

"That's another story too."

I shrugged my shoulders, "Well if you don't want to talk about it."

There was a long pause. I decided I must have overstepped some boundary when I heard a very low voice, almost a whisper. He was looking beyond the walls to his past.

"I was left. I don't remember anything about my parents. I almost remember being in the alley behind the restaurant. I was pretty young. Mama's husband, Henry found me and brought me into the kitchen. They discretely checked for missing children. He heard that a lady with a baby had been in the area, no one knew much about her. Mama made arraignments for me to stay. Later I heard that she applied to foster me. Since no one had any objections I stayed on. I wondered about my mother. What she was like. Why she left me. I stopped wondering a long time ago. I figured out that I was better off. That's all I know. Magpies has always been my home."

I had tears in my eyes for the little boy he'd been; for the man he was. I turned to him and looked into eyes. I bent down and I kissed him full on the lips. He was surprised but that didn't stop him from responding. Lightly at first and then deeper. I drew my face away and tried to breath. We were both surprised.

The mood was shattered when the doorbell rang, followed by a loud knock. I didn't know if I was disappointed or relieved.

"That's Grady" he said. He looked at me, and let me go.

I went down to answer the door. Before I let Grady in, I gave him a hug and thanked him for the VW. I told him I had christened it the Grady-mobile and it rode like the wind. He laughed at the idea and asked about Jess.

"Well he's still up there, chaffing at the bit."

I reached in the Fridge and took out a beer and set it in front of him

"Grady, I have to go out for a while. Only a couple of hours but I need to check out an address. Can you stick around until I get back?"

I was putting some Lasagna on a plate and put it in the Microwave. I set the timer and took out a pie and cut him a generous wedge and set it on a separate plate in front of him. The timer went off on the microwave.

I turned around and took the Lasagna and waved it under his nose. "This is from Mama's."

Grady looked at the steaming Lasagna. "So this is something I don't mention to Jesse?"

"Why Grady this has nothing to do with Jesse, this is about my business. I have to pick up a cell phone from Margaret over at Rosie's. Then I have to check an address. I shouldn't' be gone long. Can you do it?"

"CJ, I'd do anything for you, But not behind Jess. You tell him you're going out. I'm moving the TV from the office into Jess's bed room."

I gave him a kiss on the cheek and told him I'd be right back. I ran upstairs. Jesse was lying on the bed with his eyes closed and I thought he might be sleeping when he said "Hey kid, I didn't mean to bum you out."

I sat on the bed and I told him that he did not *bum me out*. I was honored that he shared a part his life with me. I didn't feel sorry for him. I was proud of him. He was very lucky, and it made me see the kind of man he was. He held out his hand and drew me down to him. He kissed me, and I returned it. As the kiss began to draw deeper I pushed myself away.

"Your buddy Grady is downstairs scarfing down Mama's Lasagna. You better get well fast or there won't be any left. I am going over to Rosie's; I had Margaret pick me up a cell-phone. I'll be back soon. You enjoy your time with Grady. If you can't be good I will have to make you take a pill." I did get him two aspirin.

"You got Grady sitting me? That's low CJ."

Grady showed up at the door with a television in his arms. "Hey. Baby face you got any cards?" He took it to the dresser and plugged it in.

Laughing at the picture they made I waved from the door.

"I'll be back in a flash." I grabbed my jacket out of the bedroom and left.

Chapter 14

My first stop was Rosie's. I met Margaret at the door. Rosie was excited about Margaret's job and invited me in for some iced tea. I thanked her but told her I had to get back to Jesse. Her eyebrow went up and she looked knowingly at Margaret.

"I just came over for the cell phone."

Margaret handed me a bag. "I charged it for you. And I programmed every number I thought you might use. There's a car jack and a wall jack. Your number is on the box."

I thanked them both and jumped back into the G-Mobile.

I drove over to the Wiggins neighborhood. It was just beginning to get dark. I parked just beyond the closest street light. I had a good view of the front of the house and a part of the side.

The lights were on and twice I saw a shadow pass a window. The television flickered from the front window downstairs. I marked it as the living room. A faint light come out of window on opposite side of the door. I figured it was from the kitchen beyond.

I thought I'd wait and see if there would be more traffic. It was still too early to be out partying.

I pulled out the phone bag and looked in the box. I swore under my breath; a *pink* telephone? I plugged the charger into the cigarette lighter and saw that it was charged. I played with it checking all the numbers that Margaret had programmed and was not surprised that she had the number of everyone that was listed in our files or knew.

I dropped it when it rang. I answered and heard Margaret's voice "Hello CJ, just checking to see if you figured out the phone yet."

I told her that I was fiddling with it and just about jumped out the seat when it rang. She laughed, and told me to let her know if I needed any help. As I hung up I had the thought that pink might grow on me.

I sat the phone on the seat and pulled a notebook out. I started a list. I listed all the people I knew. My new friends seemed to be part of the friends and family of Jesse. The few friends I had made were results of my first wanted poster, again this circled back to Jesse.

I was laughing at myself when two cars pulled in front of the Wiggins's house. Two men got out of the front car. A woman and a man climbed out of the back. They were carrying several grocery bags; they all met at the walk and went laughing into the house.

The men were dark. One could have been Max he looked heavy enough. I figured the woman for the sister. She was as wide as she was tall. She had a lot of frizzy unkempt hair, her face wasn't visible. But she had a very distinct waddle. Two shadows, one male and one female crossed the living room and headed toward the faint light in the back of the house.

I started to get that feeling. it was now or never. I left the car and moved toward the house. I felt the warning grow as I felt myself dim. I walked down the street past the house and crossed when I got to the corner. I slipped through the hedges bordering the driveway past a dismantled car that was in the side yard, parts of it were scattered around it. I moved toward a back window. The rooms light showed bright on the yard. I went up to the window and heard one of the men growl.

"Get that damn dog outta here! The little rat piss-ant."

The dog gave a squeal as someone shood it out of the room. They were talking about Max and how it was to hot for him to stay around. The woman piped up and said that Esther would put him up. He nixed it.

I now had a line on his voice. He said that he might go to Steve's. He owed him.

"Max you go over there and they will bust you for sure. Steve's so stoned he would invite the cops in." There was a burst of laughter.

"Well not Esther, she's a nag."

"So did you get the goods?"

"I'll get the rest tomorrow. I'll take Kayla. No one suspects the fat lady." A younger voice spoke up. I peeked over the window ledge to match faces to voices. It was the boy. I missed what he said he was leaving the room.

"Luke, you can't go. You stay here and keep Stacy busy. Maybe you two can clean up this dump."

"Look Ben, don't go telling me what to do, we're bringing the money in."

Now that I had an idea of the players I thought I'd lay low and wait for them to drive off. I went back to the G-mobile and wrote down what I had heard. I worked on a list of *Things I need*.

It was another forty-five minutes before two men came out and climbed into the lead car. I let them pull out and get to the end of the block before I turned on my car. I waited for them to turn the corner before I turned on my lights. I followed the car for twenty minutes or so. They pulled into a driveway. There was an outside light illuminating them as they walked up to a door. One was Max. They pounded on the door until the porch light came on and they went in. I couldn't see a face but I heard a voice. This must be Esther. She didn't sound happy to see them. I wrote down the address. I drove off. I was tired, and I found out what I needed to know.

I got back to Jess's about 11:30. I stopped in the kitchen and poured a glass of iced tea. I went looking for Grady. He was in Jesse's room sleeping in a chair cards were on the bed and floor. The TV was on. Grady snorted awake when I turned it off.

"Hey Grady, did you two have fun?"

"Yeah we talked about you. Jesse wanted to know every word we said."

I laughed and told him that had to make for a short evening. He said it did but cards and a ball game kept them awake.

"Jess, dozed off just a while ago, before the news. He might wake up he wouldn't take a pain pill, said he'd wait for you. Call me after the doctor leaves and let me know how he's doing."

I told him that I would. He saw himself to the door.

I went into the bathroom and stretched. I brushed my hair and teeth, washed my face and put on a nightshirt. I thought of going to the other bedroom when I stopped in my tracks. Jesse was leaning up on his elbow. He had been watching me through the door. I could feel my blush start at my toes. I also felt a tingling begin. I felt no danger, I had no urge. I looked at Jesse and I slowly closed the door. Standing in the bathroom unsure of what I should do.

I had never dimmed unless someone or something was in danger. I didn't feel the urge that came with the tingling, unless it was Jesse, and at the minute he was no threat.

I walked to *my* room and sat on the bed. Was I in danger? Was Jesse in danger?

I walked the house and checked every room, every door. As I made the rounds the tingling faded and then stopped. I came back to Jesse's room.

"Please CJ, tell me what's wrong."

The tingling had stopped but it bothered me that my dimming could come on with no urge or threat. I felt lost, tired and confused. I looked to Jesse. His eyes were pleading.

"Nothings wrong Jesse, I'm just tired."

"Baby, just come over and lay beside me, I promise that I will mind my manners. Give me that damn pill. I promise I will sleep."

I brought water to him, opened up the pill bottle and watched as he swallowed it. He leaned back on his pillow and watched me as I walked to the end of the bed, double back to the other side, fold down the blanket and climb in beside him.

"Thanks CJ" His arm across his brow, I pulled the cover over us.

I placed my hand on his chest, not so much for him, I wanted to for myself. I listened to our breathing. Synchronized, we both entered sleep. I dreamt I had faded and Jesse didn't know I was near. Sadness washed over me.

I woke in a haze. I looked at Jess and he was still deep in sleep. When this was all over I might borrow one of Jesse's magic pills.

I looked at the clock and it was 4:30 a.m. I was to awake to go back to sleep and it was too early to start the day. I carefully left the bed and went into the bathroom. Normal actions, washing my face and brushing my teeth, small things that you could do as your mind wandered.

I looked in the mirror, why did I start to fade? Did I fade? I remembered turning and watching Jesse look at me with a look of such tenderness, such intensity. I found my self responding, the familiar tingling. I felt myself respond to Jesse.

I shook my head. I had resigned my self to being alone. Friends meant explanations and I had no answers. There was no reason for me to have this ability. Therefore it needed to be hidden.

I left the bathroom by the door to the hall. I walked to his office, sat at his desk and turned on a small desk lamp. I grabbed a tablet of yellow notebook paper and leafed through it until I found a blank page and started my list.

Dimming	*Jesse*
Tingling—hands and feet	tingling, hands, chest, head ????
Fading	unknown, I think so
Faster if urgent.	No urge or danger
Urge directs	more like a pull to Jesse

I reread and tried to sort out what it all meant. I stared at my list for a long time. No real answers came. But who's to say what's real.

I needed *not* to think. I went downstairs and started a cup of tea. I had brought the paper with me and I started to make another list.

I made notes on the day before. I studied what had been accomplished and I started to feel better. I thought of my new car, the new cell phone, the wonders that Margaret had accomplished. Do we have a coat-rack yet? I bet myself we did. I had a business and I had things to do.

I went over everything about the Wiggins family, their house and Esther. I knew that Max wasn't happy staying at Esther's so he would probably bolt soon.

I thought of the kids in the house, they seemed proud of their line of work. Ben seemed to make the plans; the sister organized and set it up for the kids to target. I guessed Max, maybe with Bens help went for the money. Nice little family business.

I picked up my cup of tea and carried it into the living room. I took the afghan from the back of the couch and wrapped it around me.

The doorbell was ringing. I Tripped on the Afghan and fell off the couch. Wrapping the afghan tightly around me I hurried to the door. Dr. Wenz was standing on the porch; I welcomed him in and asked if he would like some coffee.

Gathering the corner on the afghan ad throwing it over my shoulder I told him that I had checked on Jesse around 4:30 and he was sleeping soundly then.

Dr. Wenz looked closely at me. "How have you been sleeping? It's very tiring taking care of a convalescent. Has he been annoying? He was annoying when he had the chicken pox." He continued to ramble on as he went up the steps.

I made coffee and poured three cups. I set the tray on the dresser and watched as Dr. Wenz examined Jesse. He had already finished with his head and was working on his shoulder. The blankets were thrown aside. The doctor explained that he was healing nicely and would be able to get up for a couple hours at a time if he used the walker.

"You need to stay off that foot. Baby that ankle, and don't break those stitches. Take your antibiotics and watch that eye; it looks better but you don't want to take any chances. I want you to wear this eye patch until we get you to an eye doctor." The good doctor fitted it on his head covering his eye.

"CJ here looks tired. You haven't been running her have you? Take the pain pills as needed. Don't be a hero. You still need them, every 6-8 hours."

The good doctor talked without waiting for an answer. He seemed to know that his orders would be followed.

"I want you to come in on Monday and we'll do X-rays to make sure your healing right."

He was working on Jesse's foot and ankle. He massaged it as he went down his leg. He took care around the injury but seemed to touch every inch of his ankle.

He straightened up and gathered his equipment and placed it in his bag. He came to the dresser and took a cup of coffee.

"He seems to be healing nicely; just watch that he eats well, and make sure he stays off that foot. His ribs are still tender, we'll know better Monday. About 9:00 at my office."

Jesse had retrieved his blanket and pulled it up to his rib cage. He looked like a very tired pirate. I walked the doctor to the door.

"Call me if there are any major changes. I will see you both on Monday."

I went into the kitchen and made some eggs, and then some pancakes. While poring out orange juice I spotted the fruit, I cut up small pieces of apples and bananas and a couple of maraschino cherries for color. I warmed the syrup and put it on the tray.

I carried the tray up the stairs and placed it on the dresser. I went over to the bed and put my arms out to Jesse. He opened his arms and I pulled him up to sit comfortably.

I smoothed the blankets and carried the tray to the bed. From the time I entered the room neither of us spoke. Jesse's eyes watched my every move. I made sure the tray was secure on his lap. I broke the silence as I brought my plate to the bed and sat beside him leaning on the backboard.

"Good morning Jesse. I sure hope you have an appetite."

We ate comfortably side by side enjoying the breakfast, the solitude, and the company. I told him that I liked his eye patch; it made him look rakish and not so helpless.

We went over the doctors instructions and I told him that I would take him on Monday. My hours were the most flexible. We both avoided the *open door* incident.

When we finished I loaded up the tray and said I would be back with some coffee. Meanwhile, he needed to think of something he might like to do, I didn't play cards.

When I came back with the coffee, I asked him if he had a plan. He surprised me.

"I really would like to take a shower."

"Well. Cowboy, I can't help you there. I can give you a sponge bath."

His eyebrows went up I quickly added that they really weren't as refreshing. I was trying to change the topic and come with a *safe* subject when I had an idea. I made an excuse that I needed to call Margaret, and pulled my new pink telephone out of my apron pocket.

I walked to Jesse's office and started flipping through the numbers on my phone. I found the number I wanted. I got who I wanted and I asked if it would be possible if he bring a friend and come to lunch. I got a big "YOU BET."

When I came back into the room Jesse asked about Margaret. I told him that she was a wiz at the office. He laughed at my pink phone and had me program my number in his. We talked like friends. No sexual overtones. No embarrassing talk about our latest sleeping arraignments. I told Jesse he needed to rest and that I needed to clean up the kitchen.

I was turning on the dishwasher when the door opened and Bass came in with Grady trailing behind him.

"Hi boys how are you doing."

"What's for lunch" asked Grady while Bass looked in the oven.

I turned to both of them. "That's the question. I'm sure your going to love it but first you have to work for your lunch." I sat them down and explained what I wanted them to do.

Several minutes later I heard a "Hey, What are you guys doing?" I listened to a rumble of voices. Grady and Bass were laughing so hard I almost ran up to look. Meanwhile, I pulled out Mama's home made soup, put the last of the Lasagna in the oven and made a salad.

If anyone came to the house at that minute they would have thought the roof was caving in. I looked up at the ceiling waiting for it to fall down around my shoulders.

Their voices were loud and laughing. I could alternately hear snatches of conversation. A lot of swearing and some mumbles from the trio.

I went to the back yard where it was quieter and called Margaret. She had everything in order.

"A Mr. Vince had called asking if you had anything yet."

"Call him back and tell him I'm on it and will get back to him. I need you to find out what you can about Ben and Max Wiggins. Also a Kayla Wiggins, Married, but I don't have the married name. I don't even know if the hubby's in the picture. Two teenagers, Luke and Stacy, hers I think. No last name, Check on Esther, older in age, lives on 442 N. Oak, Max is staying there now."

"There's a guy by the name of Steve, Ben doesn't trust him, but Max likes him. Vince might be helpful, but don't press him, I don't trust him enough to confide in him, He's probably got his own goon squad looking for him."

I could picture Margaret writing everything down in her precise handwriting. She would call back when she got the information. She would start with Vince and then city records.

I hung up and started to walk back to the house. An idea began to form in the back of my brain.

I walked in the house and it was quiet, too quiet. Then I heard some low mumblings. I figured Bass and Grady had succeeded. I grabbed the clean clothes off the dryer and went upstairs. I put the basket on *my bed* and carried fresh linen into Jesse's room. As I stripped his bed I could hear them talking in low voices on the other side of the bathroom door.

I made Jesse's bed. Found some clean blankets in the closet and was fluffing his pillows when I heard a grunt, a rush of splashing water and Bass yelling "Hey man I gotta go back to work."

There was some muffled laughter. I quickly picked up the room and left.

The smell of Lasagna filled the kitchen. I took it out of the oven and set it on the counter. I cut large pieces and waited for the boys. It wasn't long. They walked down the stairs holding their shoes. Both men were dripping wet and had the look of *Mission Accomplished* on their faces.

"Have a seat fella's, you look hungry."

I waited until they were seated and asked if it all went well. In between bites I heard the story.

Grady started, "Bass went to start the water, got it all nice and warm. We tried to think what would work best with all the bandages. I said shower. We could hold him up and cover the bandages."

"I told Grady a bath," piped up Bass, "he could soak and relax, and I could put some nice little bubbles in the water. We would re-tape his ribs and ankles and redo his bandages." Jesse was sleeping and grumpy when they woke him. He argued that he didn't need any of their help.

"Jess wasn't going for it."

"I told him it was going to happen one way or another, his smelly ole body was going to get wet."

"Well ole Jess said he wasn't have'n either of us share his bathroom. From there it was kinda a free-for-all. Jess is stronger then he looks. I think he's malingering since he has such a pretty nurse."

"Don't forget the drugs." piped in Grady.

"We were being careful with his wounds." Bass continued. "I'm afraid we might have been a bit rowdy."

Bass was quick to clarify that they checked his stitches and they looked okay. "But you better look."

"I'm sure Jesse will tell you all about it. We told him it was your idea." Bass said as avoided looking at me.

"Thanks fella's, now he's going to yell at me. Finish your lunch; you both did a good thing. For bravery beyond the call there's apple pie warming in the oven. I hope you wore him out. I'm heading up to the lions den."

I picked up the tray and started up the stairs. I called over my shoulder "You can let yourselves out. Be sure to lock the door."

I quietly entered the bedroom. The curtains were drawn. Jess was lying on the bed with his arm over his face. I went to the bed and sat the tray on the night stand.

"Hey Jesse, How are you doing? I brought you some lunch."

Jesse raised his arm from his face and he held his hand out to me. I took it intending to help him sit up. He held it, and made no effort to sit up. He pulled me down to him and I sat next to him on the bed.

"You are one strange woman. I mention a shower and you arrange for two goons to manhandle me into the shower."

"Yeah, I thought it was pretty clever, your wish was my command."

"That was pretty clever. As soon as those two thugs get back to the station it will be on the evening news."

"Poor baby, you know that you feel so much better. Hey, they didn't hurt you did they?"

I started examining every little hurt. Bass and Grady had rewrapped his ribs and ankle. The fresh bandages were crisp and white. These guys must have had lots of practice; each bandage was neat and tidy. The swelling on his face had gone down. He could speak easier, clearer. The bruises still looked hard and nasty but were edged with a yellowing tinge. His eye seemed clearer, not as red, and the swelling was half of what it had been. He looked especially sexy with the eye patch. He was freshly shaven and smelled so very good.

"I'm doing fine. I'm sore, but right now it's just an ache. It feels good to be clean. I haven't used my muscles in days, and they are letting me know it. The hot water helped."

"Eat something Jess and then I'm giving you a pain pill. You are going for quality sleep and I'm going to help you."

Jesse finished the soup and half of the lasagna. He looked exhausted. I took the tray and set in on the dresser. He swallowed his medicine and I helped him lie down and get comfortable.

He went to pull up the sheet when I pulled it out of his hand and I turned it down over his feet. I started at his feet. I rubbed them working my way up his legs. Avoiding the bandaged places and working on any tight muscle I found. I heard his intake of breath as I worked up his thigh. I massaged his hips and lower back. I went as far as tape on his chest and then moved to make myself available to his neck and shoulders. I rubbed his head, caressing behind his his ears and neck.

"Jesse, I would like to give you a back rub, do you think we can turn you over?"

He moaned "Oh . . . Baby."

I went to the other side of the bed and pulled down the sheets. I rolled him onto his good shoulder and then over to his stomach. I straddled him but took great care not to touch him with my body.

I started at his head, went down to his neck and shoulders and finished rubbing down his arms. I slipped lower down his body kneading muscles. Listening to the sounds he made, feeling his response to my hands letting me know when more care was needed with a knotted muscle. His sighs and moans continued as I started on his lower back, his hips and buttocks, down his legs to his feet. When I finished he let out a long sigh.

"Thanks baby."

I rolled to the side and placed a pillow under him to cushion his ribs. I slid into the bed with him and pulled the sheet and blanket up and covered us both. My last thought I had was that I had felt a slight tingling in my hands as I moved them over Jesse's body. I put my hand on his back, feeling a slight vibration. It felt different, comforting. We both slept.

I woke to a moan in the wee hours of the morning. I was instantly awake when I heard an intake of breath, followed by a painful groan.

"Jesse? Are you all right?" I turn over to see a grimace on his face.

"Oh Jesse, you have to be uncomfortable. Let me help." He was face down on the bed.

"Oh, please, I seem to be frozen in place." His voice was gruff with sleep and pain.

I rose from the bed as gently as I could an idea already shaping in my head. My biggest concern was his shoulder and rib cage.

If I could turn him as I propped up his upper body, he might be able to help by using his good leg for leverage.

"Jess, we are going to do this, but I need your help. We'll do it quickly." I began to massage his arms and leg, getting all the kinks out, loosening his muscles while telling him what I had in mind.

I raised him and slipped behind him on the bed. Together we rolled him over and up into my lap. I carefully pulled him up by lifting under his arms. I eased out while placing pillows behind him.

It went rather smoothly. His strength was returning and the help he added made it easier to slip out while padding his back and shoulder. I straighten him out and smoothed the bedding. I could see the relief he felt at having changed positions.

"Does that feel better?" I asked.

Jesse looked at me "I feel so much better. How did I luck out, the girl in my dreams wakes up in my bed?"

He had a point as I sat next to him in nothing but my panties and t-shirt. Jesse went on "It seems you can do anything."

He held my hand and said "You are a dream come true. Sometimes I think I must be imagining you that I will wake up and find I only dreamed you."

"Jesse, I need to talk to you about something. It's kind of personal. I need you to have an open mind."

"Honey, you can talk to me about anything."

The stars outside the window were bright. It was that time of morning that my thoughts were most introspective. I walked to the window and opened the drapes. The room was fully illuminated from the full moon. The stars shown bright as I stood staring into the night.

"What do you need to say baby?" He held his hand out beckoning me to his side.

I went to the bed and as I took his hand I felt the tingling in my fingers.

His eyes were on my face. His words went straight to my heart. At this moment all I wanted was in front of me. As battered and bruised as he was he was he most beautiful man I have ever met.

I looked back to the window.

"I have been confused since the day I walked into the station. I don't know what I feel because I have never felt like this. I want to be with you and run away at the same time."

"Honey, I don't know what to make of us either, I have never met anyone that could make me feel so right. From the first time I saw you and I didn't even know your name."

"I don't know what to do."

I leaned into his arms and rested my head on his shoulder, my whole body wanting to be near him.

"CJ let me show you."

He began rubbing my hand massaging each finger. It felt erotic, I felt myself respond. Each motion increased the feeling in my hands. I looked at him and tried to pull away. He pulled me gently to him and he dipped his head to kiss my lips. It was a soft and tender kiss.

He lingered, gently mating our mouths teasing my lips lightly making mine open to his. His tongue flicked across my top lip and as his kiss deepened I opened my mouth to let him in. With deep moan he intensified the kiss.

My body responded. I fell into the kiss, giving as much as he gave. It was a new awakening and I wanted more. Somewhere in the back of my mind warning single but as I felt Jesse's hand on my breast these were washed away with sensations. I felt his fingers brush across my nipples hardening them with his touch. He moved lazily, slowly taking his time.

A deep churning heat started deep inside me. Gently he massaged my breasts touching each in turn. Teasing with his fingers first softly and then harder. Gently circling my nipples making them peak.

"Lay back baby, let me touch you."

My body responded as overwhelming sensations reached into the core of me. My heart beat faster, I felt breathless. I opened my mind and let myself feel. Heat was building within me as my body searched for some unknown goal. Red hot fiery emotions flowed through me. I wanted, not knowing what.

As I explored the sensations that engulfed me I slowly recognized the familiar tingling.

I didn't want to think, old fears of being discovered invaded my thoughts. The tingling seemed to mingle with my new found emotions. The urge I felt was an overwhelming need to respond to Jesse's warmth. I slowly lifted my hand and placed it on his shoulder.

I gasped and then froze. "Jesse, Jesse! Let me up; I have got to get up!" I must have sounded hysterical. Leaving the warm bed I ran into the cold bathroom. I closed the door and leaned against it. *How would I explain this?*

I went to the sink and turned on the water. Looking in the mirror I saw color begin return as I felt my heart break. I splashed water on my face trying to calm down.

I realized that the compulsion I was waiting for wasn't there. I didn't know how long I waited. My mind was racing, Oh God was it the emotions that I had to Jesse's touch that had started my fading? I closed my eyes, trying to stop my tears.

I sat on the side of the tub dabbing my face with a cold wash cloth. I had a vision of Jesse holding *nothing?* Oh yeah, this should pretty much solve my relationship problem.

Too many thoughts, too much emotion, to damn much of everything, I started to pace as I did my deep breathing, I kept the water running as I splashed handfuls on my face. I began to feel calmer as I felt myself returning.

I looked in the mirror. My eyes were red and puffy. I had no idea how I was going to explain.

Squaring my shoulders I turned off the water. I walked back into the bedroom hoping I looked calmer then I felt. Jesse was looking at the door and followed me with his eyes as I came back into the room.

He was sitting on the edge of the bed. He held out his hand and motioned me to sit next to him. The stars illuminated the room enough that I could see his confused expression.

"I'm sorry Jesse. I don't know what to say."

"Don't say anything, you don't have to explain."

"Are you all right? How's the shoulder?"

"I'm fine, my stitches itch and the shoulder aches but not like it did. Thanks for the rub. It only hurts when I laugh."

There was a pregnant pause where neither of us spoke; I was starting to panic again when Jesse asked.

"CJ, what's wrong. I know you care, you're here and you don't have to be. You give me signals you want me and then run away every time we get close. I'm not imagining this. It's not the drugs. CJ, talk to me, trust me."

My heart was heavy as I listened to his words. My chest ached. I felt his hand on my face. I looked up to see he had wiped a tear off my cheek. I hiccupped.

"CJ, I'm making you cry? I'm hurting you and I don't know why. Talk to me; tell me how I can help."

"I'm not like other people, I have . . ."

"You have what CJ?"

"Jesse. I can't explain it. I have never been able to explain it. I don't know what to say. You have jumbled up my life. I'm confused, I haven't . . . I don't . . . Jesse I can't talk about it."

"CJ, we don't have to talk if you don't want to. You wouldn't be here to help me if you didn't want to be. Your actions, your body tells me that you care. I want to know everything about you."

He laid his head on my shoulder. I was hurting him. I was hurting me. We sat in the night. It was so quiet and the sky was beginning to dawn. I looked up at the ceiling and sighed. Maybe I should leave. Spare us both any further hurt. Jesse was the only man that ever wanted to be in my life. Not to mention the only one I had ever been attracted to.

In less than two weeks I had lost my plan to live happily ever after—*by myself*—out the door.

What could I say? *Hey, Jesse just wanted to let you to know that I'm a total freak . . . . Ya see, I get these rushes that make me do things . . . . Oh, I decided to do them on the side of good . . . , give me a minute while I change into my invisible suit. Don't Blink. Damn,* Damn,

"Damn!"

"CJ, I see a shadow of you, I get a glimpse, and my heart beats faster, just knowing you are here and not a dream."

"Jesse. You don't know," I started and stopped. He would see a shadow? A glimpse? Had he seen my shadow?

"CJ, what's so terrible that it keeps you from me?"

"Jesse, I need you to understand. It's not you. It's me. I never thought there could be a . . . *Us* . . . or anyone before. You make me want an *US* but . . ." I dropped my hands in my lap, I couldn't find the words.

"Stop CJ, it's enough that you feel something for me." He put his hand over mine.

"We will go slowly. Just being here tells me so much about you. You have a big heart. Don't forget Grady, he couldn't shut up about how rude you were. Now you have him lapping at your feet. Hell, the man gave you a car! I see your heart. Whatever you need to tell me will come in time or not at all. Either way I like who you are. If there is never an *US* I want you to always be part of my life."

When he stopped talking I lifted my head and stared at the wall. How does one respond to something like this? All I could think to do was thank him. To thank him! How lame was that when he was baring his heart to me.

Suddenly he asked, "You don't have a husband do you?"

I laughed so hard I almost fell off of the bed. "Come on Cowboy; let's get you some breakfast."

Jesse was seemed content to talk about simple things while we ate. The work he should be doing, the weather, the price of eggs. I told him that I wanted to re-stock some things we needed, milk, eggs, bread, making a mental list as I rattled along.

"I'll stop at the store. I need to check in at my office. I shouldn't be gone to long."

"There's some cash in my top drawer. Let me know if you need more. Drive carefully." He pulled me close and kissed me.

"Are you sure you'll be ok?"

"I'm feeling much better. Mama called yesterday and said she might stop by. I will laze around and try to read, but I will waste away if you don't come back soon."

"Oh, poor baby, just make sure you follow directions or I will defiantly make your life miserable."

Chapter 15

I came back to find Jesse's lean body framing the kitchen doorway, he was so handsome. Wearing a pair of jeans and cotton shirt he looked almost like his old self. He had a cup of coffee in his hand, his face to the sun soaking in the warmth of the day. It was good to seem him upright. Jesse was healing. I would miss him. Even unconscious it felt good to be around him.

"I missed you." He said as I walked to the door. He held the door open for me and I put the groceries on the table.

"I'm so glad to see that you're up. I was thinking of ways we could get you down those stairs."

"Grady and Ben stopped by to clean out the refrigerator. They helped me get it together. I feel much better. Mama stopped by and she brought some muffins and stew. But your backrub was my miracle."

"You give me too much credit." I put the milk and eggs in the refrigerator. "You're looking better everyday; as soon as you get that doorstop off your foot you'll be just fine."

Jesse came up behind me and put his arms around me. "You need to give me a ride in your tinker-toy."

I laughed, "I don't know about you Detective Keyes. I think you want to get out of the house."

"You're a mind reader too. You bet I do."

"Is this afternoon to soon? I still have to stop at the office. You do know that there is no way you'll be able to make my stairs."

"Don't be so sure, I'm a new man. You know, I'd like to stop at the Station, there's some work I can pick up, maybe then I won't be such a bear."

I ducked under his arm and told him to be ready in fifteen minutes.

We hobbled out to the G-mobile. He hesitated when he saw how far down he'd have to sit and the lack of space for his feet.

"We can take the Nova?"

"Oh, no . . . You want to see how my wheels turn." I slid the passenger seat as far back as it would go.

"Come on Cowboy, let's ride." He hobbled into the seat. His poor legs were up to his chin. I was beginning to have second thoughts. He filled up the whole side of my little G-mobile.

Jesse had to be reading my mind. "Come on slick, let's roll." He hauled in the cane Grady had given him. It took a minute to angle it into the back seat.

As we drove into town; we decided to drop Jesse at work first. When I finished I would come by and pick him up.

We were in the Station parking lot laughing as we un-folded Jesse from the car. He *fell* with his arms around me and kissed my neck. I pulled up and ducked into the seat and grabbed his cane. "Come on Cowboy, let's go see the troops."

I left him at the front desk with Dombrowski; He came down from his throne to give Jesse a big bear hug. He picked up the intercom and shouted "Bass, front and center!" I gave a salute to Grady and a wave to Jesse and walked back to the car and headed for my office.

Missing my office and ready to get down to work I didn't expect to see Margaret already at work. I walked in just as she was watering the plant.

She had made a couple of changes that really made the place comfortable. Magazines were on the coffee table. *We had a coffee table.* She had found two prints for the wall, both of Sherlock Holmes. One had him looking through a magnifying glass and the other ole Sherlock was holding a wine glass up to the light solving mysteries. I thought that they were clever and I congratulated Margaret on her taste and humor. I turned to the wall and saw a coat rack. "Margaret I love it! It's perfect!" I hung up my coat.

Margaret beamed. "I have some messages. Why don't you answer your phone?"

I followed her around the office explaining that I kept forgetting that I had a phone.

She flitted into the kitchen, talking the whole time. "I called Mr. Vince; he said that he would ask around. He didn't know much. He wants Max real bad. Hates the sister, she has been arrested twice. Kayla Wiggins Hastings Martin is her full name. She's 40 years; she's the one that handles the money, pick up and deliveries, that's drugs, weed, and prescriptions, anything they can steal and sell. Her girth hides a multiple of evils. She's also got an evil tongue. When Vince called her she told him she didn't know where the *ass hole* was and then called Vince an asshole for giving them bail in the first place. Larceny, Drugs a public intoxication, oh, and batterment. She beat her first husband almost to death. The second isn't in the picture; I bet he *RAN* out for cigarettes. She scopes the targets then acts as a look out for the kids. The kids rip stores blind."

"The kids are hers. Luke 17, Stacy 15, last names are Hastings. Stacy has made two accusations of statutory rape. They got a good price off of one. The second was dropped when he opted for jail instead of a payoff, they didn't show for court and charges dropped. Luke's been in jail at least four times. Two are sealed, but drugs, theft and robbery are public knowledge. Both are problem children, truancy, probably expelled at every grade level. Word around is that they are into something big. Both are on probation."

"Ben, the older brother, 56, got out of prison two years ago. He's paid to break legs. He butts head with Max a lot. He's got the connections with the shadier elements of the city. He's the brawn of the group. What he says goes."

"Lastly there's Max, age 38, and the baby of the clan. He does what he's told. But he does it his way, that's how he got caught. Last time there was a witness and he's talking, hence the bail. It's embarrassing for the City Councilman. Max has a temper, and a big mouth. He likes to hit. They all hang out at the *8 Ball*, that's his cousin's place. Not a place you would want to go alone."

"Esther Morris, 62, She's the aunt, she hates them all. Her husband died years ago. Her house is paid off and she lives on a pension, I talked to a neighbor. She says Esther is quiet. They get together on Thursdays to play canasta. She didn't make it last week. She saw a car off and on in the driveway. Esther won't talk about it. Says she doesn't feel well. Her friend called several times, Esther says she fine, just under the weather. She wouldn't let her bring soup."

"Steve Mitchell, small time drug dealer, doesn't hold a job. He lives in his mother's basement. I have the address here. He's been busted several times for drugs."

"I have a lead on Art, I think he's fairly new in town, but I'll keep digging. Rumor has it that he was in prison the same time as Ben. I'm pretty sure it's the same guy Ralph hung out with a few times. I think all three are from the fraternity in the penal system. I should hear something soon."

I was following Margaret to the kitchen as she rattled off this information. I was amazed at her connections. Someday I might ask.

Not stopping to pause as she made coffee. We sat over coffee, talking about the information, adding to it. Guessing what their next move would be, and planning our next move. Margaret had brought out cookies and I noticed that she had put curtains up in the kitchen. It looked like she stocked it with real food. I had to admit that she was an ace at decorating. She gave me typed pages that contained the information she had gathered.

"Margaret you have accomplished so much. You're making yourself indispensable, you need a raise."

"That's the plan. Someday CJ you'll have it all. I love what I'm doing. A week ago I wouldn't have thought it possible that my life could change so much, so fast. I owe you girl."

The phone started to ring and Margaret went to answer it. I grabbed another cup of coffee and headed to my office. On the way through I saw Margaret had a *look* on her face. I stopped to listen and I saw her go white as she handed the phone to me.

A raspy voice full of venom was on the other end.

"Listen Bitch, your dead, I know where you are. Tell Keyes to stop or he'll regret sticking his nose where it don't belong."

I felt the tingling; the caller was near. There was no number on the caller ID. I motioned to Margaret to stay put and keep the line open.

The tingling went to intense. I ran out the door and rushed to the street, looking both ways I saw nothing out of order. The closest pay phone was at the newspaper stand and I headed that way. I didn't see any suspicious persons milling about. My urge didn't lead me to any one person. I walked up the street as I felt the tingling begin to lessen. Whoever made the call had left the area.

I ran back to the office when I opened the door Margaret looked up and I saw the look of surprise on her face. I looked down at myself and groaned as I realized I had some explaining to do.

"Uh, Oh, God, Margaret, we need to talk."

"CJ, are you okay? What's happening to you?" She rushed from behind her desk and began touching my shoulders and my head.

"CJ, you okay? What's happening to you?"

"Oh Margaret, let me explain. Please, I don't want to loose you, can we sit down? I will try to explain everything."

We both went into the kitchen. It was late morning; Margaret took two wine coolers and set one before me as she sat down.

"CJ, Explain what I just saw."

"I don't know where to start. Look, I'm sorry if I freaked you out. I'll understand if you don't want to work with me."

"Whoa girl, Do I looked freaked? I mean, yeah, I am a little, but come on, what's up with you?"

"I don't know why this happens, it just does. It's complicated."

"So try, come on talk to me. You have to admit it's kind of trippy."

I looked at Margaret's face. I could see the concern in her eyes. If we were going to work together I would have to be honest. I decided to spit it out.

"Margaret, this happens when I feel something bad is going to happen. I don't have much control over it but I have pretty much learned to work around it. I kind of fade and get this urge. I have to follow it." I took a breath. "This is so hard to explain. The guy who called was close; I tried to follow him and lost the trace. I forgot that I was still faded until I saw the look on your face."

"Wow, CJ, that's pretty unique. Have you always had this? How do you do it?"

"Look Margaret, I can't explain it. I will understand if you don't want to work for me, I will pay you as soon as I can. I'm so sorry."

"You're firing me? You're firing me because I know your little secret? That's a pretty shitty thing to do!"

"You want to stay?"

"What do you think, I like the job, I like the office, and I like you, not to mention you saved my ass. So your not really *here* sometimes. I'll hang a bell on your neck."

"I'm freaking now. Are you sure? I mean most people aren't like me."

"Yeah you are a strange one alright. CJ, you have to tell me everything. Can you show me now? Can you just do it? I've seen a lot of trippy things in my life and this pretty much beats the hell out of all of them."

I was totally amazed that this didn't seem to faze her at all.

"Margaret this is not something that comes up around the office cooler."

"CJ, your telling me nobody knows about this? Honey you should have told me sooner."

"Margaret, I don't tell anyone. My parents know but it wasn't discussed. It wasn't something to be talked about. It was too weird."

"I can't imagine. I won't tell, but you have to tell me everything. Ya know it's kind of neat to have an *Invisible Woman* for a boss. I wondered why you chose to be a private eye this has got to be the best disguise."

Tears were streaming down my face "Oh Margaret, thank you."

"CJ, this is a good thing. Strange for sure, but good. How did Jesse take it?"

"He doesn't know. I don't know how to bring up the subject."

"You'll know when. Get him while he's drugged."

We both laughed and everything thing seemed right. Margaret knew and she was okay with it.

"We still don't know who the caller was."

"Remember that call from Pete? Think it could be him?"

"Did it sound like his voice?"

"I erased the recording; I really couldn't tell this last call was so hateful."

"I could check with the boys, see if there's a file for manic callers and see if the name rings a bell."

We both cracked up at the word *bell*. It was nice that someone just accepted. "I'm glad you know."

"Me too but be prepared, I'm going to have a million questions when it all sinks in. Meanwhile, I'm going to see what I can find out about a man called Pete."

Margaret went to her computer and added the notes that we had just talked about.

I went to my office and saw a ledger with expenses on my desk. Each penny accounted for. When I finished calling around, holding for most of the time, my cell-phone began to ring. I looked on my desk, then at Margaret's desk. She pointed to the coat rack and I found it in my jacket pocket.

"CJ here."

"Hey Babe, Are you just about ready? I'm with Grady and we're heading your way, we'll be there in about fifteen minutes."

Margaret and I finished up and then finished the coffee. We were in the kitchen when a double knock came to the door and I heard Jesse enter. Grady was right behind him.

"So you had some help with the steps?"

"Naw, he just went real slow. Didn't you hear him thunk up the stairs? You have fourteen thunks." I almost slung him over my shoulder."

"I'd pay to see that. Did you get what you needed?" I asked.

"He got a whole shit load of stuff. I got two boxes in the car. It's not gonna fit in that soda can you drive."

"Jess wants to stop for some party stuff. I thought I'd drive because the boxes and Jess won't fit in your car."

I looked from Grady to Jesse, "A Party? Are you having a party Grady?" Grady looked at me and then to Jesse.

"Well just a couple boys from the house. Seems Jess is doing real well, and Bass is picking up Annie." He was looking at his toes.

Was he asking me for permission?

I laughed, "Grady, I want you boys to have fun. You all need a change of pace. It's been a rough week."

Jesse popped up, "You'll be there. You have to come. If it wasn't for you there wouldn't be a party."

"Of course she'll be there." Margaret came from the kitchen; wiping her hands on a towel. She took in the group, Big Grady, Bruised Jesse and me. "You know a party is what everyone needs."

Jesse looked at Margaret, "I hear you're the one to call for organization, CJ says you run this place."

"Oh, I don't know, it's easy when you're just starting out. CJ knows her stuff."

She was staring at Jesse's face "you look like you've been to a knuckle party already."

Grady started laughing, "I heard a lot about you Margaret, I'm Grady. So it's true, you keep CJ in line?"

He held out his hand to shake hers.

"I don't know about in line. I like working for her. She's pretty gutsy. So you work with Jesse?"

Jesse took my hand and we went into my office, leaving Grady and Margaret behind to rate our assets. He turned around and sat on the corner of the desk and pulled me in his arms holding my body between his legs. He looked in my eyes.

"Baby, can I take you to a party tonight?"

"Are you having a party Cowboy? Are you sure you're up to it? I don't want you to hurt anything."

He was nuzzling my neck and pressing me close to his body. I felt his hardness pressing into me. I felt his hands lower to my hips and press me closer.

"Baby, you have to come. What if something happened and I needed my nurse?"

I pulled away and said "You just dial 911."

"Oh CJ, will you go out with me tonight? I know where there will be a nice party with some really nice people."

"Why Mr. Jesse, Are you asking me out at the last minute again? Am I always your last resort Detective Keyes? I'll have to check my schedule. I may already have plans."

"Honey you're my only resort."

Grady and Margaret filled the door. "CJ, Grady just invited me to the party, I really have to get going I need to change."

"Wait a minute Margaret; I'll give you a ride." I turned to Grady. "You're in charge of the patient."

Grady was looking at his feet.

"Ahh . . . Margret, we can drop you off on way."

Margaret looked very interested. "That's very kind, CJ are you ready to leave now? I can grab a ride with these guys."

"That would work out better. I have some things to do here. Why don't you call when you are ready and I'll pick you up and we'll go over together."

Margaret grabbed her coat. "I'll call you in a little while." she called over her shoulder as she followed the boys. I counted the 14 slow muffled thunks fading to the bottom of the steps.

In my bedroom, I looked around, Margaret hadn't touched it. Maybe I'd ask her to, it was damn depressing. Stark and dark.

I turned on the light and went to my closet. Not much of a selection, no all purpose little black dress. I settled on a pair of black jeans that were in the back of my closet and a soft deep crimson sweater. I laid them on the bed and went into the bathroom.

Margaret had hit the bathroom, potpourri, baby soaps. Nice fluffy towels. Man, that girl defiantly needed a raise; I started to draw a bath in the ancient claw foot bathtub. As an afterthought I brought in a candle, and checked the kitchen and found the wine coolers.

All right, things were looking up. I added some bubbles, lilac, not bad. I slowly submerged my body in the water. For the next 35 minutes I laid back and did the girlie things girls do. This was the first truly alone time I had for a while. Oh yes . . . .

The water was cold and I was wrinkly when I decided to climb out. I dried off and started dressing. Grabbing my big purse I started putting the tools of trade in it. I was pulling on my boots when I looked up into a mirror. I took another look at my hair and headed to the closet and pulled out a hat when the phone rang. I was as ready as I would ever be. It was time to pick up Margaret.

Chapter 16

Rosie was sweeping the porch when I arrived and I had the feeling that she was waiting for me. She had a worried look on her face. She asked about Jesse, and wanted to know who this Grady man was and if he was a nice man.

I told her that Grady was a very nice man, just a little rough around the edges. I followed her into the house hoping to calm her fears.

Margaret met us as I entered the room looking ready to party. Her hair was upswept and she wore black spandex pants and black scoop neck sweater. Her a wide red belt with matching heels and jewelry made her look like a model.

She took in my outfit shook her head.

"Hey girl we're going to a party, you need accessorizing!"

She disappeared into a room and came back with a black leather vest and dark red almost crimson scarf. I put on the vest as she tied the scarf in my hair.

"You have to burn that hat." she said as she shoved me in the bathroom. "Look! Look at you! You look fantastic."

I looked at myself and turned to see the back.

"Oh yeah, I'm sure, gypsy girl here."

"No Fashionable." She was poofing up my curls around the scarf.

"You really have to let me take you to this girl I know who does great cuts."

Rosie brought out a gold chain and put it on my neck. While Margaret brushed some blush on my cheeks.

"You have to invest in some lipstick."

"We gotta go Margaret." I said shaking my head. I gave Rosie a hug, and headed for the door.

We had developed a game plan for later in the evening we had to alter it to accommodate the party. Margaret was up for it. I might have to make her a partner. We discussed it on the way and we didn't see any problems.

Jesse's house was lit up. Every light seemed to be on and you could hear the music from the street. We had to park a few houses down.

We walked through the door and Margaret exclaimed "A few good men? It's more like the whole station!"

We entered a room of wall to wall bodies.

Grady spotted Margaret had headed straight to her. He started out stuttering about how nice she looked, he glanced at me long enough to tell me that Jess was waiting for me on the day porch.

I walked through and saw a couple of familiar faces. Annie and Bass were with Jesse and they seemed to be in deep conversation.

Annie spotted us and left them to meet me. "I don't know what Jesse would have done with out you. He hates hospitals. He looks so good."

"He looked good before I met him Annie."

She laughed. "You know what I mean, he has *that look* He's head over heals."

I was saved from commenting when Jesse hobbled up and put his arms around me.

"You look beautiful." He seemed a little shy among his friends. They seemed to be very interested in our interchange. He led me to the porch and into the darkest corner.

"I have been waiting for you. You look damn good." He pulled me to him and kissed me. "I'm so glad you're here."

"Jesse. You sure you're ready for this? It's been less then a week, you need to go slow."

Grady came out to the porch with Margaret. He had a soda for Jesse and a wine cooler for me. Grady was introducing Margaret to everyone. The music was loud. I met many of the faces I had seen at the Station along with their wives or girlfriends.

There were big laughs when Bass and Grady told the story about Jesse's shower. They fed on each other's interpretation adding more and more to their outrageous version.

Jesse took the ribbing adding tidbits about the two *gorillas* that invaded his bathroom.

I listened as they tried to out do the other and laughed when I realized that I had never been around this kind camaraderie before. It was nice to watch it up close.

I heard many stories of Jesse and his years at the precinct. I was thanked over and over for helping him. *It was nice that Jesse had a girl.*

They seemed to know a lot about me. There were a few good hearted comments. One of the officers wanted me to *detect* a woman for him.

When I was asked why I chose this line of work Margaret spoke up and told them that I was up for the adventure and I didn't like sitting behind a desk. It seemed like a good explanation.

Moorings ghost came up. Most thought it was a ploy for an insanity defense. I offered little to it; I got some compliments for bringing him in. Someone brought up Jesse's kidnapping. He didn't want to talk about it. Jesse got ragged about being set up. I learned that BA was behind bars but still able to do damage. I felt shivers up my spine. It had been so close. We had never discussed the house incident. I was leery of bringing it up because I happened to be there. Jesse didn't do *shop talk.*

As the party went on Jesse caught me looking at my watch. "You have some place you need to be?"

"No, just thinking you must be getting a little tired."

"You want to take me to bed?"

"Cowboy, after today, I think you can manage for yourself."

Jess laughed "Aren't you afraid of a relapse?"

I caught Margaret's eye and she came over to us.

"Well Mr. Jesse, you look as fit as a fiddle. CJ says you're the best kind of patient. You sleep a lot."

"Margaret, she is the best nurse. Gives lots of TLC, has a great bedside manner, I don't know how I got so lucky."

"I know what you mean she makes a terrific boss, stays away all the time, and lets me do what I want."

I couldn't listen to them anymore. "I need to use your little girl's room."

I turned to Margaret. "Margaret, can you make sure Detective Keyes here doesn't fall into a coma?" They both laughed as I made my exit. I hoped Margaret could keep him occupied for a while.

I was heading out the door when one of Jesse's friends stopped me "Your not leaving are you?"

"Oh' no, I'll be back in a bit."

The evening was clear and cool. After being around all the chatter and close bodies it felt nice to take a breather from it. I had less then an hour to accomplish what I had planned.

I started my mental checklist as I pulled into the street. I checked my watch, time wise; I figured I would check out the Wiggins Homestead and be back before anyone missed me. It was the time of night that the Wiggins would be the most productive;

I drove past the house twice. Several cars were parked in front. Jesse's party wasn't the only one going tonight. I pulled up the block and wrote down plate numbers, and a description of the cars.

On my second pass I concentrated on the several men talking and laughing on the porch. Ben looked like he was having fun. There were three men talking, I don't think they felt any pain. One could hardly stand up.

Through the open door I could see shadows of people milling around inside. The upstairs windows were lit up but I didn't see anyone pass them as I waited.

I parked up the block and thought of Max's baby face when I felt the tingling begin. I walked back to the hedge separating their house from the neighbors. There were several shadows moving in the kitchen and the blinds were down. I crossed the hedge in the front of the car-lawn ornament and I stood at the window. My sight was limited to a small break in the blinds.

There seemed to be an argument going on. I heard Kayla squealing in a tinny grating voice for someone to get out of the room. "I don't give a shit what you think you're not going back!"

A male voice bellowed back "Bull shit! I'm doing it, there's no one home! I talked to the gardener next door he said they were going out to some fancy place, some awards thing."

Kayla whined "Do you even have the alarm code? You plan this at all?"

"I can get in and out before the alarm goes off." was the reply.

"You're not doing it. You wait until things cool down. You wait until you can get the damn alarm code."

"Ma, Kayla, I checked it out. They're out. I might not get another chance like this. They feel safe now."

"They felt safe the last time, you botched it asshole, you're not going."

"Stupid bitch!" he mumbled as he walked away.

"Maxie, he's getting to be a cocky little shit. We do good because we think of everything. He's going to fuck up. I want Stacy watching him."

The back door slammed and I could see the tip of a cigarette in the dark, the red glow allowing me to follow his path. He was pacing and muttering to himself.

The door banged shut again and a female voice call out "Luke you out here?"

"What cha want Stacy? Get away from me. Man I want to strangle that bitch!"

"Ah, you know Ma; if it ain't her idea it's a no go."

"Stacy, you don't get it. I have someone on the line that will pay $25,000.00 for it. I have to meet him tonight. That's cash Stacy."

"Luke, you can't do it alone." She put her hand on his shoulder.

"I need one other person. I got the combination. I been working this one, it's a no brainer. I was there this afternoon. I'm serious Stacy these people are prime."

"It seems a little too easy Luke. What did Ben say?"

Luke hit the tree with his fist. "He's been with Art all day. They're as drunk as skunks. I tried to talk to him but he ain't hear'n nothing."

Stacy snorted with disgust. "They're all being assholes; Kayla got Art in her room and then kicked his ass out. She was stinking drunk He's on the porch with Ben. I heard them talk about going to the *8*, seems they have business."

"What's Max doing?"

"I'm dropping him at Steve's so he's gonna be stoned out. He's pissed that he's got to lay low. Ben beat him a new one when he caught him hanging out at the *8* last night."

"What about the fat bitch, she gonna to go too?"

"Probably, she's still on Arts ass. You hear him laugh at her when she told us to call her Kayla. She wants to be our aunt now, she thinks hav'n kids our age makes her old. Art told her she was old and looked older." They both started to laugh. Luke seemed to have lightened up.

"Yeah she's gonna be dogging his ass all night."

They both went back toward the house. I had a fix on Max. Some business was happening at the *8 Ball Bar*. And Luke might be burgling.

The *urge* surged, it was coming on strong. I ran to the front of the house where Ben, Art and the other man on the porch were standing by one of the cars.

"He's supposed to show after one. I need you to meet him before he comes in the bar. Kayla will come in bitching at me to get back home and kicking my ass out. I don't want anyone to know we were near him tonight."

"Think he'll back off at the trial?"

"That or dead."

I thought I might be sick. These guys were killers. The only trial I knew of was Max's; I didn't know who the witness was. But I knew where they would be. I watched as they drove off. I looked at my watch, time flies.

I crossed the yard as Luke, Stacy and Max came out with Kayla waddling after them. Her body jiggled with each lumberous step. She was one ugly woman. She was screeching over the music. "Drop off Max first! Don't let him out of your sight till you get to numb nuts house! I should a let him rot in jail. Stacy, Luke, you get your asses right back here. No stupid moves. You do as I say or I'm going to make sure your hurt."

Stacy piped up, "mom, er, Kayla, I need to stop at Nancy's I told her that I'd drop off that *purse* she wanted to borrow. We'll be back as soon as we can."

"I want all the money Stacy, don't you go borrowing any of it."

Kayla was the only one left at the house and I knew where she'd be. I decided to follow Luke and make sure he tucked Max in.

They stopped at a small house. Max was so drunk Luke and Stacy had to carry him to the door.

I went up to the side window and listened. "Hey man, good to see ya bro."

Stacy asked, "Steve you got it for me? I told her I was on my way."

She gave him a wad of bills that he counted and stuck in his pocket. He grabbed a brown paper bag and gave it to Stacy. She took out a baggy, looked at it, smelled it and said thanks.

They were leaving when Max slurred, "Hey, dickhead, you doing the Fitzsimmons?"

Luke looked at Stacy, "Naw, Kayla would have a litter."

They looked at each other as they left the house.

At the car Stacy said, "Okay, Luke lets do it. I get half, and nobody knows but us. I ain't shar'en with no one. I want to get out of this town so bad. I gotta loose these assholes and make a life. Tonight, with money in my pocket, I'm book'n it."

Everything was rolling. I needed reinforcements.

I called Margaret "Hey, girl, where are you, Jesse been asking for you, I ended up telling him you were at the office and would be back 20 minutes ago, I can't hold him off much longer."

"Margaret, I've got a three ring circus going on. I need to talk to Bass, away from Jesse."

I could hear the party going on, damn, I was missing it. Margaret handed the phone over to Bass and shoved him outside.

"Hey, what's going on? CJ, where are you, upstairs?"

"No Bass I'm driving around town, I need to talk to someone who's not toasted. Do you see Grady around?"

"Yeah, he's on the patio with Margaret. She's really nice. She's your secretary?"

"No she's my Office Manager. Can you get Grady?"

Grady seemed to be right there.

"What you doing to Bass, the ways he's waving you'd think he was back on traffic detail . . . ."

"Grady listen to me. Ben Wiggins is going after Max's witness at the *8-Ball* tonight. He's got a set up to grab him in the parking lot at 1 a.m. Kayla and Ben will be in the bar. Write these license numbers down. If you don't get there in time their taking him to an unknown location.

"You need to get someone over to Councilman Fitzsimons. I going there now, I need a police car to meet me. The Wiggins kids are going for grand larceny. Grady, please do it now. If I dial 911, I'll waste time . . . you have a whole house full of connections there. Oh, If there's anyone with a price on their head its mine. Can you get me to Margaret again?"

I waited a minute and Margaret came back on. "CJ, Jesse wants to talk to you."

"Margaret, tell him to talk to Grady and Bass, Can you have Grady drop you at Steve's?" Remember the address? I'll get you home. I meet you there in half hour."

I was following the kid's car through a classy neighborhood where life was measured by expenditures. I could see how Luke and Stacy would want to leave the nest when all they had ever been taught was how lie, cheat and steal.

"Okay Margaret, put Jesse on?"

I hadn't finished the sentence when I heard his voice.

"CJ, where the hell are you, what do you think your doing?"

"Jesse, wait a minute and listen."

Jesse interrupted, "I just talked to Bass and Grady and you have stirred up a roomful of hornets. Where are you, I'm coming to get you!"

"Jesse, listen to me, I hear the sirens now. I'm in front of Fitzsimons house; the kids are still in there. The 8-Ball is all yours, I'm going to pick up Max, when I'm done, I'll fill you in."

"The hell you are!" He shouted at me. "I'm coming now!"

"Jesse, you can't drive." I gave up. "Grab a ride with Grady, Margaret's got the address. I'll meet you there, and Jesse, stop yelling at me." I hung up.

I looked up and saw a shadow running across the yard. I jumped out and tackled Luke as he reached the tree line to the adjoining property. I whipped out my handcuffs and grabbed his wrist and closed them. He started to panic as I yanked his arm up in the air and locked the cuff to a good size tree branch. He started to yell for help and struggled to get out of the cuffs.

Stacy was right behind him

"Luke, lets go . . . COM' on, let's go . . . Luke?"

She couldn't understand why or how Luke was hanging from the tree. As she stared at Luke I locked another pair of cuffs on Stacy and cuffed her to a lower branch. I left them as the red and blue flashing lights pulled into the driveway. They both were freaking and screaming. They would be easy to locate.

I raced to my car and drove back over to Steve's. The basement was lit up. I walked around the house and went into the back entrance. I came into a room that was thick with the smell of smoke, cigarette and weed. Beer cans, pizza boxes, fast food and clothes were piled everywhere.

Max was passed out in a chair. His baby face still looked innocent, especially with the drool oozing out of the side of his mouth. Steve sat on the other end of the basement. The music was blaring and the TV on. His head was tilted at an odd angle to the side. He might be sleeping. That wouldn't last long.

I went back to Max and tied his ankles with a length of clothes line. I started to tie his wrist with another splice when he harrumphed and snorted and shook his head. He looked at his hands wiggled his fingers and passed out again.

I walked out and stepped to the side of the house. My hands on my knees I started to deep breath, I felt myself start to come together when I looked up and saw Grady staring at me.

He stopped in his tracks. "CJ, you okay?" he stepped warily to me as he checked the light around us and patted my shoulder. He looked confused. I went for distraction.

"Hey Grady, thanks for coming, where's Margaret?"

"CJ, what's going on here?"

"I have Max in the basement and the Steve guy, for harboring a fugitive. I would like to take them in. If there was just one I wouldn't ask but as long as you're here . . . ." I was hoping that I sounded glib.

Margaret and Jesse were rounding the corner. Jesse was leaning hard on his cane and his face would have be unreadable except that his good eye looked like he could spit fire. He was not a happy pirate.

"Hey Margaret, Jesse nice of you to help, I have my car but it doesn't hold too many. I could use some help getting these goons down to the station."

Grady was looking at me strangely. "Come on CJ, I'll help you get them."

Grady carried Max out like a sack of potatoes. Max starting sputtering and swearing, not comprehending what was happening to him. We left Steve behind. They would have him picked up later and add a bit more then harboring a criminal.

We put Max in Grady's back seat. After a bit of haggling and realizing the hassle he'd have of getting in and out of the G-Mobile, Jesse rode with Grady. I could tell he was upset with me. I felt bad as I watched him angrily stab his cane in the ground with each step as he walked back to Grady's car.

Margaret rode with me. I let them lead the way to the police station.

"Jesse is really upset. I thought you were only going to case the place." Margaret slid the seat belt over her shoulder.

"It started that way but things just snowballed, their pretty pissed huh?"

"Oh yeah, but you did great. They can't stay mad forever. When you get down to it, it's your job. You should have seen them organize after you called though. What a sight."

We met at the station. I filled out the paperwork and got my receipt for Max. As we were leaving as I saw officers bring in Luke and Stacy. I wondered what they'd say about being handcuffed to a tree.

I walked away thinking of their future. What would happen to them? If they ever had a chance to do it right would they take it? Would that much money change their lives for the better? Or would they squander it, and drown in disappointment?

We walked out of the police station and Jesse didn't have much to say to me. I didn't know what to say. Grady was hot and cold. I only hoped that we could talk in private.

Margaret pointed out that there was still a party. I began to suggest that they all go ahead without me when all three said "NO" simultaneously. Margaret opted to ride with me, Jesse rode with Grady.

Margaret spoke up. "You Okay CJ?"

"Yeah, I think we did okay. I just wish that Jesse wasn't so ticked off."

"So, how did you get the whole family?"

"Blind luck Margaret, Thanks for taken my back. I'm sorry Jesse was so hard on you."

"Honey, compared to Ralph, Jesse was a sweetie. He's angrier you didn't tell him that you left the party, and why. He's a hard man to distract; he figured out that I was stalling real fast."

We had arrived at the house and the lights and music were still going but most of the cars had left.

"Let's go face the music honey." Margaret sighed as she unbuckled her seat belt.

We got out of the car and went into the house.

When we arrived at Jesse's I tried once again to exit. Most of the party had left but the few that stayed were waiting to hear what had happened. Jesse took my hand. "We need to talk."

I followed him as he dragged me upstairs. No cane; he pulled himself up the banister with one hand and had a hold of my wrist with the other. One step . . . thunk . . . At a time.

He pulled me into his office. This was another facet of Jesse. I didn't like the idea that his anger was focused at me. No personal distractions in the office.

He was glaring at me, his poor eye, so black and blue. He was still so battered. I wasn't ready to see this side of Jesse.

"Jesse, I know we should talk, I'm sorry I left your party. I thought I'd be right back. Tonight is not a good night. I'm tired and I really need a shower. I hope I didn't ruin your party. I . . . ." I didn't get any farther.

"CJ, your right, we won't talk about it tonight."

He took my hands and pulled me to him. "I don't know what to say. Now that you're here, in one piece, looking like you stepped out of a dream, I relieved. I have never been so confused, hurt, scared and pissed off in my life. I'm only going to ask one thing. If you walk out tell me. If you have to work just keep me in the loop. I don't know why you didn't confide in me but I care, I didn't know I cared so much. You tied me in knots tonight."

"Jesse, I . . . ,"

"Don't say a word, will you stay the night? I promise to be a gentleman; I promise we won't talk if you don't want to."

I felt the last of my strength go. I sat on the edge of his desk. "I promise."

Jesse leaned down and kissed my forehead. "Thank You."

I looked up and he kissed me. He stood up and I leaned into him. He just held me. He was holding me while his hands began rubbing up and down my back. He moved his hands to each side of my face.

"I have never felt this way before."

We stood there enjoying the feel of each others warmth.

I pulled myself away, "I have to get Margaret home."

"Grady's doing it. He's clearing out the house. Its 4:30 and the patient and his nurse are getting some sleep."

We were at an awkward moment. I decided to stall and asked if I could use his shower. I turned to leave when Jesse's phone rang. He answered and I made a swift exit.

I stalled as long as I could in the bathroom. I went into *my bedroom* and pulled on Jesses t-shirt and walked slowly into Jesse's bedroom.

He was leaving the bathroom, drying his face with a towel. He had taken his shirt off and I could see the yellow tinge of healing around his wounds. His bruises seemed to look less raw. He had taken the bandage off his shoulder and the stitches stood out dark on his skin. I walked to him taking in the shape and form of him I kissed his stitches. I could feel quivers run through him and into me. I could smell his scent and god help me I wanted him.

He took me in his arms he kissed my neck, ears, eyes, and the tenderness making me weak. I felt so wanted, so special. He hobbled to the bed. It was good to see him so mobile. He sat on the bed and then laid back.

"Come here CJ" I laid beside him my head on his shoulder. I pulled up the corner of the blankets and covered us. I kissed his neck as he put his arm around me. I snuggled close. I was asleep before I could tell him how sorry I was.

Chapter 17

I was almost noon when the aroma of coffee entered my sleep. Jesse was not beside me. It was Sunday. I took a deep breath there were other aromas wafting up the stairs. I sat up, stretching my tired muscles that had tightened in the night. I heard a low mumble coming from his office. I went to the bathroom taking my time waking all the way up. I was brushing my teeth when Jesse knocked on the door.

"Coffee and breakfast come and get it."

I dressed in jeans and t-shirt and went barefoot into the kitchen. Bacon eggs, toast and juice were on the table. He was pouring coffee for me. "Thanks, this looks delicious, I didn't know you could cook."

"It was lucky for me I had good training at Magpies."

"Well, your coffee is excellent."

"Come on try the rest. It's nice to pay you back for all the times you cooked for me."

"If I were totally honest Mama's deliveries made me look good."

We both were eating in a comfortable silence when Grady knocked and then walked in the door. He grabbed a cup and poured himself some coffee. He looked at the stove and the table. "Help yourself Grady."

We watched as Grady proceeded to clean up every morsel. I started loading the dishwasher and cleaning the kitchen while we listened to Grady tell us about what a *fine* woman Margaret was. She was so lively and beautiful he rattled of a long list of her attributes. He also had a date for the afternoon and asked if Jesse and I would join them.

"You want us to tag along?" I asked.

"Well, I don't know what to talk about. Margaret's smart; I don't want her to think I'm an idiot."

"Too late for that." said Jesse, "Where are you taken her?"

"Well I thought the park, maybe a picnic, or a movie. I don't know that's why I need you guys. What do you do on a date?"

We looked at each other and I replied "Gee Grady we have never been on a date."

"I think it's about time" Jesse kissed my forehead.

"What do you suggest CJ?"

"I don't have a clue, why don't I call Margaret and see what she's up too?"

I needed to speak to Margaret for several reasons and I needed to be alone when I did it. I went upstairs and found my little pink cell-phone and dialed.

"Hey Margaret, How's it going? Grady's in the kitchen terrified to go on a date; He invited Jesse and me to go along."

Margaret went on a tangent of what a great guy he was; it was almost word for word what Grady had said about her. He was handsome instead of beautiful. She would love to go on a double date. I told her to pick out some activities and we would figure something out.

I changed the subject and asked her if she got home okay. "What did Grady say about seeing me at the house?"

"Grady didn't really talk about it. He asked me if you were feeling alright. I played dumb. That's for you to spill. He was upset that you took off, Grady, that is. I guess we should have had a cover story for that. But Jesse was relieved when he saw you. He couldn't believe you did it all alone, I think he would have been impressed if you hadn't pissed him off. Both of them said you should have taken one of them with you."

"Well, maybe I will next time. Every thing just unfolded. But it worked out okay don't you think?"

"I do," said Margaret "our part went really well. I think their biggest gripe is that we didn't include them."

"Margaret, when you get down to it, we did include them. They are not on my payroll but next time maybe we'll give them a heads up. They did come in handy"

We talked a while and Margaret was surprised to hear Jesse was so calm. "Be thankful for small favors honey, he cares for you a whole lot and you didn't let him polish his knight suit."

"It's that simple? He's wall to wall bruises, there's no way."

Changing the subject I told her that I would have Grady call and maybe one of us could come up with a plan.

I went to the kitchen and Grady and Jesse had their heads together drawing some kind of map and talking in low voices. I went to the coffee pot and poured out the last drop. Grady looked at me strangely.

"Margaret said she would love a day out, we didn't come up with a game plan, but she's ready for anything."

Grady's smile lit up his whole face. "We thought maybe the park? They have a carnival this week, starts today."

"That sounds like fun. I have never been to one."

"Well it's about time then. Maybe we should call Bass and Annie." Grady creased the paper that they had been working on and put it in his pocket.

"Great idea, Grady you call Bass and Margaret. I'm going to go clean up." Jesse replied rubbing his stubbly chin.

I started setting the kitchen right, cleaning the counter and feeling very domestic in Jesse's house. The thought startled me; I have never felt domestic, not even in my own house. It felt a bit strange.

Grady came in from making his calls, he walked into the kitchen turned around and walked back into the living room. He came in again and sat down with a loud sigh. He stretched his legs out in front of him, filling up half the room.

"CJ, what did I see last night?"

I thought about playing dumb, but I wasn't blond enough. I needed to find out what exactly he saw.

"Grady, it's hard to explain. I'm not sure if I can explain it. It just happens."

Grady looked at is hands and picked at his fingernails. When he looked up he said "CJ, I could see right through you. I know what I saw."

I had to know. "Did you talk to Jesse about it?"

"No, I was hoping he would talk to me. He didn't. I figure he doesn't know. So what's the story CJ? I wasn't drunk and I didn't get hit on the head."

I sat down and I put my face in my hands. "I don't want to talk about this. It's something that I've had to work with everyday of my life. I don't know how to explain it."

"Just say it CJ. You are one gutsy broad; I have a lot of respect for you, and I think I'm your friend. But there's something you're not saying and I want to know what it is. We are your friends you know."

I raised my head and took a deep breath. The afternoon light through the window was warm. I looked him in his eyes.

"I don't know why this happens. I can't stop it when it does. Grady, I will tell you that for me it's normal, but it freaks people out. Will you look at me differently?"

I was up and pacing the kitchen. I wanted to bolt so badly. "I have been trying to find a way to explain it to Jesse. But I have never been able to explain it to myself!"

"CJ," Grady got up and put his arms around me, "CJ, whatever it is, you need to let it out. Jesse loves you. I kind of like you too. We're your friends, that won't change."

"Grady is it enough to say that your not crazy? That sometimes I have a problem with being seen?"

Jesse chose that moment to walk in the kitchen. He took in the scene, Grady and I in an embrace and the tears on my face.

"What the hell is going on here?"

We jumped apart and must have looked guilty.

"Jess, its nothing man, I just wanted CJ to know how much I respect her."

Jesse had a strange look on his face. "Grady, that's my girl and I do the hugging."

I looked at Grady and I knew I would have to explain myself to Jesse soon.

Grady put his hand on Jesse's shoulder. "Hey Jess, she is one fine woman, and pretty too. You're lucky she's not my type, I'm going to call Margaret, now she's my kind of woman."

Jesse was holding me he smelled like aftershave, his face was baby-butt smooth.

I held on to him. My secret was out and I had to tell him. I don't know where it came from but it jumped out of my mouth before I could stop it.

"Grady said that you loved me."

He held me away from him and said "You couldn't tell? CJ, I have loved you since the day I met you."

He kissed one eye and then the other tasting my tears. "I didn't want scare you off, sometimes I think your afraid of me."

"Jesse, there is something you need to know. I've wanted to tell you. You might change your mind."

Jesse kissed me long and deep pressing me into him. I could feel his hardness and his moving hand under my shirt was making me shiver. I returned his kiss. It was so intense I felt myself I melting.

Grady chose to come in at that moment speaking loudly to warn us of his entry.

"We have to pick up Margaret. Are you ready? The Carnival closes at midnight. Bass drew duty and Annie's working. They'll meet us when they get off. We can take my car it's the largest and we all fit."

Grady was embarrassed about catching us in our intimate embrace. I slipped out of Jesse arms and gave Grady a peck on the cheek, "I'll go grab my purse." I jogged up the stairs, relieved that I dodged another bullet.

We rode over to Margaret's; all three of us were ignoring the elephant in the back seat.

Grady went to the door as Margaret came to the porch. Rosie waved from the door telling us to have a good time. Grady held the car door open and made sure Margaret was settled in her seat belt before he bolted around the car.

"Grady is such a gentleman." I said.

"Hey, I'm a gentleman," Jesse admonished "or don't you remember last night?"

"Oh, yeah" I said as he put his arm around me.

We pulled out and headed toward the park. The sun was out. The sky was clear; it was a perfect day to spend at a park.

We had driven a couple of blocks when Margaret asked, "So . . . What happened at the *8 Ball* last night?" She had voiced the question I had wanted to ask. I just didn't want to be the one that opened that can of worms.

Jesse spoke up. "It went like a charm. The department had the witness already under surveillance. When he left the banquet the call came in for a heads up and undercover was ready."

"Bass called in a squad to watch the bar. When the witness pulled in they waited until he was pushed into one of the cars and got them all."

Grady laughed and said "Bass got the short stick when he got stuck with Kayla. He said that she was the nastiest person he ever laid a hand on. Yelling that she was being molested, you'll have to get Bass's take on that one. He wrote reports until daylight. I think the lady hurt him."

Jesse went on, "Bass called last night, he said that it took four officers to get them out of the bar. The rest were already locked in squad cars when they came out. He said that Kayla swore at Ben, Art, anyone that was around. She kept fighting, spitting and biting. He put her in Murphy's car. Murphy's not talking to him now."

I could picture Kayla waddling, kicking and spitting. I have never laughed so hard. The way the guys told it we missed the best part.

"She wouldn't calm down, she screamed as they dragged her into lock-up."

I asked about Luke and Stacy. They were under arrested for grand larceny. They had the goods. The house had a silent alarm installed two days earlier. Luke had the wrong code. But he was right when he said that he'd get out before the alarm went off.

"You have to tell us how you worked this out. You did a months worth of police work in one night." Grady was bad at being subtle.

"Honest guys, I just left for a minute to see where Max might move to. The whole thing took on a life of its own. I just happened to be at the Wiggins and heard what they planned to do on a Saturday night."

Jesse looked at me. "Next time just let me know. You had most of the department at your disposal. Do you know how many pagers went off in my living room? Margaret, what was your part in this plan?"

Margaret turned around and looked and me. Since Jesse asked the question and Grady was holding his breath I just raised my eyebrows and shrugged.

"Well Jesse. It was such a simple one. CJ had a location on Max. We had a lead that he was changing residences. CJ was going to make sure that he was snug as a bug and beat it back to the party. All I did was to make sure that nobody figured out that she left. We didn't want to ruin your party but it took longer then we planned. You know the rest."

Go Margaret, simple and says it, I felt I was off the hook.

Jesse turned to me and said, "You went to the Wiggins house?"

"The logical place to start" I said. "Max was staying at his Aunts house. He didn't like it there. I needed to find out where he would go next. I lucked out."

We had pulled up to the park. Walking through the parking lot Margaret talked about how long it had been since she had been to a carnival. We walked around taking in the sights. Brady won Margaret a white rabbit. Jesse won a teddy bear for me. We laughed on the Ferris wheel and we watched as Grady and Margaret tried to demolish the bumper cars. We ate hot dogs and pretzels and laughed at the strong man. We teased Grady telling him we would like to see him in the tiny red and white muscle underwear.

When the lights came on the park turned into kaleidoscope of color.

We rode all the rides again, the colors mixing and blending into a world of make believe. Jess and I had taken several turns on the Ferris wheel when Grady and Margaret ran up and said that we had to hear the band. They were warming up and they were good. We hobbled to the bandstand and sat on the grass.

I had never been to a carnival. I had never sat so happily in a man's arms. I could feel Jesse's breath on my shoulder as we leaned into each other. The canopy of stars and wisps of clouds floated above us. The moon was playing peek-a-boo through the trees. We were swaying to the music. I couldn't remember ever being this content as the band played on.

The wind began to pick up and I stiffened as I felt my fingers start to tingle. I didn't want to move from my cozy warm cocoon. I felt my feet join my fingers. I knew that I would have to leave.

"Jesse, I need to find the restroom."

"Not without me, you might not make it back without a police escort."

"Jesse I said I was sorry, you stay here. You'll never make it on that foot."

Margret spoke up. "I'll go with you CJ; the restrooms are on the other side of the shooting gallery."

I was tingling and creaking as I rose from the ground.

Grady's phone rang as we made an exit. I sprinted past Margaret; "I really have to go."

We ran in between the buildings and raised my head trying to find a direction. I stopped at a tree line and saw two shadows that seemed to be surveying the area. The urge was getting stronger . . . bingo, I spotted my target.

The two men cut off the path and headed in the direction we had come from.

"I'll meet you back at the bandstand. Tell Jesse that one has on a camo shirt and black hat, the other one has a black t-shirt and beard. They're heading toward the far side of the band stand!"

"How do I spot you?" asked Margaret. I left her at a run. "I'll make sure to find you, be sure to let Jesse know. I'll be back as soon as I can."

I followed the men as they made their way around the crowd to the opposite side of the park. As I scoped the area I saw that Jesse was standing up scanning the crowd. I watched Margaret as reached Jesse and spoke to him. His head came up again and I could see that he was intent on looking for the men Margaret described.

He had his cell-phone to his ear. I didn't see Grady until Jesse looked toward the side of the bandstand.

We spotted him at the same time. He was shaking his head *no* at Jesse. Grady headed across the front of the bandstand.

I spotted the two men cut cross the park and watched as they split up. I trailed the one that followed Grady behind the bandstand. Grady was tagged.

Jess spotted them as they split up he said something into his cell-phone then stepped back into the shadows.

Jesse spoke to Margaret she looked around as she stepped into a shadow away from him to an area that Jesse gestured to. She looked alert and was also intent on looking over the audience.

I followed the trace in Grady's direction. The shadow man was moving stealthily toward him.

I shouted. "Grady! To your left!"

Grady looked up as the man lunged. He turned just in time to dodge a knife. The man turned and then twisted and stabbed again this time the knife sliced into Grady's arm. I heard him grunt. I made a kick to the back of his legs that knocked him to the ground. He went down hard. I stood with my foot on his back as Grady handcuffed him.

"You okay? There's one more, I'm going to Jesse."

Jesse was waiting for the distance to close. When the man closed in Jesse stepped out of the shadows just as I was gaining on him. I watched as the target closed in.

There were too many people in the area; the possibility of someone getting hurt was considerable.

A knife flashed in the moonlight. Jesse was ready, but went down when his ankle gave way and threw him off balance. The knife flew out of the assailants hand as I rammed into him and he went down. I stayed on him as Jesse hobbled over with his cuffs ready. Jesse was scoping the area trying to find what had brought him down.

As he snapped the cuffs closed he brushed up against me. Startled he ran his hand along my thigh, an invisible barrier. A look of surprise crossed his face. He moved his hand up my body and smelled the air as his hands followed the curve of my hip, he strained to see what he was touching; He shook his head and said "CJ?" I was speechless.

I was about to answer when Grady came up to us. Margaret was trying to examine his injured arm. He shrugged off an answer and hoisted the man up with his good arm. He couldn't see me and I fell to the ground with a grunt.

Jess was looking around and said in a low voice "CJ, where are you? Is this what you wanted to tell me?"

I was shocked. Why wasn't he? Without thinking I said. "I'll be right back."

I heard the sirens and saw the flashing lights as I ran to the restroom. My mind was flashing as fast as the lights. I locked myself in a stall I bent over and did my heavy breathing. I kept thinking that this was it. I had been foolish to start a relationship. When I explained myself I would be treated like a freak, I didn't want to face my friends.

My friends, well that didn't last long.

Well, Margaret took it really well. She did waylay Jesse. No questions asked.

She fell in with the plan. I never had a girl-friend it was nice. Grady now knew for sure ... . Jesse was probably at this moment wondering what the hell I was.

I needed to get away. Just bolt. Ready to run, I was startled with a knock on the stall door.

"CJ, come on out. You have to come out sometime."

"Go away Margaret, I can't talk right now."

"Well, I could do that but your boy friend will be here in a minute and you have to be ready. I don't think he'll be as patient as I am."

"You go tell him I left. I can't talk to anyone right now."

"Are you crazy girl? That man is worried; right now they are out there sorting out what happened. When he gets done he'll be looking for you."

"Tell him you couldn't find me." I snorted. "Yep, that's it, you didn't see me."

"Get your butt out here. I need to see you, you can be seen right? If you think I'm giving up a job because my boss has a little problem."

"A little problem?" I outright laughed. "Damn Margaret, A little problem!"

"Yeah, a little problem. He will either deal with it or not. My bet is that he loves you enough to at least listen."

I knew she was right. I had tried to tell him, it was time to tell him the truth. "Okay, let's get this over with."

I opened the stall door and went to the sink and started to splash handfuls of water on my face. My eyes were red and my face was blotchy from crying. Margaret had toweling ready when I finished.

"So your secret is out."

"I don't know as I would call it a secret. It's more like an affliction."

"Come on CJ," she led us to a low-fence and we sat down. "It's not that bad."

"Margaret, I have lived with this my whole life. I can't find anything that remotely explains it. I've never heard of anyone who does this. It's my SECRET, I have kept it hidden. I don't want to be a topic of conversation about some sub species, monitored, dissected and still labeled a freak!"

"Okay, let me help. Just spit it out. Is it physically hurting you?" Margaret was exasperated with me.

"No, it's more mental . . . it's always been mental, do you know that you're the first friend I have ever had that knows about it?" I didn't want to admit that she was the only friend I ever had.

"Well you're stuck with me. What does Jesse know?"

"He knows I have a secret and he's had a lot of clues. Tonight he called my name while I held that guy down. I have wanted to bring it up but there wasn't a good time."

"You have to tell him. CJ, look at me. You saved my life. You saved my mothers life. I owe you. If you never paid me a dime I'd still work for you. Jesse will understand."

I looked at Margaret's face long and hard. What she said was true. I could only hope that Jesse could understand it.

"You're a strange woman Margaret, I've tried and every time I chicken out. You have to admit that it's a strange subject to open. Right now I don't know what I feel about Jesse. I care and that scares the hell out of me. And, I, umm . . . seem to fade in the *heat of the moment*."

"Oh my god! Honey, you have to say something to him. He's crazy about you. You know if Grady figured it out then Jesse and Bass are not far behind."

"That's my thinking too. Jesse has *sensed* me a couple of times. He recognized me tonight, said my name. I freaked out because he's going to piece it all together. And when he does it won't be about just tonight. That's a lot of explaining."

"CJ, He loves you. Any fool can see that. Even beaten and bruised your all he could think about. Tell him, if he can't handle it, we'll deal with it."

"Yeah, yeah I know your right. I need to be in the right place to do this. I have been waiting for the right time."

"There is no time, make it happen. It will work out."

We started walking back to the guys. Margaret started talking about Grady's knife wound. "He says it mostly his jacket but I want to see it for myself."

We made it back to the site. Everyone was talking to someone. The band forgotten was breaking down their equipment. What was left of the audience was mulling around the scene. Jesse spotted us and broke away from his conversation and limped up to us.

"CJ, are you all right?" He studied my red nose and blotchy face, "You're not hurt?" Standing back looking at me, he surveyed my body for injuries.

"I'm fine Jesse." I looked down at my feet. He took my chin in his hand and raised my head to look at me. "Baby, is this what you couldn't tell me?" He pulled me to him and held me close.

Grady finished making his statement to the local boys. He walked over with Margaret who was concerned about his arm. He was so macho "It's just a scratch." He looked at me and said "Thanks for the heads up."

"Who were those men" Margaret asked. "What did they want?"

Grady gave her a big hug. "Ya know, I'm really hungry, why don't we go somewhere and we'll tell you all about it."

"There's a lot that needs to be talked about." The last part he said as he looked straight at me.

The park was pretty desolate. The band was packing up the last of the equipment.

As we walked to the car the lights from the carnival were winking out. Nobody was speaking. We all seemed to be lost in our own thoughts. We got back in the car when Grady spoke up. "Where do we eat?"

Margaret wanted to go to the hospital and check out his arm. Grady wasn't going for it. "It's fine Margaret, but if you nurse anything like CJ, I have a room open."

Margaret said that she wasn't going to go anywhere unless his arm was seen too so we decided to go to Jesse's and have something delivered.

Jesse's cell-phone rang and I listened as he spoke to Bass. Jesse was telling him what he knew about the evening's *happenings,* and that we were heading for the house to patch up Grady and get something to eat. Bass had to go to Magpies' and pick up Annie he volunteered to pick up food too.

Chapter 18

As soon as we entered the house; Margaret grabbed Grady and led him toward the stairs. "I want to see that arm, right now!" Grady was being pulled behind her sporting a big grin.

"Uh, Jesse, I'm going to use your shower." Grady called as they left the room. He was dusty and dirty, his hair matted, his shirt was torn; the sleeve from his wounded arm was wrapped around it and saturated with blood.

"There are some sweats in my bottom drawer." Jesse called after them.

Jesse and I were in the kitchen. He was as messed up as Grady. He was staring at his cast. It was stepped on dirty and mangled.

"Jesse, we need to look at that foot" I pulled up a chair and lifted it slowly to my lap. The grimace on his face showed me how painful it was.

"Jesse, this looks really bad, you'll be lucky if it's not broken."

"It's not broken, but it hurts like hell, I have that appointment with the Doctor tomorrow and I'm sure it just swollen." His face was white and etched in pain.

"Jesse, the cast is cracked. More then half way, it needs to be replaced."

"I need to take it off, I need to see it. It feels huge."

I looked it over, it was a mess. Dirty and raggedy, the split went almost all the way up the cast in a jagged pattern. "I don't know. I could hurt you more."

Jesse looked around the room and focused on a cabinet in the laundry loom. "In the second drawer there are some tools. Can you get me the utility knife?"

I started to protest. "Please CJ, it's really throbbing." I put his leg gently on the chair and went to get the knife.

It didn't take much to cut through it. My main fear was cutting him. As I uncovered it I was amazed that he walked on it as far as he had.

"Oh, Jesse, this is really bad." I looked at his face and it was an ashy white. He eyes showed his pain. I was sure that the rest of his body was in agony too.

I folded a hand towel and placed it under his foot. I took a huge pot out of the cupboard and as gently as I could, lifted his foot in it. I added several pitchers of water, added a bag of ice from the freezer and some more water until his foot was completely covered.

"Jesse, we should call the doctor."

"Give it a minute; we just need to get the swelling down."

"Let me give you a pain pill, maybe half of one?"

"No, Just some aspirin for now." He swallowed four.

I sat in the chair across from him. His head was leaning against the wall; his eyes were closed waiting for the aspirin to work.

I was studying his face and I thinking about the time we spent together. I closed my eyes and waited. I was so tired.

"CJ, How are you? You took a hard butt to your shoulder." He still had his head back and his eyes closed. I leaned back to my previous position mimicking his.

"It's okay, a little tender. I could go for a good soak."

"That does sound good. Remind me to order that hot tub I was looking at. It would feel so good right about now."

I put my head up when I heard a car in the drive way.

"That's Bass" said Jesse.

I pulled myself out of the chair and went to the door. Whatever Bass had brought smelled heavenly. Annie was right behind him. They set a box and a bag on the counter and started unloading them. I moved past Bass to help Annie and he sat next to Jesse.

"Let's take a look." Jesse pulled his foot half way out of the pot and Bass whistled. "You were told to stay off of it. You need X-rays."

"Not tonight. I have to see Dr. Wenz in the morning. He wanted to do it then anyway."

"Where's Grady?"

"Upstairs getting cleaned up. I want to look at his arm, he might need stitches.

Annie had put a large dish in the oven. "Dinner will be ready in 30 minutes Bass why you don't help Jesse up stairs and check out Grady, You need to be cleaned up Jesse, you're a mess."

Annie had said it so sweetly. *Get out of the room boys.* I liked this girl. Bass hefted Jesse up and half carried him out of the room. "I should help." I said.

"No you should sit right where you are and have this." She pulled out a Berry Wine cooler for the both of us.

"Better pull another Margaret's up stairs."

"So tell me about Grady and Margaret. He's really closed mouthed. At the party he wouldn't leave her side. When I talked to him on the phone earlier he was almost shy when he said he had a date."

"Margaret's a jewel. She met Grady yesterday at my office. It was something to see, instant attraction."

"Grady's one of the good guys. He sees himself as lone wolf and prides himself on being self sufficient. He's not down on woman, but he's never brought one around. He and Jess' are a lot alike that way. Watching him at Margaret's side all night was a real hoot."

"Well at the moment Margaret is smitten. She is most efficient person I ever met. I think she reads my mind sometimes. She was pretty used by Mooring; I'm hoping Grady can show her the other side of that coin."

"You surprised us. New in town, no one knew a thing about you. But you appeared and it's like you've been around forever."

"I still wonder how that happened. Everything is happening so fast. Nothing seems real."

"It was fun meeting Margaret; she was really fun last night. She kept a running dialogue that kept us laughing. I think she was covering for you."

I looked at Annie. She was very perceptive.

"So, Annie, what's with Jesse? Why hasn't anyone snatched him up? He's fun, He looks good in bruises. He's polite and smells nice, not to mention he has a job. Why is he still on the market?"

She looked at me over her wine cooler. "He was waiting for you."

Margaret entered the room and Annie held out the cooler. She looked at it, twisted the cap and took a drink. "Those bozo's kicked me out. They said that they could do it faster themselves. It's a regular boys club up there."

We followed Annie's lead as she set up the food. We decided to keep it easy and let every one serve themselves.

We heard the guys come down laughing and talking about injuries, past and present. As soon as they hit the kitchen they headed for the food.

"This is great, you did good Bass."

"I didn't do it. Mama and Annie did it all; don't take all the biscuits Grady."

Margaret was handing out beers and sodas; we stuck with our wine coolers.

"Sit down Jesse, Let me make you a plate, the relief in his eyes was palatable, He looked tired. His foot was the huge and purple; I couldn't imagine his pain he was in. I placed a plate in front of him. Grady and Margaret went into the living room. Bass and Annie followed. I sat across from Jesse and asked if he'd like to join them. "In a minute, I want to enjoy the solitude for a minute."

"I can leave Jesse."

"No, you can't do that, you are my solitude."

That brought a smile. I realized that I had no appetite. "I'm going to call the guys to come and move you to that big comfy chair. Then I'm going upstairs and get cleaned up. Save me some leftovers."

"I'm afraid it's a mess upstairs."

"Don't bet the ranch, Margaret's in the house."

I spent a little more time getting the dust and dirt off then I planned. I wondered what everyone was talking about downstairs and then decided it really didn't matter.

The pain in my heart was sharp when I thought of Jesse. I took a very long, very hot shower. While drying off I considered my chances of walking out the door without being seen and canceled the thought. I wrapped a towel around me and stared in the mirror. I brushed my hair with my fingers, and then rummaged through my overnight bag and found my tooth brush and cleaned my teeth.

I had hidden myself for so long I was afraid to open up. I could remember the surprised faces of people who *might* have seen something but not believing it to be real doubted them selves. In a little town like mine when they saw me they would be a little wary, cross the street to avoid me. I would hear whispers and snickers behind my back.

This was to be my new beginning. Moving to a new place and starting a business. It was such a simple goal. Now it was getting complicated and something in me wanted to reach out. What if my new friends decided that they couldn't deal with my problem? I didn't have enough to start over.

Margaret took it well; she seemed to think that it was a neat thing, especially for someone in my chosen career. Would she still feel that way after she had time to really think about it? Grady seemed to be okay with it.

I stared in the mirror and decided to stop procrastinating, Get it over with. Face the music. Rip that band aid off.

My resolve strengthened I put on the cowl neck sweater and broom skirt, went into *my room* and packed the clothes I had brought over during

Jesse's convalescing. I surprised myself, I had brought more then I realized. My overnight was stuffed. I could barely get the zipper shut.

I carried my bag out of the room and stopped. I went to the door of Jess's room and took one last look. The bed was just thrown together. Such tender feelings were awakened here. I felt my eyes sting and threw off those thoughts. I the viewed the chaos the boys had left and smiled. They were good together. I let out a breath I didn't know I was holding. I squared my shoulders and picking up my bag I headed toward the stairs. I would be prepared one way or the other.

Walking down the steps I heard a lively conversation going on. Apparently Jesse had been considering a hot tub for a while.

"If you go to all that trouble you need to add another bathroom. I hate waiting in line." That was Bass.

"Yeah, you have the room." Added Grady, "Put the tub on your patio, and add a room under the stairs for the john. Don't think PINK!" Everyone laughed.

I had set my bag on the last step when Jesse spotted me. He sat in a big brown leather recliner. His foot was propped up on the foot rest and an ice pack surrounding it. He had a beer in his hand and an empty plate sat on the table beside him.

"Hey you look better, do you feel better?"

"We left the food out." said Annie, "Chicken Cacciatore, It was wonderful, Mama always has just the thing to make things right. We were waiting for you before the guy's devoured dessert. Its apple pie it's warming in the oven."

"Come on lets get you something to eat." Annie got up and picked up some plates and Margaret followed her lead.

I followed like the confused Zombie. I was waiting for the ax to fall.

We entered the kitchen and it was totaled. Annie grabbed a plate and started filling it. Margaret was rummaging in the fridge bringing out a salad. They set both in front of me. They rinsed the dishes, loaded the dishwasher, and wiped the counters. They seemed to be old friends bantering back and forth. When they finished they sat at the table with me. Margaret replenished our wine coolers.

As I ate they filled me in on Grady's arm, Jesse's foot and the plans for the hot tub.

"I think a Jacuzzi sounds better." Annie said as she took a sip.

"What is the difference between the two?" asked Margaret "I need to look that up."

I looked at my plate surprised I had finished. The comfortable atmosphere and the Chicken Cacciatore worked its magic. I was totally sated. I wanted to go home and crawl in my own bed in my little tiny bedroom and sleep.

I was lost in this thought when Annie turned to me with two slices of apple pie alamode. Margaret had a tray with steaming coffee, "Let's give these guys their reward."

I followed them into the living room. I handed Jesse his pie. He looked up and thanked me. Margaret had given Grady's his piece and Bass was holding his. Annie started filling cups and handing them out, I helped with the sugar and cream. As I handed Jesse his he looked at me while patting the chair cushion beside "I saved you a place right here."

As I observed the people around me, I saw that everyone had paired off. Margaret was sitting next to Grady on the couch. Grady was sprawled up its length, *the wounded warrior*, they looked comfortable together, her head resting on his shoulder. They were a good looking couple.

Annie and Bass were sitting on the loveseat. They were good match. I watched as they arraigned the coffee and pie on the table in front of them. They moved without speaking, reading each others thoughts.

I sat next to Jesse in a small comfortable overstuffed chair. It had been moved out of its place next to a reading lamp and placed next to his. The room was transformed into a comfortable circle for small a gathering. Just like this one.

Small talk prevailed as we enjoyed the pie. Margaret picked up the plates while Annie refreshed the coffee. I was trying to help, but seemed to get in the way. Margaret took the plates out of my hands. I felt like they were conspiring to make sure I wouldn't bolt out the back door. *The thought had crossed my mind.*

I watched as everyone settled themselves. I heard the dishwasher start. Its churning low hum seemed to accentuate the quiet that had settled in the room. Margaret came back in and took her seat next to Grady and I saw him lower his head to her shoulder.

Grady started to say something then hesitated and look at Jesse.

Jesse turned his head and took my hand. "CJ, you are Rosie's guardian angel."

I didn't know what I expected but it wasn't that. My mind was racing back to connect Rosie and Jesse. I remembered the day we checked out bondsmen and he almost made the stretch. It was written in her complaint the night that Rosie turned herself in. She was so frightened I had hoped that part wouldn't be taken seriously.

I looked at my hands in my lap; I nodded as I said "yes" I didn't know how to explain it but guardian angel sounded much better the ghost.

He squeezed my hand and said "you're my guardian angel too."

"Jesse, I am no guardian angel."

"But I hope that you're my angel, CJ, I don't know what you do or how you do it I only want to understand it."

"Jesse, there is no explanation. I have looked for one little fact that could explain it. I haven't found anything."

"I think its pretty handy." said Grady, "It's kind of un-nerving but I could get used to it. So what happens? Does it hurt? Do you have to mumble some kind of magic words?"

Bless his heart Grady was taking it to the absurd. Even though the laughs were uncomfortable it did get every one talking at once.

"So, you are mom's guardian angel?" Margaret seemed surprised. "CJ, you changed her life from a scared old woman to a vibrant hopeful human being. She was afraid to go out of the house. Why didn't I make that connection?"

"It's not something that I can control. I have to work with it when it happens."

"Does it hurt you?" Annie's voice was full of concern.

"Only when I mess up, like if I land wrong."

"How's the shoulder, you landed on it hard." Jesse asked. He was still holding my hand. He was listening to every word and I could almost hear gears grinding in his head.

"It's doing alright. I might get a little black and blue. I'm fine."

Jesse looked at me and tugged my arm. "Sit on my lap." I must have looked surprised when he added "the ribs are okay."

I hesitated and he pulled my hand. I got up and sat on his lap. I was surprised at how natural I felt in the company of friends. They wanted to know about me. The dim lights and flickering fireplace allowed us to be alone yet together.

Sitting in Jesse lap I laid my head next to his on the headrest. The chair was big and my feet crossed his body and rested close to his thigh on the seat.

"CJ, Tell me about it."

I looked around the room every one was cuddled with their significant other. They were attentive but not staring.

I put my head back on the chair. I was talking to Jesse. I wanted him most of all to understand. This little secret was me. It formed my life. Changed my life and pretty much confused it. Everything else was background.

"I have always been this way. I call it Dimming. I used to think everyone could do it. When I found out differently I had to hide it. People who knew or suspected that I was different stayed clear of me."

I told Jesse everything. About the physical manifestations, the tingling, fading the urges. I decided to give all the facts. I would let him decide if he could live with it. As I went on it seemed that I was telling a bed time story, my audience listening to my voice waiting to hear the end.

When I finished Jesse turned his head "Thank you, baby. Is that your big secret?" His kiss curled my toes.

All at once I was getting questions. Not about *it* but about cases.

"If you were mom's guardian angel, then you must have been Moorings ghost!"

"I wonder how that's going to affect his insanity plea."

"Oh, wait a minute." said Bass. "You were at the house with Jess and me. This explains what happened to third man. I thought Jesse was nuts when he kept asking for you at the house."

I saw a light in Jesse's head go off and could hear practically see him making connections.

"You're going to give me grey hair. I know I was drugged the past few days but I swear I knew you were with me and Bass that day I could smell your perfume.

"I don't wear perfume."

"Oh god," he leaned over a smelled my neck, "you smell so good. But don't go changing the subject. When I asked you about how Mooring got tied up you did a slick job of evading the question. I knew it. What a dunce I am. That was you! You were there. You were the ghost! What a woman you are!"

I was waiting for him to freak out at me. I had lowered my head and was waiting for the lecture.

He wasn't' freaked out. He just accepted. When I raised my head he had a twinkle in his eye. "I knew you were special" he whispered in my ear.

"Bout time you figured it out" said Grady, "I knew you were bright. I didn't get it until we picked up Max. I went back that night just to check the lighting again."

"Don't forget the Wiggins kids, you really get around," Bass was proud of himself to make that connection. "You cuffed them to a tree?"

This led to a discussion of some consequences. Jail time verses mental time. I yawned. I was half listening and trying to rally energy to answer all the questions that were asked.

I felt the anxiety flow from my body as the conversation drifted through the room. I had told my secret and nobody cared.

"Jesse, I have to go home. I am so tired and I'm sure you are too. You have to be at the doctors tomorrow."

"I can take you home when I take Margaret. I'm going with Jess in the morning; Doc has to take a look at my arm."

Jesse looked at Grady and said "No. CJ's staying here."

Then he turned to me" CJ, please stay here with me tonight."

"One more" I sighed.

Everyone got up to say goodnight. I got a hug from Bass and Annie. Bass leaned into my ear and whispered. "Jesse always said you were special." He gave me a kiss on my cheek.

Ever practical Margaret said. "Hey guys get this one up-stairs; we are not going to let him walk on that foot."

Jesse protested that he could walk as the two gorillas lifted him and between them hobbled up the stairs.

Annie came to me and said that she was glad that I spoke up; she had no idea that I had such talents, but it cleared up a couple of loose ends for Bass.

"I'll take care of business tomorrow CJ; you make sure the doc looks at Grady's arm. You call me when you're done. We need to turn in that receipt."

The boys came into the kitchen. Grady said he'd be by about eight. "I took your bag back up," he whispered in my ear.

I stood at the door watching until I couldn't see their tail lights anymore. I locked up and went upstairs. I was sleepwalking as I entered *my* bedroom.

I heard Jesse call. "Not there baby, in here. I promise to be a gentleman."

I walked to the door; he was holding the blankets up for me with a big smile. I turned out the light, took off my skirt and sweater and climbed next to his warm body. I was asleep as soon as my head hit the pillow.

Chapter 18

Light butterfly wings feathered my face, the sky blanketing us in a starlit canopy while gentle winds rocked us in the moonlight. Longing and happiness filled me as I opened my eyes to find the face from my dream looking into mine.

Dark, grey-green eyes so tender looking into mine so lovingly. Running his fingers down my cheek he leaned forward and kissed me. "Were your dreams sweet? You have a sweet dreamy look."

I smiled. "Hey Cowboy, they were, and did you sleep all right?"

"Sure did, do you know that you snore?"

"I never stayed up to see. Do I really?"

"It's cute to watch. You have the cutest little snore."

I knew I was blushing. "Well, Cowboy, you snort. That's cute too."

"Huh, I do, do I?" He hit my butt and said "we have to get up, that appointment with Doc Wenz; when Grady says eight, he means eight."

"What time is it?"

"Oh . . . 6:10"

I threw the cover over my head. "I can't get up, I'm sooo . . . tired. Give me a half hour more?"

"Sure thing baby." He said as he threw the covers over of us. He held me close and started to kiss me. His hands were caressing my shoulders and back, he pressed me tightly against him. I felt his hardness through the sheer fabric of my panties, hot and throbbing forcing my body move to the heat.

Moving his hands down my hips I fell deeper into his kisses. He nuzzled and nipped at my ears and neck stoking the fire he started deep inside me.

A trembling deep within me began to surge demanding more, wanting more. He was hot and throbbing with only a thin sliver of silk separating us. I moaned as his lips continued to tease me, returning time after time to my mouth each time lingering longer and deeper.

His hands were caressing, kneading my breast, softly rubbing and gently pinching sending ripples of sensations through me. Making me shudder and crave more.

Soft kisses on my neck and ear. His tongue lingering as he made his way down to my collar bone. His hot breath was sending waves of heat through me. His lips returning little licks, gently suckling making me rise to his mouth. My body responded as I pushed myself to him. I felt him throbbing against me. I felt him grow harder against me. Curious, not knowing what to expect and already feeling more then I ever imagined. Wanting what I had never allowed myself to dream of.

His hand would alternate on my breast leaving one bereft while the other rose to the warmth. Pressing and rubbing his thumb over my nipples, so hard and tender.

He gathered up the hem of my shirt. "I never want anything between us." He stripped my off shirt and threw it across the room His body replacing the warmth of the fabric.

Flesh to flesh. I reveled in each sensation. I wanted to feel each and every sensation. I could feel the contour of his hard member pressing to break through the thin slip of fabric the only barrier between us. I groaned as the heat deep within me surged to new heights. I ached as my passion grew.

Sparks were coursing through my body. Kissing me he pressured my thighs gently apart his hands teasing me, brushing close to my core that craved his touch. Heat flared as I felt myself give into to the passion. I was so willing, wanting him to show me the way. I heard myself begging, "Jesse, show me what to do."

I ran my hands through his hair, his face, down his arms, feeling his tight muscles, kneading them as I explored his body. I wanted him to feel what he was doing to me. My body responding to his, reaching for the unknown, wanting more and not knowing what it was I wanted. Giving into the mindless sensations as I reacted with each touch, each kiss brought me closer to some unknown reward.

I reached for him. "Jesse, what do I do?" I heard him groan as his weight shifted.

"Love me baby, touch me. Let me love you."

"Oh yes," I sighed. I didn't want to stop my body's urging him to do more. To quiet the roaring beast that was raging inside me wanting the unknown. He placed my hand on his pulsing member. I felt it grow as it pulsated in my hand. Slowly his hand on mine, showing me how to give him pleasure.

I moved my finger and circled the tip making it moist and glisten. A deep groan came from his depth, encouraging me to explore more. He watched as I measured his length and width with my hands, moving down exploring the silky rod that was throbbing and growing in my hands.

Responding to my touch, he touched me, creating rushes, making me burn. I felt as his breathing increase as he slipped his hands down to my inner thighs brushing his fingers against the wet fabric, pushing against it, rubbing his fingers up and down the thin slip of material pushing harder and harder against the barrier. The sensations he created making me frantic. I wanted so much more.

"God, Jesse, help me!" I was pushing my body into his hand. He moved the wet silk down my legs and I felt his finger tracing up and down my womanhood, slowly entering his finger into me and then withdrawing. His hand molded to my mound. I pushed myself into his hand. Heat flowing through me, using my hands on him returning the frenzy he gave me. Mindlessly I let my body take over. I reveled in the sensations and followed wherever it led me.

"Baby, spread your legs a little more, let me in." My body burned as I opened up to him. His hands were holding my legs apart, rubbing up and down my inner thighs stopping before he touched the burning core in me. Slightly raising my legs he pressed his finger into me. Electricity flamed. His hands spread me farther. I pushed toward the pressure wanting more. I felt him slip another finger into me.

"O GOD! Too much; oh; please more!" I lifted off the bed. Pushing myself into his hand and begging him to give me more. I wanted everything.

"Oh baby you are beautiful, so ready for me. I want to fill you with me. I want to be in you, I want you."

He moved his finger deeper exploring my inner places. He pulled his finger out slowly and sliding it back into me. At the same time flicking at a spot that set me on fire. Making me bulk against is hand begging for release. I felt the pressure as a second finger entered me.

"Your, so warm, so tight, are you ready for me baby? I need you to be ready for me baby." His voice was raspy with emotion his words vibrated in my head. I pushed my body harder and harder onto his hand; I wanted him to fill me. I didn't know what to ask for. I was surrounded by sensation.

"Jesse, tell me what to do, tell me what you want! Please baby, show me what you need."

"I have waited to hear you say that. All of you baby, I want all of you. Does this feel good? Oh baby you are ready for me? Common baby, let me in baby."

He was looking at my face and he seemed to be studying me. His eyes were dark and clouded. He was looking at me as if I was the most precious jewel. I could feel my blush start at my feet and climb to my face. He kept staring at me as his finger increased the tempo, as my crotch rode his hand. I wanted him to climb inside me. I felt myself start to tingle and I stopped.

"Jesse help me!"

"Baby, my love." He took his fingers from me, I cried out at the loss, before I could draw a breath he put his mouth to me and suckled and nipped until I screamed out for more.

"Oh Jesse, what are you doing? Jesse!?"

"I'm loving you baby." The deep hum of his voice was stoking my frenzy. "Oh, baby, we have just begun."

I could feel the plunging of his tongue making me rise again to the overpowering needs that I didn't know I had. My head was spinning with the sensations that he was creating.

"That's it baby; I want you to cum for me. I want to see your face as you give yourself to me. Baby, touch me. See how hard I am for you? I need to be inside you."

He fingers reentered my body, fast and hard, I felt him spread my legs wider, his hands holding my thighs open. I almost wept as I screamed for more. I felt myself floating. I wanted to stop and feel each sensation, I wanted to go harder and faster. I couldn't breath, I couldn't think. Oh god, my body heat kept rising. I felt a surge deep with in me.

"God Jesse . . . More, Jesse, Jesse! . . . . Jessseeee!" I exploded. I melted as I came off the bed, his arms holding my hips tight drinking me in as I felt hot liquid flow from me. I rode the sensation until there was nothing left of me. I fell back on the bed trying to catch my breath, my heart beating wildly. My body was limp with no urge to move.

I felt him as he moved up me. Stalking, catlike, slowly moving upward I felt his breath on my face as he said "You are my heart, I want to love you."

I didn't want to open my eyes. I heard him breath and then felt his arms pull me close and hold me gently. I felt loved and cherished. As the frenzy within me started to calm I opened my eyes to find him looking at me. His eyes were masked in deep grey.

"You are so beautiful. I want to be in you."

There was more? Oh God how could there be? I was a puddle of myself.

He settled his body beside me. Moving his hands down to my sensitive area, his fingers were again tracing up and down my folds, lightly caressing me. I moved to accommodate his hand amazed that my body could respond when my mind would not. I sighed turning my head to look into his eyes. I was full of wonder.

Jesse's weight shifted and I could feel him as he entered me. I felt him throbbing. I felt him push, hot and pulsing into me. My body tensed. When I held him in my hand I thought that he would never fit inside me. With him breaching my entry I felt that he would split me open.

Jesse felt my hesitation. "Relax honey, you want me. Just relax and open up to me. Let me show you how much I love you."

Jesse looked at my face as his hands guided himself into me. He was rubbing up and down my womanhood. Slowly he slid in a bit farther. I felt him stretch sensitive membranes. I held my breath.

"Hold on to me baby."

"Jesse, it hurts! You're too big!" I tried to push away from him. "Jesse?" I couldn't let him stop, I wanted so much more "Jesse, please . . . help me."

"Its okay honey, you're so tight. Relax, baby, let me in, I don't want to hurt you. You've never loved like this before. This will only hurt for a moment and then you'll never have to hurt again, hold on to me baby, I need to love you."

"Jesse do it, please Jesse."

I held on to him as he started to pump softly as he slowly entered. I could feel myself melt to give him more way. I felt the heat push into me. I felt my body respond by pushing back. His thickness filling me tight, his length pushing onward, I felt my womb stretch to accommodate him but I was too small. I wanted to cry.

"Baby doll, its okay, we'll go slowly."

I wanted him in me. "Please Jesse, please help me!" His arms went around me and held me tight. "Oh baby, you are mine. I love you." He plunged hard, he broke the barrier. I screamed and tried to pull away.

"Oh honey, Hold on . . . ," He kissed my face and neck while he paused holding me tight, waiting for me to catch up to him.

"You okay baby? Oh baby, hold tight baby, you feel so good."

I had been holding my breath, I was full with him. The pain that seared through me eased to a throb when he started to withdraw, I held my breath as he pushed into me again.

Jesse started to slowly move with me the pain replaced with pleasure. I held on tight. I felt him move. He gently moved inside me, pulling out and plunging into me again.

"Oh, baby you feel so good, so good, my sweet baby."

Friction was building as he picked up the tempo. Our hearts beat in synchronized rhythm. I felt him fill me. I felt myself meeting him, elated with the sensations he was giving me. We built to a crescendo. I felt my body fill with a throbbing need to release.

"Oh God, Jesse . . . . JESSE!" My world exploded in lights. He plunged as I released over and over. I was numb to my toes. My heart was beating so wildly I couldn't catch my breath. I felt his release, filling me with molten hot liquid. Holding me close I felt him fill me.

Sated, he fell on me "Oh CJ, I have waited so long for you."

It was then that I felt tingling. Jesse's eyes were closed his arm over my chest and his face close to mine.

I wondered, I didn't want to know. I raised my hand and looked. It was mostly solid, but I was either working into a fade or maybe out. I had no wish to move. I felt Jesse move. I turned my head to face him.

He took my hand in wonderment and kissed it. "CJ, what is this gift you have?"

I turned my face to the ceiling. "I truly do not know." He put his arm around me pulling me to him. We both fell into a deep exhausted sleep.

Chapter 19

The phone was ringing, I felt Jesse move as he groped for the phone on the night stand. "Keyes" he answered.
"Hey man, I'm there in ten minutes."
"Grady. Yeah, uh . . . we'll be here."
"Are you still sleeping? Come on you mummy get a move on."
Jesse dropped the phone "Ten minutes."
"Grady?" I asked.
"Yeah, he'll be here in a few."
"I don't want to move."
I sat on the side of the bed and took in Jesse. Poor baby, His bandages were hanging on him, black blue and yellow bruises standing out on his skin. I looked at his ribs and the bandages were really ragged. "How's your ankle? Did you hurt your ribs? How do they feel?"
He let out a little snicker, "Numb like the rest of me."
I had gathered the blanket around me and headed for the bathroom and started the shower.
Jesse had grabbed the walker and was standing in the middle of the room stark naked. What a disheveled bruised, patched, beautiful sight. He looked rugged with his day old beard and ruffled hair. His body was strong and muscular, his shoulders wide. His hips narrow, with strong sinewy legs. A satisfied smile was on his face as he motioned me to him. I went him and he took the blanket and dropped it to the floor. He gathered me into his arms and held my naked body next to his. "CJ, I think I'm going need some help," he said with a sigh.

While I adjusted the water Jesse had removed the scraggily bandages from his ribs, his foot looked painfully black and blue. I lifted his foot and let him lean on me until he was in the tub. His hand was leaning on the wall to keep his balance.

"I hope we didn't hurt you. Jesse, I didn't stop to think about your injuries."

"Baby, it hurts so fine. How are you doing, you have to be sore."

"Baby, it hurts so fine." I echoed.

We both laughed as I followed behind him and together we let the hot steamy water flow over us. Standing this closely, watching as the water sprayed over him I saw all his wounds. I looked at his back and shoulder. The bruises were fading. The stitches in his shoulder were tight. I soaped the wash cloth and ran it over his back as he let the water beat on his head. The soap was bubbling and running in rivulets down his back, moans of satisfaction coming from him as I soaped his body, down his legs everywhere my hand chose to travel.

"You like that Cowboy?" I heard his intake of breath. "I never bathed *with* a patient before."

"You are one hell of a nurse."

I started to soap his chest. The water was making pathways through his hair and down his neck and shoulders. I added more soap and lathered my hands gently rubbing his body.

I watched his member grow as I played peek-a-boo through the soap. I felt my breathing increase. My hand followed the swollen flesh to his velvety soft orbs. He was keeping pace with me. He had soap in his free hand and was rubbing it on my chest, my shoulders and neck. I felt his finger slide into my womb. I groaned with the pleasure of it. All the muscles that protested when I got out of bed were melting under the manipulation of his hands in the hot soapy water.

Our pleasure was interrupted when a gruff came from the bottom of the stairs. "Jess you just about ready? We have twenty minutes." We both started laughing, Jesse called down "Start the coffee Grady, we'll be right down."

We rinsed off the soap and dried each other, I dressed as he shaved. We hobbled laughing down the stairs. Grady was at the bottom of the stairs with a big mug of coffee and looking at his watch, I wondered if he'd ground us for being tardy.

He was really trying to keep a straight face. "Coffee's in the kitchen, maybe after we can grab Margaret and go to breakfast."

"That sounds good to me." Jesse replied.

I walked around Jesse and went into the kitchen. Grady was holding Jesse up as they hobbled in. I handed Jesse a cup, and leaned on the counter listening to them talk about Dr. Wenz, wondering when he would authorize Jesse to go back to work.

We all climbed into Grady's car. Jesse had his cane and a slipper on his foot, there was a grimace on his face with each step. We arrived a little late but the good doctor welcomed us with open arms. He had Jesse sit on the table; I wanted to hear what was said and Grady *the mountain* just stayed, Dr. Wenz didn't seem to mind.

He had his nurse take Jesse into another room for x-rays while he looked at Grady's arm. "It should have had stitches" he lectured as he cleaned it, medicated it and bandaged it. Doctor Wenz continued to lecture ending with instructions to keep it warm and dry and to return on Friday. "It had better not be infected."

Jesse came back in the room. The doctor took the stitches out of his shoulder, looked in his eye and told him to go to an ophthalmologist just to make sure but he was *on the mend*. Jesse told him that he had very little pain in his ribs. When the doctor looked at his foot, he scowled when asked why his cast was removed. Jesse was hesitant about telling him the reason.

Dr. Wenz had really good people skills. He kept everyone distracted talking about everything. He asked questions while he poked and probed every injury. He spoke about the boy's past injuries, broken arms, broken bones, Grady swallowing a marble. Bass breaking his head open when he fell off a second story building. He had taken care of guys since they were kids. They seemed to revert back to their childhood behavior when they were around him.

The X-rays showed that his ribs were mending nicely but his foot was a mess. Nothing broken, but definitely sprained and Jesse needed to stay off of it as much as possible. "You must have not heard me when I said to stay off of your foot." Doctor Wenz wrapped it in a soft cast and to keep it dry. "Don't overdo it." He looked at me "I expect you'll make sure he follows orders."

Before I could tell him that I was not one to enforce orders Jesse piped up and said. "I'll follow her orders doc, don't you worry."

Grady added. "She's a regular Florence Nightingale."

Dr. Wenz's attention focused on me. He asked me how I was feeling. I felt a blush rise up and wondered if our morning escapades showed on my face. He told the boys to wait outside and asked if I would mind staying behind for a minute.

He looked at me. "I know you didn't come in to see me, but since you're here is everything all right with you?"

"I'm fine, I'm rarely ill." I replied.

Dr. Wenz raised his eyebrows. "I would like you to set up an appointment. When was the last time you had a physical?"

I told him years ago.

He said that I was due. "If you prefer a woman doctor I know someone who would see you. It would be wise to see someone, especially if you are having relations."

I know I turned a bright red but agreed that it was a good idea and I wouldn't mind making an appointment with him.

He looked at my bruised shoulder and asked about my parents and where I was from. He inquired if I ever had any major hospital visits or broken bones. He moved my arm to the back and then pulled them out in front of me. "Do you have any pain?"

As he examined my arm he massaged and pressured it from my shoulder to my wrist. He took my hand and told me to be careful. We walked me out to the guys and told Jesse to come in Friday with Grady. We left with the warning for Jesse to stay off the foot. I walked out feeling confused that he had taken such a personal interest in me.

He stated that Grady and Jesse would be off on medical leave for the week.

Grady was anxious to see Margaret. He expounded on what a fine caring woman she was, a classy dresser, what great eyes, wonderful personality. When he took her home they talked into the wee hours of the morning. "She is such an interesting woman. Do you think she likes me?"

"What's not to like?" Jesse replied. "A big bear like you, just show her you finer side Grady, wait until you know her better before you start growling."

I laughed "Yeah Grady the first time I met you, you had me shaking in my shoes."

"That ain't true CJ; you stood there like you were gonna bite my head off. You were one scary little spitfire."

"Grady, you are a gentleman. Once I saw under your tough exterior I found out you were a pussy cat."

We had pulled up to my office building and Grady helped Jess with his cane.

I ran ahead to get the doors. We walked into the office as Margaret came from behind the desk. She had a pencil in her hair and I could tell she had been hard at work.

Her eyes lit up when she saw Grady. He was blushing, actually blushing!

Jesse took my hand and said "How about a cup of coffee?" We went into the small kitchen and I made a cup for each of us and sat down across from him.

"You have a really comfortable office. You've made it homey."

"Its getting there, its all Margaret's doing. In fact she did it all except for the furniture you loaned me."

"Is this your apartment to? You never gave me the official tour."

"There's not much to see. It's comfortable. Beyond that door there is the bathroom and then a small bedroom. Sometimes it's nice to fall out of bed and go to work."

"Do you mind if I look?"

"Go ahead; be careful it is small, watch your foot."

Jesse stood up stretched and walked through the bathroom; I heard my door open and a few minutes later it closed. He appeared in the doorway and looked at me. "CJ that room is a closet. Don't you have claustrophobic dreams?"

I laughed. "Jesse if I am in that room I am darn near unconscious. I sleep."

Grady stepped into the kitchen "Who's up for breakfast?"

Jesse stomach growled. "I could eat a horse."

We hobbled to the car, and took off to a little café that served great coffee and decent food. It was almost ten o'clock. The day was bright and beautiful.

Chapter 20

We had a leisurely breakfast. The café was fairly empty, the breakfast crowd had left and the lunch crowd hadn't begun yet. We sat enjoying our food while we filled Margaret in on our visit to the doctors. Grady was off until Friday and Margaret was happy to hear that his arm was going to be fine.

My legs were still wobbly; I kept having sensations if I moved just right. My mind kept wandering to the night before. Jesse had his arm around me holding me close. It felt so natural to have him beside me. I had never imagined myself this close to anyone. My emotions were on my sleeve and I basked in the feeling that lingered inside me. I hadn't been to work yet and Margaret probably did a whole days work.

I did know that if I didn't get to work soon I would have to put Margaret on the street with a cup of pencils.

Grady had given Margaret a list of the men arrested during the Wiggins fiasco. They were discussing who was involved and if any of them had a reward on their head.

Margaret asked Grady he had figured out who Pete was. He said that he had a lead he was checking on. It was on the grapevine.

"Who's Pete?" asked Jesse.

"Just someone who called the office and threatened CJ, She almost collard him the other day, but he got away."

"Someone threatened you? What did he say?" Jesse was looking at me.

"He wanted you, said to tell you to back off, that you were a dead man and I would be too."

Jesse's eyes turned hard, he was trying to stay calm. "When were you going to say something to me?"

Grady piped up and said that he already told Margaret what a bone headed move it was.

Margaret bristled. She pulled away from Grady and turned to speak to him face to face. "You listen to me Mr. Grady Dombrowski, I am a grown woman and I don't plan to have another bone headed man tell me what I should or should not do. I asked you to check it out didn't I?"

Jesse and I looked up at this exchange. I was trying not to laugh, but when I looked at Jesse he had an expression on his face that looked like he might agree with Grady.

Grady was astonished that his girl just told him off. "Look sweetie, we need to know when things like this happen. We take care of our own. Look what happened when CJ went after the Wiggins's alone."

Now my feathers were ruffled. "Grady, Margaret and I didn't go into that hap-hazard. We figured that it would take about 25 minutes, an hour tops. I was just going to scope out the house because I knew Max was changing addresses. We lucked out. I heard their plans. Grady, just who did we call? And don't you forget that it all worked out. I have never had to answer to anyone so I didn't think to do it then. My main concern was to do my job."

"Why didn't you tell me?" asked Jesse.

"Mainly because it was a simple look-see and because you had a party, and the big one . . . and you happened to be injured."

Jesse took my hands in his. "CJ, I need you to keep me in the loop."

"I will if possible, but Jesse, You have your work, I don't expect to know every detail of what you're doing."

"We have to talk about this."

"We will, but not right now. I want to know about the park, what happened there."

"We got the names of the two in the park. Bass called and said that there was a rumor that BA had put a contract out on them. He was told that they were hired to finish them off. Jesse and Bass were the main witnesses and put him in prison. Bass was following the lead. They knew Jesse was hurt and they must have been watching the house. They followed Grady's car to the park.

"So, you two went to a park and you were aware that something *might* be happening and you didn't think to mention it?" Margaret asked.

"It was police business, and it was only a theory."

"Yep, your right guys, we are going to have to talk about this."

I started to laugh, "Look guys, we all have our work. I hope we can work together in the future, but right now we're at a stalemate and I'm sure in time we can find a compromise."

The arm around my shoulder pulled me close as Jesse gave me an earth-shattering kiss. He whispered in my ear, "My little peacemaker." He put his hands on mine "Baby we'll talk later, Right now I just I'm just thankful that every thing worked out."

Once again this calm reasonable man surprised me. I didn't know what to say. I thought of all the secrecy and fear I grew up with. Here was someone who made no judgments, just accepted me. My relief must have been apparent; he looked at me quizzically and pulled me closer. "Let's get out of here."

We decided to go to Jesse's and pick up my car. Margaret and I would visit Vince and turn in the receipt on Max, and check one of the others that were on Grady's list.

Grady was going to check in at the station and lay the groundwork to pick up a receipt on Art Terovolas. He was $300.00 in our slowly growing business fund. Jesse was going to work at home.

Standing by the car waiting for Margaret Jesse's pulled me to him while he did strange and wondrous things to my ear and neck. "CJ, baby, your comings back this afternoon aren't you?" It was hard to say no. I told him I'd call him. I was really tired and I did need to sleep.

"After this morning I can't promise to be a gentleman. I want to be with you, hold you. If you say no I may have to come to your little closet and we can sleep like spoons."

I laughed at the idea of both of us in my little closet room. I told him that I would call him and let him know what I was up to.

Grady and Margaret came out of the house. She looked a bit rumpled and Grady had that Grady smile, a sure clue that their budding relationship was defiantly blooming.

I wondered what they could read of our faces.

We stopped at Vince's first. I introduced him to Margaret, and explained that much of our business would be handled by her. We presented him with the receipt for Max and informed him about the outstanding reward we would be expecting for Art.

Vince gave us his sleazy leer and said that he would mail the payment.

I leaned on his counter and told him that I would have my payment now. I would be back with the other receipt on Art Terovolas and I would expect payment as soon as I returned. I did not accept checks.

"If you want us to work for you in the future you damn well pay up." He finally agreed and then asked her out to dinner.

She looked at me. Amazed, she looked him straight in the eye. "I'm so sorry, but if I did that my boyfriend would have to kill you."

He was grumpy about paying out the cash for Max. I figured it was his regular temperament. Margaret had spoken to him several times on the phone and had stressed payment on demand.

We deposited the cash. I gave Margaret $300.00 and told her to mark it as a portion of pay owed. Margaret wanted to get back to the office and finish the paperwork to close the file. We discussed our next move and clients. What we needed and what needed to be done.

Margaret looked up at me, "Uh CJ?" I raised my head from the poster I was reading and looked at her. She had a worried look on her face.

"Yes Margaret?" "What's wrong?"

"CJ, I think Grady really likes me."

The relief had to show, I was not ready to talk about Jesse yet.

"I have to agree with that. I don't know him all that well, but one glimpse of you and he lights up."

"CJ, he's a cop; my life has been . . . well . . . complicated, I did a lot of things that I wished I never had. I was with Ralph for goodness sake. How will he feel when he finds out about me?"

"Margaret, he has seen so much in the life he's led. Good or bad whatever you have experienced in your life is what's made you, you. Your intelligent, vibrant, a totally gorgeous woman, He's probably wondering why you'd want a loud, overbearing, paunchy, giant of a man who thinks your too good for him."

"He's not paunchy, he's solid."

She saw the half smile on my face and grinned. "Ya know what? I'm just going to ride my "*Grady train*" until he puts on the brakes."

"That's my girl, you know and I know that he likes what he sees."

"Just like Jesse and you. That man thinks the sun rises and sets in you."

It was my turn to blush.

"YOU DID IT! You did the deed!"

My blush had to be a deep crimson.

"Don't be embarrassed baby, He's a wonderful man, even back and blue he is one fine specimen."

I started to laugh; Margaret had a way of putting things in perspective.

Were we both in the same boat? Waiting for our guys to decide if they can handle our past? "You know what? I plan to ride the Jesse train too."

I stood to take my coffee in the kitchen and gave Margaret a big hug, "Margaret, I couldn't run this place without you."

The phone rang and Margaret's cheery "CJ's Private Investigators" She listened on the phone and then spoke low into the receiver, when she hung up she had that dreamy look.

"Grady I'll bet."

"Yes it was. He's going to come and take me home. Mom's going to make dinner and put him on the spot. He's nervous about it."

"I'll bet he is. I would love to be a fly on your wall."

"Oh, I haven't said anything about her guardian angel and I don't plan on it unless you think I should."

"No, she's happy. It makes her feel good that someone is taking care of her. It was hard enough to explain it to my closest friends."

Grady showed at the door. He gave Margaret a kiss on the cheek and asked if she was ready to go, He seemed a little uneasy about the night's upcoming events. I went up to him and gave him a hug. "You know what Grady? Rosie is one of the kindest people I know."

He looked at me, and then Margaret, "I hope she likes me."

"What's not to like" we both replied in unison.

I had tidied up the kitchen and filed the files I was working on. I was stalling. I knew I was doing busy work, trying to ignore and maybe sometimes encourage the sensations that my body sent me.

I answered my cell-phone lost in thought.

"Hey baby, Come on over. I have dinner on and it's almost ready."

"You made dinner? You're supposed to be off your foot. Did you get any work done?"

"I did try. But I had this vision of a beautiful woman lying prone in my bed and it kept distracting me."

"Maybe you should call her?"

He snickered, "If your not here in fifteen minutes I'm going to come and get you. I spent most the afternoon working on dinner."

It was my turn to laugh, "I'm on my way."

Chapter 21

Jesse had set a wonderfully romantic table. Table cloth, candles, china settings, silver, napkins and crystals set out in perfect order.

He had the lights dimmed. Standing in the doorway he stood watching my face as I took it all in. It was lovely.

He wore a pair of brown slacks, a casually unbuttoned shirt showing a peak of hair on his chest. I felt my body responding. His corduroy jacket finished the package. He looked good enough to eat.

"Jesse, it's beautiful, you have worked so hard."

He came up behind me, "All for you baby."

I turned around in his arms and was holding him back. "Thank you Jesse."

This seemed so wonderfully natural. "Jesse, I need wash my hands, give me ten minutes?"

"If I came with you, you could take as long as you wanted."

"Oh no you don't I'm famished, the aromas alone are making my mouth water."

I moved away and went upstairs in *my* bedroom and reached for my overnight bag. I unzipped it and found a serious lack of formal clothing. I really had to buy that all purpose little black dress.

I grabbed a peasant blouse that I rarely wore and after slipping it on I remembered why, the neckline was a little low; I changed into my favorite peasant skirt

After tying my sandals I looked in the mirror. I needed to buy some makeup when I went out for that little black dress. I looked like I felt, pale and nervous. I brushed my hair, and took a deep breath and went down to dinner.

I had taken the first step when I saw him leaning on the newel post at the foot of the stair. He waited for me to reach him his eyes following my progress down the stairs. He took my hand and kissed it. Then placed my arm into the crook of his and escorted me into the dining room. He held my chair and after I was seated he kissed my neck and went to his.

Pouring the wine for each of us, he lifted his glass to toast.

"To us, you are the missing piece of my heart."

He touched my glass to his, the candle light reflecting off the crystal sending prisms loose in the room. Our eyes locked and I was speechless.

I opened my mouth to speak and nothing came out. He brought the glass to him lips and set it on the table. He reached over to take my hand. "I love you babe."

He broke the contact, took his napkin, shook it out, and placed it on his lap. "I thought you were hungry?"

Cold crisp salads were on the table and small talk was about his culinary talent. I asked if he had any help from Magpies. He laughed as he said that he made it with his own hands and I would have to take my chances. He refilled our glasses and went into the kitchen.

He returned carrying a tray of condiments, bacon, onions, sour cream, and cheese. These were to garnish baked potatoes. Little tiny corn on the cob, seasoned and buttery was his vegetable of choice. He removed the salad plates to the kitchen.

I met him as he brought big thick steaks out of the broiler. "Here, let me take that, you need to be off that foot." He started to protest but surrendered and followed me to the table. Jesse poured more wine.

"Jesse, this is so much. It's really outstanding. I hate to admit that I'm not a very good cook." The small talk started small. "You seem to be maneuvering on you foot better. The swelling seems to have gone down too."

"Well, I have stayed off of it most of the day. I propped it up while I worked. Doc knows his stuff."

"He's known the three of you all since you were children. I remember something he said about the three of you jumping from a rope, one of you breaking an arm, and how you walked like little men into his office to have it fixed."

"God yes, It was Bass's arm, no tears allowed, we were HE-MEN tough. It was bent in such a way it hurt me to look at it. We wrapped his arm in Grady's shirt, he was always larger then life. Mostly to cover the bone that was showing. Bass has still has the biggest scar."

"Doctor Wenz asked me to come in, any idea what that's about? I've never had a Doctor ask me to come in." I knew I was fishing for information, it sounded like I was fishing.

"Doc's a special guy. He can look at someone and *know* things. I think a lot of its observation, but sometimes he seems to know so much more."

"Sounds ominous, I feel very well, I rarely get sick."

Jesse looked up from his plate. "It couldn't hurt. He doesn't say things he unless he has a reason."

"So you think I should go?"

"Hey, I'll go with you if you want. I think he wants your body."

"Jesse, He's got to be in his sixties."

"I'd say closer to eighty, he's been around a long time."

I felt there had to be more. "Jesse, what are you not telling me?"

He looked a little sheepish; I was twirling the goblet in my hands. He polished his off and sat back.

"Doc Wenz is special, he has great bedside manner, he can tell you every bit of gossip you would want to know. He's tight lipped on the important stuff. Never says anything mean or medical stuff. Mama would call him a healer. He has a special place in our world."

Our world? What an odd expression? I felt Jesse was trying to tell me something. I waited for him to elaborate.

He was trying to form the words he wanted to say, I knew he would get there in his own sweet time. Right now I had the time

"CJ, First I want to tell you how proud I am of you. I can't imagine what you went through to grow into such a fantastic woman. I can understand your secrecy and I want you to remember that we all have things we need to hide."

I sat up straighter in my chair. I was all ears.

"Did you notice that when the good doctor was examining me he would concentrate and rub specific areas? He smoothed my ankle from leg to toe. My ribs he started at the outside and gently touched all around my rib cage. My eye especially, he pressed and smoothed it all around. That's when the healing really began."

I looked up startled. "He did that to my shoulder this morning. I really didn't pay much attention but it hasn't hurt all day."

"My ankle is throbbing but nothing like it did last night." He paused and filled our glasses. "He was upset about the stitches. He didn't think the emergency room doctor did the job he would have."

I found this amazing, "So good ole Doc Wenz is a healer, a magic man?"

"I don't know if I would call it magic, but he's got the healing touch and he sees things that others don't. To tell you the truth we take him for granted, he's just there when we need him."

"So why do you think he wants to see me? I feel like he sees something that I don't and it's kinda freaking me out."

"I'm as surprised as you are, maybe he felt something. We did talk about you getting banged up. Or maybe he feels your special abilities and is curious. We all have gifts in our own way. It couldn't hurt."

"Well maybe I'll go see him, I do need a physical."

"It's up to you, but if my vote counts its better safe then sorry and I want you safe forever."

"I'll think about it." Maybe I'll go with you on Friday and talk to him. There are several things I would like to inquire about."

"There's not any thing wrong is there? Are you sure you okay?" I could hear the concern in his voice.

"No, I told you that I rarely get sick, just girly stuff." I think I actually saw a light bulb go on over his head.

"CJ, we didn't take any precautions!" He sounded a bit alarmed.

"Jesse, no I didn't. You were there. I really haven't had the need until just recently."

It was my turn to watch him turn red. He stammered "Oh CJ, I didn't think, Honey, I should have."

"Jesse, stop it. We will be more responsible. As a matter of fact Margaret helped me out there. She thinks of everything."

Jesse had a nervous laugh, "Margaret knows?"

"Jesse I have been walking funny all day. I can't stop touching you. I want to be with you when I'm not near you. She's a fairly observant woman."

Jesse sat back in his chair with a look of shock. Slowly a wide grin crossed his face.

"Jesse?"

He stood up and took my hand, and walked me through the living room and out to his day porch. Candles were flickering around the room. A small fire pit with a steady flame glowed at one end of the room. The plants gave the room a dense jungle like atmosphere. There were large overstuffed pillows on the floor. He fluffed a pillow and motioned for me to sit; he sat next to me and put an arm around me. When I looked up I saw the night sky. I had never seen this room in this light or at this angle.

"Oh Jesse, it's beautiful."

"I'm thinking I should put the Jacuzzi in that corner, I'm taking the advice of the gorilla brothers and adding a bath and dressing room. I'm still working out the details."

"It will be beautiful."

Jesse had reached in an ice bucket that he had placed under a tree and poured champagne for the two of us. He tipped his glass to toast, when I stopped him.

"Let me Jesse." I toasted us. "From the moment I saw you I was afraid of you. I'm not afraid anymore, I'm petrified. I don't know the rules. I know that being away from you hurts. Please don't hurt me."

We both took a sip and Jesse took my glass and put both of them on a low table. He took me in his arms and kissed me.

"CJ, we will learn how to love each other together."

My heart was pounding, Jesse's face was close to mine, his kiss was deep and mind sweeping, I took me a minute to realize that I was tingling and the maelstrom of overwhelming emotions was pulling me to Jesse.

Jesse was nipping on my neck, he had started at my ears and the sensations ignited a heat in me deep and erotic. My body responded without any thought. I followed Jesse's lead and mimicked his actions.

"CJ, I love your body, I love the leanness, your strength . . . ."

His lips were on my neck, his hands caressing up and down my body as he nipped and rolled his tongue on my nipple, I felt it harden and strained for more.

I held his head to my breast; I was brushing my finger through his hair, feeling the different textures of his neck and shoulders. I was mimicking his actions, doing to him as he did me, holding on to each sensation that charged through me. Wanting more I pushed my body into his. I wanted to blend with him. I raised my head and saw the stars above me. I put my hand toward the sky, and froze. I had dimmed and the star I was reaching for was on my hand. I froze.

Jesse was startled. He looked up when he felt me pushing away, my feet trying to find purchase to scramble out from under him.

"CJ, Stop."

The sweet feelings of our lovemaking had changed, first by embarrassment and then fear.

"CJ Stop baby, come here baby, let me hold you."

"Jesse," I couldn't talk. I looked at Jesse and he was looking at me, maybe even through me. He seemed to be studying my face. His hands were running up and down my arms, I didn't trust myself to touch him; I felt tears come into my eyes.

I saw his lips move before I heard his voice. "Hey honey, its okay, your Okay; I dreamt one night that you were so close. I could feel you, I could feel and smell your hair, I love your hair. I hope all our kids have your hair. When I opened my eyes you weren't there, yet I felt your hand on my chest. The other night when we talked about your ability, I thought *it was real,* you were truly beside me. It wasn't a dream. This morning all I knew was this marvelous woman wanted me as much as I wanted her. Baby, I always know when you're near me."

"Jesse, it's not that simple."

"Sure it is, I love you, and you love me. We belong together. Look, there are a lot of special abilities out there. I believe that everyone has special talents. Some are just more prominent, evolved. I have a sense of rightness. A gut feeling that lets me know if I am on the right track, and my gut feeling tells me we are oh so right for each other."

"Jesse, If what I feel is love, then I do love you, but this happens when something is wrong. I have always thought it happened because I was meant to help. I made my whole life's decisions around it. If I disappear when were together does that mean we're wrong?"

The tingling had stopped and Jesse's hands left my arms to hold my hands. The look on his face was unreadable.

"CJ, look at me. I am here. I'm ready to take on any demons we come across. We are not wrong. I think it's because you feel so strongly for me. It's so strong and deep that you physically manifest a change. Have you ever loved anyone?"

"No, I always kept my distance. I broke my own rule and let you get close."

"CJ, I'm glad that you did. I want to be with you. I love you and I want to be the father to your children. CJ, I love you."

"Jesse, slow down, how can you be so sure, it's so much, I am so confused!"

"I knew you would be mine when I saw you stapling your fliers to a telephone pole, before I knew your name. I would catch a glimpse and my heart would beat faster. I knew before you walked into the station, if you hadn't come in that day I would have made it a point to look you up."

"You weren't surprised when you found out. You would have figured it out sooner if you didn't have so many drugs in you."

"Back to *US*, Maybe it's because you care for me that it happens. And let me tell you something this fading, this dimming thing you have going? It's a definite turn on."

"You are loco, your nuts. This isn't funny. Look, I freak you out and I can't handle watching that. I think I better leave."

"No, don't go, stay. You surprise me but you don't freak me out. We will adjust and work it out. Its kind of neat to know your girl cares enough to *change* for you."

"That's not funny Jesse. It's not a joke. I have been living this thing. I am the most warped woman you will ever meet."

"I was hoping that you would be *my* warped woman."

I began to relax; maybe we could work it out. Maybe my biggest fear was having someone find out about me and turning away, calling me a freak. I never dreamed of finding what I had with Jesse.

"I think we should call Dr. Wenz in the morning. I think he can help. I will be right there with you." He said as he nuzzled my neck.

I looked around at Jesse's beautiful room. I had lost the glow of the evening. I was embarrassed, exhausted and frightened. I wondered if when the wine wore off he would have second thoughts.

Jesse shifted his body and pulled me into his arms. "Look at the sky CJ, Look at the stars. There are as many differences in people as there are stars." He pulled me to him and pulled the afghan around us. We fell asleep in each others arms watching the sky.

Chapter 22

"Hey Baby, are you going to sleep all day?"

My nose caught a whiff of coffee, I groaned as I rolled over. "Hey you, what time is it?" I was struggling to a sitting position. Jesse had a cup of coffee and was watching me as I stretched to get the cricks out of my bones. He had already showered and shaved and looked like he just walked out of GQ magazine. I could imagine what I looked like. I pulled the Afghan around me and took the mug from him. I took a sip and savored the flavor as the warm liquid slid down my throat. "Thanks Jesse, How long have you been up?"

"Just a couple of hours, you looked so sweet, I didn't want to wake you." Jesse handed me his robe, "When you're ready, I have breakfast waiting in the kitchen."

"My, you have been busy. I don't think I can eat a bite after last night." With that remark the night before came to mind, I could feel a blush come over me. Jesse took my cup and held out his hand. He pulled me up; I rose holding the afghan around me as I stood.

"I have to get you fueled up; I have the whole day planned."

"Jesse, I have to get to work. I have been really slacking off and I have things to do."

"I know baby, go get cleaned up, we'll talk about it over orange juice. You ready for another cup?"

He kissed my forehead, turned and walked from the room. I slipped on the robe, grabbed my clothes and ran up to the shower. As the water flowed over me, the events of the night ran through my head, as I went through my mental checklist one thought stood out. Jesse knew and he still cared. I felt my smile spread and the last vestige of sleep vanished. I dressed quickly, jeans and shirt; I added a rarely used lacy camisole and wondered at myself.

Jesse was on the phone when I came downstairs; he looked up with the most glorious smile. "Thanks Bass, I'll try to pick it up later." He pulled me to him, gave me a kiss "Morning babe, did you sleep alright?"

We walked to the kitchen; there was the promised orange juice. I sat down while Jesse made me a plate of sausage and eggs. He sat across from me with a cup of coffee and started talking about the plan for the day.

"Bass has all the names of the 8-ball arrests. One was Matt Dawson; he's the guy that Freddy wanted so badly."

"That's the one he would pay double on?" That's great, what else is happening?"

Jesse looked at his plate. "I made an appointment with Doc Wenz."

"Jesse, did we hurt your foot?" I had noticed earlier that he was leaning heavily on his cane; He had it covered with a sock.

"No," he hesitated; "I made the appointment for you, at 1:30, and before you protest I am asking you to do this for me."

"What's the rush Jesse, Why the urgency?"

Jesse took my hand. "The doc can explain it better then I can. He has the ability to heal, Mama says both for body and soul. If anyone can enlighten us about your abilities he can."

"Are you telling me that he knows something about my dimming? He can tell me what's wrong with me?"

"That's what we are going to find out. He was really anxious about seeing you, when I called this morning he was ready to cancel all his appointments."

"Now I'm worried, why the special treatment? Does that mean he thinks I have a problem?"

"Don't jump the gun. I'm just saying he knows things and I trust him, I want you to be happy. If he knows something we need to know what it is."

"I have to call the office." I ran upstairs and grabbed my phone. I sat on *my* bed and tried to sort out what I had just agreed to. I was terrified; my affliction was what defined me. Did this mean curing me? Would it go away? By making it go away would I would be normal? What the hell was normal? It's the one thing I always wanted to be wasn't it?

I dialed the office. That lady had to be sitting on the phone. "Hey Margaret are we still solvent? How's it going?"

"CJ, as a matter of fact it's been pretty busy. I had a Ms. Jamison call she wants you to find her son. She saw a flier and said that she hasn't heard from him in five weeks. She's checked everywhere including hospitals and missing persons. I have her number."

"Grady called and said that he just talked to Bass, he's bringing me some papers on a guy we can collect on from the Wiggins bust and red hot poster. Bass also found Pete. He was one of the guys at the park. No paper on him, but at least he's caught."

"That's great, Jesse, said we had Matt Dawson, he's one of Freddy's and worth double. Give Freddy a call and give him a heads up, We'll go over and I'll introduce you to him. He's such a sweet man. Give Mrs. Jamison a call and have her come in tomorrow morning. Get as much information as you can. Last known address, Social, and driver's license. If you have time do a cursory on him, oh check and see if he's wanted."

"Sounds like a plan, I'm on it."

"Hey, how did Grady get along with your mom?"

"I think were in direct competition. She's really taken to him."

"I don't know when I'll be in; call me if anything comes up." I have an appointment at 1:30 with Doc Wenz."

"That's interesting, not to mention a good idea, you feeling alright? Grady mentioned him last night. He said he was a great doctor. He didn't elaborate, but he had such reverence, if that's the right word, in his voice. I need to meet him. I could use a good look over."

"I have my reservations but I do need to see him about personal some needs."

"Are you saying that you and your handsome cowboy are officially and item?"

"I'll catch you up when I see you, I defiantly need advice."

"CJ, just take it at your own pace. He's a good guy but only you know if he's right for you. I'll be here if you need me."

I grabbed a jacket and went downstairs. Jesse had a set of keys in his hands and said that we would take his Nova. I looked at his face and then at his foot and said sure. But he wasn't going to drive.

"I never let anyone drive the Nova but me." He stated.

"Well then I better go warm up the Grady-mobile." He looked to the ceiling and then sighed as he handed me his keys.

"You gotta know I love you if I let you drive my pride and joy."

"Come on Cowboy, I have wanted to drive your car since the first time I rode in it."

I rushed past him and went to open the garage door. There it sat waiting for me.

Jesse hobbled to the passenger side of the car and opened the door. He stood leaning his elbows on the roof of the car trying to decide if he really wanted to let me drive his precious car.

"Second thoughts?" The smirk on my face must have been a challenge.

He sighed as he slid into the passenger seat. "No Baby, lets get on the road."

When we arrived at the office there was no one in the reception room. Doc Wenz came out of his office to greet us followed by a matronly woman he introduced as Dr. Kent. She shook my hand and said she would be happy to do my examination.

I looked at Jesse who was shaking Dr. Wenz's hand. Dr Wenz turned to me and said, "I was fortunate enough to speak to a colleague of mine yesterday, he is top in his field of Ophthalmology. He would be happy to take a look at Jesse's eye. The swelling is down and he should be able to examine it properly. I can take him while Gina, Doctor Kent here, does your physical, I can assure you that she is very thorough."

I looked at Jesse and he didn't seem concerned about the change. It did sound like a practical solution, the two bird's one stone theory. "Dr. Ormond can do this at 1:30 as a special favor to me. If you have reservations I could arrange another time."

"No, no. It's probably for the best I'm just surprised is all" I replied.

"Its ok baby, his office is just two blocks up and it shouldn't take that long, unless you want me to stay with you?"

The thought of Jesse standing idly by while I had my feet up in stirrups had no appeal for me. Nor the fact that he would have sit quietly in an empty room just waiting.

"Look, let's just get this done. I need a physical; you need your eye seen too. Go, we'll be fine here."

Dr. Wenz ushered Jesse out the door as I turned to Dr. Kent. "Where do you want me?" She led me to an exam room and handed me a clipboard with papers that I was to fill out. She went to some drawers and pulled out a paper shirt. She started to take out medical items that would be used.

As I filled out the form I noticed that it was different from others I had filled out in the past. The usual questions were there, Name, address, and phone, last visit to a doctor, ailments and illnesses.

The last two pages I came to were really extensive. Parents, grandparents, aunts, uncles, siblings, ages, where and when they were born, if known how they died. Many questions were very specific. It was far more detailed then any I had filled out in the past. I was getting to the last question when Doctor Kent entered.

"I am sorry that you were not informed earlier about the changes. Dr. Wenz makes plans and most find it easier to accommodate him, I have never known a man so dedicated and driven. It's impossible to say no to him."

"You have that right. The few times I have seen him with Jesse its cut and dried. No wiggle room to argue and always so reasonable. How long have you worked with Doc Wenz?"

"Seems like forever. I came here right after med school. I have known him all my life. He was my mentor."

Dr. Kent looked to be in her forties, a small birdlike woman whose actions were swift as she went about her business of setting up my examination. She weighed me and asked me to sit, she checked my eyes, ears, mouth, neck, Took my temperature, blood pressure, Took some blood samples, knocked my knee cap, checked my hands and feet. All the while telling me that she had teenagers, she lived just out of town with her husband of 18 years. She kept the prattle up and declared that I looked physically fit.

She asked that I lay down on the exam table. She checked my head, and neck again, asked about the bruise on my shoulder, she did a breast exam and I blushed at the mark that mysteriously appeared that morning.

Next I was asked to the stirrups, her non-stop prattle continued during the exam. I was asked questions about my family if they had any cancers, if they were sickly; she asked how far I could climb up my family tree and if there were any known oddities.

I decided to be straight with her. "I don't know about any relatives, I have an aunt somewhere I tried to track her down a few years ago but didn't get far. She remarried and I never heard her married name. My parents didn't talk much about themselves or any of the family, I did try to find out more, but I didn't have much luck. I'm an only child and the black sheep of the family."

I had a feeling that our idle conversation was being scrutinized closely. Doctor Kent's bedside manner was efficient, calm and comforting. Like Doctor Wenz, a no nonsense attitude with humor.

"I know I am here for more then a physical exam, As long as we are on this personal level, let's not beat around the bush." I spoke between my knees as she continued my exam.

Doctor Kent laughed, "Tell you what CJ, call me Gina, I promise to answer your questions as honestly as you answer mine, you can sit up now."

"Well, if that's the case don't let me forget to ask about birth control."

Doctor Kent laughed "Get dressed and I will be back in a moment." She picked up a tray with used instruments and the samples she had taken. "I'll be right back." She said as she walked out the door.

I was buttoning my shirt when she knocked on the door. "CJ, when you're ready come to Dr. Wenz office, I wait for you there."

Gina was sitting at the conference table in his office going over the papers I had filled out and adding her notes. I sat on a chair across from her and discussed my personal habits and types of birth control. We had just finished when Jesse and Dr. Wenz returned. He had a new patch on his eye and I couldn't help laughing.

"Oh Jesse, how's your eye? Its okay isn't it?"

"It's fine; this is just a precaution, the eye drops that are making it hard to see." He held up a large plastic pair of dark wrap around sun glasses. "I should be able to see clearer in a couple of hours. The eye patch is temporary."

We were all seated around the conference table. Dr. Wenz opened the conversation commenting on Jesse's improvement. If he kept out of trouble and followed instructions he should be able to return to work the following week, desk duty. Jesse groaned at that but then said that it would give him time to catch up on paper work. I don't think anyone at the table believed that he would be a desk jockey for long.

Dr. Wenz had my file in front of him and said that I seemed to be very healthy; he would know more after he got the blood test completed. He looked up at me and then Jesse and asked me if I had ever traveled to foreign countries, and general geographical questions. I looked at the good Doctor and said no to all the questions and asked what any of this had to do with my exam.

"CJ, you go by your initials, could you tell me what they stand for?" This seemed like a loaded question, I had been called by my initials from the earliest memories. My name has been a bone of contention as I grew up.

"Well, it's always been CJ even in school."

"You have never used it in any business dealing, have many asked it?

"Well, yes, of course."

"And what did you answer?"

"That I used CJ, and the matter was dropped."

His eyes were locked on mine, his voice was steady and I was getting a little uncomfortable with his scrutiny. I felt beyond uncomfortable. I started to feel anxious. Both Doctors were watching me closely, Jesse seemed to sit a little straighter, his eye patch making me think of pirates and walking the plank. I didn't know why this was making me feel so strange.

"I need to explain and I want you to pay close attention to me. CJ, you are a very special person. It is apparent to me that you have lived in isolation because there was a need to hide your abilities. I believe you have had a ward of protection placed on you and this ward has protected you."

"I don't understand what you're talking about. Ward? Is that like a curse? You're beginning to really freak me out here."

"That is not my intention. I am trying to explain that you are more then CJ, you are more then a Private Investigator. The wards were most likely placed on you for protection. You are anxious because deep inside you cannot break past that barrier. I would like to help you do that."

"Oh, this is getting to be really freaky." I looked at Jesse. Sometime during this exchange he had taken my hand in his; he was rubbing his thumb on my wrist, the motion giving me stability. I started to tingle; I started to deep breath hoping to stop the urge to run.

"CJ, this is not a bad thing. But you need to be aware, and with awareness you will begin to understand."

My eyes still locked on Doctor Wenz, "Jesse, what is he talking about."

Jesse grasped my hand tighter. "Look at me CJ. Don't be afraid, I know what the doctor is trying to tell you. I told you that I have abilities, they are not the same as yours but they are part of me, like breathing. I knew you were mine the first time I saw you. I knew you were special the first time I saw you. My gift allows me to see true. I can look, and talk to a person and I know if they are being truthful, I have insight to their thoughts and that insight helps me to see the direction I need to take."

"I think," said Gina "that you have more to understand about yourself. We would like to help you do that."

Still focusing at Jesse I asked, "Where did this come from, why me?"

Dr. Wenz answered. "You were born with it, you are very powerful and I believe from the snatches I have heard and seen you did not have guidance on how to develop it. You've adapted remarkably well, but you need to understand it. To understand we must remove the wards, time and patience will help you adjust to it."

"CJ, There are many of us, each with abilities that are special." Jesse took both of my hands in his. "I was lucky to have been put in Mama's path; she recognized mine and helped me."

"Mama too? Look guys I'm reeling here."

The doctor went on. "Yes Mama too, try to keep an open mind. I know that this is a lot to hear at one time. "CJ, do me this small favor explain what's happens when your ability surfaces."

"I have told Jesse most of it and obviously you guys know some of it." I looked around the table and surrendered. I explained the actual physical changes that occurred; the urges that guided my actions, and my heightened senses.

"Have you noticed that this ability has escalated over the years?"

"When I was a little girl I did little things. I had to be very close to what I called the target. I tried to hide it as I was growing up especially after I realized I was the only one that was weird. I don't have any control, it just happens; I would have to hide until I could be seen again.

I learned by accident how to make myself come back faster. When I came to this city, with all the people and I was actively looking for work, it happened more frequently. I look for signs to help me find the bad guy. I don't know why or when but it happens. I also figured out that when I touch something I can bring it on."

"CJ, what is your name?" My gaze went to Gina.

"Why is that so important?"

"Okay with out the results of the tests. Without more information and research I'm going out on a line here. I am sure I am right. There are many people like you, maybe not with your particular gift, but with other gifts like Jesse's, or like mine, I can heal, Dr. Kent can heal, Mama can read hearts, Bass and Grady can move mass and mask the closest around them, in some cases redirect their thoughts. Annie is a reader and healer. All of these gifts come in various degrees. But all take practice and guidance. All carry a responsibility with them."

"So all of you can do *special* things, and no one bothered to let me know? Maybe make me feel better? To think I had to hide what I can do?"

I was really on a roll. "Jesse, was it fun to keep me in the dark?" I had taken my hand back and put both on my lap. I felt betrayed.

"CJ, No CJ, it wasn't like that. We didn't know what your capabilities were, you keep them well hidden. I just knew you were special, I was drawn to you. When I did find out, the reality, not the maybe, I was thrilled. I don't break my friends confidences they would have said something when they were ready. I know you felt their closeness as they did yours. You were so secretive, we all wanted to give you your space. When you told me that night everything was on the table. You trusted me. I am telling you now, but you need to hear what we are trying to say. Your ignorance of the possibilities could put us all in danger. I'm here now, and we are sharing, and all I ask is that you just listen."

I realized that they might be able to answer the questions I have searched for.

"So what do you need me to do?"

Dr. Wenz spoke up. "CJ, someone is protecting you. But the fact remains you somehow evaded detection, the powers that you have are growing, if you want to see the full potential, we need to break the wards. You are a strong woman, you were a strong child. To think of what you must have gone through alone growing up trying to understand, to make a life that included your powers, to embrace them. My admiration for your strength and courage only increases. My theory is that the wards placed on you are weakening. As a small girl, it must have been very confusing."

"These wards, you say they are breaking down, that I have had them since I was little. Who put them on me?" Why?"

"Both are very good questions, someone who loved you very much, to answer the first question. Someone who wanted you protected, for the second. You say your parents were not attentive to you. This doesn't fit in the picture. There is an explanation. When the wards come down we may learn more."

My head was swimming, too much information. I looked at Jesse, I put my hand on his, "Jesse, I am so confused."

"Honey, don't worry, this is a good thing. We'll work it out together."

"Okay, Doc. What do I have to do?"

Gina spoke up. "We could try hypnosis, a suggestion to your subconscious to release the wards?"

"I would not attempt it myself," said Doctor Wenz, "I know someone that is experienced. I would of course insist that Gina or I be present, and Jesse."

"I don't know if I'm comfortable with that. I don't want someone cruising through my head. Doc, have you ever this done before?"

"No, you are unique; you have not had guidance, or a sponsor that recognized your talent as Mama did Jesse's."

"So my bungling self has made it this far. Why can't I just keep on like I have been, I seem to be fine. If something comes up I have you to help me right?"

Gina looked from Jesse to me. "There are several problems that may arise; one is that you have been warded for a reason, knowledge gains reason. Your abilities are increasing, you need to focus on the depth of those abilities and gain control. You have said that there are times when you must hide yourself until reestablishment is complete. The fact that you stumbled on deep breathing and sense deprivation to help you is remarkable. But what if there was a way to do it faster? What if you could control it at will?"

This was too much. "Jesse I need to take a walk." I stood up. "Look, doctors, I know you want to help but I need to think." I had an urge to run, I had to get out. "I have to go."

I bolted out the door.

I wasn't thinking. I was just running. I stopped out of breath and found myself at a bridge in the park. Stopping to catch my breath I sat on the grass reviewing what had been said, knowing that there was a lot unsaid. I was a coward to run, but one thing at a time. The urge said to go. I went. I was still a coward. I sat for a long time before I remembered I left Jesse stranded, unable to walk, unable to drive and visually impaired.

I took my phone out of my pocket and dialed Jesse. "I'm sorry Jesse."

"God, I'm so glad you called, I was going to call you but I knew you wanted to be alone. I have been so worried, are you alright? Where are you?"

"At the park, I just realized I left you with no way to get home."

"Don't worry about me; Bass and Grady are picking me and the car up. We can swing by and pick you up."

I looked around; I was only a mile or so from my work. "No, I'm heading for the office. Jesse, I need to think, and I need to do it alone. I'll call you later. Jesse thanks for helping, apologize for me will you?"

"Don't worry about it, both doctors are concerned and hope that they see you again soon. I'll tell them your thinking. Oh, CJ? I love you."

I stood up and brushed the grass off of me. I started making my way to work. I was thinking about how scattered I was, I needed something to focus on.

Work . . . I had to get to Freddy's. I had to get my car at Jesse's. I needed to sort out so much. Margaret was a calm soul; maybe if I ran it by her it would make more sense. Where was a paper and pencil when I needed one? My mental checklist was not working.

Chapter 23

When I arrived at the office Margaret was on the phone, I waved at her and headed for the kitchen, I grabbed a bottle of water and sat at the table. I was exhausted on so many levels. Margaret came to the kitchen, "I just spoke to Jesse, and he's worried about you. Are you okay?"

"Margaret, I guess so, I don't know. I have too much to think about. What's happening here? Are there any monumental disasters in the works?"

"Nothing major, I made an appointment for the missing person's mother. She's coming in tomorrow at 10:00. I have done a cursory rundown on Bradley Jamison, the missing son. I didn't give her terms; I figured you would work something out."

I wasn't really listening; I looked at Margaret, "I'm sorry, what was that?"

"Your not all here CJ, what's on your mind?"

"I don't know where to begin. Have you ever been at a place where you think you have everything worked out? You have your life planned and *Wham*, it's not your life, it's nothing you could have imagined and you're so tied up in knots you can't think?"

"CJ, I have. You forget that I was trapped in a place so dark and bleak I had lost hope. I was scared all the time. You helped me. Working with you has helped. But sometimes I wake up a shaking and in a sweat. Waiting and listening for footsteps and the beating that usually came with them. Then I realize that it's over, he has no power over me anymore and I feel reborn. Yeah, I know. So tell me."

I put my hand on Margaret's and I saw the pain in her eyes. It had only been a short time and pain from recalling her past showed in her eyes. I felt terrible for making her think of it.

"Oh, Margaret, I don't know where to start. I went to see Dr. Wenz this morning. This ability I have is more then I thought. I think, or he thinks so anyway.

I met Gina Kent, who is his associate and had a physical, then everyone sat at a conference table and I was on the hot spot. They seem to think that there is more I can do about my ability, they suggested hypnosis, and for some reason I had to run, the urge had me RUNNING! I left Jesse with no way home and I ran."

"So you're against hypnosis?"

"No, yes, I don't know. It was all so sudden and they seemed to think it was so important."

"Why did they want to hypnotize you?"

"Something about wards placed on me. They might have been put on me to protect me from this *gift* of mine. I don't know, all my life I have tried not to have it, then I had to work with it and I finally found a livelihood that I could use it in, and now out of the blue it's imperative that I get to the bottom of it. I have tried and tried to find out what it was then I decided to just accept it. Now I'm supposed to understand it? Develop it? Margaret, someone put a *ward* on me? Where was everyone when I was going crazy trying to figure out why I was so different? This is just too much."

"Wow, that's a lot. Before you say anything, what do you think? What do you want? Do you think they can help? Or are you afraid of what you will find out?"

"I think that I'm afraid. I have tried in the past to find out about my past and came up with nothing, zilch. All these years and suddenly, poof! . . . Here's the answer? But the answer involves fishing around in my head. What if it's more then I can handle?"

"I doubt that, your one of the strongest woman I know. Hell, just to tackle Mooring, you put yourself in a situation that I wouldn't. Don't doubt yourself, you face things head on, don't stop now."

"I guess it just took me by surprise. I want to know, but do I need to know?"

"You know you do, don't con yourself. You need to face whatever this is to you." You don't hide from anything or anyone. Do you trust Wenz?"

"Yeah, I guess so. Jesse thinks the world of him, everyone does. So you think I should just go for it?"

"I think you should think about it. You've come this far. I can't see you just giving up. Take your time. Set your own pace. Can't hurt, you might find something that you really need to know. So explain this *ward* thing."

"From what I understand it's like a spell, or a block. A mental block, so I guess I would have to have been hypnotized to have it in the first place.

But what freaks me out is my reaction to the idea of hypnotism, I actually bolted, I didn't have a choice, I didn't want to hear anymore."

"Maybe this ward was put in jeopardy, you would have to fight it and that's why you ran away?" Who would have done this to you? What about your parents?"

"My parents couldn't help me, I think I embarrassed them or maybe frightened them. My mom, more then my dad, he's always so calm. It had to be freaky to have a kid like me."

"Did you ever ask them? They have to know something. Maybe you should ask again. You're not that little kid anymore. They may be able to help."

"You may be right. I think I should see them. I want to see their faces when I ask about it."

"Well I'm going to be there with you. Between the both of us maybe we can figure out what to do next."

We were interrupted by the telephone. Margaret went to answer and I read the list that I had made while we sat talking. I laughed that it mirrored the way my thoughts were running. Scribbled on the napkin in front of me I could see where the subject matter was definitely disturbing. I had actually stabbed through the word hypnotism.

It made sense that it had been done when I was young. Was I so young that maybe I didn't understand and therefore couldn't absorb it all? This was sounding more and more far fetched.

Margaret returned and said that Grady was coming over with Jesse, She couldn't think of a reason to put them off. I told her that it was alright, I had to get a ride to Jesse's to get my car. I went to clean up and change before they arrived.

I felt so tired, totally drained. I opted for a shower and did feel better when I climbed out. As I dressed I heard voices in the other room, the boys had arrived.

Everyone was seated in the reception area. Margaret had brought a chair out and Grady was expounding from it as I entered.

"I think it's great. I knew she was special, I remember when my mom took me to see Doc, she was so excited and it seemed such a big deal. When did you know Jesse?"

"I guess it was when I reached puberty. I had the feelings before, but then they came on really strong. I started to really feel everyone around me. I knew if someone was up to no good. I thought I was nuts, Mama took me to see the Doc. We were lucky Grady; we had people who knew what to look for. CJ didn't have a support system. She is so strong, she amazes me. She really is amazing."

I walked into this conversation and told them it was not nice to talk behind my back. At least Jesse had a guilty look.

Grady got up and gave me a big hug, "Hey Sis how are you doing? You okay?"

"Sis? What have you been smoking?"

He held me away from him and said "Look, I'm bigger then you are and your Jesse's girl so all that's left is a sister, if you ever need anything, or want someone to punch your boyfriend's lights out, I'm your man. I'm your big handsome, hunky big brother."

We all were laughing, "Grady, I truly am honored to have a place in your family."

"Okay, I hate to barge in on your family reunion but I am one hungry lady. Has anyone heard my stomach growl?" Margaret had her hand to her forehead acting like she was going to faint.

Grady dumped me in Jesse's lap and went to Margaret. "Hey princess what are you hungry for?"

Jesse looked at me and we both laughed. He whispered in my ear "Grady's got it bad."

Grady said that he felt he could eat a mule, he was really hungry for some Italian, and he knew just the place. We drove a county over to this quaint little place that had a patio overlooking a lake. Birds were circling in the air. Wonderful aromas wafting on the air and suddenly I was hungry.

We sat on the patio, wine in our glasses and breadsticks on the table. A sailboat heading in for the evening and the breeze was gentle. Relaxed and working into mellow. I listened to the easy banter that was floating around me. It seemed that we had known each other all are lives, thinking that the past two weeks I had gained friends, I had never had friends. Now I had a family.

Dinner was wonderful, Manicotti for me, Spaghetti for the boys, Margaret had a Ravioli with clam sauce. We talked about everything, except the elephant in the corner.

We sat talking for hours, watching the sun set, ordering more wine. I was leaning on Jesse admiring the picture that Margaret and Grady made. It was such a warm loving feeling, Grady moving his massive hands over Margaret's shoulders so tenderly. This little sign of affection made me sigh. Jesse heard me and kissed the side of my head. "Honey, I think its time we went home."

Grady dropped us off at Jesse's and went to take Margaret home. "Bet he takes the long way home" Jesse said as he opened the door.

"Grady lives at home doesn't he?"

"Oh yeah, He's got quite a houseful there.

"And Margaret lives at Rosie's. Where do they get to be alone?"

"I don't know, maybe the no-tell-motel, but Grady's got a huge house, He works on it all the time. His brother is a carpenter. His mom has a series of rooms, there's one whole floor for his sister and husband, they have two kids and they have their own rooms. Grady has the whole back half, with a private entrance. Everyone has privacy. They all share the kitchen and everyone meets there anyway. You'll have to ask Grady for a tour."

Jesse took some wine coolers out of the fridge as he spoke, he handed one to me and I followed him as he went out to the sun porch. He tossed a few pillows and sat. He reached for my hand and I sat down beside him. He put his arm around me and we both leaned back watching the lighting bugs, and the clouds pass over the moon. I felt at peace, and protected. He took off the eye patch and laid it on the table.

"I didn't know that it would be so hard for you baby, I'm sorry I hurt you."

"Jesse, you didn't know, and it was hard for you too. There's so much I don't know. There was a time I searched for a reason; I was driven to find anything that could help me understand. Months of checking every little thing, when I gave up, when I decided that I had to live with it like someone with a handicap, I learned to live around it. Now, I think I'm afraid to know."

"It's got to be hard, but don't you think knowing is better then guessing? It would make all those months you searched worthwhile."

"But Jess, I gave up. I have a life now. I have a *way* of life now."

"Why should that change? If you look at it the right way, it helped you choose a unique way of using it. That's good isn't it?"

"I guess we can twist it any way we want. I talked to Margaret about it. It seems there are a lot of undercurrents here. I have looked for someone like me and found nothing. I move to the city and I find a whole nest of oddities. I mean that in the nicest way since I'm one of them."

"Sarcastic are we? That's much better the broody."

"Broody! Broody? You think I'm broody? You have a lot of room to talk."

"Working that into temper tantrum are we?"

It was my turn to look at him, "I don't know what you're up to but it's not going to work."

"I'm not up to anything. I'm just here with my girl watching the clouds pass by."

"Who's being sarcastic now? How were you told that you were odd?"

"I thought about that today after you left and I was waiting for the guys. I was about 13, I was in a back booth doing my homework when

Mama sat down and told me that we needed to talk. Being a kid and being bombarded by the thoughts and feelings of everyone around me, with no way to turn it off made me angry all the time. I had headaches so severe that I would lay in the dark and wonder if I was crazy. That's when Mama told me about how I came to live there. I knew I was left and they found me. Mama knew right off that I had something. She did look for my mother; I don't think she ever stopped, but Magpies was always home.

"I could sense the truth, or if something was not true. I knew who the bad guys were. It wasn't an ability or affliction. Growing up around it just seemed normal."

"It really manifested one evening when I was doing my homework and not really paying attention to it, like I said I was in a pretty angry back then. Anyway, I was doing my homework when I looked up and saw a man come in to Magpies. I was surprised because I had never seen an aura before. I felt he had *badness* when he came through the door. He demanded money from Mama. I tensed and I was ready to help when Mama said *Sure, Here you go young man.*" She opened the register and told him that he must really need it. She asked him if he wanted some pie as she handed a whole one over to him. He just gaped at her, stammered out "*no thanks*" and ran out of Magpies."

"I saw and felt Mama's power that night. She held me in place; I don't think the man noticed me at all. She read this man, I saw his aura change from black to grey and then to blue. Mama's actions and words seemed to confuse him. She read his heart. Several months later she got an envelope with the exact amount that was taken."

"When it was over I was released and I ran to her. I told her to call the police. She said that the man needed the money more then she did. I was sitting at the counter and she put some milk and cookies out and asked me what I saw. I started from when he came in. She stopped me and said she needed to know what I saw *in* him.

I told her about the colors around him and how they had changed. That he had *Badness* when he walked in the door, but not so much when he left. She said that I was growing up and that we needed to talk. She contacted Dr Wenz, and we went for an appointment the next day.

Because I grew up around sensitive people, I wasn't surprised. It was the way it was. They both explained that my natural ability was a good thing; I didn't think anything about it. It was just me. I have worked with it. Dr. Wenz helped me to channel it. It's a real help in my job. It's probably why I chose police work."

"Wow, I can see that skinny little boy. Mama read me too didn't she?"

"Yes, but she won't pry into your life. You keep yourself really closed off. She just knows that you are terrific because I say so."

"It must have been wonderful growing up at Magpies. You are in such a large family and every ones so close."

"Sweetheart, you are family too, with or without me you get everyone. Just because you have a little talent, that's no a reason to kick you out of the nest."

"You do know that I can go home and think about this in peace in quiet."

"Baby, I want this to be your home."

"Oh Jesse, that's not fair, I'm so blown away already."

"Just stay the night. No pressure."

"Jesse, I need to go home, I want to talk to my parents."

"Can I go? It's about time I met the parents."

"Not funny Jesse, It was Margaret's idea. I sort of promised her."

"I want to go CJ; I want to see where you grew up."

"Lets go upstairs, I need to be held."

"My sweet CJ, how do you make me so crazy? Come on, baby we both need some sleep.

Chapter 24

I woke up feeling calm and happy. I followed the aroma of coffee and found a pirate in the kitchen. I laughed at his raised eyebrow. This man could convince me to walk the plank. He handed me coffee and sat a plate of bacon and eggs in front of me. He sat across from me with his. Everything seemed so right. I had slept well wrapped in his arms, no dreams or nightmares. The sun through the window was warm. It looked to be a good day.

"What's on your agenda today? Anything I can help you with, I'm off for the week and at your command."

"This morning I have an appointment with a lady who's looking for her son. I am hoping to get caught up on paperwork and I need to go to Freddy's, I want to introduce Margaret to him. I'll make plans from there."

"Call me when you get some free time I'd like to meet for lunch or something."

We both avoided talking about the day before. I needed to think more then talk at the minute. Jesse must have sensed it, "I have some work to catch up on that I brought home."

"I'll call and let you know about lunch, but I better get going. I need to go over the files with Margaret."

I took my plate to the sink and started to clean up. "Leave it CJ; I need something to do today." He had come up behind me and was nuzzling my neck. "You have a good day."

When I got to the office Margaret was on the phone, she waved at me as I went to the office. She had the Jamison file on my desk, and several messages, I looked through them and read that Freddy and Vince had called. I put them aside and read what Margaret had found out. Bradley Jamison, 26, a computer nerd and works at developing computer games for Cyber-Games. His employer said one day he never showed up. Up until that time he hadn't known of any unusual absences. He was dedicated to his work. Really bright but not a social person, He did not have any close buddies. The boss called his house several times, no answer and put his check in the mail.

No tickets, no arrests or convictions, he was reported as a missing person by his mother. He had been missing for five weeks.

Margaret had checked out his address. He hadn't been home. He paid his rent on time. He was quiet, didn't have parties. His landlord said that he needed something soon. He never saw a girl friend around.

I looked at my watch; I had another 25 minutes before Ms. Jamison was due.

I picked up the file and went to the lobby just as Margaret put down the phone. "This file is excellent. I really like the forms you worked up, clear and precise. You think of everything." I leafed through each page amazed that I had found such a friend and co-worker.

"I forgot to ask you how you billed, cost and such so I left it blank; the contract form is pretty generic. I just changed it for our needs and added a letterhead."

"You are amazing, we'll tighten it up as we go along, but you make us look very professional. I would like to take you to Freddy's today. Maybe we'll have time after the appointment."

"Grady asked me to lunch, he's still babying his arm. Dr. Wentz put him on a weeks leave. He was going to call Jesse."

"Jesse mentioned lunch too. I told him I'd get back to him."

There was a knock on the door. Ms. Jamison had arrived. I opened it to greet my first walk in client.

Ms. Jamison was a small woman. She was lost in the floral print dress, and by the way she was clutching her purse she was very nervous.

"Ms. Jamison, It's very nice to meet you. I am CJ and you have spoken to Margaret on the phone. I led her to the office and asked Margaret to bring some coffee in for us.

Ms. Jamison sat down looking uncomfortable. I opened the conversation by telling her what had been done for her. She seemed encouraged that we had done something.

"Ms. Jamison, I have a form that we can fill out together to get all the information we can about your son."

Margaret came in with the coffee and some scones. She gave Ms. Jamison a cup and sat mine on the desk with the scones between us.

Margaret left to answer the phone. I waited until Ms. Jamison was comfortable and started to ask questions.

"Did you see him often?"

"He came over once a week for dinner. He's a good boy. He calls to check on me couple of times a week. I haven't seen or heard from him in five weeks." She swallowed a cry, determined to be strong.

"Tell me about him. What were his hobbies? His likes? Dislikes?"

"He was a quiet boy, studied all the time. He loved his job. He works with computers; they are so foreign to me. He bought me a computer and taught me how to E-mail. He was so happy when I finally took to it. I love that Google thing. He liked to tinker with computers, he did something with games. Imagine that a grown man getting paid for making games. There's not much he didn't like. He's a quiet boy, doesn't go out dancing, I have tried to get him to come to a couple of my doings, the Gardening Club, Historical Society, the Spring Fling Gala that we help sponsor. He was so shy."

"What can you tell me about his friends?"

"He had some in high school; he was in the chess club. I think there was a boy he studied with in collage, but after they graduated I didn't hear anything about him. He may have some friends at work, but he didn't mention anyone in particular. They hired a new guy and he was showing him the ropes."

"Did he have girlfriends? Is there anyone special that he might be seeing?"

"No, not that I know of, I'm sure he would have mentioned one that's why I drag him to my clubs, I want grandchildren."

We laughed and talked about his habits and his routine, she handed me a picture. He looked like a studious young man, uncomfortable in a tuxedo taken at a cousins' wedding.

I asked about unusual behavior and anything that might have seemed strange no matter how small. She couldn't think of anything except that hearing nothing for five weeks was not Bradley. She signed a statement allowing me to look into more personal records. I gave her a copy of the interview sheet. I asked her to go over it and add any thing to it that might come to mind no matter how insignificant.

I gave her our fee, the first visit was free. We requested a $500.00 retainer. I would bill her $100.00 a day and expenses, I would apply the retainer to the final bill.

She took a handful of money and counted out five hundred dollar bills. "That's a lot of money to carry around, you should be very careful."

"She laughed and said, "Do I look like I have any money?"

"Just the same you need to be careful."

"Find my son Ms. CJ. Find my boy."

We spoke of his work, anyone he might have mentioned, I asked if she had a key to his apartment and if it would be all right for me to check it out. By the end of the interview I had acquired quite a bit of information.

I gave her my card and told her we would keep her up to date. As I saw her to the door she asked that I call her Ellen, and thanked us I for our help. I told her to call about anything she might remember or think of. I told her she could E-mail anytime for any reason, Margaret was my associate and we both would be working for her.

I gave Margaret the file and we went over how we would divide the work, I gave her the money and she said that she would start a separate retainer account. I sat at my desk writing my impressions, coming up with avenues we could check out.

I would start on the footwork in the morning and Margaret was already making the computer sing.

I came out of my office as Margaret finished typing out the notes from the interview. "Let's take a break; I want to introduce you to Freddy."

We left and headed to Freddy's. He was in the back working on a ledger book. He looked up and saw us and came around the counter, "CJ! It's good to see you. I was hoping to thank your personally."

Freddy, this is Margaret, she my friend and business partner. He looked at Margaret with his eyebrows raised he took her hand. "It is very good to meet you Margaret. So business is going well?" I laughed and told him that business was good because Margaret took care of all the details.

"I have this envelope and a paper for you to sign. We agreed on double, yes? So I have one thousand dollars for you. I made a check, I thought it was safer then cash."

I took the envelope and signed off on the receipt, He asked about Jesse, and was glad to hear he was healing. After more small talk we left. We headed for the bank to make a deposit.

We both decided that we needed to have some iced tea and talk about our next move. We sat down just as Margaret's cell-phone rang.

"Hi ya handsome." I assumed it was Grady. I opened up my note book and found a clean page. I started listing what needed to be done first, regarding our missing Bradley.

Margaret held her phone as she asked if I would like have lunch with Grady and Jesse, they were both stomping at the bit with inactivity.

I motioned for her to give me the phone. "Hey Grady, you guys bored? Margaret and I would be happy to pick up a puzzle and bring it over."

Margaret laughed and just about spit up her tea. "How about you meet us and you can pick out one that you like. A teddy bear one caught my eye. We should be back at the office in about thirty minutes."

I handed the phone to Margaret. She started to laugh and hung up.
"He said he didn't want a sissy teddy bear puzzle."

"Margaret, you know how we talked about visiting my parents? I need to go. When I mentioned it to Jesse, he wanted to go. I don't know if that would be the right thing. He came off as wanting to meet the parent's thing. This is a fishing thing."

"It might be nice to show off your new boyfriend. You might run it by the boys at lunch and get their take on it. We can always drop them at a bar and give them some pool money if you don't want to bring them to the door."

"Margaret, you are so wise." We left the cafe and headed for the office. Grady and Jesse were leaning against the car waiting patiently when we arrived. Jesse's eye patch would come off very nicely at my parents.

We walked over to Grady's car. Grady opened Margaret's door. He was such a gent. Jesse leaned into my face and gave me a kiss. He opened the door and asked if we had any ideas as where we might go to lunch.

Margaret looked at me and asked "What do you think CJ, What are you hungry for?"

Off the cuff I said "I know a place just outside of town that serves a mean burger. That's all they make with French Fries, onion rings and hot apple pie."

We climbed into Grady's car. As we headed for the highway the conversation flowed around our new client and how sweet Freddy was. We were on the outskirts of my home town when I pointed out a hole in the wall building with a neon light over the entrance stating that it was *JAKES PLACE*, one of the few places I enjoyed growing up

"About time, a guy could starve to death." Grady growled as he pulled into the parking lot.

We walked in and as our eyes adjusted to the dark, a voice came from the back. "CJ! Son of a gun, where have you been hiding?"

"I moved to the city Jake, I told you about it."

"You mean you really did get into detecting?"

"You betcha, I pulled out a stack of cards and gave them to him. Can you post a couple of these?"

"Sure, are ya any good?"

"Is she good? She's the best. She's got the brains." Margaret said as her finger thumped at his chest.

He looked down at her finger and said "I know she's got brains, but I never saw her detect before."

I laughed. "Jake these are my friends. Grady and Margaret and this is Jesse. Friends, this is my good friend Jake. I told these guys that you made the best burgers around."

"Well CJ your friends are my friends, find a place to sit and I'll be over in a minute. We sat in a booth. The menu was on the table. Billy's fare was simple and to the point. We ordered burgers, soft drinks and an extra order of French fries. Billy asked about the eye patch, Jesse told him he got it in the line of duty. Billy was surprised that they were detectives. Grady told him Margaret was my Office Manager and I corrected him by stating she was a Partner in the Firm of CJ and Associate Private Investigators. Margaret beamed.

We ate and laughed. We were sitting back and enjoying each other with interjections from Billy whenever he passed our table.

Jesse spoke up. "Well ladies, when are you going to let us in on the game plan?"

Margaret looked up, as I answered. "Well there is no game plan. We thought we might run it by you and then make a decision.

I want to visit my parents. Margaret is going with me, it was her idea. Jesse mentioned that he wanted to go, but not for the same reason. Grady, you're the driver in case we have to make a quick getaway."

"I want to ask them some very direct questions. I know they won't talk about it if there are a lot of people around. It might be easer if I spoke to them away from each other. It's on the table. You have any suggestions?"

Margaret said that she could help separate them. "Maybe talk gardening?"

"I have some stuff in the barn, I could get dad to go with me."

"I can be helpful" offered Jesse; "I can tell if they are hiding something. Maybe help find the right questions?"

"I want to see your barn, I want to see the structure, is it a real barn?" *Grady was excited about a building?*

Margaret looked at him. "We'll try to work that in Grady. I think CJ's point is not to swarm her parents. It's a pretty delicate situation."

Then she focused on Jesse. "You walk up to the door looking like Captain Bligh is not a soothing kind of sight . . . . Let me see that eye; is it still looking really black and blue and red?" She looked under the patch. "Keep the patch on. I think you should drop us off. We will have time to get some information, and clue them in on the Hulk here and Dead Eye Dick. We will explain that you are detectives and really good guys before they meet you."

Everyone looked at Margaret. "You are really brilliant, sounds good to me. You guys find something to do and we will call you to come and get us."

Margaret piped up and said "Hey, I might have some quarters if you want to play pool."

I laughed as Jesse and Grady scoped out the tables in the back of the room.

I could see that Jesse wasn't entirely happy but he knew it was a good plan. "I want to meet your folks, try to work that in will you?"

Jake stopped by the table and said that he saw my dad at the hardware store. "Tell him hello when you see him."

"We're going over there now. The guys here will be coming back. Hope you have a few quarters."

"Which way?" asked Grady.

"Go up about a quarter mile, Turn right and go about two miles. Can't miss it, it's an old red brick farm house."

"Sounds spooky CJ, is it haunted?"

"It's not haunted, the ivy needs to be cut and maybe some paint on the shutters. It's just a big ole house; most of it's closed off. I loved to explore it as a kid."

"You sure you don't want us to come with you?"

"Not yet Jesse, we'll call you."

Chapter 25

Grady drove us to the house, Margaret and I went around to the side door and walked in. "Mom, Dad? You home! It's CJ; hope I caught you at a good time!"

Mom almost came running to meet us. "CJ, is that really you? What a nice surprise. I didn't expect you. I'm so glad you're here. Come in, Come in . . ." She yelled into the yard. "JACOB! JACOB! Come in here right away!"

I was surprised at my mom's exuberance. She was always so calm and serene. What had gotten into her?

"Sorry I didn't call first. I was in the area with some friends and thought I would stop in. Do you still have some of my old stuff in the barn? I started an office and there may be some things that I could use. Oh! Mom, this is Margaret she's my partner. Margret held her hand out to shake moms hand she seemed shy in returning it.

"I'm so glad you came, and your friend too!" Mom gave me a quick, almost shy hug. I hoped that I didn't show my surprise, I only could remember a handful of times that I was truly hugged by mom and I was very young.

Everyone looked up when a small white haired man entered the hallway, "CJ How's my girl! It's been quiet around here since you left. And you brought a friend!"

"This is Margaret dad; she's my very good friend and partner."

"It's nice to meet you, sir."

"Call me Jacob."

"Dad do you still have my junk in the barn? I was going to see if there was something I could use for my office."

"You know I don't throw away anything. Would you like to look now?"

"That would be great; do you want to go come along Margaret?"

"No you two go ahead; I am not wearing the right shoes. Do you mind if stay here with you Mrs. Mason? I love these old country farmhouses. It's really a lovely home you have here."

This had worked out better then I thought. I followed dad to the barn, noticing how the garden was half the size. We still had a gaggle of geese, and cats everywhere. As we walked to the barn we talked about the changes that had been made. Not many, but I could see that paint was needed here and there. I looked at dad and noticed that he seemed a little worn around the edges; the years were beginning to take their toll. I felt bad for the years that I had spent away. I promised myself that I would call and visit more often. He could really use my help.

"The horse is in the pasture, you better say hello. She pined for you a long while after you left. I talk to her, but it's not the same."

We had come to a locked room and there were boxes and baskets and items I hadn't seen for years. My bicycle was hanging from a rafter and there were odd pieces of furniture. "Dad, you do save everything?"

We walked around the room looking at my past. This was harder then I thought it would be.

I was stalling, trying to find the right opening when I saw my horse leaning over at the fence.

I felt brighter, "Dad, she's still beautiful!" I called to her as I walked to the corral. "Hey Princess, how's my girl?"

I was wishing I had brought an apple or carrot with me. Dad held out his hand and it was full of sugar cubes.

"Hey, girl, you better give her these, she might ignore you out of spite." I laughed as I took the cubes and sprinted to the fence. Dad was following at his own pace. I missed that smile on his face, he missed me. I was happy, at this minute I felt like I was 12 again.

Dad followed me to the fence and watched as I petted and purred at Princes. Princess took her treats and made little throaty sounds of thanks.

We were both leaning on the fence, a horse head between us. I was trying to open the conversation when Dad said, "CJ, you came here for more then a visit. I have been waiting and I knew that one day you would come for answers."

"So tell me dad. Tell me what's wrong with me."

"There is nothing wrong with you; you just march to the beat of a different drummer."

"Dad, I missed the whole band, I'm out here floundering."

Dad looked over the fields. He seemed to be gathering his thoughts." I always knew this day would come. I tried to talk to you several times. Were you to young? What did I really have to tell you? Every time I started to talk I would loose my train of thought, or get distracted."

"Just say it dad, I've been going through this *period of adjustment* and I have whole pieces missing. I know there's more to it, and it's so over the wall, believe me, I am ready to believe anything."

"It's not that easy. You were an answer to our prayers. An old friend, an army buddy came to us one evening, He had you in his arms. You were a precious little bundle. He told us that his wife had died giving birth. He couldn't take care of his baby. He was a big strong man and I could tell that what he was asking was the hardest thing he ever did."

"He was in special ops and had to disappear. He had such love and pain in his eyes. Even then you seemed beyond your years. I'll give you all the information on your dad that I have. I didn't know your mother, but he was an honorable man. He was a man of principal."

"Tell me about him."

Dad leaned against the fence his leg up on the railing. "He came to me because I knew things about him. He had special traits that had nothing to do with his career. He knew he could trust me. He asked that I protect you. CJ, you have always been my girl. Watching you grow has been my biggest joy. We knew you were special. We didn't know how special. I'm afraid we didn't handle it well. We tried to be good parents."

"I tried to tell you one day. You were about nine or so. I couldn't find the words. I was tongue tied. Your mom said we shouldn't that it was not the right time. She said that mother's knew these things."

"Dad, you did know that mom had a hard time with me. Sometimes she was relieved that she didn't have to be in the same room with me. That's why then, I wasn't hers? Was she ashamed of me? I wasn't the little girl she wanted?"

"Honey, your mother had . . . problems, after so many miscarriages she was overwhelmed by this little girl who would cry and sometimes kind of shimmer. I tried to talk but the words wouldn't come. She didn't understand it, and I couldn't explain it. She had never seen what your father was capable of and I couldn't tell her. She was always afraid that someday he would come to claim you. But she always loved you. In the years you've been gone we have talked of it a lot. She has missed you so much."

"I couldn't help, your father said that safeguards had been put on you and you would be safe. We took it that you might be in danger. The way he showed up late at night, and left as soon as he came. We didn't know what kind of danger. When you faded, we tried to hide you from danger. It was more instinct then any clear thought. It was a confusing time. But we loved you."

You got really good at hiding, and we got good at letting you. Your mother loves you; she just couldn't understand. We couldn't understand. Every time it happened she would pretend that it didn't. I had hoped that your dad or someone who knew what was happening would come by and help us. It didn't happen. We loved you. I can't imagine how hard it must have been for you. I'm sorry that we failed you."

"Dad, you didn't fail me. I know that I have a lot of questions to ask you. But I need to know if there is any way I can get hold of your friend, its hard to imagine anyone but you being my father. I have questions only he can answer. But know this, he's not my dad, you are."

We walked hand in hand back to the house. It was funny how the deception did not really hurt. I felt honored that I grew up in this beautiful field.

When we got back to the house, Margaret had my mom in stitches, she had a glass of iced tea in front of her, and she was going on with story about Grady. I remembered the story and it was pretty racy. Mom was laughing so hard she was holding her sides.

Mom saw us come in and gestured to us to join them. She got up and filled some glasses. "Margaret is such a delightful young woman. CJ I'm so glad you brought her here. She said that you left your young men up at Jake's. Why don't you call them and ask them if they want to stay for dinner. Jacob, Margaret said that her young man likes old buildings you should show him around. Maybe he can give you some advice about that corner stall."

I have never seen my mother so animated, what did Margaret put in her tea?

Margaret winked at me across the table. "Marta said that we could use the credenza at the office. It would look really good under the Sherlock's"

It took me a minute to connect Marta to mom. "It would look nice, but mom don't you use it?"

"Not for twenty or so years all I do is dust and polish it. I would like to bring my sewing machine down from upstairs and put it there instead. The stairs are getting bothersome and it is more convenient. The lights better too."

If I had been standing, I would have fallen on the floor.

Mom looked at me. "CJ, tell me about your young man. Margaret says that he's a hero and a real gentleman."

I looked at Margaret she was on the phone letting Jesse and Grady know that the coast was clear.

Mom had started things happening around the kitchen. Taking out pans and potatoes she bustled around the kitchen giving orders to dad to *skin some corn*

She asked me to go to the pantry and get an onion and garlic.

By the time I came back up the boys had pulled into the driveway. Dad met them and was shaking hands and introducing himself before he led them into the house.

They stood in the kitchen and the room defiantly shrunk. Margaret introduced Grady and Jesse to Mom. She shook Jesse's hand and said that she was sorry he was hurt. It was a shame to cover up even one of his pretty eyes.

My mom was flirting? Hell was defiantly freezing over.

Dad asked Grady if he wanted to see the barn, "CJ said that you were interested in old buildings. This one is defiantly old. We should go before we loose the light. There were some things CJ wants to take back with her." Jesse volunteered to go along.

The three of us discussed what else would be good for dinner. Mom had me get out the good silver and set the dining room table. I felt I should go dress for dinner. She was taking out all the stops.

"CJ, is your Jesse serious?"

Margaret answered. "Marta, this man has had stars in his eyes, since the day he met her. They are really good for each other especially since they work together on occasion. Why, when Jesse was laid up, he didn't want anyone but CJ helping him."

Mom's eye brows went up as she caught the possible meaning of *helping* and *laid* up. I could see her relax just before she said "He just better treat you well."

I could not remember a time that Mom had ever been this comfortable around me. Maybe it was Margaret's continual banter of questions and observations that kept everyone busy talking.

The guys came in the kitchen; Grady was animated about the *space* in the barn. He and Jesse offered to come back and fix the corner of the stable. Jesse commented on Grady's skills, how talented he was and told dad about the great job he did on his patio and the plans they were discussing about remodeling his house.

I was caught in a time loop. This house that had never felt like a home was now comfortable. The furniture, even the wall paper was the same. Everything was in the same place, nothing much had changed. It was the people, it was this group of friends that came in and made it a lively place.

It had been almost six years since I had left home. Classes and starting a business had kept me busy. The few times I did return had been tense. Was I the one that caused the unhappiness? The few phone calls I made had been stinted.

Dad had always tried to be understanding, keeping the balance between mother and daughter. As I watched my mom I was surprised by her. What had happened to make such a transformation?

Margaret came over and startled me out of my thoughts. She put her arm around me "CJ, your folks are very nice. This house is a real trip. Your mom said you'd give me the grand tour after dinner."

I shook off the past and smiled "I'd love too, should we see go check on the boys?"

Talk around the kitchen was animated. Jesse was talking to mom as she dished up some green beans to take it into the dining room. Grady was sitting with dad at the formica table in the kitchen, talking about what would be needed for the stable and sketching it on a piece of paper. Margaret had grabbed a bowl of potatoes to place on the dining table.

Mom turned to me and said "CJ, I'm so glad your here, I have had this ham and it was way too much for just the two of us." Jesse passed me with the beans and mom handed me a gravy boat.

I met up with Jesse in the dining room; it had never felt so cozy in here. Jesse put the bowl down and as soon as I placed mine on the table he grabbed me around the waist and hugged me to him. "CJ, thanks for letting us come." He kissed my neck, and hobbled back to the kitchen.

We were seated at the table and everyone was in high spirits when Dad spoke up "Jesse what are your intentions regarding my daughter?" The silence was deafening. Grady looked at Margaret and stifled a smile. Jesse looked at me, and then back to Dad.

"Well Sir, CJ is the most intriguing woman I have ever met. I would like a minute to speak to you before we leave."

Mom looked at Jesse like she might be appraising him for an auction. Margaret and Grady were looking at me. I could feel a blush flow up my body. We were all waiting for dad to respond. "I'll be here, Mr. Grady, can you pass me those potatoes?"

The rest of the meal went well we talked about how Jake's son mowed the yard and helped out with chores on the weekends, the same chores that used to be mine. I looked at my parents and they looked so much older. I left home without looking back. I thought that leaving would make their lives easier. The few phone calls, usually around the holidays were not happy ones. I mailed presents. So what had I missed in my past that I was sitting in an atmosphere that I never would have imagined?

I was brought back to the real world when Margaret asked if that would be a problem.

"What? Problem?"

"I was just telling your folks that we could come with Grady and work on the ivy. This house is amazing and I would love to see it without the jungle in front."

"That would be great. Count me in."

"That's settled." Mom was smiling, "I will expect you for the weekend."

We finished with homemade pie, made with cherries from our orchard. The local gossip had everyone laughing.

We finished the dishes and I was standing on the back porch watching as Princess made her way to the barn. Mom came up and asked if I'd like to sit with her for a minute in the Gazebo. She handed me a glass of iced tea and I followed her out to porch swing. The fireflies were blinking on and off. The moon lit up the yard. We were both stalling neither of us knowing how to begin.

Mom cleared her throat. "CJ, We, I have missed you. Your dad told me that you have questions. I wish we had answers so many times. You were so beautiful, always quiet, studious, and so unusual. After you left your dad and I would talk about how quiet the house was. I kept trying to think of what I could have done to make your life better."

"We wanted a child; you were sent from heaven, a special gift. Your dad and I had given up on having children. One night you were brought to us."

"You father, he was a big man, very imposing and strong. It was very hard for him to leave you. He wouldn't let you out of his arms until he had to go. He trusted us with you. When he said you were special I wasn't really listening. I was looking at your sleeping face and watching as he looked at you. He had so much love and sadness in his eyes. After he left it was as if he had never been here. You were our child."

"Early on I noticed that you had a way of shimmering when you were upset. There was no way to explain it. It scared me. I almost dropped you the first time it happened. I thought for a long time that I must be crazy. I kept away from people just in case it happened in front of them. I just had the bare bones truth and no instructions."

"I missed you so much and you were gone for so long. I couldn't say when I started badgering your poor dad about you. He couldn't tell me much, just what we were told when you arrived."

"You were a serious girl. You kept to yourself. You were happier in the barn or with your animals. You turned into a beautiful woman CJ. I wish I could have done more for you."

I could feel the pain that came with her words. As she spoke the emotions churning in me were coming to a front, I thought of how I avoided her, how I didn't want to make her feel bad.

"Mom, I'm sorry too. I didn't know, I didn't think. I never knew what to say. I would see sadness in your face and knew I put it there. I am so sorry."

"No need for that. We are what we are. I know that I missed my girl. And she is here now, my girl has come home."

We both had tears in our eyes. Each of us understood a little bit of the pain we had caused the other and could now put it behind us. We were holding each other and crying when mom pulled away. She reached into her apron pocket and handed me a small book. It looked like a diary.

"This was left by your Father. He didn't say anything about it. It was left on the table by the chair he was sitting in when he brought you to us. We didn't notice it until he had left. I didn't think about it until one day I was looking for a table cloth. It was in the drawer and it made me think of you. It was about that time that I started trying to find answers. Your poor dad, we didn't have a reason but since I found that book it seemed important. I'm glad you showed up. I was going to use it for an excuse to call you."

I opened the book and saw a lock of hair taped to the inside cover. It was written in a language that I couldn't read. The beginning was written in a woman's hand. As I leafed through it I saw that the writing had changed toward the end into a bolder more male script.

"Is this his writing? It is his, I can feel it."

"I hadn't thought about it in years. When I came across it a few weeks ago, I kept thinking I should get it to you. Your dad and I have been talking a lot lately. I honestly didn't remember it. I saw it for just a second that night. I didn't feel safe until I took you up to the nursery. I never gave up hope that your crib would be filled. I sat in a rocker and sang to you until your dad came in and helped me tuck you in. I do love you CJ."

"Mama, thank you. I ran my hand over the cover. Thank you for sharing our first night together. You don't know what it means to me. I promise to never let fear or anger come between us again. You and dad, you have always been and will always be my parents. I do love you, I'm sorry."

"We'll be fine. You are my daughter and I love you. Now tell me about your young man. Is that eye-patch part of the package?"

I laughed, "He's wonderful Mom and he has to wear it for a while longer. He was pretty banged up and I helped him when he couldn't fend for himself. I had help from Grady and some of Jesse's other friends. But he is special."

"I can see how you look at each other. You are happy, the happiest I have ever seen you."

We heard the back door close and watched as Dad and Jesse walked over to join us.

"Your friends are getting ready to leave. I'm looking forward to seeing you Saturday. We'll have more time to talk then. Are you two okay?"

"Yes we are Dad. I have had a wonderful day and I am so glad that we came."

Jesse held out his hand to help me up.

Dad cleared his throat, "Your young man has asked for your hand in marriage, are you in agreement?"

Mom put both of her hands to her heart; tears welled up in her eyes. I looked at Dad and then at Jesse. "Not until he gets rid of that patch."

We all laughed and walked back to the house.

We drove back into the city, my heart lighter then I have ever known it to be. I felt as if a great weight had been lifted. There were reasons even if they were unexplainable. Truth was indeed stranger then fiction.

On the way home I hugged the diary to my heart. Grady and Margaret were excited about the house and barn. All present were city slickers and they were amazed that I grew up on a farm. "Not so much a farm, more orchard and stables."

"I saw some chickens" said Grady, Margaret piped in with "Your mom said you had cows."

I laughed. "Two cows, Daisy and Elmer. Margaret, thank you for encouraging me there is so much that we never talked about. And you guys, I'll never be able to tell you how much this means to me."

"Oh, Gosh," said Grady, "twernt nothing."

I listened to them ramble on the way home. Some of the insights were right on.

Jesse was impressed with their need to know about my business. "Your moms afraid that it's dangerous, I told her you were working on a missing person. Imagine if I told her how you walked on BA's neck?"

Margaret looked at me and thanked me for taking her with me "They are good people; I can see how not understanding could cost all of you so much, you childhood had to be a nightmare at times. This gift, freaking out your parents and you trying to figuring it out step by step, day by day, how to live with it."

"Margaret, we didn't really think about it. We just did it."

"Still, I like who you are. They had a lot to do with that. Are you sure you're not an alien?"

"CJ, my heart, you are the strongest women I have ever met." Jesse hugged me to him, I was glad that it was dark and no one could see me blush. I kept my head on his shoulder and was lulled to sleep by the motion of the tires and the lull of voices.

Chapter 26

I woke in the middle of the night. Jesse was sleeping like a baby with a smile and a sweet little snore. I got out of bed, picked up the diary from the night table. I washed my face and brushed my teeth and went down stairs to make some tea. I took my cup and the diary into the living room. Snuggling under an afghan I opened the diary. The hair taped to the inside cover was soft and a bit darker then mine. I touched it as I leaned back and tried to *feel* its origin. It felt warm. I held the book to my chest, closing my eyes and it felt intimate. I didn't want to put it down. A warm blue color filled my head, a deep sea green interweaving, warm colors, close colors. I forced myself to stop and opened to the first page. I put my hand over the words. It was in a language I had never seen. I rested my hand lightly on the page and again felt colors, warm blues and soothing greens intermingling, combining and flitting around each other. The intensity rising as I let my head fall back my tea forgotten, feeling the joining of colors. I felt a part of it, lost in it, wrapped in it. I was enveloped in the feeling of comfort, warmth and love.

I woke with Jesse beside me, his touch adding colors of deep crimson, first wafting around the colors in my mind and then joining the maelstrom of textures. I felt passion, I felt him kiss my eyelids, I heard his voice. "Morning sweetheart," as he nuzzled my neck, the colors brightened and then flamed. When his mouth touched mine I raised my hands to touch his face. My world started spiraling and the colors intensified. Blending and dancing as my heart beat quickened.

Jesse felt the colors with me. Startled he pulled away with a look of disbelief. "Did you feel that? Did you see what I saw?"

"Jesse. You felt it too, you were crimson."

"Baby it was beautiful. Where did you get this book? I saw it in the car so I guessed it was yours. It looks like a diary. I didn't know that you kept one."

"This was left at mom and dads when my father gave me to them. My mom found it not long ago and gave it to me last night. I can't read it, but I can feel colors from it, glorious, wonderful, vibrant colors. You saw them? Could you feel them?"

"I felt something from you, a charge of emotion, it's hard to explain. You wouldn't let it go last night. Grady carried you up to the bed and you still wouldn't let go of it. I put it on the nightstand before I came to bed. This is some book CJ."

"It's a wonderful book." I held it for Jesse to take. He hesitated just a moment and then opened it to the first page. He saw the hair clipping, and studied the words on the page. "I have no idea what language this is."

"Put your hand over the words Jesse." He followed my suggestion, "close your eyes and open your mind." He laid his head back and waited.

"Give me your hand honey." I placed my hand on his and we both felt the color. We stayed on the page together. It was other-worldly. He raised his head and shook it. "CJ, this is one powerful book. We need to let Dr; Wenz look at this he might know someone who can read the language. Or least tell us what language it is."

"Jesse, it's mine I don't want to let it go of it yet. I feel that this is private, it was left for me. I know you're right and if someone can translate what it says I will know so much more. But right now, I feel that I need to keep it to myself."

We leafed through the book together, the flowing penmanship of a woman, then halfway through the bold deep writing of someone who wrote fast and hard.

Jesse put his hand over the man's writing. His eyes opened wide as he gasped. I put my hands over his and leaned my forehead to his we were wrapped emotions that were urgent and sensual.

We both pulled back. "Whoa, CJ, I would really like to know what this says."

"So do I, hold it by yourself, what does it feel like."

Jesse took the book and held it between his palms; turned it in his hands and opened it randomly to a page with feminine writing.

"I feel some emotion but not as strongly as when I held it with you. That was vivid, intense." He turned the pages to the more masculine writing. "This seems to be added after the original text, written in a hurry, I think by your father. I feel it more strongly. I'm sure the woman's writing may have been your mothers."

"He didn't stay very long, just long enough to drop me off and leave. Dad said there wasn't time for any explanations. No one noticed it until after he left and it was forgotten until recently."

"I think we should get this to Wenz. He might know someone who can decipher it."

"What if he doesn't?"

"I don't think it would have been left if that was the case. I think there are things that were written for you to understand. It was left for you. You seem to *feel* the pages."

"What good does that do if I can't understand the language?"

"That brings us back to Wenz. Why don't you keep it with you today and see if up can fathom anything. There has to be a key."

"We can copy a few pages."

"I have a copier upstairs; I can take some pages over to Doc this morning." Jesse pulled me up "We'll take a couple of sample pages of each type of handwriting."

As I followed him upstairs his foot seemed to be a bit sturdier, he had a solid grip on the banister as he pulled himself up. My days of nursing were drawing to a close.

We copied two pages of each type of handwriting and I went to the office as Jesse made arrangements with Grady to see the Doctor together since they both had the week off.

Margaret was as excited as I was. We poured over the book and experimented with it. She didn't get the intense feelings from it that Jess and I had when we held it between us. Her eyes got wide at what she could feel. "This is something. Kinda freaky CJ, It makes sense that its might be your mothers. I wonder what she wrote."

"I wish I knew, Jesse should have some idea soon if Doctor Wenz can recognize the language, or he knows someone that can."

"CJ, this is pretty mysterious. Why do you think it was hidden?"

"I don't know that it was. It was more like it was forgotten. I'm sure my dad would have said something. I don't think I was supposed to see this, not until I was ready to."

"That sounds more spooky then freaky" Margaret stood up and was rubbing her arms.

The phone rang as we were lost in our own thoughts; the ringing startled me back to the present. Margaret picked up the phone and I could tell that it was Grady. I got up to walk to the office and give her some space when the door opened and Jesse and Bass walked in.

"Hey babe, Can you take a ride with me this afternoon?"

Margaret had hung up the phone interloping on Jesse as he finished his question. "CJ, I need to take the day off, Grady just invited me on a road trip."

I looked from one to the other wondering what was *really* going on. "Just where is this road trip leading to? Is there any particular destination?"

Jesse was bursting with excitement. Margaret seemed as perplexed as I was.

Reaching for her purse she was ready for what ever was about to happen. I threw my hands in the air and said "Okay guys, you can explain on the way."

We were deciding who would ride with whom. When Bass said that we should go with Grady he would pick up Annie and meet us. Margaret and I were standing on the curb wondering what was going on when Grady pulled up and opened the door for Margaret. Jesse ushered me toward the car. Bass took off to pick up Annie.

"Okay fella's start talking. I have things to do and if this is just another runaway I have a client I'm working on."

"This won't take long." Jesse explained. "We showed Doc Wentz the copies and he was really excited. He called a friend of his at the University, a Professor Dunn; he's an expert on ancient writings and cultures. When the good Doctor described some of the writing he was told to bring it over. Apparently this is really something and he's anxious to look at it. I told them that you had to be there for any meeting."

"You think he can help?"

"Sure would be nice. CJ, if it helps you we have to explore it. Did you happen to bring the diary?"

"Yes, but I'm not giving it up. More then anything I know that it needs to stay with me."

Jesse hugged me. "That's a given, but I've been thinking. You know the wards that you might have? I think some were placed on your folks. Its not that they didn't want to tell you, they couldn't."

"Why now Jesse", I asked, "Why after all these years?"

"I can't tell you that honey. Maybe the book will help. One step at a time babe."

Margaret and Grady were keeping their own conversation in the front seat. "How did Bass join the party today?"

"He took a personal day. He's got a gazillion of them. He was bummed that Grady and I had the week off so he decided to stop and smell the roses. We were going to kidnap you two and go to Magpies for lunch so that he could ogle Annie while she worked.

"Doc got so excited when we dropped off the pages that we all decided to make a day of it."

"You'll have to talk to CJ about making a day of it, but I can't wait to see if anyone can shed some light on that diary."

"Pull up to that building Grady, his office is on the second floor." We were helping Jesse out of the car when Bass pulled up with Annie. We waited for him to park and went into the building.

Dr. Wentz greeted us at the elevator. "You boys run all the red lights?" He glanced at Bass and Annie and said they might have to get a bigger room.

Professor Dunn was ready for us. He seemed very excited about this discovery and couldn't wait to meet me. I felt uncomfortable and a bit shy when he took both of my hands in his and thanked me for the opportunity to see the papers Dr Wenz had shown him.

"You can read them? Understand what they say?" I was so excited that my mouth took off. "What do they say? Was it my mother and fathers writing?"

"I have seen four pages and no, I cannot read them, however I have copies of a similar language. I need to know more to translate them. I am having them faxed to a friend and we should have an answer shortly."

He must have seen the disappointment in my face. I heard Grady ask him about wards and Professor Dunn say there were many kinds. The banter was around me but I didn't feel part of it.

I was disappointed. I was ready to have someone tell me what was written, not *maybe* find a key that *might help* them. I was feeling disappointed and sad when I felt a sudden urge and a full-blown tingling.

I looked around me and I began to focus on the hundreds, thousands of books and papers that were crowded in Professor Dunn's office. They were stacked in piles and on chairs. Some were dog-eared and marked with post-it notes, or a book marking a place in another book.

I felt my feet walk toward an unsteady pile of books and papers in a corner. My hand reached out to brush the stack of books slowly from top to bottom. I felt my fingers pull a slim book black with gilt edging out of a stack. It seemed to be very old. It felt old and valuable. It shouldn't be in such a lost and lonely place. It should sit proudly on a shelf, behind glass with locks and bolts. I picked up the book and felt the golden edges of the pages. I held it close. I was alone with the book in a roomful of people. I heard Jesse's voice. It seemed so far away.

"CJ? Hey CJ!" I heard him call me. I felt him hold me. "Baby, what's happening? Talk to me CJ, Listen to me baby." He was holding me tight the book between us. I felt him blend with me. I suddenly became aware of the others around us staring at us in disbelief. I felt myself visible. I watched as Jesse as he wavered and became visible with me.

Margaret was the first to take action. She came up to us and held us both while asking if there was a place we could sit down. She delegated Grady to get some water and then followed the professor to a conference room down the hall. The Professor allowed all the friends to sit close together while he took a seat at the end of the large oval table.

When everyone was seated Dr. Wenz checked us out, shining a light in our eyes and then checking our pulses. He sat down next to us. Grady and Bass sat on either side of the table with Margaret and Annie. Professor Dunn spoke first. "What happened to you CJ, can you tell me?"

I looked up with no words. I had never been so careless. I never made a public display or *un-display*. The urge was to fast and the tingling was immediate. No warnings of danger, just an unstoppable need to follow my instincts, which happened to lead to a well buried book. I shook my head; I didn't know how to explain.

Jesse spoke up. "Whatever happened was really strange." He had his arm around my shoulders but I couldn't remember when he put it there. I just looked up, I was drained, scared and waiting for someone to scream out that I was a freak.

Dr. Wenz asked Jesse in a calm voice. "What happened to you Jesse?"

"I'm not really sure. I saw CJ walk across the room; she seemed to be vanishing with each step. I could see stacks of books through her. I had to get to her before she vanished completely. I needed to be with her. My whole being had to be with to her. When we touched, I felt what she was feeling, I felt the tingling she described and I could see so clearly. I wasn't scared; I wanted to be with her. I felt that she had something important to do. I just couldn't figure out what, I needed to keep her safe. This is really hard to put in words."

"You're doing just fine." Professor Dunn looked at me. "CJ, can I see the book you found?"

I didn't realize I still had the book. I was holding it close to my chest; I felt that it was very important to me. I didn't want to let it go.

I looked at it. The cover was dark black pliable leather, it was very old. It had a strange inscription on the front, fairly worn and hard to decipher but I knew the symbol. I had seen it before.

I looked at the professor and I knew that it was his, it was in his office. It was old and valuable and there was no way I would be allowed to walk out with it.

He held out his hand and I carefully handed it to him. He gently took it. He reverently ran his hands over the binding; turning it over in his big hands. It looked fragile. He opened the slim book and the pages were yellowed, the paper seemed fragile and transparent, the words looked similar to the words in my diary.

I slowly opened my backpack and took out my red diary. I held it close and then looked at the professor. "This was left for me. This will explain to me what I need to know. It is mine." I opened the pages, past the lock of hair. On the third page was a symbol matching the one on the black book.

"CJ, can I see your book? I promise to return it. This is where the copied pages came from isn't it?"

"Yes, Can you help me read it?"

"I don't know. I know that you do, somehow this book will let you know what it says, but I need to do more research. I wish I could keep your book until I find something out, but it will be safe with you."

"What about the black book. Will it help us figure out CJ's?" Jess was running his thumb up and down on my shoulder as he spoke. That small touch of affection spoke volumes to me

Grady turned in his seat to the professor, "What are you saying Professor, We have another link? What about *wards* and such. It's just a mental block right? How do we unblock her?"

"Good question. I would venture to say that the wards, as you put it, are breaking down. From what I understand, she has been aware of this ability since childhood, the fact that she has worked around it, incorporated it and used it to create a livelihood is remarkable. All of these things have added to the break down of the wards."

"Legend has it if there are protective wards put in place, a word or phrase can open the vault so to speak. Sometimes, especially on a child the wards will break with puberty, or be removed when the danger is past. We don't know of any danger. Puberty doesn't seem to be a factor, although it may have accelerated it. It may be that it was placed as temporary or perhaps hurriedly and maybe some phrase or part of the ward was not applied. That would account for the early manifestation of the ability. Mind you, this is conjecture. Has something happened in the recent past that would allow this ability to grow and expand?"

My mind was trying to grasp what was being said. I looked at Jesse and I could see that he was trying to understand as well.

Margaret was the one to grasp the meaning. "CJ, maybe being in love broke the dam! You said that you always held yourself apart because you were always afraid people would find out and freak. But now you have us, you have Jesse. Now you're not alone it doesn't have to be a secret!"

"I'm still amazed," Professor Dunn was studying Jess as he spoke, "that Jesse was part of your manifestation. He faded with you. Has this ever happened before?"

We both shook our heads no. Jesse hesitated and pressed me closer to him as the professor continued. "I think that this is just the beginning. The good doctor told me that you struggled to stop it, and actually developed ways to slow it down. There is much more we need to know."

"I will investigate the language in the diary; I would like to copy each page. I'm going ask that you document each time something happens. Both books seem similar, but this one," he motioned to the black book "was written by a different author, and seems quite a bit older."

"Uh, Doctor, Professor," Jesse looked intense. "I would like to point out that whatever wards were put on CJ were put there for a reason. She might be in danger. The fact that she was placed in a *safe place* pretty much tells me that she still might be." Jesse was adamant, his grip on my shoulder tightened.

I looked at Jesse; he was in full cop mode. I looked at Grady and Bass and saw the same expression on their faces. "Until I know that she's safe, I want to keep all this under wraps. Use a different name on any correspondence that I am sure is going to be flying around. Once your investigation really starts someone's going to ask questions."

"That's a very good point. We need more information; do you know the names of your birth parents? Do you have any records or papers that we can backtrack with?"

This interview was going way to fast. Before I was just odd, now I might be in danger? I looked at Jesse and then Margaret. "I'll try; I will look through my papers. I'll check with my parents. Look, I need to get out of here. Can I have my book? Can I borrow the black one? I promise to get it back to you."

The professor looked at CJ; "Can you copy the pages in your diary for me? I will do the same with the black book. I didn't even know I had it here. I have never seen it before. I have a feeling it was put here for you to find, and I'd like to know by whom. The uncanny way that you located it would suggest that *it* found you."

I took my book from his hand; I put it in my backpack as I walked to the door. "I'm glad I met you, but now I am freaking out and I really need to get out of here." Jesse was at the door opening it and calling over his shoulder that we would get back to them.

Grady's chair squealed on the floor as he rose. "Sorry Doc, I'm the driver, Ready Margaret?" Bass and Annie flanked them.

Chapter 27

The ride back to the office was a quiet one. Everyone seemed to be deep in thought. Jesse held me close and by the time we got back to my office I mumbled that I needed to be alone. It turned out that I did nothing. I wrote no notes; I didn't even make one of my copious lists. I did nothing, I went to my bedroom stripped down and climbed into my small bed. I slept.

I woke to the smell of coffee. After washing my face and brushing my hair I walked in to the kitchen. I poured a cup coffee and walked into the lobby. Margaret was typing, she looked up and smiled and said she had put the Jamison file on my desk. She went back to her typing. I wandered into my office sat down and began going over the file. I read and re-read the file in front of me, nothing was making sense. I looked at the clock and decided that the day was over. I thought to go to Bradley's work and interview his boss and co-workers. Margaret had added a profile for Cyber-Games; it was too late now.

Margaret came to my doorway, "Hey CJ, Annie just called and wants to know if we can come out and play. Seems like the guys are having a card party and we are on our own."

"Is that right? Did she have any suggestions?"

"Not really, just said no dives."

"Do you have any suggestions?"

"Not yet, but we'll come up with something, so it's a go?"

"Yeah, call her back, as long as its casual I'm game."

We picked up Annie at *Magpies*, and decided to go to a bistro. None of us had eaten all day and we were ready for food.

"Slip In" seemed to be a nice place. It was new and crowded. We had come at the right time, Ladies Night and Happy Hour. Apparently this was the place to be, tables surrounded a small dance floor and a smaller stage. The crowd was lively and the band, a trio, was pretty good. We had ordered sandwiches and fries and a beer all around. The beat of the band was lively and I felt my spirits rise. Margaret and Annie were animated. It felt good to be out. It was good to be out with friends.

We laughed and danced and drank our beer. We didn't talk about work or that afternoon. We barraged Annie with questions about Jesse and Grady. She had an uncanny way of answering. Mimicking the guys as she talked, she was hysterical; she had each one down, gruff Grady, stoic Bass, and Jesse, with his slow quiet grin. We were hysterical with laughter.

Sometime during the evening we switched from beer to shots. Every shot came with a toast to the guys. When it came time for last call we were disappointed that the night had to end. Margaret seemed to be the only one sober enough to drive. On the way to the parking lot we decided that we would take ourselves over to the poker party and win all the guys' money.

The game was at Bass's. I had never been to his house; it was the same house he avoided growing up. It was left to him when his dad died. He gutted it and with the help of his friends rebuilt it into a nice home. Annie leaned on the bell while Margaret and I held the beer and snacks that we brought with us.

Bass opened the door and barely caught Annie as she stumbled into the house. Margaret and I followed and were met by two surprised men coming from a back room. Grady took one look at Margaret and said "You're all soused! What have you girls been up to?"

"We had a girl's night out." Annie stated as Jesse took the bags from me. Margaret had walked up to Grady and gave him her bag, pulled his head down and gave him a big sloppy kiss. "We had a grand time. We danced all night!"

We were led into the kitchen where the air was filled with cigar smoke, beer cans and cards.

I was surprised to see Dr Wenz sitting at the table starting a game of solitaire. I went and kissed him on the head surprising everyone. "What have you gotten me into you ole goat?" He looked at me stunned and then surprised when I fell into his lap and then to the floor.

"It's good to see you too; I can see that you girls have been having a good time."

Apparently we had broken up the card party. Annie and Margaret were standing by the sink giving Grady hard time. Bass was standing with his back to the counter his arms folded in front of him laughing as Jesse sat me in a chair.

Dr Wenz's face was red from my sloppy kiss and he got up to leave. "I don't think I can handle the activities of young people these days, you two," he said as he stared at Jesse and me "I need to see both of you in my office first thing . . . better make ten or so. I can let myself out, seems you fellows have your hands full."

"So guys, did we break up your game?" Margaret said as she leaned into Grady and patted his chest. "We came over to play poker."

Bass and Jesse started laughing, Grady joined in as he said that all the money had just left with Doc. He had won it all. At that moment, in my somewhat drunken haze, I realized that I was part of these people. They were my friends and I was feeling really good about everything.

Jesse and I woke up to the alarm ringing. I didn't remember the ride to Jesse's house, I didn't remember leaving Bass's. I didn't remember how I got into Jesse's bed but here I was and even through the sluggish brain cells I felt happy.

Jesse rolled over to face me, "Hey sunshine, time to rise." I opened one eye, rolled over and pulled up the sheet, "no, no, I need more sleep." Jesse kissed the back of my neck, nuzzling my ear he said "Baby, you were so cute last night, but we have to go see doc this morning."

I sat straight up, "Oh Jesse! . . . The doctor! . . . . I remember calling him names."

'That you did, an old goat, and he turned beet red when you kissed him."

"Oh Jesse, I can't go, I'm so embarrassed." It all came back, at least the part where I fell on the good doctor and called him an old goat. I sank back into the bed and covered my head again. "I can't go Jesse, I can't face that man."

Jesse snickered, and then started to laugh. "Are you kidding? I'll bet he enjoyed every minute. You have to face the music sometime."

"I have to go to work, I have things to do."

"We'll go as soon as we're through with the Doc. I doubt that Margaret is going to be on top of things this morning. Apparently the three of you had a real good time."

"Oh Jesse, can't I just sleep?"

"Yeah, later, Jump in the shower and I'll make some coffee, we'll grab some breakfast on the way."

My head was still fuzzy on the way to the Doctors. I was not ready to confront the good ole doctor that morning. Jesse explained that the main topic at the poker game was the two books.

"So you talked about me all night?" Recalling the way we poked fun at the guys the night before. I could imagine what they might have said about us.

Jesse had the grace to look a little sheepish. "It wasn't like that at all. Hey honey, I was worried about you."

"You could have waited until I was around." I was working up to angry.

"Sweetheart, you weren't around. You didn't want to think about it. We were at that meeting too. It wasn't planned, it just happened. And yes we talked about you."

"So what did you figure out?" I was still hot, but it was understandable. I spent the night not thinking about it, I guess that when they got together that would be the main topic.

"Doc still thinks it's connected with your name, he's convinced the answer is in the books. He wants to do a couple of tests on you. He was really amazed to see you disappear. I was too. It was a trippy feeling. It was like sharing the diary but without the colors. One seemed to be a maelstrom of color and the other was the total absence. But what I felt was intense in both, and the tingling was intense when I touched you. Or maybe I was just overcome with the lack of color and the texture with the book and the strange feelings. The urge to protect you was overwhelming. Is that what you feel when you have the need to follow a lead? It was like and overpowering need to move?"

I listened to what Jesse was saying, the tone of his voice, I watched his face as he spoke, searching for the words to explain what he felt and saw. He knew what I felt. He was the only person that had ever come close to understanding what my life was like.

"Jesse, you know, you actually know, and you're not running for the hills?" I could feel the tears start to rise. When did I turn into this weepy weak female?

"CJ, you know I'm amazed that you could keep this to yourself all these years. And we didn't talk about you as much as we talked about the fact that to keep this secret you had to have some help. Grady thinks that your mom and dad were protected too, that's why they couldn't explain anything or understand. Your birth father showed up one night with a baby, asked for their help and left. He couldn't have stayed long. He was in a hurry, maybe in trouble. He found a safe place for you and left making sure that your and your folks would be safe. I think that the diary wasn't forgotten, it was hidden until you were ready for it. Even Dunn said that he didn't know that the black book was in his office, but you found it. You went straight to it. It's all there we just have to figure out how all the pieces fit."

I listened while Jesse talked; I was checking it against my mental list, comparing it to what I had suspected and what I knew for a fact. Adding his theory's to mine and finding that in the past few days we had gathered a lot of information.

The fact that there were others who believed me, believed in me made everything so real. I was not a fluke of nature. There were others that had abilities. Did this mean that they had to hide theirs as mine was hidden? Why was everything such a big secret?

This last question I must out spoken out loud, Jesse looked at me and said "I don't know why it's a secret. You father went to a lot of trouble. I think that he meant to come back. I would like to talk to him myself."

We had arrived at the doc's office, Jesse and I went to the door hand in hand. We stopped at the door and Jesse looked into my eyes. "We'll figure this out. Someone somewhere will help us discover the truth."

"I don't know if I want to know the truth anymore Jesse, So much has happened in the past few weeks, The only thing that I ever wished for was to have friends that would understand and accept me."

"Oh Baby, you had me the first time I saw you."

"Let's get this over with."

We walked into the office just as the good doctor was ushering a small boy and his mother out of his office. "You take your medicine and try to stay out of old buildings. He'll be fine" he said to the mother, "call me if you need me." I noticed that he had a bandage on his arm. I thought of Jesse at that age with that same sad face.

As they left the doctor ushered us in. "It's good to see you two. I hope you're both feeling well."

I hoped he couldn't see an aura of alcohol that surrounded me.

"CJ, I would like to have some additional tests run on you. The routine tests came back and you are a very healthy woman."

"I want to talk about what happened to Jesse and yourself yesterday. It was quite interesting. You both seemed to disappear. Can you tell how this happened?"

"Not really, I call it dimming. It happens when something is about to happen. I get a tingling like my hands and feet have fallen asleep and are beginning to wake up . . . but stronger. I feel that I have to move, sometimes it gets intense. If I try not to follow it, it gets more urgent, I do what I am led to do. When the danger is past I fade back in. I have never had another person with me before. I'm as confused as you are that Jesse could do it too."

The doctor was listening as I struggled to explain, he turned to Jesse, "This has never happened to you before?"

"These past weeks, when CJ was at the house I thought I saw a shadow of her once or twice, I marked it down as very good drugs. I think I felt her, or more smelled her when Bass came to the house when I was set up. I know when she is near me."

Jesse stopped for a minute and looked at me. "CJ, remember the other night when we were together and you kind of freaked out because you were dimming, I got a slight feeling in my hands that night, but did you notice if it happened then? Did I fade with you?"

I looked from one to the other "I honestly don't know. I have always tried to avoid people when it happens; I was to upset waiting for you to run screaming out of the room that I really didn't notice."

Doctor Wenz looked at both of us, "Uh . . . the next time you two are together it might be something you want to jot down."

We both looked at him, a little shocked, his red face gave him away, he was looking toward the floor and I had to laugh. "This is all in the name of science, right doctor?" I could see the doctors blush deepen as Jesse snorted as he tried to stifle a laugh.

The doctor straightened himself up and harrumphed as he got back his composure, "Have you given any more though to hypnosis?"

"No I have not. But I will think about it. I would like Jesse with me *if*, and that's a big *if* I do. Oh, and Margaret too. She has an uncanny way understanding things."

"That she does. I would like to set some tests up for you; they will test your brain waves and see if there are any abnormalities that can be seen. It won't take long but I think it would be good to rule out anything unforeseen."

"Do you expect anything *unforeseen*?"

"It's just a precaution, or more like elimination. From what I have heard from you and your friends and what I have seen we know that your abilities are genuine. We know that you have coped, and learned to incorporate it into your life. I will venture to say there is more to your abilities than you have explored."

I looked at him and said "What if I don't want to know more? What if I am where I am at and that's good enough? I do want to know what the book says and I do want to know who my parents were but I don't know about this. It took a long time to get comfortable in this skin. I just found out that people can accept me, some people, but it's not like I want to add it to my letterhead. I feel that hiding it is the right thing to do."

"I think so to, but don't think of it as hiding it. Jesse has the ability to read people in unfathomable ways; he has developed it to a great degree. He has incorporated it into his life to the point where he uses it in every part of his life. It is just Jesse. You know him on the inside, you know it's true. The same will be for you. Just as Jesse may read a fact, he still has to find the fact. These abilities come with responsibilities. And you young lady are the type that also finds facts. If you don't do it now, sometime in the future you will have to follow that *urge*."

We had all known that it would come back to that. I had very little choice. Even now the diary was burning a hole in my jacket pocket. I found my hand on it as I made my decision. "I will do whatever is within reason."

"Good girl. I will make an appointment for next week. I will get back with you when everything is arraigned."

"I'm still not sure about the hypnosis thing. I can't see anyone prying in my head when I don't know what's in it."

Jesse laughed, "I'll be right there if you want."

"Maybe that's the point, maybe there's something in there that I might not want you to know about."

Jesse looked offended, "Well . . . there is Margaret."

"Yes there is, but before I do anything I need to think about it and I really need to get to work. Doc, Thank you. You seem to always bring up more questions then answers."

The doctor laughed, "As do you young lady."

We rose to leave when Jesse turned to the doctor and said "When are you going to let me win my money back?"

"Soon Jesse, I like the way you fellows have poker parties, I especially enjoyed the entertainment."

I could feel myself blush as I walked out the door. "You ole goat!"

Both of them broke up in laughter.

Chapter 28

Jesse was dropping me at my office when he spotted Grady's car parked on the street. "Well looks who's here. True love reigns."

Is that what they have? True love? How can you tell?"

"I see what they feel. They just shine together."

"That's true. They do don't they."

"Bass should be here. He's still on time off. We planned to meet and do something today."

"You won't do anything about my problem without me will you?"

"We talked about going fishing the other night; I think that it would make a nice relaxing day and maybe a nice fish dinner."

We started up the stairs just as Jesse's cell-phone rang. I noticed earlier that he had removed his eye patch and soon you wouldn't even know that his eye had been seriously injured. His limp was better and soon he wouldn't need the soft-cast on his foot. It was looking pretty raggedy. My nursing days were definitely over.

Grady was still talking when we opened the door; they were talking to each other when they met face to face. "Bass called, he's on his way."

Margaret was in the background, ever efficient she had folders on the corner of her desk with posted notes on them.

"So how did it go? Get anything figured out?"

"Not really just more questions."

"I've been thinking." Grady was rubbing his chin looking thoughtful. "If all we need to unlock your brain is your name why don't we experiment? Maybe it's Calamity Jane?

I looked up at him and sneered. "Keep thinking big boy, Margaret would you hand me my gun?"

A knock on the door interrupted our banter. Grady pretending to make a quick get a way opened it to Bass who first words of greeting was "Hey you guys ready? Let's get going times a wasting!"

Margaret gave Grady a hug and said "I expect fish tonight."

"Come on cave man, let's go." Bass called back to Grady as he pushed Jesse out the door.

The office fell silent as we listened to the footsteps grow fainter as they went down the stairs. Margaret looked at me and said "Well, you look no worse for wear. How are you doing?"

"If I don't think my head doesn't hurt as much." I replied; "unfortunately that seems to be all I can do. You don't look like your suffering much, what's your secret" I fell on to the couch and laid my head back. "I'm not very good at this partying thing; I don't remember how I got to Jesses."

"That was the easy part. The ride home was the fun part. All the way home you talked about how pretty Jesse's eyes were and how cute the doctor looked with his hair all messy. You messed it up by the way. Did you know you fell off his lap?"

"Oh my god, he never mentioned it this morning, neither did Jesse. How am I going to face him now?"

"Well you already have. You probably made "the old goats" year."

Margaret handed me a cup of coffee. Sitting there wasn't going to change anything. I looked at Margaret and asked if there was anything new on the Jamison case.

"I made an appointment for you at Cyber-Games. Jamison's boss is Wayne Whitmore, He started the company with a game he invented called *Tag Team*, they have developed several since then and he's made a lot of money. Bradley has been with him for the last six years."

"I don't know much about the game world, I have seen some advertisements, and they are pretty brutal and bloody." I took the folder from Margaret's desk, my eyes went wide as I read that Cyber-Games had made over four million dollars in the last year. "Wow, seems to be a booming business."

"I planned on picking up the latest one and checking it out. Its called *Doomed Defense* doesn't sound cheery;" Margaret replied. "Your appointments for 2:30, is that a good time?"

"That's perfect. Let me freshen up and I'll get over there. What do you have on Whitmore?"

Margaret landed me another paper out of the folder. "This is his background. He sounds bright, intelligent and has money. Best schools, nothing here about a wife or girlfriend. He's from Los Angeles."

"Well, it's a beginning." I replaced the file folder on Margaret's desk.

"Oh, how's Annie? Have you talked to her today?"

"I called her just before Grady got here. She sounded very hung over. She's stopping over after work to meet Bass. She is one really funny lady. I loved the way she took on the guys personalities. She fell asleep on Bass's sofa, or maybe passed out is a better word. She said to be sure to call next time we go out."

"I don't know if that will be any time soon. My head is still muddy."

I left to freshen up, thirty minutes later I and was ready to go. I hoped I looked better then I felt. Fresh air would do the trick. I looked at the address for Cyber-Games and decided the drive to the outskirts of town was just what I needed. The air was fresh and I felt the last of the cobwebs leave as I left the city.

Cyber-Games was housed in a big ugly brick building that seemed to dwarf the area around it. It wasn't hidden but it wasn't really noticeable until you turned down the drive. As I walked from the parking lot I thought: *it was a dark and stormy night.* It was glad that I came during the daylight hours. It was a long walk from the parking lot. I passed several cars some were pretty expensive.

I noticed that security cameras were set at intervals from the parking lot up to the building. I entered into a large, tastefully decorated reception room. Framed copies of the games Cyber-Games produced lined the walls.

A bored receptionist was filing her nails at the front desk. She had on ear plugs and didn't seem to notice my entrance. As I came to the desk she looked up startled to see me standing in front of her. She removed her ear plugs and I could hear the beat of a base drumming from them.

"Welcome to Cyber-Games. Can I help you?"

"My name is CJ Mason; I have an appointment with Mr. Whitmore."

"He didn't mention an appointment to me." she was looking at her appointment book. "Are you sure?"

"Would you please let Mr. Whitmore know that I am here?" I turned and sat on a comfortable chair that overlooked the lobby. I was reviewing my notes when the receptionist called over to say that Mr. Whitmore would see me. I rose and the receptionist apologized that Mr. Whitmore had forgotten to inform her of the appointment. I was to follow the corridor and take the elevator to the forth floor. Mr. Whitmore's secretary would meet me. I thanked her and went to meet Cyber-Games creator.

As the elevators door opened I was greeted by an older woman with styled hair and a no nonsense business suit. She apologized for the confusion. The appointment was made, but was not relayed to the receptionist.

"My fault really, I usually pencil in the appointments for her when I leave. I just haven't had the time to get downstairs this morning. Mr. Whitmore will see you now." She led me to a door, opened it and announced me. "Ms. Mason is here to see you Mr. Whitmore."

Mr. Whitmore looked about 18 with a baby face. When he rounded his desk to shake my hand his deep voice gave way to an older man. As I shook it I could see that he was indeed older. Although not tall, he was not short. He was dressed casually but expensively, if he added a jacket and tie and he would be ready for the board room. He had a firm grasp on my hand as he asked me to have a seat.

"What can I do for you Ms. Mason? Please call me Wayne. Although my Office Manager thinks we should look and act more like the corporate image I prefer informal. Can I get you some coffee or tea?"

"No thank you. I'll try not to take up much of your time." I said as I took out my notes. "I'm here at the request of Mrs. Jamison, Bradley Jamison's mother. I was hoping you could fill me in on what Bradley did here."

"Brad is one of our most productive workers. I hired him when I first started Cyber-Games about six years ago; he's a wizard at what he does."

"I know that you produce video games for computers. What part did Bradley play in that role?"

"Oh, Brad was involved in every aspect. His game was our beginning. We have brainstorming sessions, everyone's in the actual production and development. We all throw out ideas or help to develop or expand another's idea. Some are rejected, some are considered and some just take a life of their own. Brad was a genius on all levels; he was quiet until he had something to say. These sessions are informal and most people would think we are playing games. But it is the core of our creativity."

"How many people attend these sessions?"

"Anyone that's available. Sometimes one is involved in a project and doesn't show, other times they may be stumped and show up to get a different perspective. Like I said we're very informal."

"Did Bradley have a project that he was having trouble with?"

"Let me explain. Brad was involved in a project. This past year we haven't seen much of him. When he's on a roll he rolls with it. He's created four very successful games for us and creativity isn't something you can pigeon hole into a 9 to 5 time slot. He was organized. He kept his own time schedule and was productive. I didn't interfere."

"It took a while before you realized that Bradley was missing. Why was that?"

"Again, we go back to the creativity of our people. I don't harness them in. I don't ask them where they go. We pay very well and as long as they are productive I'm happy."

"Bradley had been working on this particular project almost a year. Is that a long time?"

"Not really, it took two and a half years to develop the prototype for our first game. It took almost another year to have it developed and on the market. I lived on peanut butter and crackers. But in the end I made enough to start Cyber-Games and hire the most talented people."

"So when did you hear that Bradley was missing?"

"His mother called, she was looking for him. She said that she hadn't heard from him. I told her that I would check into it and get back to her. I did, I told her that Bradley was not in and that he hadn't left any messages with us. When she told me she was going to file a missing persons report I agreed that it was a good call. I did check out Brad's office I didn't see anything that looked suspicious, I spoke to the police officers we cooperated as much as we could. I don't know where Brad is. I am as concerned as anyone else. I just don't know what I can add to it."

"You said that Bradley had been working on his project for quite a while. Do you know what it was? Did he leave it behind?"

"That is the question. I don't know. Brad had his own codes. This is a highly competitive business and we have good security. Our best security is our employees. If Brads work is in his office we cannot unlock the codes he created for it. Believe me we have tried."

"Can I see his office? Just to get a feeling of the kind of man Brad was?"

"I'll take you there myself."

"Who did Bradley associate with here, any close friends, girl friends?"

"He was friendly with everyone. He didn't have close friends, no drinking buddies. I don't think I ever heard him talk about a girl friend. But you never know."

"Could you give me a list of your employees?"

"I'll make sure you have one this afternoon."

"Do you know anyone that worked closely with him?"

"Brad worked with anyone who needed help. He wasn't sharing a project with anyone. We all want to get to the bottom of this. We gave the police this same information. I have a meeting in thirty minutes let me take you to his office."

We walked to the elevator and went to the third floor. I noticed that each side of the hall way had key card locks. There was a plaque on the door stating that we were at Brad Jamison's door. Mr. Whitmore opened it with a key card. I walked into a spacious office. There were several computers and a large white board on one wall. A bank of windows flanked an outer wall. The area was pretty neat. Everything seemed to have a place. There were no personal pictures but several awards hung on his walls. His desk was tidy. I checked his drawers and they were locked. There were several large files that held large flat paper, also locked. I tried to read the white board but it was done in computer code. Nothing in the garbage can but they could have had the office cleaned many times considering the length of time that Bradley had been missing.

"Did Bradley leave his keys behind? How many people have access to his office?"

"We haven't found any keys, but I had a duplicate made of his door when the police came to check it over."

"What was Bradley's project about? Are all projects cleared through you before they begin? Do you receive reports as it progresses?"

"Brad's project is top secret; competition in this field is amazing. He was pretty much a lone wolf and had proven to me in the past that he was capable and reliable. He gave me verbal updates, but work in progress is work in progress."

"Well, I have taken up enough of your time. I would appreciate if you would send that list as soon as possible."

"Anything we can do to help. I do need to get answers. We need to know if his work was involved and if it had been compromised. Brad was a good employee, his work is important."

As we walked I noted that he said Bradley's name in the past tense. I also noted that he mentioned the work that needed to be found. As we rode down the elevator, he offered the latest game to me. It hadn't been released yet. We went directly to the front desk where he told Chrissy to fax a company employee list to the number on my business card. He followed me to the door and as he shook my hand and held it as he hesitated "It's been very nice speaking to you, please let me know if you hear anything."

On the way back to the office I thought I would stop at Bradley's apartment. Mrs. Jamison had sent his keys to our office. I stopped at the landlord's apartment first. As I knocked I was hoping that he could give me some personal information, something he may not have repeated to his mother.

The door was answered by a middle age woman. She informed me that Harry, her husband, was up fixing a leak in a dishwasher. I told her I didn't want to disturb him and asked if another time be more convenient.

"You didn't come to rent an apartment?"

"I'm sorry, let me introduce myself," I gave her my card. "I'm from CJ Investigations. I'm here investigating the disappearance of one of your renters."

"Oh, you mean Mr. Jamison, Bradley. He was such a good renter. My heart goes out to his mother, she was here looking for him. There wasn't much I could tell her. He paid his rent on time like clockwork, he never had wild parties. Such a polite boy always offered to help if he sees me with groceries and such. You're looking for him?"

"Yes I am" I replied, "His mother hired us to investigate his disappearance. She told me that she would contact you and let you know that I would be stopping by."

"I do believe that she talked to Harry. But I can take you up now. He's on the second floor. He wanted to be toward the back because of street noise. I think he worked at home a lot." She seemed to be the motherly type, friendly and interested.

"Ms . . . I didn't get your name."

"I'm Betty, Harry and I have run this place for the last thirty two years. I've seen it all. It's a real study of people; you'd be surprised what people do."

"It's good to meet you Betty." She stopped in front of Bradley's door and opened it for me. As soon as we stepped in we were assaulted by the mess that was in front of us.

"Oh my goodness, this wasn't like this when I let his mother in." Betty was visibly upset.

The furniture was torn apart. Cushions from the chair and sofa were shredded; the TV looked kicked in and anything attached to it was torn from it. I could see from where we stood that the same had been done on the kitchen. I held Betty back and told her to call the police. I pulled out my little pink cell-phone and dialed Margaret while Betty hustled back to her apartment.

"Margaret, CJ here. Listen hon. I'm at Bradley's apartment and it looks like it's been ransacked. I have the police coming in but I need you to grab my camera and get on over here pronto. Do you have a way over?"

"Yeah, Annie's here we'll be there shortly."

I didn't feel any danger. I crossed the threshold and looked around the apartment. Pictures on the wall were stripped from their frames and tossed. I walked into the bathroom, towels and toiletries were strewn about. The top of the toilet tank was lying on the floor. The medicine cabinet was open.

His bedroom was shredded, the pillows were slashed open and stuffing covered the floor, the mattress was tossed to the side and shredded. I looked into the closet and it was more of the same. Whoever had come here was defiantly looking for something. I wondered if they had found it.

Betty came back to the apartment followed by a man in a white t-shirt and tool belt. "Oh my" he shook his head, "what happened here?" I came back to the door and Betty introduced me to Harry.

"Harry, you didn't hear any noise coming from this apartment?"

"No, and usually I hear everything eventually. But this, I had no idea."

"Anyone come by looking for Bradley? Has anyone come by that maybe looked out of place?"

"No, I can't think of anyone. The last time I was here I brought Mrs. Jamison to look at the apartment. It didn't look like this."

"When did you notice that Bradley was missing?

"When he was late with the rent, He always paid on time. I left messages here then left one at his work. I couldn't get hold of him that's when I had Betty call his mother. She's his contact number. She came over and looked around. Bradley was a real tidy fellow. This is a real mess. All this glass, and his TV, they even broke his computer."

I had already noticed that his computer had been dismantled and the hard drive was missing. Betty started to pick up a cushion when I stopped her. "You have to leave this until the police get here."

Margaret showed up just before the police arrived. Annie was right behind her. I introduced them to Betty and Harry. I took the camera and started to take pictures. It looked as if whoever went to all this trouble was looking for something that was small and created the mess to look like vandals. I wondered why they didn't just take the valuable stuff and make it look like a robbery.

I finished as the police arrived. The squad car pulled up and two patrol officers climbed out of the car. They both had been at Jesse's party and were surprised to see me and even more surprised to see Annie. I introduced Betty and Harry and explained why we happened to be there. They went through the apartment and said that they would try to get some prints. I gave them the background on Bradley, and told them that Ms. Jamison had been there the week before and nothing was out of place. The officers said that the apartment was off limits until it was dusted. They were going to send for another unit to interview neighbors. They updated Bradley's missing person to foul play in their report.

"There's nothing you can do here." The officers were getting their equipment out of the car. "When we get done we'll let you know. You have any idea what they were looking for here?"

"Something to do with computer games I think, but it could be anything. I'll have to update his Mother. Can I get a copy of the report?"

"You know better then that CJ, it's under investigation. But I'll keep you in the loop."

"Thanks we'll get out of here then. Harry, Betty, I plan to come back later. Mrs. Jamison gave me a set of Bradley's keys but I'll let you know when I come."

Harry kept shaking his head back and forth. "Mrs. Jamison paid the rent for another month. This is some mess." He was looking at the door knob. "Who ever got in here didn't have a key."

Betty looked at me and then at Margaret and Annie, "You all private investigators? I bet you'll get to the bottom of this. If you find Bradley you tell him he will always be welcome."

We left deciding to meet at the office. I had no real information to give Ms. Jamison. I wondered how I would break the news of the break in.

We were sitting in the kitchen sipping on our wine coolers and waiting for a pizza. We were looking at the pictures that Margaret had downloaded and printed. "Whoever did this was looking for something. Think they found it?" Annie was looking at the bathroom pictures.

"I don't know, maybe but I don't think so. I think that they made the mess because they couldn't find whatever they were looking for." Margaret said as she headed for the door. The pizza had arrived.

"How do you figure?" I asked as she returned.

"Just a hunch, the place was trashed. Not just ransacked, but trashed. If it has to do with computers I can see the small stuff, but the bed? The computer is understandable but to smash the TV screen?" She was looking at the pictures and asked "did you see his alarm clock? It's on the floor next to his bed frame, upside down? It says 1:32, I wonder if that's AM or PM?"

I took the picture from her. "Interesting, I know that we need to get back in there. Wonder how they are coming with the prints."

We sat around and ate pizza while I filled them in on my interview with Wayne Whitmore, my take on him and my thoughts and suspicions. "Whitmore has a card key to Bradley's his office, but didn't seem to have one for the files or desk. I don't think he was telling the complete truth. If I had a missing employee who had been missing for weeks and happened to be working on a gazillion dollar project, I think that I would have the files unlocked as soon as possible. I think he knows what's in the files but he's playing dumb."

Annie grabbed another piece of pizza. "Ya know, I read that Cyber-Games is one of the fastest growing gaming companies. This Whitmore guy started it by the seat of his pants. He lucked out with the first game."

The phone started to ring and Margaret went to answer it. She came back and said that Mr. Whitmore was on the line.

I went to the phone "CJ here, how are you doing Mr. Whitmore? It was nice meeting you too. What can I do for you?"

"Oh, well yes Wayne, we did receive your fax, I haven't had the opportunity to go over it yet. I will keep you posted. Please call me if you think of anything that might help us locate Bradley. Oh, I'm afraid that at the moment I'm really tied up, perhaps some other time."

I walked back into the kitchen. "What did he have to say?" Annie asked.

"He wants me to call him Wayne, and he wanted to know if we got his fax. I put it on your desk Margaret. It's the employee list for Cyber-Games. He wants us to keep him informed. Oh, and he asked me out to dinner."

Margaret choked on her wine cooler, as Annie passed her a napkin she asked me if I accepted.

"No I didn't. He seems nice enough but he doesn't trip my trigger, thank you very much."

Annie replied, "What did you tell him?"

"I'm really tied up and I have no free time"

"Jesse will love that one" said Margaret as she dabbed at the wine cooler on her blouse.

"Jesse doesn't have to know about it yet. I might need to ask some questions and I don't want to alienate him at this point. Sometimes it's easier to get answers away from the work scene. I'll tell Jesse. But at the minute there is no need to as I have no intention of going out with him."

Margaret's cell phone started to ring. She looked at the Caller ID and said "It's Grady; I hope they didn't catch to many fish, this pizza is filling.

She answered and I could hear Grady's voice come through loudly, at the same time my phone rang and another phone in the waiting room from Annie purse rang. We looked at each other and laughed, I heard Grady's grumble as I answered mine.

"Hi Jesse, did you catch any fish?"

"What have you girls been up to? We just got a call telling us that you were at the scene of a burglary."

"Wow, your guys are slowing down, that was a couple of hours ago."

"What are you up to CJ? How did all three of you get involved?"

"Look Jesse, Grady and Bass are harping at Margaret and Annie as we speak. Why don't we meet somewhere and I'll explain the whole thing. We were in no danger. I'm sure the rat that turned us in told you that much."

"We have to come by there to get Bass's car, we'll talk then."

"Sounds good to me, see you in a bit."

Margaret came from the reception area as Annie came back to the kitchen. We looked at each other and started laughing. Margaret started to hiccup. Annie was holding her sides leaning on the counter and said "They were together fishing when Bass got a call about a break in, when they said that you two were involved they all called at once."

"Fastest cels in the west" hiccupped Margaret.

Tears were flowing we were so hysterical. Gasping for air I stuttered, "Something tells me that we're about to have a dis-cuss-ion."

"All three of us are here that's some force they have to reckon with" said Annie.

"Hey I don't expect Jesse to call every time he goes out on business."

"You forget," said Margaret. "He hasn't been to work for awhile, and the calls he had before he was injured you were *unofficially* there."

"How many times were you *around* that he doesn't know about CJ?" This was from sweet little Annie?

"Not that many, I haven't known him that long."

"Well he respects you and your work, it will work it out. It's nice to know that they care."

"Did they say if they caught any fish? Maybe we should order another pizza; if we feed them they might not be so irritable with us." Margaret was dialing as she spoke. Annie was taking plates from the cupboard.

"I need a bigger kitchen. Should we get some more beer?"

Chapter 29

The guys came in just as we sent the pizza boy away. They smelled like fish, and were loaded for bear. Grady went right to Margaret and asked her if she was out of her mind. She handed him a beer and told him to sit down. "If you want to speak to me, you keep civil Mr. Dombrowski." Grady closed his mouth and sat.

Annie was at the table and handed a plate to Bass before he could say a word but if looks could talk I would have to say that he was using all of his restraint to keep it to himself.

Jesse entered the kitchen, I couldn't read him but I knew that he was thinking of what he could say that wouldn't get him tossed down the stairs.

I didn't give anyone time to speak as I reached over the table and handed Jesse a beer. "Hey Jesse, You catch anything today? Have some pizza." I handed him a plate.

"I hear the three of you have been busy today. Want to fill us in?" Jesse said as he took the plate.

"We were following up on our missing person. Apparently someone ransacked his apartment. We were doing our civic duty and reported it."

Bass voice boomed out "And you had to involve Annie?"

"Wait just one minute Bass," interrupted Annie. "I involved myself. Don't you dare blame CJ; you know you're just pissed off because you heard it through your buddies. You want to get mad? You get mad at them because you know they were pulling your chain."

"It was embarrassing hearing your ole lady was at the scene of a crime." Grady looked a little repentant, but he wasn't off the hook. Margaret rose to her full height; she looked Grady straight in the eye and poked him in his chest with her finger.

"Ole Lady?" Margaret was really upset. "Look buster I'm no ones *Ole Lady* and if you keep thinking your Neanderthal thoughts you can just go out and find you one." She turned and walked out of the room.

"Look guys," I said "we followed protocol. We were just gathering information; Annie was there to drive the get away car."

Annie cracked up; I cracked up, Jesse eyes started to smile. Even Bass was trying hard to keep a straight face; Grady got up from the table and went to look for Margaret.

"You do know that we would have told you about it. We've been organizing the information."

"So, did you catch any fish?" I went to his chair and put my hand on his shoulder.

"Not any that we could keep, we tossed quite a few back. But it was nice to get out and enjoy the day. Thanks for the pizza, hits the spot."

Margaret and Grady had returned to the room, Grady took another piece of pizza, "I think we should order another one. Fishing makes me hungry."

I looked at Margaret and she winked. Everyone was back on track. I asked Margaret to hit the redial.

"So what led up to all this excitement? This was the missing computer guy right? Did you get any leads?" Bass had Annie on his lap and the kitchen was getting smaller.

"Let's go out to the lobby. We have more room and I can show you the pictures." I grabbed my wine cooler and led the way. "Grab those chairs and I'll get the one from my office."

We moved the end tables together and Margaret cleared off her desk. Bass went for more beer and wine coolers. I got out my notes while Grady and Jesse started looking at the pictures. Annie and Margaret were making cleaning noises the kitchen. We had circled in the area when Bass returned with the drinks and Pizza. "Met the kid downstairs, he said this was his third trip here. You're keeping him busy."

I told them of my visit with Whitmore, my impressions about Bradley's office and the locked cabinets. I pulled the game out of my backpack and gave it to Margaret. "This is the latest one; it's not on the market yet."

"This is the building that's out past the interstate? Old, brick, you have to look to see it?" Grady was getting excited. "That building was vacant for years. It was a mess. I heard that someone bought it. They had to do a lot of work to make it usable."

"I know that place. It used to be a factory. The owner died and it was abandoned. Guess no one wanted to operate it." Bass reached for another piece of pizza, "that was years ago. I didn't know anyone bought it."

"It looked old, and kind of scary, but when you get inside its pretty nice, open and airy. They have security cameras every where. Whitmore said there always a chance of espionage. Guess games have big competition."

"Big bucks for sure, even the government is interested on a lot of levels. Think that Bradley is involved is something shady?" Jesse leaned in from the sofa and pointed at the picture he had in his hand. "This wasn't a random act. It was targeted."

"Ya know" said Grady. "Anyone that works for a company like this has to sign a confidentiality statement. They also sign that anything produced belongs to the company. His office belongs to the company. I don't think Whitmore would have to wait to check out the files. It's his property. But even so, this guy has been missing long enough that the company would be within their rights to check out that office. So what is Whitmore waiting for?"

"I got the feeling Wayne already knows what's in that office. They have a problem getting into his computer. Bradley is a genius; everyone agrees with that, whatever he was working on he's the only one who can shed light on it."

"Who's Wayne?" Jesse asked.

"That's Whitmore;" said Annie.

"He's working on his corporate image." Finished Margaret as they both started laughing.

"It's not a big deal. He wanted to impress me. You know the money doesn't change the man thing."

"Ok," said Bass "Bradley is part of an espionage thing and has taken off for parts unknown letting no one know, including his mother. Or, Bradley was abducted and is being held ransom or maybe forced to finish a game program?"

"So you all think that Bradley's disappearance is connected to his work. He is either in on it or being held because of it." Margaret was counting the points on her fingers. "His mother was the first one that missed him. I don't know but the impression I got from his mother and the landlord was that he was quiet, tidy, polite and hardworking. I can't see him trashing his own apartment. I don't think he's missing by choice."

"Add to that pot his boss didn't report him missing although his projects make him billions of bucks, and he wasn't concerned enough to break a couple of easy locks?" I was sorting through the pictures, "Margaret you have the magnifying glass?" I found the one that Annie pointed out earlier; can anyone tell me if this is AM of PM? I'm going to visit the apartment again, I think the sooner the better." I started gathering up my notes, grabbed my note pad and got up to get my back pack.

Jesse had an amazed look on his face. "You don't plan on going right now, this very minute, do you?"

"Well, yes. I'd like to see it before the landlady decides to clean it up. Besides, it's still light and I have to walk off this pizza."

"I'm going with you. There is no way you are going alone."

"Good, because I wanted your impression up close and personal."

Jesse grabbed his coat off the back of a chair. "We'll catch you guys later. Come on babe, I want to see you in action."

We took the G-mobile. I knocked on Betty's door and introduced Jesse. I told her that we were going to look at Bradley's apartment.

She had a look of concern, "You don't think anything has happened to that nice boy do you?" I gave her a hug. "I sure hope not Betty; I'll do what ever I can to find him."

I had to jiggle the key to unlock the door to the apartment, "Harry, Betty's husband noticed that the lock had been worked on."

It still looked ransacked but different as the police had moved items; fingerprint dust was every where.

"I didn't touch anything earlier, only took pictures, I didn't want to disturb the crime scene. I want to go through everything; I want to find something, anything that will give me an idea where to start."

Jesse was walking the perimeter, "Do you have the pictures handy?"

I dug them out of my back pack and handed them over. I left Jesse in the living room and walked into the bed room. The clock was by the closet, it had some fingerprint dust on it. I noticed the face. The alarm was not set. AM or PM was still in question.

I stood up and looked around the room. The dresser was dusted and bare. Everything that was on it was strewn about the room. The closet was destroyed, clothes looked searched and thrown to the floor, shoes had their linings and heals cut out. Boxes that had to have been on the shelves were emptied. Pictures and school memorabilia were trashed and walked over. I felt sad that Bradley's life meant so little to these people."

Jesse came into the bedroom; He had one of the pictures in his hand as he said "Hey CJ, can you come in here for a minute?"

I followed Jesse back into the living room. I saw that he had changed the room somewhat. He had moved the sofa, tossing the cushions back on it. He had done the same with the easy chair. He had up righted the coffee table and several lamps.

"What did you find Cowboy?"

"I placed the furniture as close as I could to the original spots. You said that this guy was methodical. In one of the pictures he was sitting on the couch with his mother that gave me the general placement. I used the markings on the rugs to match where the furniture had been. These three pictures were on that wall. He pointed over the sofa. The edge of his desk is in the right hand corner. They threw the papers out and then checked the drawers and desk. I think they knew what they were looking for. I was going through the papers and there's a lot of computer stuff that they tossed aside. Whoever did this knew it wasn't what they were looking for. I think they were searching for computer codes. Maybe to open the computer they took."

"That makes sense but it doesn't really tell us what they were looking for or if they found it."

"Here's one of the pictures you took, look at this picture, this is the one I used to place the furniture with what do you see?"

I studied both pictures and then took them into the kitchen turned on the light and placed them side by side on the counter. "I still don't see it Jesse."

Jesse came into the kitchen and stood behind me. He wrapped his arms around me and put his chin on my shoulder. "Okay, Baby, follow me here. I was in your world for a minute, follow me into mine. Look at both pictures and then close your eyes."

I followed Jesse's direction and felt myself start to respond, Jesse was holding me close. I felt color surround us. "Think of the picture baby; see how he sits with his mother? She's smiling at the camera. She's proud of him."

"Yeah, I can see that. There's a cake on this counter. Maybe it's his Birthday? No not birthday, some kind of celebration."

"Think of his face. What does it look like?" My eyes were closed but I pictured Bradley's face in my mind. He looked handsome but distracted. He was staring past the camera, he was focused on the counter that was in front of him. The one that we were standing behind not focused on the counter but below it. I felt the urge begin, I felt Jesse respond to it. "What do you feel CJ?"

"He hid it. It's hidden. It's in front of him." As I spoke I moved back into Jesse, He turned with me and we went around the counter and looked at the front of it. There didn't seem to be much to look at. There were electrical plugs on each end. They didn't seem to be disturbed.

I walked bent over down the length of the counter. I looked at Jesse as he pressed his hand to the wall feeling his way along. He stopped midway. "CJ feel this wall and tell me your impression."

I put my hand on the wall next to his, "I don't fell anything, just the wall." He put his hand over mine and I felt a heat." Jesse is that you?"

"Now feel lower." we both went to the base board. I almost lost my balance when I felt a deeper heat. "What are we feeling Jesse?"

He pulled up the carpet, and then felt along the edge. The tack stripping had a gap in it. He felt deeper and pulled out a small rectangular item. "What is it Jesse?" He held it by the end and looked at it closely, "It's a jump drive. I'll bet this is what they were looking for."

We both sat with our backs to the wall. "What are you going to do with it Jesse, are you going to turn it in?" He looked at me and said, "It's your find, let's download it and then turn it in."

"How did you know Jesse? How did you know where to look?"

"Honey, that's hard to explain. I could call it a lucky guess, but that's not quite it. It works better on a live person; I can tell what they are not saying. The look on Bradley's face and the fact he wasn't exactly happy in the family photo didn't sit right. There was a receipt on the floor from a bakery and if you look in the picture you can just see the reflection of a cake on the counter in its reflection."

He handed me a receipt that was dated a month and a half ago. Close to the time he disappeared. These pictures were on the floor. It's the same party. The other lady might be a friend of his moms, she seems to be the about the right age. He's looking under the counter and he looks intense. It felt wrong. That's the only word I have to describe it."

"That doesn't explain it. How did you know?" I looked at him questionably, "He's missing and I thought you needed to be with the person you question."

"He is here, everything in these rooms belongs to him, you helped, you focused on him and what we were looking for. I think he knew that he was in trouble. His work is the key to this. We have to figure out how."

"Whoa Cowboy, how did I help you, I didn't feel any hiding places. I think I felt the wrongness, but that was because the rooms are trashed."

"When I held onto you and felt your strength, I thought of the way you focused on the book. I tried to concentrate on that feeling. I knew we were close. You helped me follow his thought pattern."

"That sounds far fetched. I didn't pick up on any of that. You're saying that you used me as a kind of conduit to channel him? Way too weird, how did you ever think to do that?"

"Beats me, but one thing I have learned is to follow my instincts. And, well . . . I really wanted to hold you."

"Lets get out of here; I wonder if Margaret is still at the office, I'd like to see what's on this thing."

I started to rise and watched as Jesse put the carpet back. "You think their coming back?"

Jesse patted the carpet down; you couldn't tell it had been disturbed. "They might. They didn't find what they were looking for."

I turned to go to the door when he stopped me. "One more thing while we're here, I want to try something." He looked around the room and then followed the short hallway and looked around the bedroom; He studied the floor and picked up what looked like a class ring.

"Come over here CJ," he turned around in the room and looked at the messy surroundings. He sat a chair upright and sat down. I came over to him and he reached for my hand and he gently pulled me to his lap. He held the ring between us.

"I want to see if we can connect with him. I'm going to concentrate on Bradley and where he may be. I want you to do the same." He put the ring in my hand and held my hands between his.

I closed my eyes and felt Jesse as he put his forehead on mine. His arm was around me, his hands securely around mine. I took a deep breath and concentrated on the face I saw on the photograph. The shape of his head, his hair style, the angle of his head, the way he held himself. I thought of his office and tried to picture him in it. I was beginning to think that nothing would happen when I started to feel cold, and then I felt color, I recognized it as Jesse and myself fusing into a mixture of what was us. I concentrated on Bradley and I felt a frightened and angry feeling. The colors changed to gray and puce as they entered the mixture and suddenly the feeling of being bound caused me to fight the binding. I pulled myself from Jesse and opened my eyes. "Jesse, did you see that? He's in trouble. We have to find him."

"I felt it CJ, I felt him, let's get out of here. Take the ring," He picked up the photos and the receipt and he followed me out the door.

"Will we be coming back? I need to turn the keys into the office."

I dropped the keys off and thanked Betty. I told her that I would be talking to Mrs. Jamison, but since the rent was paid up leave it as it was for a while, we might need to come back.

The ride back was quiet, both of us thinking about what we had found. The intimacy that came with our combined color melds was overwhelming. I kept rubbing my wrist. I could still feel the bindings. Jesse took my hand. "Baby, you're awesome."

"Why don't you call Margaret and see if she's around. We have to get this downloaded. I have to turn the jump drive in as evidence."

I called and left a message, and then called her on the cell phone. Grady had taken her over to his house and she would be tied up for a while.

"Let's go to my house. I'll put it in the safe. You know, I have a lot of room at my house, there's plenty of room for the both of us."

I looked over at him and I said "Jesse, you don't need my help anymore, you're almost totally healed." I was being vague on purpose.

I hadn't thought that far ahead. I was still wrapped up in Bradley's apartment and the mixture of feelings and the intimacy we had shared. I had so many feelings that I hadn't even begun to sort out.

"Would you mind staying tonight? We can get an early start in the morning go to your work and have Margaret download and then I can take it to the station. With two heads working on it we might be able to figure out what's going on." Jesse's tone had taken on an edge. He knew that I had avoided answering him.

I drove to his house and we went in, I followed him upstairs and watched as he opened his office closet and started to fiddle with the combination. "You think we should try to open it on your computer? I asked as he opened the safe. This guy had guns and money, papers an odd assortment of miscellaneous things like a watch, rings and small boxes that had to be jewelry. He must have heard my gasp. He looked up as he closed the door and spun the lock. "I'm not sure I want to tamper with evidence. Right now I am too wound up to look at it."

"Gosh Jesse, that's a lot of cash. You always keep so much on hand?" I blurted out. I could have turned my back as he secreted it away.

"It comes in handy. Hey baby, I really have to take a shower, I still smell like fish. I'll hurry and then we'll have a small bite to eat."

"Sounds good, I'm going slip into something more comfortable. This is my *Interview Potential Suspects'* outfit."

"You do look terrific. Want to join me? I still have this mini cast thing that might give me problems."

"I think you'll do just fine. I'll find a baggie to keep the water off while you shower." I hadn't felt this self conscience since I first *moved in*.

"Don't bother; I have some in the bathroom." He turned and went across to his room. He was really upset with me. I decided to go to the other bedroom and see what there was to wear. I changed into a broom skirt and tank top.

I walked downstairs and looked in to the refrigerator. It was full of Magpies specialties, but I had no appetite. I was tired. It had been a long day. I grabbed a wine cooler and went outside. In his backyard I could see the light from the bedroom spill over the lawn. There was a nip in the air and the moon was almost full. I sat on the grass and leaned on the tree. I pulled my legs up and just sat there absorbing the night. I wasn't thinking, I was just feeling the night. I don't know how long I sat, eyes closed, feeling the moon and breeze.

I felt him sit beside me. Close but not touching. He spoke into the night. "I thought you had left, I looked through the house. I was relieved to see that your car was still here. When I saw you in the moonlight you took my breath away. You look like a fairy princess."

I opened my eyes and I looked at him. His face was in profile and he looked so strong, he was looking at the moon, the clouds slowly dancing around it. I couldn't read his face. I didn't have to. It was a powerful face. I knew that I would always be safe with him.

I slowly got up and stretched my self. He watched without a word. I put my hand out and helped him to his feet. We walked back into the house.

"Are you hungry? I can promise you *Magpies* best. It won't take a moment to warm something up."

"No, baby, thanks the pizza filled me up." He looked at me and sighed. "Let's get some sleep."

We went up the stairs and I went into the bathroom, I turned off the lights and went to the far side of the bed, I slipped off my skirt and climbed into the bed. "Thanks CJ,"

I lay on the bed and felt him fit his body to mine. He held me close and kissed my neck. "Sweet dreams baby."

Chapter 30

I woke up to a feeling of emptiness'. I looked toward his pillow. A note on his pillow read. We w*ent to get the cast off . . . back soon. Love, J.*

I was alone in the house. I wandered downstairs and found another note by the coffee pot. *Breakfast is in the oven. Enjoy. J.*

I took out the plate and took off the cover. Biscuits in gravy, smelled great. I opened the fridge and saw a fruit cup next to a glass of orange juice with another note *Enjoy J.*

I sat at the table enjoying my breakfast and making my list for the day. Writing down what needed to be done and what should be done, when it occurred to me that I was totally alone.

I gulped down my coffee stuck my notebook in my bag and ran upstairs. I looked at the unmade bed and decided that would have to wait. I went into the bathroom and started to draw a bath. I ran into my bedroom and grabbed my travel bag that held every toiletry that I would ever need. All the while imagining the soothing waters dissolving the aches that I had in my body and calming the myriad of random thoughts in my head. The room was filled with steam, I used his shampoo to create bubbles, I slowly lowered myself into the warm, soapy water, I felt the heat immediately wrap around me.

I let my head fall back. I closed my eyes and started my breathing exercises and let my brain empty of any outside intrusions. I felt the warm waters drain the aches from me. The thoughts of the past few days faded as I inhaled the scents around me. Jesse's shampoo, Jesses soap, Jesse seemed to be filling my head with thoughts of him.

I shook my head; I wanted to empty all thoughts. I submerged my head and felt the warm depth surround me.

I came up from water and laid my head back. I felt the tension leave my body and my mind. I wanted no thoughts, only the sense of ease and relaxation.

I slowly let my mind wander to the colors that came when I held the diary and felt a warm sense of being. I felt no sense of urgency, I felt safe and well. A wash of warmth surrounded me. I felt cradled and loved, basking in the feeling of peace. The colors were slowly moving within me. They seemed to touch my every cell, every muscle, every bone and as they whorled through my body.

Changing into a denser more encompassing pattern I felt drawn into it. Allowing the colors to change increased the motion of the pattern. The slow melding of color and motion intensified as I felt my body respond to my inner turbulence.

My mind separated from my body and reached deeper into the mesh of swirling sensations that was being drawn into me. I felt rather then saw images appear in the pattern. It was a kaleidoscope of images changing within each swirl, they were not clear, they were hazy. It was like looking through a thin gauzy veil rippling with each movement making any feature indistinguishable. An outline of a woman appeared with flowing hair, standing on a precipice that changed into a rocky crag surrounded by flowers. Another vision emerged of a small stone house; sitting in the shade by the door with a basket doing domestic chores. Glimpses of her life seemed to appear with no definition. A contended feeling surrounded me. One that was caring and loving. I seemed to be following her life. Feeling more as my colors blended and meshed with hers. I knew her, she was in me.

My visions suddenly change. The tempo of hazy swirls sped up and I felt her running. I could feel her panic. I tried to sense her danger but a soulless black vortex was whirling toward her propelling her to go faster as the colors deepened and intensified. I could feel her fear. It roiled in waves as I reached out to help her; I tried to call, to reach her.

I heard my name. "CJ . . . Hey, CJ! Come on baby wake up, CJ wake up for me baby."

The colors faded as the crimson color of Jesse entered; I heard his voice from a far away place. I screamed. "Jesse. Jesse! Help her Jesse!"

"It's ok Baby, I'm here, wake up baby, open your eyes and look at me." Jesse's arms were around me. He was holding me close, speaking in my ear. "Come on baby wakeup. Your okay, I'm here . . . come on baby."

I slowly opened my eyes. I didn't want to leave the cocoon that I had been in. I wanted to help this woman who had allowed me glimpse her life, who so desperately needed help. "Oh Jesse she needs us. She needs our help!"

Jesse had been rocking me in his arms. We were on the bathroom floor. I was naked and Jesse was soaking wet. "Let's get you dried off baby, you can tell me about it." Jesse reached around me and grabbed a towel. He tucked it around me and carried me into the bedroom. We sat on the bed as he pulled the blanket around me. Taking the towel he dried my hair and held me.

"You ready to talk? Can you tell me what happened?" The concern on his face was palatable.

"Oh Jesse, It started so beautifully. I felt the colors, like the ones in the diary. I felt them drift around me and they felt wonderful. I floated with them, they were part of me. I can't explain it. It was all so, so encompassing. I saw a woman, she was so content, so in love, I couldn't see her face and the pictures kept changed, I just got glimpses of her life. I could barely see her; it was like looking though a thick veil, no features only the outline of her body. She was beautiful. She moved with such grace. She made me feel so loved."

"Oh Jesse, suddenly she was afraid. She was trying to run, she was holding hunched over holding her stomach. She was so afraid; the wind was blowing hard making it darker and harder for me to follow. I couldn't help her! I couldn't reach her! I was trying so hard and then, then I was here, and you were here. Oh Jesse, I couldn't help her!"

"Oh, sweetie, I'm so sorry. You said it was the same pattern that you felt in the diary?"

"The pattern changed with each emotion. On the cliff she seemed to be waiting, the wind billowing through her cloths, the way she stood it felt as if she was waiting. At her cottage she was serene, content, still waiting.

When she was frightened she was in such turmoil, the urge to flee seemed to be her only option!" I felt what she felt, I was running, out of breath and so sad."

Jesse held me close, he soothed me with kisses, rubbing my arms and my back. "We'll work it out baby. Lay here and rest for a minute."

Neither of us spoke. I closed my eyes. The soothing motion of Jesse's hands comforted me as he rocked me in his arms. I eventually calmed. The colors around me slowly centering me. The unique blend I recognized as us. Words were not needed.

Somewhere in the perimeter of my mind I heard the ringing of a phone. I strained to find the direction when it stopped. Shortly it began to ring again. Jesse had begun to rise when the distant ringing stopped and his cell phone on the night table began to ring. The moment was over; I felt the loss. I began to rise as Jesse reached over me to answer. It was Margaret.

"Hey Margaret, what's up? Yeah she's here, give me a minute and I'll get her."

Jesse handed me the phone. "Sorry Margaret, I got hung up, what's going on?" I was sitting on the edge of the bed and was surprised to see that it was 11:30. I was way off schedule. "I'll be there within the hour."

I raced to the bathroom, and closed the door as I dropped the blanket on the floor. I hurriedly dressed, brushed my teeth and hair and marveled how bad hair days seemed to be my norm. Grabbing my bag I headed downstairs.

Jesse was downstairs talking on his phone. He had changed out of the wet clothes and had his keys in his hand. I looked from his hand to his foot and saw that he had on a pair of shoes. He watched me as I stared at his foot, when he hung up he raised his foot and said "Look baby, no doorstop."

"That's great Jesse, how does it feel?" I asked.

"It feels so much better, I told Grady I'd meet him and Bass, we're working out a plan for Saturday. Were still going to your folks aren't we?"

"Uh yeah, I guess so." I suddenly realized it was already Wednesday and I had a lot to do.

"So you're driving now, that's good. I need to get to work, let me know what you guys plan for this weekend. Bass is going too?"

He started walking me to my G-mobile, "Annie's taking the weekend off. Grady got the measurements and he's getting his tools together. Bass said something about taking his van."

He opened my door and gave me a kiss, "Be careful baby, call me if you need anything." He had the jump drive in his hand; here you go, I'll be by later to get the information on this."

"I forgot. Oh Jesse, I don't know where my head is" I needed to get it together.

"Be careful, are you sure you're ready to go to work? You had me worried." He stood in the driveway, his hand resting on my window. "I'll be fine, you take care, call me." I said as I backed out of the driveway.

Chapter 31

Margaret was on the phone and typing when I arrived. She waved as I hung my coat and went into my office. I started going through the file folders on my desk. She added two more bond skips, one from Jacobson. I started to read the new information and the notes she had written. She called from the door, "CJ, conference in the kitchen?"

I met her as she turned on the coffee. I had my notes out adding to them when Margaret placed a cup of coffee in front of me and one for herself. She placed a plate of donuts on the table as she sat down.

"CJ, you look like hell. What happened?" I looked up at her, "Margaret I don't know where to start."

"Trouble in paradise? How's Jesse? She said as she took a sip of coffee.

I let out a sigh and decided that we could play twenty questions all day. "No, Jesse and I are fine. He doesn't need a nurse anymore. Were doing okay, I'm just taking things day by day. I just need to focus."

"What do you need to focus on?" She raised her cup to her lips and waited for my reply.

"Margaret, Jesse is not a problem, its how we can do things together. I have had so many things happen in the last few weeks and they all connect in a screwy kind of way. Take this thing, I held up the jump drive. There was no way it should have been found. But Jesse's mind . . . Look, we need to see what's on this thing. Jesse needs to turn it in, its evidence, but we need to look at it first." I was rambling and knew that I wasn't making much sense.

"Okay girl, let's do this." Margaret was up; she took the jump drive from my hand and walked to her desk. I sat on the corner of her desk and watched as she inserted it and brought it up on her screen.

As she fiddled I told her how we found it. "Jesse was so intuitive; he was like a blood hound. Gathering and eliminating information. Adding it to the equation or discarding it."

Margaret watched the screen and set it up to print. "Grady told me he's good at what he does. Jesse always seems to find the answers; the hard part is putting all the pieces together."

The monitor showed a screen of jumbled numbers letters and symbols. The printer started to spew out papers. We both stared at the screen as she scrolled down page after page. "There are 212 pages; I need to get more paper." She went to the supply closet and retrieved a ream of paper. I moved to her chair and strained to see what was written.

"Margaret, you know anyone that can read this?" I scrolled down farther and saw that the pattern had changed but still unreadable.

"It's Greek to me. We can check with the professor, he may know someone at the university, a computer geek, someone like Bradley?"

"Well, I'm sure the police have someone. I know that Bradley's in trouble. I just hope that we find him before its too late. He hid this really well. I'd like to know if someone goes back and does a real through search of his place. They know what they are looking for."

Margaret had started to make copies of the sheets that had been printed. They were still spewing from her printer. "I'm making two copies, I want to hide these really well, It would be our luck that they might try to follow up with us since you two went there after the cops did their search."

"I have been thinking about Wayne, a multimillion dollar game is missing along with his star game guy. He doesn't report either of them missing. When confronted he does a cursory check of what might be missing but doesn't bother to break the locks in the office. I don't believe that for a minute."

"He knows a lot more." Margaret said as she fed the copy machine another handful of papers. "We have to figure out a way to get him to slip up."

I got up to get my notes when my phone rang. "Hey Jesse, how's it going? I have your little do-hicky here, ready to be picked up." I turned to Margaret as I hung up, "the big boys are coming over."

We were shuffling through the papers trying to see some sort of pattern. I told Margaret about our combined efforts at the apartment and how it seemed to heighten both of our abilities. I tried to explain how Jesse seemed to draw *something* from me that helped him focus on his thoughts. "Its way to hard to explain." I was rubbing my forehead; I had a small headache, something that I rarely had.

I took the ring out of my backpack and placed it on the desk. "I'd like to go back to Cyber-Games and snoop around. There are four floors and I would really like to see what I missed. The top floor is where the offices are. There is a large glassed in conference room. The only solid walls were in Whitmore's office. I don't think he uses it much. It looked more for show, maybe for big power meetings. His assistant has an office next to his. I never saw inside her office. Come to think about it, she never gave me her name. Do you have that employee list?"

As Margaret bustled about in her office organizing, I went into my office and updated all my notes and started a file on what I labeled my freaky file. This file now held the incident at Bradley's apartment and the one that happened this morning. I made a note that both included Jesse.

The first thing on my list was to find more about Whitmore's personal habits. The employee list had been updated; Margaret had added addresses and phone numbers to some of them.

We sat down with coffee and discussed how we would start. We divided the numbers and started to make plans on how to proceed.

Jesse and Grady arrived and after looking at the copies decided that they didn't have a clue about computers. The idea of contacting the university was the best anyone could come up with. I was going to look into Whitmore's background and wanted interview several of his employees. Margaret had done a partial check but could only go so far. She looked at Grady and asked if there was anyway that he could check through the list and see if there were any names that he recognized that would help narrow the list. She was at the copy machine and made a copy for them.

"I can look into it. I don't know any computer-geeks."

He started to survey the list. "Do you know who they have for security?" Margaret looked through the notes "Ace Security did the security badges and door cards. Would they use the same company for security guards and cameras?"

"Let me look into that one," Jesse was looking at the employee list. I have a friend that works at Ace; I want to keep this under wraps as long as we can. We still don't know why Bradley's missing. You're working on a high dollar company. It might go farther up the food chain."

"Whitmore didn't seem too bright." I said. "The fact that the cabinets were locked and he didn't realize one of his employees was missing, that's like two big red flags. Bradley made a lot of money for him. I would think he would be more concerned."

"Unless someone else is calling the shots, and that opens a whole new can of worms." Grady was looking at the names on the employee list. "Hey Jesse, why don't I go with you, there's something I want to check on. Where are you girls starting?"

Margaret and I were looking at each other. I turned to the boy's, "We were discussing that when you guys came in. Here's the jump drive, we'll fill you in later."

Jesse looked frustrated. "What do you mean? Fill us in? We were going to help you with this."

"Look Jesse, I'm sure you want to help, but we have this under control, you need to get that do-hicky to the police department and we have to do our thing."

"We're going to check the security angle," Grady was a little peeved, "You can use our help on this."

I looked at Jesse, "Grady you are helping. But you know that there are things that you can't do, you have to follow the letter of the law, and I have some flexibility. If you get involved you will have to follow procedure. Jesse already feels guilty for not reporting the flash drive."

Jesse was angry. "Damn it CJ, I'm not going to do anything that isn't legal, but I'm not going to let you get caught in the middle of this. Right now this looks like a kidnapping. It involves a lot of money and the bad guys are not playing games."

"I agree, but this is my case. He's been reported missing and the police have the same information I have. Jesse, I will keep you in the loop, but right now I have to follow my instincts."

"And just what are those *instincts*?" asked Grady, now he was really getting angry.

Margaret grabbed the ball. "Right now we plan to check up on the employee list. I think the security angle is your part. We don't plan to exclude you but give us some credit fella's! You know if we need help we'll call you."

Grady seemed to know when to back off. "Okay, okay, but this might be dangerous. Let's get going Jesse; we need to get someone to look at this *do-hicky*. If it's ok with you girls I'm starting with the University."

Margaret went to give Grady a hug, "If you find anything you will let us know won't you?"

Grady shrugged, "Margaret, it goes both ways, just keep us in the loop."

"Okay ladies, we'll do the same.

I'll call you later CJ," Jesse came and gave me a hug. "Are you doing alright baby? I have some thoughts about this morning, maybe we can talk about it later."

"I'll work it into my schedule" and gave him a kiss on the cheek.

Chapter 32

When they left Margaret looked at me. "What happened this morning CJ? You came in looking a bit haggard."

"We can talk on the way Margaret. I'd like to go over to Cyber-Games and put faces to some of these names and maybe check it out a little closer. You feel like coming along? I could use an extra pair of eyes and your keen sense of observation."

"Try to keep me away. What's the plan?"

"I want to talk to as many people as we can. Get a gauge on who does what, any hostilities, any thing that feels out of place."

I went into my bedroom as I was talking and reached for the bag that I kept in the back of my closet, I placed it on the bed and took out several small canisters of pepper spray. I reached in again and brought out a small tape recorder and a stun gun. I reloaded the recorder with a fresh cartridge and explained that it was voice activated. I had a small camera that I put on my sweater and grabbed a gaudy pin that covered everything but the lens. The button to the shutter went under my sweater on a long cord that I could manipulate from my pocket.

Margaret had picked up the stun gun and held it in her palm. "This is cool. I didn't know that you had an arsenal back here."

"We have to plug that in; it will take less then an hour to charge it but if push ever comes to shove it will buy us time to get away."

Margaret found an outlet and plugged the stun gun in as she read the directions. "This is cool; it would have been handy with Ralph. Is it legal?"

"It is in this state. Strictly self defense Margaret. Put that and the spray in your purse. We need to get another recorder, stun gun and add a carton of spray."

"I'll put that on our list. CJ, do you use these often?"

"I always carry the pepper spray. I've used it once on a particularly mean dog. It was close he had the upper paw until I got to the spray. I keep it in my pocket just in case. The stun gun I haven't and hopefully won't use, *Be Aware and Be Prepared* that's my motto."

"Do you think we will have to use these?" Margaret was examining the pepper spray.

"Hopefully not, but I figure getting away from a problem is half the solution. I don't want to kill anyone but I won't mind causing hurt to someone who's trying to hurt me. First and foremost Margaret keep yourself safe."

"So we go in guns blazing and peppers spraying and we take them all down until one of them confesses that they have Bradley." Margaret was laughing as she pointed for index fingers at me like she was shooting a gun.

"Afraid not hon. we're going to go in as professional women who are seeking answers. Between the both of us I hope to find someone who can give us information, while we scope out the building. I want to know what and who's where, if anyone seems nervous, or maybe wants us to avoid an area. It's going to be a little fact finding tour."

"Well, that sounds simple enough; I'm going to get that employee list and a notepad." Margaret was still talking as she left he room, "Whitmore didn't know what he was working on? How does he know what projects he has going on? They didn't separate the list by departments."

I met her in the kitchen, I poured the last of the coffee and we went over how we could possibly split up to get our information. What questions we could ask that wouldn't alert them to the information we had.

Margaret grabbed her coat and purse. She had a way about her. Where I was more casual, she was dressy. Where my hair wouldn't comb, every hair had a place on her head. Her hands were manicured and she stood tall. I was skinny and short. There were so many differences in our personalities. We did make for a strange duo.

I watched as she placed the stun gun in her pocket, "Ready CJ? I can't wait to see this place. Grady seemed to think it was architectural anomaly. The guy that built it designed it himself way back when."

"It would be handy to have a set of blueprints. You ready to go?"

We drove the same route I had taken the last time. We had discussed how we would divide and conquer. As we drove toward the building Margaret looked at me and asked. "This monstrosity was innovative?"

The grounds around the structure took on an even more eerie feeling as the trees had shed most of their leaves allowing all the harsh angles of the building to stand out.

We left the car and I reviewed the cameras that I had noticed at my first visit. We entered the reception area and I went up to the desk to inquire about Mr. Whitmore.

"Do you have an appointment? It was the same girl with the same earphones and the same bored expression.

"Chrissy, right? I was hoping he'd have a moment to see me. He told me I could stop by at any time."

"Oh, well let me see if he's available. Please have a seat." Chrissy was watching Margaret as she strolled around the room. "She's with me." I said before she could ask. Chrissy shrugged her shoulders and started to dial the phone.

Margaret walked around the reception area, checking out the posters that advertised the games. She stopped at a picture that was on a side wall and was studying it when I came up to her.

"Chrissy is checking to see if he's available. This is interesting," I said as I looked over her shoulder. "It looks like the original building."

"It hasn't changed much." I was looking at the façade, "They made a few of changes," answered Margaret, "the new windows seem to make it look even more ominous."

"Look at the plaque. The building was new. This building is 52 years old and looked decades older at its conception."

"Can you read it? It's a pretty old photo" I strained to see the lettering.

"No, it was taken a ways away, maybe to get the whole building in the picture?"

We were interrupted by a voice I recognized. "Ladies, can I help you with something?"

Whitmore's assistant was behind us, looking prim and efficient and not to happy to see us.

We both turned "I'm sorry if we came at a bad time but I was hoping to speak to Mr. Whitmore. This is Margaret Cross my Associate and we happened to be in the area. Margaret, this is Mr. Whitmore's assistant, I'm, sorry but I did not get your name."

"I'm Louise, Good to meet you Ms. Cross;" she shook Margaret's hand reluctantly. "Mr. Whitmore is tied up in a meeting and won't be available for another hour or so."

Margaret didn't let the opportunity pass. "I was so excited to come here; it was really my fault that we just dropped in. My boyfriend has a passion for old buildings and when CJ mentioned that she had been here he went absolutely crazy, I was looking at this photo," She motioned to the picture. "It looks the same from the outside except for the windows. What did they manufacture back then?"

Louise looked from Margaret to the picture. She seemed impatient, "Originally it was a factory for work boots. They also made work gloves. Unfortunately it went out of business when the owner died. It was vacant until Mr. Whitmore came in and renovated it for Cyber-Games."

"When did the owner die? Was it vacant a long time?"

"He died in 72, and it was vacant until Cyber-Games began seven years ago. Two of those years were restoring the building for our needs and bringing it up to code."

Margaret excitement was infectious, "I would love to see what you have done. I mean the outside looks kind of old and gnarly, but looking at this area, you guys have made it look airy and modern."

"We don't give tours, this is strictly operations only." explained Louise.

"Oh, you should reconsider. My nephew has all of your games. I would think that any youngster who plays them would want to know what it takes to create one. I was looking at the graphics on the last game and I tell you I was impressed. I even wanted to know what it takes to create such innovative, action packed games." Margaret had taken control of Louise's arm and led her back to the center of the room.

Her rhetoric had thrown Louise off guard and the spotlight she had placed on Louise seemed to make her more animated.

"I'm sorry, we don't give tours." Louise seemed to think that would put Margaret off.

Margaret looked downcast but before Louise could shuffle us out the door she said, "Louise, look, we have at least an hour to wait for Mr. Whitmore, would it be possible for you to show us around? I know a lot of the questions we have are on how these things are made to work. A general education of the process would probably answer some of our questions without disturbing Mr. Whitmore."

"I don't know, most of the work here is done on computers. It's not very interesting from a layman's point of view. It's the finished product that's exciting."

Margaret was not to be put off, "Is there a delivery place around here? I guess if we must wait we might as well not miss lunch. Do you have a cafeteria?"

Louise was now getting irritated. I could almost feel the wheels churning in her head. She realized that we were going to stick around until Whitmore was available, or she could show us what we wanted to see.

"I hate to disappoint you ladies. I know that you are trying to find Brad. We have been so distressed by what happened. I don't know how knowing how the games are made will help you I don't understand most of it. But I have a bit of time, but we'll have to be quick."

"Louise that would be wonderful, we promise not to interfere. But sometimes getting an idea of what one does helps us to understand how that person thinks."

"I doubt it in this case. Sometimes I think these guys are from another planet. There are times when I'm not even sure that they are in this reality."

Margaret had a big smiled as she again shook Louise's hand. "Thank you so much, my nephew is going to be so excited when I tell him what I did today."

"Don't thank me yet, you don't now how boring it can be watching a think tank think." She turned to walk away when she stopped and asked "Have you made any headway with Bradley's case? We miss him."

"Not yet," I answered. "We seem to be hitting blank walls, Did Mr. Whitmore ever go through Bradley's files; I know he couldn't find the keys."

"I believe he did. He had a locksmith come up." She was cautious with her reply.

"Did he find anything interesting? Anything that would give us a clue to what may have happened or what he may have been working on?"

"I'm sure I would have heard if there was. I was told that his project has been placed on hold. He's a very valuable employee. I hope you find him soon."

"I hope so to; thank you for setting this up. Anything that might help is welcome."

"I have about a half hour before my next meeting. Let's start with the offices. I know you've seen Brads, I'll introduce you to his co-workers."

We started at the third floor. She went to an office and introduced us to Carl. He looked like a gangly boy still growing into manhood. Jeans and t-shirt, glasses and unkempt hair, he had a bad case of acne and seemed to be very shy. He didn't hear us when we entered and was surprised to see us when Louise interrupted his train of thought.

"Carl these ladies would like to know how you create your games, Step by step."

Carl looked at his feet. "I don't know how to explain that. We just get ideas and then we work them out."

"Well let's start there. Where do you get your ideas?" I asked as Louise stood leaning on a desk looking impatient. I was fingering Bradley's ring in my pocket. Hoping it would lead me to a clue or insight. The metal was warm in my pocket but I felt nothing emanating from it.

"Lots of times they just come to us. Sometimes we bounce ideas off each other. Sometimes we get a good lead and sometimes not." Carl wasn't a social butterfly and I could see him try to work into words what he was trying to say.

"What are you working on now" asked Margaret.

"Uh . . . , I have a glitch in my program and I'm trying to figure out how to get it to work right. It keeps looping around and messing with the scoring."

"Is that an unusual thing?"

"Oh it happens all the time. Sometimes it's an easy fix sometimes you have to tear it apart and start over; this one is in the first stages."

"How long does it take to create a game?" Margaret asked.

"A really long time sometimes, the last one I did was three years in the making. I had to revamp it four times that took another two years. Then I came here and I had all of the technology I didn't have before. It was on the street in six months. Cyber-Games has all the latest technology that makes it a lot easier.

"So you came to Cyber-Games with a work in progress, and then you finished it, and then Cyber-Games marketed and packaged it. Who carries the patent?"

"That would be Cyber-Games. They made it possible to get it to the market. I got a sign on bonus and a weekly paycheck and residuals from all my games."

Margaret looked at the computer screen, "The money must be pretty good then."

"Yeah, I paid off my school loans got me a house and I helped my folks pay off theirs. That felt really good."

"So how long have you been working here?"

"I've been here almost two years."

"Do you know how long Bradley has worked here?"

He looked uncomfortable at the mention of Bradley's name, "He was here before me. From the beginning I think. He was really smart. He helped me a lot when I first started working here." I could hear the sadness I his voice.

I changed the subject;" Do you work together on projects? I was walking around his room looking at the equipment. There were several computers and notes everywhere.

"We work together when we need to."

"When was the last time you worked together?" Margaret asked as she picked up a slinky and passed it from one hand to the other.

"Brad was supposed to meet me in the conference room. He forgot. He came out of the offices and got on the elevator. He didn't even look up."

"Did he forget a lot?" asked Margaret.

"Naw, he was good at getting things done. He might be late, but he always showed. I waited a while but he didn't come back. Greg came in and we worked it out."

I was watching Louise and she seemed to be surprised at his answer. She stood up straight, looking at her watch she said "Shall we continue? I have a tight schedule this afternoon."

"Carl, it was very nice to meet you. I still don't know how you do it but it's really awesome." Margaret returned the slinky to his desk.

We started to walk to the elevator. "How many programmers work here?"

"There are five including Brad." We passed doors, some were open the one with Bradley's name on it was closed. The ones that were opened had a space much like Carl's and Bradley's. Each had a name on the door. Each opened up to a huge room that had windows covering one wall. We passed a open room that held another programmer. The name on the door said *Greg Adler;* it looked like a collage student's room. Computers were piled with papers and the work space was cluttered. There were pizza boxes and other food product residue littering the area. A fooze ball was lying on the floor. A large easy chair was in the corner next to a state of the art sound system. Tapes were haphazardly strewn around the area. I saw a head surrounded by a stack of papers behind a desk.

Margaret walked right in. "Some place you have here, I guess the cleaning lady can't find this room."

"I don't like the cleaners to come in here. I can't find anything when they leave. I'm afraid they'll throw out something I need. I only let them in when I finish a project."

Louise stepped in "This is Greg. He's also a programmer." Her irritation was showing, her foot was tapping as she looked at her watch.

"It's good to meet you Greg; I am getting an education here. How long have you worked here?" Margaret had already made it to the middle of the room and held out her hand to shake his.

"Almost two years." He finished what he was doing and stood up. Short and stocky with a ratty flannel shirt, baggy jeans and hair that needed a cut and a comb. He shook Margaret's hand; it was not a gesture he was comfortable with.

Louise explained that she was showing us the facility. She was looking at her watch and looking antsy. I knew our time here was short.

I asked. "Did you know Bradley well?"

"No. Not really well. He kind of lived in his own world. If I asked him something he would always answer, sometimes days later, but we never like went to lunch. He brought his own. Can't tell you much, I didn't know him well."

"He was a quiet studious type?" Margaret asked as she looked at a computer screen. "Did he have any friends? How about a girlfriend?"

"I don't think so, no one that he ever talked about, He was getting a lot of calls for a while, but I don't know who."

"Greg, what are all these little symbols? Margaret asked as she pointed to the computer screen. "Looks like a lot gobbelty gook."

"That's the program I'm working on. Its not so mysterious, once I get it done it will program a part of a game. He started to explain and it was way over my head. "So this is just a little part of the whole?" I asked.

"A very little part." He answered.

"So how long before this game is finished?

"About a year give or take any complications. We're in the early stages."

I looked at him, "A year for each game"?

"No, the one I'm working on now is the first one I started cold since I've been here. The last was one I had been working on."

"So, your game was a work in progress when you got hired on?"

"Mine was, but like I said, this one is in-house."

"It was the same for Bradley?"

Greg looked at his feet, "I think his first one was. He's designed four since, the latest one was almost finished when he took off."

"How do you mean *took off*. When was the last time you saw him?" I asked.

"I'm not sure, I heard him in his office and he was grumbling to himself. I didn't see him. I know that Carl was piss . . . upset because he was stuck on something and came by asking me if I could help him."

I turned to Margaret "Did you get a chance too look at the game that Mr. Whitmore gave us?"

"Grady has it; his nephew was crazy for it. He loves it; you guys did a great job. I'm afraid that there is too much violence for me. How do you make the characters do what they do?"

Greg started on the explanation when I turned to Louise, "Is there a restroom near?" I asked.

"It's down at the end of the hall; just take a left out the door."

I left them while Greg continued to explain to Margaret. I scoped out the offices on both sides of the hall. I passed Bradley's and jiggled the knob. It was locked. Another office had *Matt Slater* on the door, it was closed. I returned to the hallway, went down the stairwell, and followed down to the next level. Through a window in the door I saw one huge room lined with computers, large spaces with tables cluttered with papers and pens, many drawings were pinned to the walls. I recognized pictures that were in various stages of some the published games. I counted seven people in the room all working, some together some alone, two were sitting at computers.

I walked the stairwell down to the next floor. I was back in the lobby. I continued down and found myself on the basement floor. This door had no window, it was locked. I put my ear to it and didn't hear any sounds. I wanted to see what was on the other side, maybe storage or the computer mainframe? Time was running out, I turned around and ran back up the stairs.

Margaret was still asking questions and looked relieved when she saw me enter the room. Louise looked irritated. With a plastic smile she apologized, "I'm sorry ladies, but I really have to be in a meeting."

I looked at Margaret, "Gee, I hope that Mr. Whitmore can give us few minutes."

I could tell that Louise's patience was at the end of its tether. "Follow me; I'll see if he can fit in a few minutes."

She started toward the elevator her body language screaming that she was ready to strangle us.

Margaret was on her heels thanking her for the tour and complementing her on the efficiency of Cyber-Games. She was sure Louise had to be responsible for its remarkable success. Taking care of details is essential in any operation. Margaret was laying it on thick and I could see Louise relax as she took in the compliments. By the time we left the elevator Margaret had smoothed most of Louise's feathers.

As we left the elevator Louise asked that we wait in the conference room while she checked with Mr. Whitmore.

The conference room was glass enclosed. It sat in the corner of the building and was bordered by windows. I stood overlooking the grounds, a utility shed sat to the side. The surrounding area had pathways through the trees that led to a small picnic table. Nice place for a nature hike when one wanted to go out in the open air.

Margaret interrupted my musing "This room is kind of creepy, so impersonal." I looked around it and noticed that cameras had been placed in two very visible places. One camera covered the room while the other faced the grounds. There were no papers, or cups. A stark room with no pictures only the view of the grounds. A large table and six chairs sat in the middle of the room. When you came here you brought your own materials. The windows and the glass enclosed walls made me feel like I was standing in a fish bowl.

Louise came out of an office and we both watched her progress as she walked to the conference room. "I'm sorry, but Mr. Whitmore is still busy. He has another appointment in town in about an hour. "If you'd like I will call you after I schedule a meeting for you."

"That won't be necessary, but if you could have Mr. Whitmore call me I would appreciate it."

We began to walk to the elevator. Once we entered I asked "You were the last person to speak to Bradley?"

She looked startled at the question, "I don't believe so. We're not sure what day he left." I looked up at the camera in the elevator. "With all these security cameras, I would think there would be one that would show him leaving."

"I'm sure the police already have that information."

"What was the disagreement between Bradley and yourself?" I asked.

"I'm sure I don't know what you mean." Her features had hardened and I noticed that she had taken on a defensive stance. "I don't remember speaking to Brad before he disappeared."

We had reached the main floor. Louise was anxious for us to leave.

Margaret turned to her "Thanks for the tour. I'm not sure if I understand how you make a game but I have a new respect for the work that goes into one."

"Thank you ladies, I do hope you find Brad soon. We miss him here."

We were well in the parking lot when Margaret spoke up. "She knows something."

"Do the police have the security tapes?"

"I'll ask, but if they don't I'd like to see them first."

"They have cameras on every floor and in all the main rooms. I didn't see them in the offices but I'll bet they have them."

Margaret turned to me, "Did you get to check out the building?"

"Not as much as I would have liked to. The second floor looks to be the art design side of things. Lots of drawings, I took pictures through the door; I hope I got all the faces. There's a floor below the lobby, locked up tight. No window, No sounds. I would like to see what's there. Since they have computers coming out their ears I thought maybe the mainframe, or storage, I wanted to ask Carl but I didn't want him to know I was snooping. Oh, and there are cameras in the stair well too."

"I'm sure we've both been well photographed. I'll bet you Louise is watching our every move right now."

"That I don't doubt. Did you get an education from Greg?"

Margaret gave me a go to hell look. "Actually what didn't go over my head was kind of interesting. I think that whatever happened to Bradley is connected to this place. Greg told me that Bradley was almost finished. That he had found a problem and was working it out. He didn't know what it was about but maybe that's what's on the jump drive."

"It seemed to me that Carl knew something, I wonder if he told the police about the meeting with Louise. She knows something."

"I agree with that. We have the boys until the end of the week. Maybe we should put them to more use. I really hate the idea of having to answer to them if they don't agree with our decisions."

"CJ, all we have to do is listen to them. Then we do as we please."

"And hope we don't get caught. I have never had a partner in any sense of the word. I'm still getting used to you."

"That's because you know I listen and then do what I please."

I laughed and looked at her, "That's because we both have been on the same page."

Chapter 33

Back at the office Margaret started on the phone messages and I began and updating my notes. With all of the security at Cyber-Games there had to be some record of Bradley's last day there. I compared the name to the employee list and came up empty. I sat thinking of what my next move might be when Margaret showed up at the door. "Hey girl, you have a message or two here. Jesse called, he dropped of the copied pages of the diary to the professor, and they have a program writer going over the jump drive."

"We need to call them and see if they have security tapes. Especially the day that he was to meet Carl. I want to find out more about Louise, she bothers me."

"I can do a general check, maybe the boys can help there." Margaret was making notes as she talked. "We should check out Whitmore a little more closely too."

"We have to be a bit more cautious. I think that Louise knows we suspect something." We were interrupted by the phone; Margaret picked it up "CJ Investigations" I listened as she spoke. "Yes she is in; can I tell her whose calling? Just a moment please."

Margaret put the phone on hold. "Speak of the devil, Whitmore's on the line."

I took the receiver from her "Mr. Whitmore, What can I do for you?" Margaret stood by the desk with a smirk on her face listening as I spoke to Mr. Whitmore.

"Yes we were there this morning; I was disappointed that I didn't get a chance to speak with you. Well, yes, I would like to get together and discuss the case. I'll have to check my schedule; I'll have my secretary call and make arraignments. It was good speaking to you Mr. Whitmore, yes of course, Wayne. Goodbye."

"That sounded good. What's the plan CJ?"

I was taping my pencil on the desk, "Apparently he was disappointed about missing us today and wants to get together. He mentioned dinner; I sure would like to get back into Cyber-Games. Oh, and he wants me to call him Wayne."

"Imagine that," replied Margaret, "he wants to get to know you better."

"It's more like he wants to know what we know. We need to download the pictures we took today. I would like to get a closer look at what we might have missed."

"I'm on it. Did you get the impression that Carl might know something?" Margaret had the camera and was getting it ready to download. "Either that or he was the only one genuinely upset about Bradley."

"What happened when I left the room? What impression did you get about Greg?"

"That's when I got the impression that Louise knew more then she let on; every time I would ask a question about what Bradley was working on she would make a comment and sidestepped it. Greg seemed to be a little put out about the third time he got interrupted. I think he knows what Bradley was working on."

"What makes you think that?" I said gathering up the files and placing them in the cabinet.

"It was one of the questions I asked him that Louise jumped all over. I was curious about the glitch that Carl had, the one that Bradley stood him up on? I asked Greg how they fixed it. He began to explain that Bradley had developed a program that could go through it and check all the variables and target the problem, Louise jumped in and changed the subject. Greg looked a little sheepish and after that wouldn't talk about it anymore. Louise is hiding something I just know it."

"I trust your instincts, any ideas on what our next move might be?"

"I think we should call our guys and get some lunch, I'm hungry. Maybe they got a lead."

Margaret started to dial the phone, her face lit up when Grady answered. I could hear his deep muffled voice as he spoke. I gave her some privacy as I went into the kitchen. She followed me as she hung up. "Grady's picking Jesse up now. He's at the Station. We're going to meet at the *Four Star Bar* in half an hour."

"I've never been there, isn't it around the corner from the Station?"

"I've never been there; it's one of those places I avoided. But it's one of the safest places around. The owned by retired cops. Considering my past associates I steered clear of it like the plague."

I laughed as I grabbed my jacket and notes, "Margaret, your going to have to tell me your life history."

"You'll have to wait for the book to come out." Margaret said as she followed me down to the G-Mobile.

We arrived just as Jesse and Grady pull up. Grady got out of the car went right to Margaret. They were so adorable. Jesse came around the car and gave me a hug. "This place has the best burgers. Are you hungry?"

"Starved" I replied as I walked through the door that Jesse held open.

It was a dark room and I could just make out the bar and some scattered tables. As I waited for my eyes to adjust as a hefty man came out of the shadows and gave Jesse big hug.

"About time you came around Keyes. We were wondering if you were on your feet yet." He had an apron tied around his waist and a big grin on his face. It was hard to judge his age but his balding head and white mustache told me he was no teenager. His smile lit up the place. "Come on, sit down, and let me get you some lunch. You need to tell me how you two lucked out and found such beautiful ladies."

As he led us to a booth in the back Jesse introduced us to Mack, not only was he the cook, but he was part owner. I noticed that he moved with severe limp. "I very happy to me you CJ, and Margaret," he said as we were seating ourselves, He looked at Margaret and then Grady and said "I don't know what you see in this grizzly ole cop, he has a lot of hard edges."

Margaret looked at Mack and said, "That's the challenge, smoothing those rough edges out."

Mack left the table shaking his head and laughing "Your one lucky dog Grady."

Jesse gave me a kiss and handed me a menu. "The food here is good. I'm getting the burger and fries." I looked at the menu, it had good plain food. I settled on a BLT with coleslaw. Grady and Margaret decided on the cheese burgers, fries and onion rings.

Mack took our order. As we waited for our food the boys gave us the background on the *Four Star Bar*. Mack had been injured on duty. When he recovered he was restricted to desk duty. He decided to retire and invested with two other retired officers and started the Four Star. The forth star was to symbolize all the officers that died in the line of duty.

I was looking at the pictures that surrounded the bar. All were of officers and their families, weddings, promotions, all aspects of duty and leisure.

When our food came it was hearty, plentiful and very good. We took our time as we discussed what everyone had done.

Jesse had dropped off the jump drive at the station and stopped at Ace Security. He had a long talk with his friend and found out that additional security had been added since Bradley's disappearance and he would fax the changes to our office this afternoon. Jesse stressed the importance. Hopefully something concrete would turn up.

Margaret explained our return visit to Cyber-Games. We both made it clear that we didn't trust Louise; we felt she was hiding something. Margaret explained how Louise interrupted whenever the conversation strayed to Bradley. We both agreed that Greg knew something about Bradley's program. It was fairly new and no one else had access to it.

"Security cameras were everywhere and we were sure that one had to show Bradley's last day there." I questioned why a camera would record picnic table and the utility shed. I described my snooping through the floors and the secured door in the basement. Jesse's eyes hardened and I could tell he was not pleased. I drew the layout on a napkin as I outlined the interior of the building.

Grady pulled out the employee list from his pocket. He was looking at it while we related our escapades. "There is no Louise on this list. What's her last name?"

"She never said," answered Margaret. "But give me a minute and I will find out." She took out her cell phone and dialed Cyber-Games. "Hello, Chrissy? This is Margaret; I was visiting Cyber-Games this morning with my friend. I wanted to send a thank you note to Ms. Lois for taking the time to show us around. I didn't get her last name, could you help me out?"

We all watched as Margaret spoke into her phone. "Oh that's right, Louise, not Lois where did that come from? I'm glad I called; it was so interesting although I didn't understand all that much. That's Connor? C-o-n-n-e-r. Thanks Chrissy, you've been a great help. Thank you dear." She hung up her phone while the three of us gaped at her. All I could say was "Margaret you defiantly need a raise."

Grady quipped in "You could charm a snake."

"Charmed you didn't I big boy?" Margaret answered as Grady choked on a French fry.

Jesse started laughing and we all joined in. Mack had come to our table with apple pie ala mode for all of us. "Lunch is on the house. I'm really glad you made it Jesse, we were all worried about you."

"Thanks Mack, I'm glad it's over, can't wait to get back to work."

"Well, you guys be careful out there. Don't stay away so long. Nice to meet you ladies, you are welcome anytime, preferably without these two."

We took our time over the pie. Jesse called Bass and asked if he could do a background on Louise Connor and Greg Alder. He asked if there were any security tapes from Cyber-Games and if not it might be a good idea to get a court order.

"Whitmore called today and was disappointed that he missed us."

I wasn't sure how Jesse would take me going out on a date. "He invited me to have dinner. I'm thinking that it might be a good idea to find out what he can tell us away from work. I want him relaxed enough that he might give something away."

"CJ, that's not a good idea. My bet is that he's fishing to see what you know. He might be setting you up."

"Jesse, I realize that, but if I can get some information it will be worthwhile."

"Makes sense," Grady was waving his fork in the air. "If CJ can get a clue on where to look we can get a warrant for a search."

"I don't like it, he's up to something." Jesse was getting up from the table; he pulled a large tip out of his pocket and tossed it on the table.

Grady followed suit while he said "I think she should do it, we'll just stay close and see what develops."

"I still don't like it." Jesse picked up my jacket and held it out for me.

"I looked up at him "Jesse, I need to do this. We'll just make sure it's a well lit public place."

Grady put his arm around Margaret. "We'll be right there. We won't let anything happen."

"Let's go over to your office and talk about it." Jesse waved to Mack as he opened the door. "It was great Mack! We'll be back soon."

On the way back to our cars Jesse stopped and turned me to face him. "I don't feel good about this CJ, not at all."

I looked into his beautiful eyes, "I don't think we have much of a choice."

In the office Margaret put on some coffee and I retrieved the notes that we had worked on. The bottom line was that Bradley was still missing and we had no clue why, or where he might be.

"Okay" Jesse barked, "but you don't go anywhere without us. "Make the *date*." he literally spat out the last word.

"Why don't I make reservations at the Blue Oyster, it's the closest place to Cyber-Games, Maybe we will get a chance to go back there afterwards without anyone looking over our shoulder."

Margaret was already looking up the number.

"He doesn't know us, but you're probably on the security tapes." Grady was looking at Margaret, I was thinking that he was having second thoughts about her involvement.

"That's not a problem, you'll see. Say 8:30? Dinner reservations, you can meet him there and have your car."

"After the lunch we had today I don't think I'll be that hungry." I was trying for levity.

"Grady, you and Margaret try to get a table close to CJ; I'll scope out the parking area and find a place where I can see you from the bar. CJ, baby, be real careful. He may look like a nerd, but I don't trust him."

"Jesse, grab the fax. Maybe your friend sent us something we can use. Margaret, make the call. I want to get this over with. I need to get dressed so you guys go get ready."

"I'll give you a ride to your house." Grady said as he picked up Margaret's jacket.

Margaret followed me to the kitchen with the coffee cups. "Margaret, take the items I gave you this morning, just in case."

"Reservations are made. I'll see your there." she replied as she went to meet Grady waiting at the door.

Jesse was brooding as I entered the room. "Don't worry Jesse, its just dinner."

He looked up, "I don't like you dating other guys."

"Jesse you goon, this is business. You're going to be there. If he gets out of line you can punch out his lights."

He pulled me to him and I could hear him laugh in my ear. "I might do it anyway, please be careful. I have to go meet Bass. I'll see you tonight."

I spent the rest of the afternoon cleaning up the kitchen, updating my notes and thinking of ways to get Whitmore to give himself away. By the time I was finished and dressed, I still didn't have a clue on how.

Chapter 34

I arrived at the Blue Oyster ten minutes late. I didn't see any familiar cars and wondering if my backup was running late. Mr. Whitmore was waiting in the lobby and came to greet me as soon as I entered.

"I'm sorry; I'm running a little late." I apologized as I shook his hand.

"You are well worth waiting for." He stood back and looked at me and then put his had on my waist and led me to a table. "Your choice of restaurants is excellent. I often take my clients here and I have never been disappointed." He had extended my chair and took the one across from me.

"I have always wanted to come here, I'm happy I made the right choice." I discretely looked around for my team, taking in the ambiance of the room. It was dimly lit and the décor bordered on romantic. Large leafy potted plants used as partitions made each table an oasis.

"I took the liberty of ordering, I hope you don't mind but the salmon is excellent here. I hope that is all right with you."

"That's fine," I replied. The waiter came with the wine, pouring it and waiting as Whitney tasted it with great relish.

"I've been attracted to you since you walked into my office. I've wanted to ask you why one as beautiful as yourself would choose your line of work."

"That's a question I get often. I don't like sitting behind a desk. I like having my own business and my own hours."

"How did you decide to start Cyber-Games? It's a long stretch from designing to running a company as successful as yours."

"Not so much. I like designing, but it's all-consuming. I like the business end of things. The combination of both makes for a good fit. I know enough to sell our games and at times I contribute to the creative side."

"That makes sense. How do you recruit? I spoke to a couple of your programmers and they said they had been working on their own project when you hired them"

"I'm pretty finicky there. I like to recruit from the University. But the last two have been word of mouth. I want bright, self motivated people. I give them the freedom and the technology to do their best and I reward them well. They may have something that is good and given the opportunity it becomes great. In return I give them a large sign on bonus, a good salary, and use of the best technology. These guys are innovators. They come here in debt with huge student loans. I require a five year contract, and rights to all work produced. It's the standard business contract. Its win-win for all involved."

"But each one has a something to bring to the table before the contract is signed." I sipped my wine, as the waiter placed our salads.

"Yes, that is the one requirement and why I have such large sign on bonuses. I get to preview what they have and at the same time judge their work to see if it's up to our standards. You would be surprised by the amount of applications we reject."

I nibbled on my salad as he talked. He sounded sincere. I decided to change the subject. "Louise gave us a tour this morning. What is her position in your company?"

"Ah, Louise, I don't know what I would do without her. She does the day to day. I require updates every week. If there is a problem or a new piece of equipment the employees tell her and I will do what is necessary. If a project is stalled I want to know about it. She does the books and works with the accountants, manufacturers and sales."

"She's been with you a long time? I took another sip of wine. As I looked up I saw a beautiful woman walk by and sit at the table behind Whitney. It took a second to register that it was Margaret and she looked fantastic, I almost choked on my wine. I saw big broad shoulders on the other side of a palm plant and knew it was Grady. I felt myself relax a bit.

"She's been with me for about three years. She answered an ad I placed for an assistant. She seemed to know her stuff and she become indispensable. After she started I found that the day to day things that I did were done before I got to them."

"Do you know what Bradley and Louise were arguing about?"

H looked surprised. "I wasn't aware of any conflict between Louise and Brad, where did you hear that?"

"It was brought up in regards to a missed meeting with one of your employees; apparently he left her office and was upset enough to forget about the meeting. It was the last time anyone saw him. Surely, Louise said something."

"No, this is the first I've heard of any conflict. If it were serious I'm sure I would have been told."

"Was Bradley a temperamental person? Did he get upset?"

"No, no he wasn't. He was intense but in a low key way. I don't remember a time that I've seen him upset."

Either he was a very good actor or he really didn't know about the incident.

The waiter came and took away our salad plates. Whitmore asked "Do we have to talk business? I was hoping that we could get to know each other on a more personal level."

I looked up and explained "I don't involve my personal life with my business. I'm afraid that's just not possible at the moment."

"And ethics too. I don't believe I've ever met a more beautiful, smart, woman. I hope we find Brad soon. I would like to get the business part out of the way."

"We'll talk about it when the time comes." The salmon was placed on the table.

"So, let's get back to Louise. What can you tell me about her? Where did she work before she came to you?"

"I don't really remember some big corporate think tank. She wanted to get away from the big headaches. She had all the right credentials. After she started it was like she was always there."

"What's a think tank?" I took a bite of the salmon, it melted in my mouth.

"You find projects or come up with ideas, collaborate, and make them happen, you set it up with a manufacturer and packager and distributor and get it sold. It's kind of like Cyber-Games, but we're low key. We only have one product, we just need to figure out the next trend and make the game better then the last one."

Wayne tipped his glass to me. He had three glasses to my one. I looked up to see Grady stand up and excuse himself. He lifted Margaret's hand and kissed it before he turned and walked past my table. He looked good in suit and tie. The Wyle Ole Coyote had some moves.

I must have been smiling when I looked back at Wayne. He had a look in his eyes that I had only shared with Jesse. *Get back to work.* "Wayne, what was Bradley working on?"

"He had project he called *Galaxy*, it was different from what he had done in the past. I asked him about the mechanics and research, it was a big change, but I could see the value. We talked quite a while. He wanted to merge game with education. I was surprised because the way he explained it, kids would have fun, learn, and not be aware of it. I realized he was bored with the same-ole-same-ole. I didn't doubt that he could do it, it was the time line. I need a game a year that makes a reasonable return to keep Cyber-Games up and running. Technology alone is outdated every six months. But we have one near completion so I agreed."

"Bradley's contract would be up in another year."

"Brad kept us going. He didn't want management. He wanted freedom to create. He was shy and he had a hard time speaking to anyone unless it was work related and then he was passionate. If I hadn't passed his office on that day, at that time, who knows when he would of told me about Galaxy. I knew he had already started the research, not because he told me, he would have put out another game, but he would worked on it between projects or at home"

Wayne stopped to fill our glasses, his fifth my second. "But this idea was a good one, I was excited about it"

"You miss him." It was more of a statement then question.

"And she's perceptive too. Yes, I genuinely like Brad. He's quirky and shy but the things he can do. Create, and not think of the fortune that could be made. Money just kept his lights on. He developed this tracking program that could trace errors and suggest possible solutions. He only used it in-house; It would never enter his mind that it might mean millions. He developed a tool to make us better, he shared it."

"Did you ever think he might sell it?"

"The first thing I think when I see something new is its worth. I thought about it, and this could be a huge benefit to us. I figured we had something here that would keep us ahead of schedule; it's practical and would probably be developed by someone with Bradley's intelligence within a year. When that time came I would go to Brad, offer him a partnership and place it on the market. I don't want to loose him. He is few and far between."

"What could this program do outside the gaming industry?"

"It's got all kinds of practical applications. In any industry, the fact is by the time someone else developed it Brad would have something even better in the works."

The waiter came to the table and asked if we wanted desert, I declined and asked for a coffee. Wayne followed my lead.

"Wayne, how did you come by the start up money for Cyber-Games? Why would you build your company here?"

"I've been waiting for that question. My great uncle owed the business. He left it to me when he died. When I came of age I received the property and over Two-million dollars. I found out on my 21st birthday. I had no idea. I never really knew the man. I was born just before he died."

"I was at a place where I had nothing, was going no-where, wondering how I was going to finish school. Out of the blue a boot factory saves my ass. I met Brad in my last year of school. He was brilliant. I had a half-assed idea. He had the talent, Cyber-Games wouldn't have happened without Brad. We made it work; I drew up a business plan in my last year of school. We developed it into Cyber Games. The first two years it was just the two of us. He did his thing and I did mine. We had the time and the money to do it. The only stipulation was to finish his game, our first, within 6 months. We got what we needed for the program first. Then I went out and found producers and merchandisers, the business end of things. It took seven and a half months to finish and two months to produce. But it really took off, faster then either of us imagined. We were both amazed. And we grew. I miss the ole days. God I miss him. Where do you think he is?"

"I don't know yet, but we'll find him." He seemed so desolate that I didn't realize that I put my hand on his arm. I immediately moved it; this man did not need encouragement. I told him that I had an early morning and really needed to leave. I hoped he understood. He stood up and held my chair and helped me with my jacket, holding my elbow as he walked me to the door. Jesse walked past me an out into the parking lot. He had a great poker face. I hoped mine held up as well.

Wayne returned and opened the door for me. He placed his had lightly on my waist as he walked me to my car. I opened my door to get in when he stopped me. He took both my hands in his and looked me in the eyes as he said "This has been the best business dinner I have ever had. You're really terrific." When he bent over to kiss me I ducked into the car hoping that Jesse wasn't paying attention.

I started the car and drove off watching my rearview mirror to make sure that Wayne went to his car. Jesse was no where to be seen.

I drove a mile or so down the road and pulled behind a huge tree. I pulled out my cell-phone and called Jesse. "Hey Jesse, I'm in place"

"Hey babe, how was the salmon?"

"It was terrific. What did you have?"

"Two beers and some bar nuts."

"Poor baby, I should have brought you a doggy bag."

"Here's Margaret and Grady, I'll meet you. Your boy friend took off, looks like he was heading to town."

"Hey, you guys want to go exploring? I would like to check out that utility shed."

"I'll ask the kids, but it looks like they want to ditch me. How much wine did they drink?"

"See ya soon Cowboy"

Chapter 35

I had changed out of my skirt and was tying my tennis shoes when they drove up beside me. Margaret was likewise trod. "Hey girl, how was your date?" Before I could deck her she said "We're taken Grady's car, its dark and big enough for all of us."

On the way to Cyber-Games Jesse started talking. It was amazing to hear him plan.

"We'll go in two teams. I'd like to avoid the driveway so we should cut across the field. Grady, find someplace close but hidden to park. First sign of trouble, we head for the car and wait. Set you cells to vibrate. I'd like to head across the field the back way and from two directions, CJ, Margaret, you two lead you know the camera angles. I want us to end up at the back of the shed."

Grady piped in "single file. We don't want to make a wide target, low and slow to the ground." He parked his beast of a car on the opposite side of the road in a grove of trees. We all got out and scoped the area around us. The building stood out stark and black in the moonlight, the night security lights were casting dark gloomy shadows on the lawn. The wind was picking up and the sudden gusts picked up leaves and whirled them into the night.

We walked across the street and angled toward the back of the building before we crossed the large expanse of lawn. Trees were scattered, most of the space we traveled was open. We stopped by a lilac bush that gave us enough cover to stop for a moment, Grady and Margret behind us.

I pulled out Bradley's ring and handed it to Jesse. "I tried using it today and got nothing, I wished I had you with me then." He gave me a swift kiss and said "I'm here now baby."

"Grady, you take the left and see if there is a way in, we'll take the right. Avoid the front. CJ, wait here for a minute." We watched as Grady and Margaret slunk off into the night.

"Hey baby, hold my hand and concentrate on the ring. Think of Bradley, describe him to me." I closed my eyes and told him my impression of the tall gangly guy with horn rimmed glasses. Drawing from what I learned from Wayne, a shy, dedicated, creative soul, a boy never in a hurry. A genius who's only goal was to find the next solution.

I began to feel color, my cool blues to teal green; Jesse's crimson to red to deep purple, moving together, combining. Heat started coming from the ring. I felt the familiar tingling and knew that Jesse was feeling it to. I looked around and my vision had changed to black and white. Jesse was a shadow like me. Together we made our way to the shed. Grady and Margaret were waiting at the back. I spoke first; to warn them that we were in place. "Any luck?"

"There's a front door but no windows." Grady answered in a low tone.

"We're going to try the door, keep a look-out." Jesse was pulling me toward the front of the building. The door was padlocked; I watched as Jesse pulled out a tool and jimmied the lock. "Hey Cowboy, that's breaking and entering."

"I'm off duty, are you going to report me?"

"No, but I think I'll hold it over your head next time I want something."

The lock opened and we slipped through a small opening hoping that if the camera was running our movements wouldn't be noticed. As our eyes adjusted to the darkness we saw a lawnmower, rakes, shovels, and a wheelbarrow on one side of the shed. Large bags of grass seed, soil and fertilizer stacked in appropriate piles. I pulled a penlight out of my backpack. I slowly moved it around the room. Nothing seemed out of place until I came to the back of the shed. Partially hidden was a work table loaded with large pots, gardening spades and other utensils. The area just beyond the work table was empty. It had been cleared out. We moved closer to the corner and I moved the penlight over the area breaking it into quadrants illuminating every inch of the walls and floor. "Stop" Jesse pointed to the corner. "What's that?"

We both eased into the area, trying not to disturb any evidence that might be present. "He was here; the ring is really hot."

"Let me have it for a minute." I traded the ring for the penlight, "Jesse, look at the cabinet low in the corner."

Jesse stooped down and brushed at floor by the work table. "Someone was here; bring the light closer, what is this?" I stooped behind him, "It looks like initials, *BJ*, and it looks fairly fresh."

"We need to get out of here; we know he was here and I don't think he strolled in here by himself." I was getting that familiar urgent feeling.

We stood up to leave when we heard voices outside. Grady's voice came out loud and slurred. "We were just looking at the building. My girlfriend was here for a tour and told me how neat it was."

Margaret chirped in, "We were having dinner down the road and I thought I'd bring him here and show him this big ole spooky building. We didn't mean any harm. But ya see, he lives with his mom and I live with mine and we look for places to be alone if you know what I mean."

I was embarrassed for Margaret. How much wine did they have?

We listened as the security guard said. "This land is posted, didn't you see the signs? You're trespassing. You two come along I need to check your ID's."

"Honest officer, we don't mean no harm, can't you just let us go, we won't come back." Margaret was laying it on thick. I pictured her batting her lashes and looking really blond.

"Get going, that way" he said pointing his finger toward the building

"Another one of you hair-brained ideas" ragged Margaret, "We couldn't go to a motel, no, we had to go see the ole spooky building." Margaret could whine with the best of them.

"My idea! You went on and on about this scary building, it ain't scary, it's downright ugly. Why do I listen to you?" Grady angrily complained, not to be outdone.

Jesse and I slipped out of the building and locked the door. We followed, entering behind the guard. He directed them down the stairs into the room that I wanted to check out that morning. It was huge. One wall contained computer banks. There was a room on the side it contained desk, chairs and monitors for all the camera's that were installed on the premises. I spotted the one for the shed at the moment there was nothing to show. I noticed a wall that stored security tapes. I was wondering how far they went back when Grady spoke up.

"Hey, this place is really neat. It sure has a lot of security; I think I'd really like a job where I could just look at TV all night. Is this how you found us?"

"No, I like to walk around, check the premises and rattle the doors. Sometimes I like to sit at the picnic table and have lunch. It gets pretty boring in here. I just happened to see you out of the corner of my eye. Let me see some ID."

Margaret whipped hers right out. "That's me big boy. Can't you give us a break?"

Jesse and I were checking out the tapes. Looking at the dates, I picked one labeled with today's date and slipped it in my backpack. I saw Jesse pull two and place them with mine. These guys were really organized; everything about this place was controlled. I saw Grady looking at a stack of tapes that were not filed yet. I continued checking the dates and noticed that there were gaps in several places. I moved past Grady and used his bulk to get a closer look. I pulled four out of the stack and replaced them with some that I had in my hand.

"Look man, give us a break, I gotta get up early in the morning." Grady actually whined.

"To late fella, the boss lady is on her way. You might as well get comfortable."

"Boss lady? Who's the boss lady? Is she that nice lady that gave me a tour this morning?" I wanted you to meet her honey; I told her how you liked strange buildings. Your nephew would have loved that tour." Margaret babbled on distracting the security guard.

Jesse was checking out a door attached to the room, it was locked. I felt the ring burn in my pocket and I knew we were close.

The phone on the desk rang, the security guy said he'd "bring em'on up" and hung up.

"We're going upstairs. I want you two to behave."

While Grady and Margaret started out in front the guard, Jesse picked the lock to the room. The only item in the room was a cot, possibly for the security people. I pulled back the blanket and under the pillow there was a small piece of paper. No words, just a symbol. Similar to one that was scratched into the sheds wall. I picked it up carefully and put it in the front zipper of my pack.

Jesse was looking in every corner of the room and under the cot. "He was here, and not too long ago. Give me your hand, you have the ring?" We placed it between our palms and I felt us meld, fast and hot. "Think of him CJ; think about where he could be."

"I feel coldness, darkness, not damp, very humid. What do you feel Jesse?"

"He's close, I think he's sick, Come on CJ we can find him."

I thought of the symbols, the torn sheet of paper, visualizing the one scratched into a cabinet. "Jesse, are there any more floors?" He stood in front of the bank of monitors, checking each one. I saw the floors dark with no activity. Every office seemed to be monitored.

One door had a camera focused on it. There didn't seem to be any thing to monitor but the door. It was labeled with a code and Jesse picked up a notebook matching cameras to codes. Each camera was assigned to a hallway or room. This one faced a door. He took the fax out of his pocket and compared it to the notebook. He turned the page and compared them to the codes that were added in pen. These included the shed, and the door and several more offices.

I was looking at the monitors and saw the guard in the hall outside of Louise's office. "Jesse, they're in Louise's office."

"Let's move it. What floor is that door on?"

"Looks like this one, but I don't think it's on this end of the building." Jesse was looking at the diagram "there seems to be a space beyond the back wall."

I walked toward the back of the room passing the computer banks. "Nothing's back here, just a blank wall."

"I have an idea; let's go to the other side of the lobby. There has to be a stairway from the lobby down to this floor if this schematic is right. They had to be able to mount that camera."

We tipped toed through the lobby. I was certain that it would be really hard to pick us up on the camera; we were both shadows of ourselves but I wasn't sure about motion detectors. The elevator would make noise. I was hoping for stairs. We stood looking up at the stairway that led up, there was no door under it and Jesse began examining a wall behind the elevator. "CJ we can enter the elevator from the back. "It's going to make some noise."

I whispered. "Looks well hidden, let's go." He pushed a button hidden behind a plant and the door opened. We entered and I pressed the only button going down.

The gears sounded like thunder and it seemed to take forever to descend one floor. It opened to a narrow hallway facing a lone door. I looked up and saw the camera mounted in the corner. I pointed it out to Jesse. He shrugged, there was no way we could avoid it unless we dismantled it and we didn't have time. I had a passing thought of Margaret running out of words, and shrugged it off. Not our Margaret.

We walked toward the door. I felt like I was walking in an optical illusion, watching it grow larger as the walls seemed to separate with each step. Jesse had his tool kit ready when we reached it. He opened the door silently.

I saw a very dim light on the opposite side of a narrow room. Jesse propped the door open and took out my pen light. The room was small without windows. The floor was concrete. Jesse flashed the light over the area and we both saw the cot with a huddled figure on it.

I went over and gently nudged a shoulder. "Bradley, Are you okay? We have come to take you out of here."

The figure moved and tried to focus. He started to grope around, shaking his head back and forth and seemed confused.

Jesse handed him his glasses and helped him sit up. "Bradley, I'm a police officer, we have been looking for you."

"Who? What??" Bradley was weak. His body would not respond as he kept looking around, he seemed frightened.

"Let us help you up big guy." Jesse had raised him to his feet but he couldn't stand by himself.

"Jesse, he's either really tired or drugged, we have to carry him out of here."

Together we raised him up, propping him between us as we dragged him to the elevator; across the lobby and leaving the way we came in.

The night air seemed to help. We helped him stagger around the corner of the building. Jesse pulled out his cell phone and called Bass.

"Help is on the way." He dialed Grady's phone and let it ring twice. This was the Keystone Cop's secret code for reinforcements.

We sat on each side of Bradley, watching as he deeply inhaled the night air. "You think Grady and Margaret's doing okay?"

"I hope so; she's really clever, how long before the troops arrive?" I asked as I tried to adjust under Bradley's weight.

"Shouldn't be to long, I'm going back for the tapes. I don't want them to know that we were here." Jesse went back into the building.

I had a vision of Bradley floating down the hall with his toes dragging. I felt a nudge at my side. Bradley was trying to wake up. He took in a deep breath of fresh air and tried to focus. I was rubbing his back and telling him that he would be okay. His head fell to his chest and he was out cold again. I looked up to see Jesse returning with tapes. I watched as he approached his shadow filling in with each step. I was relieved that Bradley was still in a stupor. I didn't want to explain this to our drugged friend.

"We can wait here or get him to the car. Bass is about ten minutes out. What do you want to do?"

"I shook my head, I don't know, I don't want to leave the guys."

"They should be alright. How you doing Bradley? I think your colors coming back." He was gently shaking him trying to rouse him for the long walk down the driveway.

"I'm going to call Whitmore. I think he should be here when the sparks start to fly." I started dialing as Jesse tried to raise Bradley again.

I called Wayne and told him that I had a lead on Bradley and asked if he would like to meet me. He jumped on it and asked where. When I told him Cyber-Games he hesitated and asked if I was sure. When I answered yes he said he was on his way.

"How far away does your boyfriend live?" Jesse choked out.

"About ten minutes, that new condo *The Cypress Estates*. He is kind of cute, don't you think?" Jesse growled at me.

Bradley was trying to focus and talk at the same time. "It was Louise, you have to find her."

"It's alright we have her. We're waiting for reinforcements. You think you can walk? We have a car on the other side of this field that you can wait in until the police arrive."

We half walked, half dragged Bradley to the car. He fell asleep as soon as he hit the back seat. I was leaning against the car when Jesse came up and pulled me into his arms. "Your one gutsy broad, you know that?"

"Thanks, I think. I would love to be a fly on the Louise's wall; Margaret has a way with words."

He bent down to kiss me when we heard the sirens in the distance. The Calvary was on the way.

I looked up at Jesse. "You want to stay here with Bradley, might not look good that both of you guys were trespassing, breaking and entering, kidnapping and stealing tapes."

"You have a point, how do you explain your presence?"

"Margaret called to tell me she was showing Grady the building and she sounded tipsy. We'll wing it and let you know."

"I'm going to flash Bass and you update him on the way so he doesn't go in cold." He leaned over and flashed the headlights. The lead car came to a stop and Bass got out. "CJ needs a ride to the building; I have the kid in the car. She'll fill you in."

We went through the back door, Jesse didn't miss a trick. It was propped open with a tape. I led them to the elevator I really didn't care how much noise we made. When it stopped on the fourth floor the security guard was surprised to see four Police Officers exit the elevator.

I headed for Louise's office and the guard shouted for us to wait. The first officer cuffed him and stood him against the wall. Louise must have heard the guard's shout; the door opened as we came to it. I stood back while Bass backed Louise against her desk. She was protesting the *intrusion*. When she spotted me her mouth slammed shut, she looked at me with daggers in her eyes. "What are you doing here?" she practically screamed.

"I'm just taken care of business Louise." I turned to Margaret and Grady, "You guys need a ride?"

I had given Bass the short version of what happened, I told him about the shed and the hidden room. I wanted to take Bradley to the hospital and get hold of his mother. "Is it all right if we give our statements later?"

Bass looked from Margaret, to Grady and then to me. "Yeah you'll need time get a good one together" he said under his breath. Then louder, "That's tonight folks. I want the facts while they are fresh."

Margaret rose from her chair; Grady took her elbow and the started for the door when Wayne arrived. "What's going on here?" He looked at me and then Louise who was standing with handcuffs and a really ugly face. Bass was reading her rights and another officer started to question Wayne taking his name and information.

I turned to Bass who stood next to Wayne; "We'll be at the hospital. Bradley was drugged with something. Wayne looked up surprised and then angry. "Where is he, is he alright?"

"He will be. Why don't you go down to the station and we'll meet you later." I turned and left the room.

We spent the rest of the night and part of the early morning at the hospital and then the police station.

We did come up with a pretty good story, Grady and Margaret and their great love for ugly architecture. Margaret's call, totally inebriated and telling me what they were up to. My arrival as the rent-a cop took Margaret and Grady in. I called Jesse to help with big ole tipsy Grady. Simple, I hoped.

Jesse came up with noticing the room with the door. Watching the monitors and seeing our friends then noticing the book and somehow figuring out there was a camera focused on a door. I wanted to find the room and took off. Jesse was concerned and followed me. There were only a couple of gaping holes in the story. It was too early in the morning to try fill them all in. I was exhausted.

I called Bradley's mother and sent a cab to pick her up. We left her at the hospital where Bradley was sleeping soundly. Grady and Margaret went to the station, their drunken story had preceded them and it would be a while before something better came up on the gossip mill.

Wayne stayed at the hospital, He was a basket case. I called Chrissy and had her pick him up. He did take notice of Jesse's possessive stance not to mention the fact that Jesses hand was on my shoulder, or at my waist, or holding my hand every time Wayne was near. I caught the look on Wayne's face the moment he realized I had a boyfriend. It was a bad night all around for him.

He did impress me with how he arranged the best for Bradley and his mother. If he had a part in the kidnapping I didn't *feel* a connection.

We all decided that we would sleep in and sort out the facts in the morning. Jesse drove my G-mobile to his house and the last thing I remember was falling into bed.

Chapter 36

I woke up to a barrage of noise, I bolted upright and slowly distinguished the ringing of my cell-phone, Jesse's home and cell-phone, and the doorbell chiming with a steady ding-dong. Someone was beating on the side door and I heard Bass shouting from the yard "Jess, get your ass out of bed!"

I sat up. "Jesus Jesse, aren't any your friends house broken?" I looked around confused and trying to find something to cover myself with. Jesse was up and swearing as he ran for the bedroom door looking as bedraggled as I was. "Jesse Wait!" I cried out . . . "grab a robe."

Jesse looked down at himself, naked except for his briefs, "You do look adorable." I said as he grabbed a robe off of the bathroom door and stomped down the stairs.

He went to the door and was greeted by Grady and Margaret. Standing beside the door was O'Riley, his thumb ready to hit the doorbell again. Jesse glared at him "You touch that bell one more time I'm gonna shoot you."

"Rise and shine sweetheart, where's CJ?" Margaret said as she pushed past him and into the room.

What's going on here? What are you doing here? Jesse watched as Grady and O'Riley rushed by him. Closing the door he stomped behind them. I had staggered to the kitchen door opening it to Bass and Annie. "Don't you know where the spare key is?"

"Not there, we looked, how are you CJ, did you sleep well?" Bass had a big shit eating grin. Annie was a little more demure, but her excitement was barely contained.

I closed the door behind them and followed only to meet the others in the dining room. "Will someone please tell me what going on? What are you doing here?" Jesse was still trying to waking up.

"Why Jesse, we wanted come over and give you the good news!" Bass waved a bottle of Champagne in front of him.

Jesse lifted one eyebrow "I'd rather have coffee!"

Annie came from the kitchen wiping her hands on a dish towel, "Coffees on and I'm making a brunch, you two go get cleaned up. It will be ready by the time you are."

"Let me help you with that" said Margaret, "Get going you two, times flying!"

Jesse grabbed my hand and stomped back up the stairs. "Jesse, don't you want to know what they're talking about?"

"No, I want to crawl back in bed and wake up properly by making love to my lady."

"Like that's going to happen. Aren't you the least bit curious?"

"I'm getting there. I guess a quick cold shower will have to do."

A quick shower it was, we conserved water and dressed. The coffee wafting up the stairwell helped hurry us along. Loud voices and laughter from below motivated us to find out why we were having a party.

We came down the stairs and Jesse was still scowling and had his arms crossed over his chest.

"Okay, spill it. Why are you guys here? Didn't we agree we were all going to sleep in this morning?"

"Change of plans ole man." Bass came over to me and grabbed Margaret as she was passing through. You, Ms. CJ and Margaret here are being honored for rescuing Bradley Jamison. There was a news story this morning but the Mayor and Chief of Police want to officially commend you on your work. He's set up a news conference in his office at One O'clock." Before I could answer everyone was congratulating us.

"Wait a minute;" I interjected. "We didn't do it on our own. We had a lot of help."

"That may be so, but think of the advertising for your business. Mrs. Jamison will be there. She wanted to thank you both personally."

"That's all well and good but I really don't want to be high-profile. The less people that recognize me the better off I am."

"CJ, it's your fifteen minutes of fame." Annie said as she started picking up coffee cups. "It will blow over and all will return to normal."

"Do you think I have time to buy a new dress?" Margaret asked as she looked at her watch.

"Come on you guys the brunch is on the table and we have just over an hour to make it downtown." Annie was hustling us all into the dining room.

I grabbed a muffin and an orange juice and went back upstairs. I put on my broom skirt and blue tank top with a short jacket. I was tying my sandals when Jesse came in. "You always look so good." He went to his closet and pulled out a shirt and jacket and started to replace his jeans with dress pants. "I feel weird about this Jesse, you and Grady and Bass had a whole lot to do with this."

"Baby, it was your case, we just helped."

"Jesse you guys did more then help. We couldn't have done it without you."

"Thanks baby, but I have a feeling you would have figured it out, we only helped expedite matters."

"Damn and he's modest too. You are too good to be true . . . . You look really handsome."

"Lets get this party on the road, we have some unfinished business." Jesse growled as he looked at the unmade bed.

The Mayors office had a party atmosphere. There were people everywhere. I saw the local news station interviewing the Mayor in the lobby. The Mayor was standing beside the Police Chief and other VIP's I didn't recognize. The lights from the new crews were bright and we kept getting flashed by photographers. Questions were thrown at us. "How did you do it? When did you know it was espionage?"

Espionage? I didn't get time for it to register. Margaret and I were hustled through the crowd. We found ourselves standing between the Mayor and Chief of Police. Mrs. Jamison was behind the podium with Bradley sitting tall in a wheelchair. He much more alert then the last time I saw him. I leaned over to ask him "How are you doing Bradley, you look so much better."

"I'm doing fine Miss CJ, thanks for finding me." Bradley handshake was weak. "I want an update Bradley; I'll stop by the hospital later, you to take it easy." Mrs., Jamison put her arms around my neck "Thank you CJ, Thanks for finding my boy." She was trying not to cry.

The Mayor cleared his throat and motioned for me to join him at a podium, Margaret was already in place.

He introduced us and began his speech. "I would like to congratulate the tireless effort that was made to make our streets safer. I commend the brave women of *CJ Investigations* who stopped terrorism in our little corner of the world by breaking up a ring of saboteurs. Dangerous people, who tried to sell a valuable program created by Cyber-Games to the highest bidder, their actions led an undercover operation to capture and arrest the responsible parties. I would like to thank both of you on behalf of the city, and present you with the key to the city."

I was stunned; I had missed a couple of details while I slept. Margaret looked just as stunned but she had the presence of mind to accept the Key to the City.

I missed his introduction but I saw Wayne Whitmore take the podium. He turned to Margaret and me. "Ladies, you have no idea how happy I am to have Bradley Jamison back. He is a great asset to Cyber-Games and one of my best friends. You have saved my company and my reputation. I posted a reward for the return of Mr. Jamison and I would like to present it to both of your for the work you have done. Thank you. I am also presenting the police department with a matching check for their work in helping to solve this case." He turned and picked two bundles of roses from somewhere behind him and gave one to each of us.

I looked at the roses and then realized everyone was waiting for me to speak. I opened my mouth and nothing came out. I took a deep breath and tried again.

I looked up at Margaret and I thanked her silently as she spoke up. "We, of CJ Investigations wish to thank you for acknowledging our work and giving us the Key to your city. We are grateful that our efforts, with the help of your local law enforcement helped bring a happy solution to everyone involved."

Bless you Margaret and your gift of gab.

Flash bulbs popped and questions came from all directions. The Mayor answered some of them before he told the crowd that an official statement would be made available. We were then ushered us into his office. The contrast from the questions and flashing bulbs was emphasized by the cool quiet of the office. It took a minute to realize that there were two men standing in the room.

Dark suits, thin ties, somber expressions. The atmosphere changed from a party atmosphere to strange. There was a knock on the door; The Mayor opened it to Jesse and Grady. "Their okay" said one of the suits.

"If you don't mind we need to speak to these folks alone" The other suit said as he looked at the Mayor.

"No, No, that's alright. Take your time," he replied. The suits stared at him until he left.

When the door closed the two men came around the desk. They shook our hands and introduced themselves as Agents Baker and Morse, FBI agents that were in charge of investigating Cyber-Games for selling technology to underground sources. They had been working in tandem with Mr. Whitmore. "We read your written statements and we have several questions." He looked at Margaret and then me. "Ms. Mason, you began investigating at the behest of Mrs. Jamison. At that time Mr. Jamison had been missing five weeks. What made you suspect that Cyber-Games was involved."

I looked at the agent and replied. "Bradley was missing and Cyber-Games wasn't as concerned as I would be if a valued employee, worth millions disappeared."

Margaret looked at the agents and said "There was a matter of locked cabinets, and the fact that Bradley's absence wasn't reported until Ms. Jamison demanded that it be. Five weeks later."

"When I spoke to Mr. Whitmore, he seemed more alarmed that Bradley's work was missing, then Bradley." I added.

"Why did you focus on Louise Conner?"

"I learned that she had words with Bradley that seemed to coincide with time that he went missing. When I asked her about it she tensed up."

Margaret was trying to figure out why we were being questioned. She raised the Key to the City and pointed it at the agents. "Look Fellas, we're darn good at what we do. A lot of the work was down right tedious, but the bottom line is that we are professionals. CJ here has good instincts. Now why don't you tell us why you brought us in here because I didn't see either of you crawling around in the grass in the middle of the night!"

Agent Baker cleared his throat; he was trying to cover a laugh. "We've been tripping over you girls since you started. I have to admit that you're good. We had our suspicions and we had a suspect. We just had to find the proof. We were following from the buyers end. They wanted the program. When the trail led to Cyber-Games there was a kidnapping in progress. That's when we started to trip over you two. No one knew about the underground room. That was Connor's doing, under the guise of broken pipes. The work was completed and no one knew that a room had been built. You found it, just by looking at a door on a monitor? Good instincts there."

"That was Jesse." I wanted to give credit where credit was due. "Grady and Margaret bought us the time to look for it."

"Louise Conner and her accomplice were arrested last night. The buyers were arrested at the pick up point. Louise gave that away just before she came to Cyber-Games. If she hadn't been in such a hurry to get there she wouldn't have forgotten to scramble it. That was when we heard you were on the premises. Cyber-Games is in the clear and you folks are heroes."

"So why are we here?" asked Margaret.

"We wanted to meet you personally. There are a few questions we would like to clear up, as I said we have read your statements and there seem to be some questions."

I spoke up; "I don't know how we can add to it. It was mostly hard work and dumb luck. I will be happy to go over it with you but right at this minute I am overwhelmed, exhausted and I have a date with my boyfriend."

"That's it? You're not going to grill us?" Margaret asked as she waved the key to the city at them. "You're not going to arrest us?"

"Not at the moment" said Agent Baker with a grunt of a laugh. "But I would appreciate it if you didn't mention this meeting. I know we won't."

You two have been a pleasure to work around." They both left through the back door.

"What was that all about?" I asked.

Grady pulled Margaret to him "That was weird; somehow knowing that they are taking a personal interest in you girls' bothers me."

Jesse face mirrored Grady's thoughts. "Let's go home."

We met Bass and Annie by the car. "What was the meeting all about?" Bass asked as he opened the door.

"Let's get home Bass." Jesse's voice was dead pan, a sign that whatever he had going on in his mind at the moment he was not ready to share.

When everyone was settled and Grady had pulled out into traffic, Margaret looked into the backseat "Nice roses. That was really nice of Whitmore, what's in the envelope?"

I handed the roses I had to Annie who was sitting on Bass's lap. "I don't know I'm still processing what happened. I know I put it in my pocket."

Bass sneezed at the flowers that were now hiding his face. Annie was trying to move them, when Bass sneezed again he put them in the back window.

"I opened the envelope and took out a letter. I unfolded it and a check fell in my lap. I picked it up and looked at it. The check was for One Hundred and Fifty Thousand Dollars. My mouth fell open, as I held the check up for Jesse to read. I was speechless.

"Well" asked Margaret, "what does it say?"

Jesse took the check from my hand and handed it to Margaret. For once Margaret had no words. Her eyes popped out and she kept opening her mouth to speak, nothing came out. "Jesse you read this," I handed him the letter.

> Dear CJ and Associates;
>
> Thank you for saving my employee and my business. This reward was posted for anyone who provided information leading to the capture and arrests of responsible parties in regards to the disappearance of Mr. Bradley Jamison. You have done so much more. Thank you for finding him. If I can be of any assistance in the future please do not hesitate to contact me.
>
> Sincerely;
> Wayne C. Whitmore
> CEO Cyber-Games Corporation.

Margaret showed the check to Grady; he whooped out a loud cry, she passed it to Annie and Bass who spoke at the same time congratulating us. Jesse was smiling; He hugged me close and gave me a kiss that curled my toes. "That's my girl, Baby, let's go home."

When we arrived at Jesses everyone was jubilant. It had been a harried, brain draining day. We were all too hyper to settle down but none of us wanted to face any kind of crowd. We settled on ordering pizza and going over the days events. Sitting around the living room we dissected the events that led up to today and decided it was all a matter of dumb luck.

Bass brought up the visit to my folks. He had his van ready and loaded. Grady had assembled all his tools and everyone looked forward to a weekend in the country. He said he'd pick us up at six a.m. and to be ready. Grady and Margaret would meet us here. By the time everyone left we were ready for sleep.

Chapter 37

We woke up excited about the day ahead. I made a quick breakfast while Jesse showered.

I had just finished dressing when the rest of the work party arrived. We all had dressed for work in jeans and t-shirts.

Bass quickly stored our overnight bags and we were on the road within the hour. Bass's van was really sweet. He had a small trailer loaded with the wood that Grady had purchased for the barn. Annie sat in the front, Grady and Margaret sat in the middle and Jesse and I opted for the half seat. It was a comfortable ride and I marveled at all the fall colors. It was exciting to go home.

Grady started looking through his bag, "I know I put it in here somewhere" he said as he pawed through the bag. Margaret leaned over the same bag, unzipped a side pouch and lifted a manila envelope out. "Is this what you're looking for?"

"You are so great." He turned in his seat to face us. "I had this yesterday, but with all the commotion I forgot to give it to you."

I reached for the package with a questioning look.

"It's the pages from the black book. The professor still hasn't been able to decipher any of it. This is your copy."

"Oh, thanks Grady," I hesitated before I took it. My friends seemed to realize that I wasn't ready to deal with it yet. It still amazed me that so little time had passed yet these wonderful people understood and accepted me.

We arrived mid-morning. Dad was coming around the corner of the house as we drove up. He looked at the trailer with the wood and various tools, "I cleaned out a large area in the barn the trailer should fit and still give us plenty of work room."

We climbed out of the van, Jesse and Grady grabbed the overnight bags, set them on the porch. The women *folk* took it from there. The guys disappeared into the van and headed down to the barn.

Mom held the door open as we entered. I introduced Annie and gave mom a hug.

Margaret dropped her bag and gave her an even bigger one. We were all talking over each other. Mom asked me to locate a room for everyone. There were three bedrooms upstairs, and a sewing room I wasn't sure how she'd go for us cohabiting so I didn't bring up the subject. Annie was thrilled with the house. I let them pick the room they wanted. We sat the bags on the floor and went downstairs to join my mother.

Mom was in the kitchen pouring iced tea and we sat around the table and talked about where we needed to start. Margaret was anxious to start on the ivy. It had to be trimmed back and the house washed before we could paint. We agreed that we would start at the front and head toward the side porch and then the back. Grady had brought pruning shears; we had moms and plenty of gloves. We decided that two would cut and the third would haul it out of the way. We would alternate clippers and haulers.

Margaret got to her feet "times a wasting" she grabbed a pair of pruning shears and headed for the porch. Annie took the first turn at hauling. We worked until mom came out and announced lunch. She told us to clean up while she went to summon the guys.

The aroma of lunch hit us as we came up the steps. My mouth started to water as I recognized ham and the smell of apple pie. Margaret went right to the kitchen and her eyes as big a saucers as she scoped out home made bread and corn on the cob. Annie was checking out the kitchen noting the large area and the huge stove. She took in the massive counters and cupboards that were well stocked with every kind of fruit and vegetable that mom had in her garden. All kinds of home canning jars each neatly dated and labeled. She turned as mom came into the kitchen. "This is amazing. I love your kitchen."

"Thank you, I will make sure you have some fresh preserves to take home with you."

"Don't forget me," Margaret started to place the plates on the table. "My mom hid the last of the jars you gave me and I think she plans to hold them for ransom."

Mom laughed, "It's nice to be appreciated, and I won't forget you Margaret." I handed Annie the napkins and she started placing them on the table when the guys came in. They were sweaty and dusty and they looked so male. They went to clean up commenting on how starved they were and how good everything smelled.

We were finally sitting, passing the corn and building homemade ham sandwiches when out of the blue my dad said, "You all looked pretty good on the News last night. I went out this morning and bought ten copies of the Gazette."

"You saw that did you," drawled out Grady, not sure it was a good thing. "I'm afraid I didn't catch that article."

"Well I saw you kids on the 5 O'clock news, I made sure to record it on the 11 O'clock news. I might pull it out this evening so you can see how you looked."

I knew my face was red, remembering that I couldn't say a word to save my life. "Oh, gosh, I don't know if I can watch that."

"Nonsense," mom chimed in "You both looked very beautiful and professional. I'm very proud of you." She then turned to Jesse. "This was just a simple missing person wasn't it Detective Keyes?"

Now it was Jesse's turn to turn red. He started to sputter, trying to let mom know they were behind us the whole time when she broke out laughing, surprising all of us.

"Mom, I would never let CJ get hurt, not for nothing. She is the most important person in my life."

"I know that Jesse, I just want you to know that I would worry about my girl if she taught nursery school. This is not a profession many women would choose but I feel better knowing that you are near."

Bass sat back and watched the exchange. He squeezed Annie's hand under the table and said. "You don't have to worry folks; we will all take good care of your little girl. She means the world to all of us."

Now I was turning red. "Alright you guy's its time to get back to work. I'm going to go cut some Ivy." I grabbed my gloves and shears off the back porch and went back to the front of the house.

Margaret came out shortly and I could hear deep voices joking back and forth heading for the barn. I was looking at the work we had yet to do.

"You don't have to be embarrassed."

"I know Margaret." I sat on the porch steps and re-tied my shoe. "I never had friends before. I never had the camaraderie that we share. It's like we've know each other forever. I just got all choked up."

Margaret put her arm around me. "Girlfriend, my life has shown me that we should cherish what we have. Be there when we can. And depend on our friends always. You led me to Grady. You trusted me and gave me a job when you knew the life I led. Jesse, Grady, Bass and Annie took me into their circle too. We're a couple of lucky women CJ."

I started to pull on my work gloves. "Margaret, I've been thinking. I want to invest half the money we received and buy the building we're renting. It would give us more room and we could even rent out part of it. I want to give you the other half of the money. I know we work well together and if you got your PI license we would truly be associates. I want to make us a Corporation. What do you think?"

Margaret was speechless. She hesitated so long that I wasn't sure that she would accept my idea. I had been staring straight ahead as I spoke so when I looked at her she had tears streaming down her face. "Margaret, I'm sorry, I didn't mean to offend you."

"Offend me? CJ, you just offered me the world. Of course I'll get a license. You bet I want to partner up with you. The idea about buying the building is excellent. I have a few suggestions there. But giving me half the money? No way. You can give me that raise that you keep talking about, and help pay for my schooling, but I want the money to go back onto OUR business and make it the best damn Private Investigation Business in the state."

Now tears were in my eyes. "Done" I shook her hand with my gloved hand and grabbed the pruning shears. "Let's get this ivy under control."

Annie came out with a welcome tray of iced tea. The afternoon sun was warm. The autumn breeze had slowed down and we were hot and sweaty. "Sorry I'm late. I was helping your mom clean up and help her to start supper. Your mom is great; I would die to have her kitchen. You grew up in this big beautiful house?"

"That I did. And it was big then too. We're almost done with the front. We can haul these cuttings to the burn pile. The side will be much easier." We sat on the porch swing and finished our tea. Mom came to the front door and walked to the bottom of the steps and looked up at the brick wall and then at all the cuttings. "My but you have been working hard. Don't you overdue it; I don't want you to get too tired."

"Don't worry; we need the fresh air and exercise. We don't get to do much gardening in the city." Margaret finished off her tea. "Okay ladies lets get to it."

Mom collected the glasses and took them back into the kitchen. "I'm going to walk some tea out to the men folk." She walked back into the house with the tray of empty glasses.

We finished the side of the house and the back was easy but in full sun. We were hot, tired and sweaty. Margaret spied the garden hose and pulled it to the front of the house; she hosed the residue of the ivy off the house and watched as the dirt from previous years washed down from the trim and windows. She then turned the hose on us and sprayed while we squealed at the assault. Annie and I tried to wrestle the hose from her and went down laughing. Annie got the hose and started spraying while Margaret was holding me in front of her. We were slipping in the mud and yelling and carrying on like grade school kids. I felt my foot slip and fell into a muddy hole. When I looked up the boys were laughing at the corner of the house. Dad was laughing so hard he had to hold himself up with the trellis. I heard the screen door shut and Mom was on the porch laughing with us.

Annie dropped the hose, looking innocent. I picked it up and I aimed it at the boys. They were covered with sawdust and sweat soaked their shirts. Margaret was right behind me, pulling the hose so that I would have more to work with.

The guys came at me like three huge linebackers. I tried to back away from them when I found myself on my butt back in my mud hole; I watched as the guys took control of the hose and went after Annie and Margaret. Grady went down with Oomph; Jesse was trying to grab the banister when the water hit him in the back of his head. Bass had the hose and was standing like a Greek god spaying everyone away from him.

Mama saved us all; going back into the house she came out the side door and turned the water off. Bass was left standing, watching the hose go limp as it slowed to a trickle. We all jumped on him making sure that he was as muddy as we were. We were out of breath pointing at each other, wiping mud off of ourselves as we slipped and fell and added more.

We came to a halt when Mama's voice called out "No one is coming in my house muddy. You all go back to the barn and hose off. That goes for you too ole man. Dinner will be ready in 30 minutes." Dad was drenched but not to muddy.

We slipped and slid until we were out of the war zone and I led them to the barn where we could clean off most of the mud. There was a makeshift shower that we used when I was girl after I had gotten particularly dirty or decided to hose down my horse. We took turns, girls first, laughing as we soaped the mud and grit off of each other. Mom had brought towels for everyone and robes that had been in my closet so long that I forgotten that I had them.

It was getting near dusk. The sky was reddish and the clouds were gathering as we walked back to the house. The wind had picked up and I felt the chill of autumn create goose bumps on my skin. We hurried into the house to the warmth of the kitchen and aromatic smells of roast beef. We ran into our appointed rooms, dressed quickly to help mom with supper.

We entered the kitchen as the guys walked in. Mom's face turned a bright red as she turned back to her stove. This was a Kodak moment.

I couldn't imagine what she might be thinking when three hunky men wearing nothing but towels strolled in and ran for the stairs. They seemed to be a bit red themselves. The three of us were at the counter laughing so hard we had to hold each other up.

We were at the table and talking recipes when the boys came down looking a bit sheepish.

Jesse spoke up for guys. "Uh, Ms. Marta, I want to apologize for our uh, lack of clothing. We didn't mean any disrespect."

"Jesse, Grady, Bass," mom began looking at each in turn. "Don't apologize for getting an old ladies heart racing. I haven't seen that much of fine horse flesh all at one time in my life. Sit down and eat."

My mouth was hanging open. Who was this lady? What did I miss?

"CJ, close your mouth and pass those potatoes, all of you have put in a hard days work and you have to be starving. Grady, have a biscuit."

We had loaded our plates and were settled into a great meal, savoring the tastes and smells when Margaret brought up our business agreement. "That's a great idea" said Grady. "You two work well together."

"Why buy the building?" Bass asked as he helped himself to more potatoes. "Why not rent down town. That new building still has vacancies."

"You mean that glitzy one on the corner?" I asked Bass. "That one is so commercial. I would have to raise my rates; people like Ms. Jamison would shy away from all the glitter and shine."

"And you would have to dress up every day" said Grady, "you'd hate that."

"I like where I'm located. Not to far in town. Not too far out of town. I don't know what it is about that building but it special."

"I like it too, the parking is good and it has a classic style. It's close to my moms; I like to keep an eye on her." Margaret explained. "We could move the office downstairs and then convert the upstairs into an apartment. Expand the rooms so that we don't elbow each other in the kitchen. Have you looked at the rooms downstairs?"

"I saw some of it when I moved in. There was a shop there. They moved out shortly after I moved in."

"I remember something there, what was it?" Annie sat back with a look of contentment.

"It was a tattoo place. I was glad when they left. What do you think Jesse?"

"You want to buy the building, and make an apartment? I think the bottom floor would be great for the business. You and Margaret work well together and it would be great to make it a Corporation, It all sounds great."

Something was bothering Jesse, "You don't sound to enthusiastic." something was wrong but I couldn't quite put my finger on it.

"CJ, you pretty much do what you want anyway." He pushed his plate away.

"Is anyone ready for pie? Annie brought this one. It looks delicious." Mom was changing the subject.

Mom stood up and started to clear the plates, Annie and Margaret got up to help. Dad said he wanted to take a walk and check out barn to "let his dinner settle before desert." Bass and Grady volunteered to go with him. He stopped at the door and asked Jesse to join them. "I want to take another look at that wall."

"You guys did a good days work today, I really appreciate what you have done. Grady you have a real talent for building." We heard their voices fade as they wandered down the path.

I started to pick up the plates around me when mom stopped me. "CJ, this was news to him, give him time to think about it."

"Mom, it's not like I tried to drop it on him. I have put every cent I own in my business. Poor Margaret has been paid a slaves wage and she's indispensable. It makes good business sense."

"Yes its good sense. That man loves you. I think that he may be upset because he wants to help you achieve your goals and feels you don't need him."

"Mom, that's not true."

"So you need to tell him that."

She picked up the plates in front of me and went to the dishwasher. Margaret and Annie were keeping busy across the room and came back to the table to clear the last of the dishes. I picked up my glass and placed it in with the others.

I needed to clear my head; I walked to the fence and watched Princes as she made her way to me. I had an apple and let her take a bite. I stroked her mane and coat. I used to tell her all my problems, she always understood. I watched as the moon played peek-a-boo with the clouds. The stars were bright and winking at me. I told her about the strange twists that my life had taken, about Jesse and how I now had friends, she whinnied as if she understood. Nudging my shoulder I told her how fast everything was changing, my parents who were not my parents, a little red diary that mysteriously appears creating a maelstrom of emotions and questions. My heart was so full but everything was happening so fast. I was waiting for the bubble would burst. Princess nudged my shoulder again and I held her head scratched behind her ears. I laid my head on hers and cried.

Jesse came up behind me. He held me close and nuzzled at my ear. I felt him reach around me to pat my horses' neck.

"Your dad just called me an idiot."

I looked at him in disbelief. "My dad wouldn't do that."

"Oh but he did, Grady and Bass think that I'm just an ass."

"Well I can believe that."

"Look, CJ, You blindsided me. I reacted badly. I can't explain what hit me. I'm not usually rude."

"I know that Jesse. I'm sorry I didn't tell you but I never had to consult with anyone; or rather never had anyone to consult with. I've always made my own decisions. I had plans for my business, I thought this would be years away. I never even considered buying a building but it makes sense. I didn't expect the money. I just saw my dream within reach."

"I know. We've never had time to sit down and talk about our personal dreams. In my mind we are together, us. I always knew you could do anything. Buying the building is a great idea. I think it was the apartment part. I was afraid of the distance it would put between us."

"Jesse, I have an apartment now."

"Yeah, but it's such a tiny little place and attached to your business. I'll bet the last owners used it for storage. I have a house and we are comfortable aren't we?"

"I was in your house because you were hurt and drugged. You're well now Jesse."

"But I like you there." Jesse said this with such a humble tone my heart went out to him. "Jesse. I like your house to. In all my life I have never had so many things to think about at one time. I never had anyone to worry about."

"CJ, I'm just saying I'm sorry for being an idiot and an ass. The idea of you having an actual apartment for yourself, one you really wanted and didn't share with an office space, it felt . . . it felt like you were leaving me."

"Jesse. Three weeks ago I didn't even know you."

"You know me now. My whole life I knew you would show up. I just didn't know when until I saw you nail that poster to a telephone pole."

"Whoa Jesse," I couldn't think. "There's too much happening to fast. Not just with you. Jesse, there's *CJ Investigations*, having the money to advertise and expand, to have a place of my own. I have Margaret, and I have a lead on my past. I'm re-uniting on a whole new level with my folks."

Then it hit me, like a bolt of lightening, like a force that was unstoppable. Everything began with Jesse! I was beginning but I hadn't flourished until I saw the grey-green eyes across a dingy squad room scrounging for my first poster. He accepted me, every part of me. He trusted me, in a half drugged stupor asked for me to care for him. He treated me and my work with respect. Who was I kidding? This was Jesse Keyes. My heart filled up and I felt my lungs expand.

My whole being was tuned to his. I couldn't breath. I was trying to get air, gasping for a breath while my heart beat for him.

"CJ, sweetheart, are you okay? What can I do baby? I'm sorry baby we'll build you the best damn office and apartment. I'll be patient, I won't rush you." He was holding me close and patting my back. He began rubbing the back of my neck.

I pulled away from him. I was laughing. It was all so clear. I felt this overwhelming, hysterical laughter bubbling up, coming from the inner most part of me. I threw my arms around his neck and kissed his face and his neck. I put my hands on each side of his face and looked into his eyes. "Jesse, if what I feel is love then I love you. Everyday, I feel more and more. It scares the hell out of me. When you were getting better I was feeling sad because I wouldn't be needed any more. So I do know how you feel. And you know what? Margaret needs an apartment!"

Jesse picked me up and swung me around. In the dark we entered our special world of color and light. We began walking the field holding each other close. We talked of what our lives were like before we met. We talked of what our lives could be. I told him what my plans were and why. He shared how he felt and what he wanted. How I had made his life whole.

We walked to the end of the pasture gazing up at the moon I shivered as I felt Jesse pull me to him and together we fell to the ground. I let down all my defenses. This man had my heart. For the first time I truly felt that I would never be alone again.

We headed back for the house. Our colors blending as we walked I felt that Jesse and I were beginning a new path together.

A piece of pie was on the table waiting for us. We carried it into the living room where everyone was enjoying the news conference that dad had taped. There seemed to be a contest of who could outdo the other on making fun of Margaret and me standing up with the Mayor. Sometime through the evening I fell asleep on Jesse's shoulder.

Chapter 38

Everyone was up early in good spirits as we argued over the bathroom, Tossing well meaning insults at each other. Discussing our plans for the day, as we rushed through breakfast to finish our work before the day warmed up.

I could hear saws and hammering coming from the barn while we washed down the house and trim. By mid morning we were ready to paint. We stopped for a quick picnic lunch in the gazebo. I told the girls about my discussion with Jesse. Margaret's only comment was it was about time I came to my senses.

Finished with the barn the guys came to check on our progress. They each picked up a paint brush and together we worked on the back of the house. The afternoon was on the wane when I started to clean the paint brushes.

I had just finished cleaning the last brush when Dad came around the house followed by a huge man. "CJ, can you come here a minute?" I looked up and looked at the man, handsome and strong, tall by anyone's standards. I straightened up and walked to them. A strange feeling came over me, I knew this man was here to see me. I stood tall and looked at Dad.

"CJ, I would like you to meet my very good friend Rengard."

I knew who he was, I knew before he spoke. I looked into his face. He was studying me with old eyes that had a look in them I couldn't decipher. It was intense, yet inquiring as if he was taking my measure.

"You're my father."

"Yes, I am your father. You have grown up well."

The betrayal that I had felt when I found out that Mom and Dad were not my real parents welled up. The anger that I thought was buried deep surged and expanded as I looked into his eyes, "You sure took your time getting here."

He stood for a moment, his eyes boring into mine. I thought I had angered him when he suddenly put his hands on his hips, tipped his head to the heavens and laughed a deep thunderous roar of a laugh that filled the air. "You have your mothers' impertinence girl, as well as her beauty."

Jesse came up behind me and put his arm around my shoulder. Rengard looked at Jesse and took in his possessive stance. He seemed to be aware of every nuance around us. Grady and Bass each took point behind Jesse. He raised his eyes to them and asked "Are these your warriors' girl?"

I raised my eyebrows. "These are my friends. Did you want to talk to me? Would you like to come into the house?"

"That was my intention. Am I welcome then?"

"Of course you are Rengard" answered my Dad. "You have had a long journey. We were just about to sit down to supper. Of course you will join us."

Rengard put a hand on dad's shoulder. "I would enjoy sharing a meal with your family. There is much we need to catch up on."

I watched as they walked to the house apparently forgotten for the moment. I sighed and fell onto Jesse's shoulder. He wrapped his arms around me. "So, we meet your father, I hope he can answer some of the questions we have."

Subdued we filed into the house. Rengard was sitting at the table he looked up as we entered and openly stared at my face. "You are your mother. I look at you and old memories crowd my mind and my heart." He turned to my mother and took her hand, you have raised her well."

I sat across from him and Jesse sat next to me. As he spoke with my parents I took in his deep almost colorless eyes. His hair was brown black with streaks of grey; cinched back with a leather tie. His cloths were comfortable, jeans and with a dark blue cotton shirt and black leather vest. The open collar showed a strong neck. His weathered face was handsome, lean and strong. The wrinkles around his eyes and mouth gave the impression of age and humor. I looked for similarities between us. There were few.

Lost in thought it took a moment to realize I was being spoken to.

"Earth to CJ!" Margaret had interrupted the thousand questions that were distracting me while I studied Rengard. I looked at her, still trying to unravel my thoughts and emotions.

"CJ, if you guys move into the living room Annie and I can set the table."

I looked around and asked where Grady and Bass were. "They finished the paint trays and their cleaning up now. They will be down in a minute. Why don't you visit until everything is ready?"

I looked at Dad and Rengard who were now standing and heading for the living room. Jesse and I followed and sat on the sofa, Dad and Rengard opted for the easy chairs. Mom came in and sat in her rocker in the corner.

Rengard looked at me. "You must have questions; I will answer what I can."

I opened my mouth to speak; I didn't know where to start. Jesse patted my hand and said, "CJ has been going through hell. She just found out that the people she believed to be her parents are not, why all the deception?"

Rengard looked at Jesse, and then me. "My wife, your mother, was the love of my life. She died fighting for you. We were caught in a war that forced me to make the hardest choice I ever made at a time when I was overwhelmed with grief. I needed to keep you safe. To keep you safe meant keeping secrets. I brought you to my trusted friend who had told me of his wife who could not have a child. They took you in, no questions asked. They promised to protect and guard you."

"That doesn't explain the deception."

"I have talked to Jacob; over the years you have realized that you have, ah . . . *abilities*. There are those who would hurt you to use those abilities. In my haste I placed safeguards on you, and your parents. I did it to keep you all safe. It was my haste and grief that put you at risk. The discovery of your abilities so early was not expected. I have done you a disservice and I apologize to all but especially to you my daughter. For leaving you frightened and alone I am sorry."

I listened without really comprehending. I wanted scream. I felt like my life was some dime-store novel. "So what took you so long?"

"I was summoned by the book. The guards that I put on it would let me know that you were ready to face your destiny. You had found your life mate."

He said this so calmly and earnestly. I was catching words like *destiny* and *life mate*. I had my destiny; I was working on my destiny. What the hell was he was talking about?

"Look, I'm not sure what you want with me. You abandoned me remember? Now you come out of the blue and tell me I have a destiny? I already have a life thank you."

He voice was hard and loud as he responded. "I did NOT abandon you. I left you in safekeeping with my good friends. I had no choice." He was angry, he sat up straight in his chair, his eyes demanding I finish.

"So what took you so long to come back? Twenty-two years and now you show up? What am I to do with that?" I was angry, hurt and ready for a fight.

"These are things we need to talk about. You have the diary? I know that you would not travel anywhere without it. I ask that you be patient and hear me out and all will become clear."

Margaret came to the door. She was nervously twisting her apron in her hands. I realized that she had been waiting to enter. She didn't want to intrude but the raised voices brought her into the room. "Uh, a folks, supper is ready, why don't we sit down and have a nice calm meal."

Grady and Bass were sitting at the table. They looked uncomfortable about being left out of the conversation. They were on alert, ready to stand behind their friend. We gathered around the table each reclaiming the seat they had chosen at the beginning of our visit. Annie set a gravy boat in the middle of the table and took her place next to Bass.

"Thank you for allowing me to share this meal with you." Rengard said humbly. My mother placed a chair next to Margaret for him. He was directly across from me.

My dad began to make introductions. "Rengard let me tell you who you are sharing my table with. This is Grady and Bass. They work with Jesse, They are police officers. Ms. Margaret is a partner with our daughter and they have a successful private investigation business. This little girl is Annie and she makes the most heavenly pies this side of the world." After he made the introductions we started to pass plates. I wasn't especially hungry; my head was still sorting out his words.

Bass looked at Rengard and asked. "What do you do Mr. Rengard?"

"It's Rengard. I am a warrior and I protect my people."

"Who are your people?" asked Bass as he loaded up his plate with potatoes.

"They are the ones that I have sworn to protect."

"That doesn't tell us much." Bass answered.

Jesse interrupted "Tell us about the book. We can't understand the language."

"The book, I would like to see it before I leave. It was very painful to leave my child and my wife's thoughts behind. You are very intuitive, have you not reasoned it out?"

"I know that the book and CJ are intricately entwined. I know that she has talents that make it possible to *feel* things in the book."

"You have talent also Jesse, as do your friends and this small one here." He said as he casually pointed his fork toward Annie. Looking at Margaret he said "You have heart, your talent lies in you compassion and insight. There may be a bit of fey in you."

"Well, that's nice to know. What's a fey?" Margaret said as she took a plate of dinner rolls from Marta.

"A bit of fairy magic, it expands your awareness, your impulses."

"Back to the book," said Jesse. "What language is it? We can't find anyone to translate it."

"It is an old tongue and not remembered by many. My daughter must open it. The binding spell was placed with her name."

Grady looked up. "That's what Dr. Wenz said; you had to use your name."

Rengard went on "I had little time to protect all of you when I came here that night. It was urgent to get you to safety. Jacob told me that the binding spell was broken at an early age by our daughter. She has a very strong will. I give her much credit that she has worked so hard to recognize and adapt it to her life."

"Wait a minute, wait just a second; you bound all of us with a spell? You made us all forget you. Forget that I just showed up on a doorstep. You left mom and dad thinking I was their child. No explanations! I grow up thinking I'm a freak. I scared the hell out of my mom. I stayed away from everyone because I'm a freak! I spend years looking for my past. And when I finally get a life, a business that actually benefits from my freakiness you show up and tell me, oops, that isn't what was supposed to happen?" I looked at him. You're too late DAD!" I stood up and walked out the door. I was confused and angry.

Jesse followed me. He caught up with me when I reached the pasture. I was so angry that I was shaking. I was holding myself not even trying to stop the tears.

"Baby," He pulled me to him. "Baby, it's alright, we'll work it out."

"It's already worked out. I have my life." I turned away from him and watched as Princess came up to the fence.

"Don't you want to know what's in the book?" Jesse leaned on the fence. I couldn't look at him. I didn't know what I wanted.

"No. I don't want to think right now. I want to go back to my life and pretend that this never happened."

"Honey you can't do that. You know you can't. We started this together; you need to know why you were placed here. Why you need to be protected. You need to know what happened to your real mother. You can't give up. You know that tomorrow, or next week or even next month you will have to come back and chew this bone. It will worry at you until you have all the answers."

"Your right, But right now I'm on overload. I can't think. Everything is mixed up inside. I'm angry and I want to hit something."

"Come back and let me do the talking. If you want to hit him your warriors will hold him down. But I need the answers as well as you. CJ, if I had an opportunity to find out about my parents I would do it come hell or high water. You can do this. We can do this together!"

I looked at him. "I know your right I have to calm down. My emotions are to close to the surface. You'd hold him down huh?"

"You bet cha, I'll be right beside you baby."

Jesse took my hand as we walked back toward the house. The wind had picked up and the night was clear. The moon was so bright that lit up the yard. We spotted him at the same time. He was sitting in the gazebo; we walked up the steps and sat across from him.

Chapter 39

I sat in the shadows of the gazebo. I was so close to Jesse that I was almost sitting on his lap. Questions were spiraling through my head, I wanted to know yet I was afraid of what I would hear.

"Tell us about CJ's mother." Jesse knew where to start. I leaned back on his shoulder my hand gripping his.

Rengard nodded his head and leaned back and looked up at the sky. He slowly gathered his thoughts and took a deep breath before he spoke. His deep voice rang out clear in the night.

"Celilia, My Celi, was beautiful. The first time I saw her she took my breath away. I knew she would share my life. She was so petite, like you, She had big, big eyes that read ones soul. She was a free spirit. She loved life. I met her at a gathering. She had many suitors. I bullied my way to her. Threatening anyone who came between us until I was before her and looking at her face, her eyes and her beguiling lips, I claimed her as my own. She laughed at me. *"I belong to no one."* She surprised me by her brashness. We danced until the dawn. Each time I told that her that she was mine she would say *"No one owns me."* As the dawn broke we walked to a nearby stream. We waded in the water, we talked for many hours. I told her that she had my heart. Every heart beat I had would be for hers for all time. She took my hand and said that her heart was mine and because she had given it freely and it could never be owned."

"We walked hand in hand back to the gathering; most were sleeping getting ready to begin again. The gathering would last two days more. Her father was a chieftain and I was a mere warrior. He wanted her to marry high in another clan. He recognized that I was Celilia's Life-Mate and ordered a contest. For the remaining days I fought any who would challenge for her hand. My love won, I was beaten and bloody but in the end we held hands as the binding cloth was wrapped around our wrists and the words spoken. We dedicated our love to each other in a holy union that declared no ownership, only lasting love."

"We lived happily; I would leave to protect our Chieftain and land, when I returned we would renew our union. One time I returned and Celilia told me I was to be a father. It was a great day. A momentous day! We were happy, awaiting the event of your birth. I stayed close during this time. In the last month I was called to the court of my chieftain I was torn with my duty and my need to be with my mate. We talked and it was decided that I would be back in four days time. Celilia said we had time but to hurry home."

"I had been gone one day and one night when I woke from my campsite with the greatest of pain in my head and heart. I felt Celi's fear. I left everything behind and rode as if followed by demons for our home. I didn't stop; I couldn't stop. My horse was half dead when I arrived. The door was open, our belongings scattered. I centered my thoughts and pictured her face, her smile, her eyes, I felt myself led. I ran until I came to a precipice. I searched the area. The urgency became unbearable. I screamed her name, I begged the Gods to lead me to her."

"I found her in a cave half way down the cliff. She had dragged herself inside. She was not conscience, I held her in my arms as I cried her name and felt for broken bones, I prayed and begged for all the gods to help me. I was afraid to move her because of the babe. She woke for me, she was very weak. She told me to help the babe. She had begun having birthing pains. She could not help much. During a woman's carrying time her powers are diminished, all strength goes to the child. What little strength she had she gave to her child. I wept as I felt her contractions expand. I prayed when she had relief. She delivered you to me in the night. I held my child and my wife, I heard your first cry as Celi' made me promise to protect you with her last breath. Her face was serene. She had given me her final gift."

"I had never experienced the anger and hatred that surrounded me in that small cave. I pray I never feel it again. I mourned my loss feeling my heart breaking, ranting at the Gods for taking someone so good away. My pain seemed endless."

"I was willing to die with my life mate, as is my right. I could have gone renegade in my rage had I not looked at your face. Your eyes, so much like Celi's. Through my grief and tears I heard your voice; I looked down and saw your grief, your loss, your mother showing in your face. My duty was to you."

"You were so helpless. Looking at you saved me. You saved us both. I held both of you in my arms. I was blessed by your birth. I wrapped you in her underskirt and I carried you to our home. I sat in a chair rocking you, half expecting my Celi to walk through the door."

"The sun began to rise when horses approached the house. My first in command reported that two homes had been raided, both carried the blood of our ancestors, the woman within had fey blood. The need of us by the chieftain was a ruse. It was a ploy to steel the women."

"My men helped me to retrieve Cecilia's body. We buried her in our ways. The hunting party was ready to search for the missing woman and child.

"My heart was torn, to avenge the wrong done to me by finding our lost, or keep my last promise to my beloved. If not for the babe my spirit would be broken. My need for revenge was overwhelming but my promise was my first duty. I fetched Celi's diary and Jacob's face appeared to me, my friend, who I trusted with my life. I came to this house to beg him to harbor my child."

"I bound you all to the book until I could come and free you. I needed to hide you from the same ones that murdered my Celi. It may have been my grief, or my anger that weakened my words. If I should not have lived to this day the wards would have broken themselves once my beautiful daughter found her life mate and then the diary would reveal itself."

I felt Rengards pain as he retold the story of my birth. I could hardly picture myself in the tale of Rengard and Celilia's love story. I felt tears as they streamed down my face. I looked at this stranger who was my father and saw the man. He was looking up into the night sky. My heart was breaking for what had been taken from him.

I leaned over and put my hand on his. "I am so sorry for your loss."

"Feel no sorrow for me lass, my love for Celi is eternal. She lives on through you. Had I known of your pain I would come long before this."

I stood and walked over to him. I leaned down a kissed his forehead. "Thank you for saving my life and telling me about my mother."

"Dry your tears girl. This is a time of joy. All the years that passed have led us to this day. When I felt the book found I knew you were waiting for me. I would like to hold the book of my wife and lovers thoughts. May I see it again? Can you fetch the book? I would want to feel my Celi's thoughts one more time."

We walked to the house and I *fetched* the diary, it now held so much more for me. Knowing what was written in it was meant for me. For a heart beat I hesitated and then picked up the manila envelope that held the copies of the black leather book. Perhaps my father could translate it.

I met everyone in the kitchen, there were cherry and blueberry pies on the counter. Annie was cutting large pieces and I could smell the coffee brewing. Mom and Dad were sitting on the sofa and I noticed that mom's sewing machine had been moved. Grady and Bass had been put to work.

I placed the diary on the table in front of Rengard. We watched as the bright red leather book was picked up and disappeared between his huge hands. He held it reverently, as if were a sacred tome that was beyond value. His eyes were closed and I wondered if he was feeling the colors as Jesse and I had.

The pie was passed and coffee poured. He put his hands in his lap still holding the book. He opened his eyes and seemed surprised to be sitting in the kitchen surrounded by so many people.

He placed the book in my hand. "She wrote this for you. Thank you for sharing it with me."

Jesse had the manila envelope in front of him. "Rengard, there's handwriting in the Red Diary. Is it yours?"

His eyes met Jesse's "Yes, I wrote it as I brought my daughter to Jacob and Marta. It contains the instructions for breaking the bindings. It also contains my thoughts and explained my actions."

Jesse slid the manila envelope over to Rengard. "These are pages that have been copied from a book found in the office of Professor Dunn at the university. CJ was led to it by her abilities. Its writing is similar to that of the red book. Could you look at it and tell us what it says?"

"First things first," Margaret had gotten up and was refreshing the coffee cups. "Rengard, Sir, could you please tell us the code to remove the wards? I believe that we have waited long enough."

"Well of course," he turned to me. "You must say your name and command all wards to cease!"

"Go ahead CJ, Say your name."

I looked around the table, every eye was on me. I closed my eyes and took a deep breath and said "I, CJ command all wards and bindings be released from this book, my family and myself." I opened my eyes and everyone was still staring at me. I opened the book a couple of pages and nothing had changed I still couldn't read a word.

Rengard looked at me. "Why do you use initials? You must use your name!"

I looked at mom and dad; this had been a conversation that we had in the past. Now I knew it was the wards. I looked at Rengard. "What is my name?"

He looked astounded. You do not know your name? Now it was his turn to look at my parents. "She does not know her name? How is this?"

Now everyone was confused. "You never said." My mother replied. "You gave us a paper with instructions of special herbs to be added to her formula. She was so small, just a minute, I'll show you."

Mom went to a book cabinet and pulled her bible out. It had been in her family forever and traced births, deaths, weddings, any major happing that had happen in her family for generations, I remember pouring over the family tree looking for anyone who shared my disability. Through my fifteenth summer I wrote everyone I could trace hoping to find a relative who might have literally faded away. I had written or visited most of the people listed in it.

She brought the Bible to the table and opened the cover very gently. There was and old yellow paper folded twice. She opened it and hand written were several words written hastily at the bottom was *1 dp—CJ*. She handed the paper to Rengard. He looked at it and smiled.

"This is the healers. I took you to her. I needed to know what I needed to travel with a baby. She gave me this and much more. The herbs were very important she made a mixture and I was to add one drop to the goats' milk. We traveled fast and hard. You traveled well little one."

"Hey, . . . uh . . . big guy! So what's her name?" Margaret was getting impatient. We all realized that the key was here. We would never have learned it if Rengard hadn't appeared.

Chapter 40

Rengard looked the table amazement. He looked first to mom and then dad. "My dear friends I have ill used your friendship. You truly do not know our child's name?"

He then looked at me. "Dear child, I am so sorry for the added burden you have suffered for my negligence."

Grady sat up straight in his chair. "Do you mean to tell us that we might never have understood anything?"

"Fate works in its own time. Jesse and Celilia share a bond. Together they would have fathomed the meanings. I can see how your auras combine. You are truly mated."

Margaret stood up. "Celilia! . . . You called her Celilia. That's your name! CJ! You have a name!" Margaret had risen from chair and was all but dancing with her revelation.

"You are truly of fey blood. I named her for her mother. I held her up to the sky and thanked the Gods for their gift."

It was my turn to be amazed. I felt that night in a deep part of me. Maybe it was Rengard's story, maybe the book that I held tight to my heart.

I heard myself remember.

"The moon was full; it lit up the water like day. I was above it all I felt the words echo across the sky. Junos, I am named Celilia Junos."

"Your name means *Daughter of the Moon*." Rengard put his hand over mine. "You are truly the Daughter of the moon."

Tears were flowing. Even Bass's eyes were red. I looked at my parents they were side by side holding each other tightly. Jesse kissed my temple and held me close. "It's a beautiful name."

Everyone looked up as Grady blew his nose. The ole pussy cat showed himself again. I laughed, I looked at Rengard and said "Thank you." I looked around the table into the faces of my friends and my family. I felt the love and friendship they shared with me.

I stood up and put the book to my heart. I closed my eyes and taking a deep centering breath I said what came from my heart.

"I. Celilia Junos, command that all spells of protection placed on my family, this book and myself cease to be from this moment forward."

My eyes were closed when I felt the book emit a heat, a deep vibration that was similar to my tingling sensations but not the same. I felt it surround me in light and awareness. I felt the light as it moved to include Jesse feeling his amazement.

The vibration expanded through me, encompassing me in a euphoric joining. I opened my eyes and saw the air shimmer as it passed to my parents and then my father. The light that filled the room moving with colors that changed as it touched each of us. I saw as it started to surround my friends. I watched their reactions as they were joined to us. Each surrounded by their individual aura, I felt elation as each touched my own. The amazement of this moment was all consuming. I felt the link that would forever be shared by us.

How I knew these things, I don't know. It was felt; a part of each of us was now a part of the other. It went deeper then friendship. More binding then words.

I don't know how long we kept this communion. I remember raising my head off the table. I shook my head and raised it to Jesse. "Whoa, Hey Cowboy what just happened?"

"Whoa is right. CJ, you did it. You broke the spell!"

I looked around the room and everyone seemed to be coming from a deep sleep.

"Damn CJ, what just happened here?" Bass was holding Annie who was looking at me in disbelief.

"I don't know for sure. I think we broke the ward."

"The ward is gone. I put a spell of protection on you, it is now broken." Rengard looked at me pointedly. "You are still in danger. You need training, all of you." He looked around the table. "You are all Celilia's guard."

"Wait a minute;" I said as I stood up. "You can't command someone to protect me. You can't order us like you would one of your men."

"I can and I have. Your mother was the daughter of a powerful Chieftain. Her powers were many and strong. She has passed that legacy to you. As her daughter you must respect and guard her gifts. The gifts that she protected when she gave life to you, the gifts she gave her life for."

"That's pretty clear" Margaret had reached for a pitcher of tea and started to pour a glass for everyone.

I was exhausted and I really needed to be alone. I rose from my chair.

"Child," Regard touched my hand as I moved away from the table. "The binding that has taken place this night is life long. Each who shared in it will forever be in link with all. You are clan."

I looked at Rengard and at the faces of everyone around the table. "I love you all. I don't understand anything yet but what you gave me before tonight helped me more then I can ever tell you. I am so exhausted. I'm going to bed. I'll see you in the morning." I picked up the diary and carried it with me to my room.

As I left the room I heard Bass ask Grady to call the day sergeant and let him know they were taking the day off. I had forgotten it was Sunday and the end of our weekend.

Chapter 41

I laid awake a long time. Reliving the power I felt in the kitchen. Closing my eyes I recalled Rengards tragic love story about my mother. Renewed tears came with remembering his faraway voice. Reliving the power I felt as we shared the fantastic light. I could feel where the others were in the house. I wondered what it would mean. I knew in my heart that we would always be part of each other. I opened the book and found that I could almost read the words. Sounding out syllables, some were archaic and sounded like Rengards speech. I slipped the book under my pillow and closed my eyes thinking of my mother as I saw her in front of the cottage. She was peaceful and content shelling peas for their meal. I watched as she looked up to the sky her face clear in my mind. I was looking in a mirror.

I woke up with Jesse spooned to me. He was gently snoring and holding me close. I lay listening to him breath, feeling the comfort. Feeling loved.

I thought about the fear I had of getting close to someone. How it was easier to avoid people then to explain. All the searching, trying to find myself. Trying to find out why I was so different. By hap-stance finding others who had abilities was amazing. These people befriended me, welcomed me into their circle. In the time that we had known each other we forged a bond that seemed written for a fairy tale. I snickered to myself. Maybe I was still dreaming and when I wake up it would all be just a pipe dream.

Jesse woke to my snicker. "Hey babe, you awake? How are you doing?"

"I'm doing okay, how about you?"

"Just fine baby, you slept well. I don't think you moved all night."

"I'm almost afraid to get up. I was just thinking that last night was a dream, I'm almost hoping it was."

"It was freaky. Your ole man is a kick. I like him."

"I wanted to hate him."

"Whatever he's done was done in your best interest. I think his grief, his love for you and his need for revenge clouded his mind. I find it ironic that you are the one who remembered your name. That's some powerful magic she passed to you."

"I hear voices in the kitchen should we go down?"

"I have another idea." Jesse said as he nuzzled my neck.

"Not here Cowboy, my folks are downstairs'."

"But baby."

"No buts, I'll beat you downstairs." I grabbed my jeans and a blouse and ran for the bathroom.

The coffee was made. Sausage and pancakes were cooking on the stove with Annie and mom sharing the chore. Margaret was setting the table.

I went to pour a cup and asked where the guys were. "They left early; they wanted to check the fence line." Margaret said as she placed the silverware. "Apparently Jesse noticed that there were a couple of week spots." Annie added "We're to send Jesse out if he ever wakes up."

"He's awake. He'll be down in a minute." I heard his steps on the stairs as I spoke.

Mom looked a Jesse, "The men are looking at the fence. They said you should join them."

I looked at mom she seemed a bit tense. This was my first inkling that something might be wrong. I moved over to the table and sat next to mom placing my coffee in front of me. "Okay ladies, what's up?"

Annie continued cooking but Margaret grabbed her cup and sat on the other side of me. Mom was waiting for her to settle. "CJ, your life has been a strange one. I want you to know that you and your friends will always be welcome here. I am old and I wish I had been a better mother, but know this girl, you are my daughter also."

"Mom, I just realized this morning that my life has been a comedy of errors. *If* my birth mother had lived my life would have been so different. *If* I had been older maybe I would have understood more. I know that Rengard did his best but we were all under the influence of something that was bigger then anyone could have guessed."

"Now we know. Now we live our lives. Like Rengard said, fate finds a way. In our case it just took its good ole sweet time. I don't think there is anything any of us could have done differently. I feel like a big dark cloud has been lifted and now I need to understand it." I placed my hand on moms, "We all did what we could, and through it all we loved each other. Its just going to get better, I know it is."

Mom patted my hand in return. "You were a good girl CJ and you grew into a good woman."

"Not to be a wet blanket but I am really hungry. When are the boys due back?"

"Margaret pulled out her cell-phone, hit a button and said "Their on the way."

Everything was on the table as they trooped in. Everyone was bantering back and forth. It felt just like family.

After washing up the guys sat down and I watched as the food disappeared from the plates. They talked about fence repair. Cleaning the eaves, changing the furnace filters.

Rengard spoke up. "I have decided that all training should be postponed until you have had a chance to read your diary. Your mother wrote about her responsibilities to her clan. These responsibilities are now yours."

"Ah, Rengard? Where is this clan? I have a life here. I don't want to go globe tracking."

"Your clan is those under your protection. Our Chieftain and his wife see to their needs."

"This will be in the Diary?" I stuttered, "How do I use it?"

"First you read it. The communion that you feel when you touch the book will answer your questions. Guard it well; do not allow it to leave you."

Grady was looking for more pancakes as Annie delivered another huge stack to the table. "Did you get a look at the pages we gave you? The ones we had copied from the black book that CJ found?"

"Yes, and I am still studying it. It is not exactly the same, however it from my homeland. I would like to know how it made its way here. I would also like to know how it was separated from its owner. These books are sacred to the clan. If there is no offspring they are incinerated in the owners' pyre."

"Pyre, you mean like cremation? Like in fire, flames ending in ashes?" asked Jesse.

"Yes, it is our way."

"You should meet Professor Dunn; he said he had no idea of where the book came from or how it came to be there."

"I would like to meet this man. I also wish to speak to your healer. But this will have to wait. I am leaving today. I will return. I would like you read your diary and understand its importance. Please understand that you are bound to each other," he turned to me "your Warriors are honor bound to protect you."

After breakfast we talked about coming back, Mom had packed large baskets of food for Rengard and for us. She doubled the preserves for Margaret, after all she had Grady.

We offered Rengard a ride to wherever he had to go but he refused. Saying he wanted some time with my parents. He would return soon.

I stood aside, I didn't know what to say to this man who had answered one question and like everyone I spoke to in the past few weeks created so many more.

He came looking for me. "Celilia, you are image of your mother. You have her spirit. It gives me great joy to see how you have grown. Jesse is your life mate, he will give good council. He is your fiercest warrior and will protect you to his death." He bent down and kissed my forehead. "My daughter, my love, Thank you for listening to an old mans reminiscing."

I had tears in my eyes as he walked away. Jesse came around the corner and saw me standing alone and looking into space; he put his arms around me. "Its okay baby, he'll be back."

We were ready to leave; everything was loaded into the van. I saw the credenza had been loaded in the trailer, along with my bicycle and few other old pieces of furniture that I had last seen in the attic.

I kissed my dad and mom goodbye and gave them both a huge hug; Rengard stood watching, I believe I surprised him when I kissed his cheek and whispered thank you. The others shook hands and kissed cheeks. We all promised to come back soon.

The drive back was filled with conversation. Margaret and Annie thought Rengard was living in the wrong century. They adored his speech.

"He said the book summoned him" Annie said out of the blue, "your mom gave it to you just last week."

"Yeah, how does that work, did he mention where he came from?" Bass looked back at me.

"No, I didn't ask. I didn't ask a lot of things. Now I have all kinds of questions for him."

"So, maybe the answers are in the book. We need a game plan." Annie looked thoughtful. "Maybe between all of us we can come up with more answers."

"After all we are your warriors" Grady was beating his chest.

"I couldn't ask for a better army, but somehow warriors don't quite fit this century." I laughed.

"Hey, I like being a warrior. In this day and age I figure being a police officer is just about the same." Grady was so full of himself.

"We are in this together. We are all equal and I can't see my life changing all that much because of this. I'm just as confused as I ever was."

"This has been one strange weekend," stated Bass. "Margaret, you are fey? That's like a fairy right? We'll have to check you out a little closer, I wondered what Grady saw in you besides the fact that you're smart, pretty and you have an uncanny way of making a point."

"Thanks Bass, I think."

"What did you girls decide about you business?" Still buying the building? My brother is an ace carpenter." Grady was excited. "I really want to see the main floor."

I spoke up, "Yeah, I think we should look into that. We know what's wrong with it that should help us make a good deal. Grady can you and your brother look at it and maybe put a couple of rough plans together so we can get it started?

"You should get it appraised; I'll look at it when you get the keys. My brother's crew would do a great job. Restoring that old building is right up our alley."

Margaret was excited. "I don't believe what's happening. I'm so happy I think I'm going to cry." I could see tears welling in her eyes. Grady pulled her to him in a big embrace. "Go ahead and cry honey bunch, your big bad warrior will be right here."

He said this so sincerely that we all stared at them. I had never heard Grady use that gentle, loving tone. It made me want to cry.

We discussed the changes that would be nice for the building. We bantered about Wayne, and the money he gave us. I learned that Margaret had more then a bookkeeping background and that we could handle our financing without getting accountant. I was happy. My life was filled with people I loved and trusted. I looked at Jesse, he seemed introspective. I took his hand and brought it to my breast. "You have my heart."

He smiled and pulled me to him. We all rode quietly the last few miles of our trip, each lost in our own thoughts and dreams.

Chapter 42

Bass stopped at Jesse's and we agreed to get together the next day. All three of our men were returning to work. Bass was taking the trailer to his house and would meet us after work at the *agency* as he called our office. Grady and Margaret walked hand in hand to his car.

Jesse's house was very quiet. He dropped our bags in the laundry room and began to snoop through the food basket. I started to put the preserves in the cupboard; Jesse was putting ham and roast beef in the refrigerator. We both felt the closeness; it was as if it had always been this way.

"I think you should go take a shower. I'm going to make us a bite to eat."

Jesse looked at me and smiled. I heard him humming as he went through the house and up the stairs.

I made some soup and sandwiches, set the table and put a load of laundry in the washer.

I brought out the diary and marveled at the texture of the cover. Opening it I felt a difference. Before I could feel the power, and I needed to draw from within me to get a reaction. Now as I held it the power all but leapt out to me, drawing me to it. Powerful stuff, I leaned back holding it. Not ready to read it.

Jesse found me holding the book, almost asleep. Hey babe, it's your turn, go take a shower."

I went upstairs and as soon as the water hit me I felt revived. I hurried through all my girlie chores and went downstairs. Jesse was in the laundry room folding the clothes when I came into the room. "You didn't have to do that." I protested.

He kissed me without an answer. We sat down and ate our supper. Afterwards we cleaned the table and stacked the dishes. We walked upstairs together listening to the chug-chug-chugging of the dishwasher

As we entered the bedroom I watched as Jesse turned the bed down.

"Detective Keyes," I said as I slowly unbuttoned the top button of my blouse. "Did you have a good time at my folks this weekend?"

Jesse stared as I unbuttoned the second button. "Oh yes, it's been an informative weekend. Hard labor, good fun, and oh yeah, I found out that I have a Life Mate."

"Did you?" And what does that mean to you?" I was on the third button. I heard him clear his throat before he answered.

"That the woman I love, in accordance to her clan laws is my wife."

I slipped my blouse off my shoulders and I stood before him in my bra. "Is that so?"

He crossed the room, and without touching me and kissed my neck. "Oh, yeah, I think so."

I had unbuttoned my jeans, the zipper sounded like thunder as I slowly lowered it. "Do I have any thing to say about this?"

Still not touching my flesh he took the waist band of my jeans and pulled them to the floor. "You can say anything you want."

My body was burning. "I want you." I sighed.

Jesse was kneeling on the floor where he lifted my foot out of the material. I put my hands on his shoulders for balance. He raised my other foot and repeated the action.

I felt his hands travel up my legs, a gentle, intimate slow action that sent shivers through me. "Oh Jesse . . ."

He lightly pressured my legs apart, his hand light and soothing. "Close your eyes baby, close your eyes and feel me love you."

I closed my eyes and felt him press against my body. He was kneeling before me and I felt his mouth on my body. Heat pulsed from me. I felt his mouth at my panty line, then closer to my rapidly warming private places. I felt his fingers lightly glide over the thin sliver of silk. Crushing his hair in my hand my balance was failing fast. "Jesse, I want more."

"Yes love." He gently took my hips in his hands and pushed me back to the bed. Still on his knees one hands slowly making its way up my body as he slowly breached the material.

"Jesse, don't stop."

"Never baby." He reached behind me and unsnapped my bra. He lowered my straps and I watched as he slowly pulled it away from me. I felt like I was a present that he was gently unwrapping. His lips were on my breast. He was suckling me gently. I felt my nipples grow hard. I urged him to take more, to do more. Every part of my body was vibrating with need for him.

His hands replaced his lips, kneading and rolling my nipples bringing me to a higher frenzy of need. Pushing me gently to the bed I lay prone as he removed the silky barrier. His hands rubbing and massaging, spreading my legs wider, "Baby, you are so beautiful." He lightly pressured my legs apart as I pressed myself into his hand, I begged him for more. I demanded more. I lay on the bed, praying for the release he was promising.

His finger slowly making its way into me, his hand pushing deeper mimicking the movement of lovemaking teasing me as the momentum increased. He moved his body onto the bed. His lips captured mine as his tongue took me. His hands kept moving deeper, touching the hidden nub that made me scream for more. Demanding more, as my passion increased. I gave way to pure sensation. I felt my body tremble and sparks seemed to surround us. His hot pulsing rod leapt when I touched him, fondling him. I ran my finger onto the small drop of liquid that escaped it. "CJ, Oh baby CJ, what you do to me. Cum for me CJ, come to me."

I screamed his name as I exploded. We were surrounded in the swirling colors of *us*. Our bodies wrapped in the vibrant hues that were ours only. I fell back spent and shaking from eruption that came over me.

I opened my eyes to find our colors enveloping us pulsing to our heartbeat, keeping tempo. I felt it waft through me, through us.

"Look Jesse," I raised my hand in the air the swirling mist went through it. He placed his next to mine and smiled as he put his hand in mine. We watched in fascination as our colors combined and wove into intricate patterns. The intensity of it made me want to weep. The old familiar urge flared and I realized it had been with me through the night. I looked at Jesse and his eyes were exploring my face. "CJ, you are mine."

I heard a whisper in my head. "I give myself freely."

He put his hand on my face. "I give myself to you, to love and protect for all time."

We both were centered in flowing colors locked into the moment.

Jesse lay beside me, looking at me with love. I felt cherished as he touched my face. I was again immersed in the feelings he created as he ran his fingers through my hair. I felt hands slowly touching my face, following down my neck to my breast, lowering his head I watched him as he suckled. His hands replacing his lips on my breast he kissed me increasing the tempo of the colors, intensifying them as he moved down my body. My hand searched and found him hard and pulsating.

I gave into the feelings that had held me captive my whole life. I gave myself reign to cast off all secrets, rising above the fears and pain that had closeted me for so long. Color burst from me, sensations of our blending circling us with our passion.

Power seemed to surge as I pushed Jesse from me. Looking into his eyes, I saw my feelings mirrored in his. "It's my turn Cowboy."

I explored him, devoured him. He lay on the bed astounded as I inspected and played, experimenting with his body. I watched as his nipples hardened to my touch. I felt him reach for me as I gave him light kisses on his mouth, his neck, his collarbone. I held his arms "Don't move baby; let me love you."

I marveled at the differences between our bodies. The hair on his chest was soft and downy. I played in it, making little swirls, standing it up and running my fingers through it, feeling the texture of him. Slowly I explored his body, moving my hands over his ribs and down his hips. He watched as my hand glide down to his stomach. I listened as he took halting breaths as I reached made my way down his thighs just missing the part of him that would unite us.

I watched as he grew engorged and searched the air reaching for my touch. I put my hand on him and heard him moan. Measuring the weight and girth of him in my hand and marveling at its size and remembering how he had fit inside of me, still amazed that he had. I felt my pulse increase as my body recalled and craved more. Following the pulsing heat to its base and feeling the soft orbs that nestled beneath. Making myself wet and hot with wanting him.

"CJ, woman you are torturing me." He tried to rise; I placed my hand on his chest and staid him. I continued my journey as I slowly straddled him and ran my hands up and down his body. Kissing his chest, I moved my hands down his arms, admiring his strength and marveling at my new found courage.

"Does this feel as good to you as it does to me?" I barely recognized my own voice. Low and husky dry with expectation. I moved down his body and once again came to his throbbing hot rod. I sat on him feeling the throbbing at my womanhood.

Jesse moved his hand, massaging me with his penis that he was now holding it at the base. "Jesse, it's my turn." I pushed his hand away. I gently ran my hand around the head. I heard him groan and I marveled at the power I had over him. I lowered my head; my tongue licked the bead of liquid. I kissed him gently and another groan erupted from Jesse. I felt it expand as my body went into overload and the colors surrounding us in an explosion of light.

I felt my self lifted and thrown in a maelstrom color, crimson hot and fiery I was suddenly on my back. Jesse was covering my body with his. "Woman, I can't wait, I need to be inside you."

I looked at his face. I heard myself answer with a deep throaty laugh. He watched me as I watched him as he took in every inch of my body. He moved my legs and with one brush of his hand as touched me. Looking into my eyes he entered. As he pushed into me he closed his eyes and sighed. "Baby, I am forever yours."

He started to slowly withdraw, when I cried out from the loss and reached for him as he plunged into me again.

We made love all through the night. I never knew there were so many ways to love. We explored every inch of our bodies. Over and over Jesse made me scream and cry and laugh and beg for more. Everything he did to me I did to him. We would fall in exhaustion and wake when one of us would arouse the other with a kiss or a touch and begin again. Every thought I shared with him. In the wee hours of the morning we fell into an exhausted sleep.

Chapter 43

I don't know when Jesse left that morning. I climbed out of bed on wobbly legs calling his name. I looked at the clock and saw that it was after 10:00, I could only wonder if he made it to work on time.

I drew a bath after a bit my muscles stopped screaming. When I finally finished and climbed out of the bathtub and looked into the mirror and wondered if the girl looking back was really me. I saw a couple of bites I would have to cover. I thought I might need bondo to cover the dark circles under my eyes. I dressed and made my way downstairs. In the kitchen was a note by the coffee pot. *Baby, I'll call you. See you tonight. Love, J.* The note set my heart aflutter.

I poured coffee, and reached for my backpack. I pulled out my notebook and started to make a list. I went for my phone as it started to ring. "Margaret, I was just getting my thoughts together to call you. I planned to be there already"

"Don't worry about it. Jesse called earlier and said that you were sleeping in. I was hoping that I didn't wake you up."

"No, I'm just about ready to leave here. I didn't have breakfast. It will be lunchtime soon. How about I pick you up and we'll get a bite to eat?"

"I'll be right here. I was just finishing notes on Cyber-Games. Why don't we both take the afternoon off?"

"I like how you think Margaret. Be there soon."

When I got to the office the steps were a painfully sweet reminder that I had abused every bone in my body. Margaret was on the phone and she looked up as I daintily walked across the floor. I didn't make it to my office and fell onto the sofa and laid my head back and closed my eyes.

I heard Margaret hang up the phone. "Do I need to set up a coffee IV? Good god girl I've seen livelier coma victims."

"Coffee would be nice."

"Jesse said that you would be tired. I could guess but I think I see all the tell-tale signs of good loving. Knowing you two the earth moved."

I snorted, "You are so intuitive."

"You stay right there, I'm bringing the pot here." I could hear Margaret as she walked into the kitchen, the rattle of cups and walk back.

"Here drink this. One cup and you spill all."

I opened one eye "You got all day?"

"I'll ask my boss, spill it girl."

"I can't explain it. I'm still in a daze. I love him so much Margaret. I never thought . . . ." I couldn't find the words,

"You don't have to. I can see it in your face and I'm so happy for you."

"You know what I want to do Margaret? I was thinking about my life. It really hasn't changed. We have a couple of answers but a whole lot more questions. What I need to do is concentrate on our plans." I pulled out the list I had started at Jesse's.

"We need to call an appraiser and the landlord, to see what he wants for the building. Oh, and get a key so we can check out the downstairs and let the appraiser and Grady in. We need to go to the bank. Did you ever figure out what I owe you in past wages?"

"Hold on girl. First of all I have the landlord coming over with the key he'll drop it in the mail shoot this afternoon sometime. I told him we were thinking of renting the downstairs. The appraiser will be here on Thursday, 1:30. Grady and the guys will be here after work, Bass is stopping to get Annie on the way. The bank is open until 4:30. And we need to get food to feed everyone."

"Wow, double your raise. Add to that list that we need to stop and change this business to a corporation, and call the guy that did my signs; he's in the address book. Oh and tell him to print the door downstairs to read *Junos-Cross Private Investigators*. Or maybe Cross-Junos like in Cross the Moon?"

"Ah, CJ, that won't work. You see I ah . . . I haven't agreed yet but I might change my name to Dombrowski. As a matter of fact the only reason I haven't decided yet is because it is Dombrowski!"

"Margaret. How exciting! When did this happen. You can keep your maiden name or maybe hyphenate it."

"I don't think so; it will take two pieces of paper to sign a letter. Besides Grady would think I'm ashamed of him. Or his name anyway."

"Well you don't have to decide today. When we buy this building, I want all the changes to be announced at the grand opening. So you have time."

"CJ, as long as we're going to do lunch, lets do the day. Remember that girl I told you about that does great hair? You really do need to do something with your head. I'll bet she would squeeze you . . . er . . . us in. We might as well get a manicure and even a pedicure. That ivy made a mess of my nails."

"I'm sure we can fit it in. I would like to stop and check out a little shop in that new gaudy building downtown, I saw the cutest all purpose little black dress in the window."